SOUP

The Future Is Past And Present

Travis Haugen

 FriesenPress

Suite 300 - 990 Fort St
Victoria, BC, V8V 3K2
Canada

www.friesenpress.com

Editor: Eric Anderson

Illustrator: Haley Craw

ISBN
978-1-5255-2928-3 (Hardcover)
978-1-5255-2929-0 (Paperback)
978-1-5255-2930-6 (eBook)

1. FICTION, THRILLERS

Distributed to the trade by The Ingram Book Company

TABLE OF CONTENTS

A Note from the Author

Hi Folks,

I spent 40 years of my life as a professional musician. The events in this book are drawn from real life experiences on numerous tours throughout Canada and the US, and from hundreds of hours of recording studio sessions.

This story was made to interact with twenty-four original songs and three addendums from the *Soup* website.

In the e-book, simply click on the familiar blue links, and you are there.

In the print copies, the triggers are highlighted in bold to indicate a link. When you encounter a highlighted song title, or a highlighted word link, please refer to the "Song Links" appendix and the "Addendum Links" appendix at the back of the book for the website link addresses, as well as below.

Online Music Link Page
http://www.soupsyz.com

From there, you can access the Addendum page. You can also download active .pdf files from the download page to serve as your links.

I pray you have as much fun reading *Soup* as we did making it.

Thanks

Travis

AUGUST 25, 1967

The weekly outing had become something of a ritual for them. Friday nights, after supper, they would head out to the country with their hearts pumping and the radio blaring, riding on a wave of blinding optimism. They'd drive for hours, most times talking and laughing about nothing at all. Other times they'd settle into a comfortable silence, speaking without speaking.

They'd been silent for some time when the boy was drawn in by a pretty song on the radio. She was lost in it too, absorbed as though in a trance. The boy looked to his mother. She looked back with warm sadness in her eyes. He felt her love wrap around him as she smiled. She was about to say something when the crunch came. The boy could almost hear the sound of her silent scream as her head snapped to the side at an impossible angle. That's all there was. He never got to hear what she wanted to say.

CHAPTER ONE — IT BEGINS

JULY 22, 1999

Right on time, Scott thinks as the van pulls up to the curb. He climbs in, taking his usual spot in the passenger seat.

"How'd all that go?" Del asks.

"Good. Real good. That Manning dude's all right, for a Yankee movie type. We got two songs done, 'I Call your Name,' and 'Give It Up.' This guy Ian played a wicked sax solo on 'I Call your Name.' I played the rest."

"Cool. It's about time you got your songs out there. I've been saying that for years," says Del.

"Nothing will come of it. Kevin's barely got enough to get everybody back to Milwaukee. I felt guilty taking the fifty bucks he paid me. It's the same with us. How we gonna follow Led Zep with one of mine? 'Glad you enjoyed that rockin' little number, folks. Now here's a sucky little thing our bass player wrote.' They'd stone us."

"Yeah, I get it. But this movie thing is a totally different bag."

"No, I'd bet the movie doesn't make it out of his basement."

"I don't know about that. Independent movies are happening these days. Never say never, dude. Gloria says to bring you home for supper. You in?"

"Thanks, but three's company. Know what I mean? You two got a good thing going and I'm happy for you, but I'm outside looking in on that scene."

"That's you talking, not her. She's from the straight world, dude, you know that, but she likes you. We just gotta tone it down a little, ease her into our world."

"I like her too. And you're nuts about her. I get that. But right now, you don't need me around."

"Come on, man. It's supper. You spend way too much time alone."

"I've never had a problem with it. Why should you?"

"Yeah, I know. The mysterious Scott Yonge, you just gotta fill those shoes."

He doesn't answer.

"You're always welcome, dude, you know that," Del says. "The rules have changed a bit—for both of us—but all those years on the road . . . We had a great time, didn't we?"

"We did, and we've got lots of music in us yet, but the road's a young man's game. There's no getting around the fact that I'll be forty-two this year, and you'll be, well, we won't go there. We did the right thing, moving here. Calgary's been good to us."

"Yep, time to settle down. That's what I'm doing with Gloria. But I'm still me, dude."

"And I'm still me."

"So you're coming?"

"Not tonight. Drop me off at the condo and tell Gloria thanks. We'll hook up another time."

"Okay, dude. Your call." Dell can't hide the disappointment in his voice.

Scott pats the side of the van before Del pulls away. He feels a tinge of sadness he can't lay a finger on, but quickly shakes it away. He skips the elevator and climbs the stairs to his third-floor apartment. He enjoys the feeling of home the recent purchase has offered him, something he has not felt since he was ten years old. Still, it feels empty in the late afternoon light as he unlocks the door and walks in. He pours a cold cup left over from the morning's brew, pops it in the microwave, and settles in with his acoustic guitar. The song flows out of him.

Some days give some days take
Some days leave your mind half-baked
But I know there's something there for me
Whatever it is it's waiting patiently yeah yeah

Same old story same old song
Getting nowhere just getting along
I know there's something there for me
Whatever it is it's waiting patiently yeah yeah

Daylight shining through
Leading me to you
Whatever it is whatever will be
I know it's waiting there for me

Nothing's easy nothing's free
Nothing's written in stone to be
But I know there's something there for me
Whatever it is it's waiting patiently

Yeah I know there's something there for me yeah yeah
Whatever it is it's waiting patiently
Waiting there for me
There for me

There's another one that nobody will hear, Scott thinks. He writes down the lyrics and punches up Cakewalk 9.0 on his desktop PC. He draws a swig of his coffee while the program boots up, then records the song like he has all the others.

The melancholy slowly creeps in as he finishes the task. Does he call her? No, that relationship is going nowhere. *I'll see her on the weekend. We'll talk then. I know what she wants. It's definitely not what I want. Why can't things stay simple, like we outlined from the start?* He feels like he's using her and he can't live with that.

He smiles to himself, his usual optimism returning. *We're on in a couple of hours. I've always got that to look forward to. Life is good buddy, life is good.*

He returns the guitar to its case and heads for the shower.

◆ ◆ ◆

OCTOBER 2020

"Does everything have to happen so early?" Carolyn asks. She yawns as they pull off Highway 33 into town. "It's not light yet. It's still night as far as I'm concerned."

"We're on nature's timetable, sweetie. We'd miss the show if we didn't abide." Michelle says.

"I'm not complaining, Mom. I'm glad we came, but 10 AM would suit me a little better. How does Mr. Millar know today's the day?"

"He's an old timer. The ritual was a part of his life long before your father came to them. He knows the signs."

"I like him. He sounded like an old friend on the phone last night."

"He's a gem, all right. A reminder of a gentler world." Michelle manoeuvres the rented car to a stop in the back of Carolyn's paternal great-grandparent's house, the structure standing forlorn in the glow of the headlights. They exit the vehicle and hike east for the last quarter of a mile so as not to disturb the quiet of the new day.

"Hopefully, we can catch a flight out of Regina later today. Riki wants to pick up one of the new Wombats. They're cool, Mom. The video is H3D and the high-end model can broadcast Halos. I want to hook up with her and check one out for myself."

"There's a hint if ever I heard one," Michelle says. "I thought yours was the latest and greatest."

"'Was' is the key word. I'll bet Hedley has got the new Wombat aced."

"He's probably disassembled and assembled the damn thing several times, figured out all the glitches, and knows how to fix them. He tries to teach me how to use the new contraption, but by the time he explains the inner workings to me, I forget which button to press to turn it on." She laughs.

They walk in silence, enjoying the crisp, early morning air. They veer off the rural road onto the dirt approach leading to an open field. They come to a stop about a hundred yards in, standing silent on an inland shore.

"Why does Dad want us to come back year after year?" Carolyn asks as she looks out over the large natural pond, a shimmering mirror reflecting the new light of the coming day.

Michelle takes in the inquisitive face and the deep blue eyes of her daughter, framed by thick, Spanish black hair tumbling to her shoulders in waves.

"I think he saw what was coming, Carolyn. I think he saw the world we live in now. He grew up in a simpler time, before the virtual world dominated our lives. He believed in the innocence of those times and lived his life through the wonder of that innocence. You were eight when he died, too young to understand, maybe, but he wanted this place to remind you and Hedley how pure and simple life can be. An awful lot has changed in the last eleven years, but the simple truth of this place will stay with you forever. That's what he wanted you to see, a simple truth to carry you through an ever more complex world. It is the one way he can stay with you. I wish you could have known more of him."

Carolyn pours another hot chocolate from the thermos brought for just such a purpose, the steam rising like a specter in the cool October Saskatchewan morning.

"Me too, Mom, I'm jealous of you and Hedley. You felt him after he died. I should have been there."

"There's no way you could have been, just as we could not have been with you and your dad that night in the yard. I believe he gave you what he gave us at the crash site. You were lucky enough to be held by him, to touch him. He touched us too, as best he could, but he was already gone. His spirit touched us, but we could not touch him back. You held him, Carolyn, you gave him great comfort. *I'm* jealous of *you*. What I wouldn't give to hold him again, to have him hold me. I have no regrets, we had him for a while, now we carry on in his name, and in your grandparents' name, and in Duke's name, and in our names. We get to make the choices now."

"I want them back, Mom. I want them all back, like it was before Dad died. I want Grampa. I don't want to believe he's gone. It's not fair, not at all."

"It's neither fair nor unfair honey. It just is," Michelle replies quietly. "I miss them too. Your father, your grandfather, your uncle Michael, I think of them every day, but mostly, I thank a greater power that I have you and Hedley. We need to live for each other, and for Uncle Darren and your aunts and your cousins, all of us still here."

"How long are we going to keep coming? I mean, doesn't it hurt to come every year?"

"As long as I'm able to make the trip, that's how long. And when I can't, I hope you keep coming, and one day bring your kids and show them this magic place. Your father so wanted to make the trip, all of us together. Look, Soup, you can almost make them out in the new dawn."

Carolyn looks out over the marsh to see the slender, curvaceous necks and graceful feathered heads against the luminous red sky.

"You never call me that. That was dad's word for me."

"Only Scott could've come up with Soup. I miss his lovely mind. Maybe saying it will help you feel him."

"I wish. It doesn't matter how many times Hedley tried, and you still try to make me see, I can't feel him. Why didn't he come to me too?"

"If there was a way, he would have found it, you know he would have. I can't pretend to understand these things. I don't think we're ready for that kind of knowledge, but I think he was trying to tell us not to worry, that everything was going to be great, even with what was coming. And it is, Carolyn, it is. Life is beautiful. Your father taught me that. He taught everyone who knew him that. Look at the geese. Listen to their soft sweet honking as they rest. Is there anything anywhere more beautiful? That's what your father wanted us to see. And maybe through them we can catch a glimpse of him. I can't help but think he's out there with them right now looking back at us with a big grin on his face. That would be so your father! He would see the humor in that. I miss him every second I'm alive, and every sweet memory pushes me forward into the future."

"I do have that, I do. When I think that I could be standing right where he stood when he was a boy, year after year, coming to see the geese just as we are now, it makes me want to cry, but in a good way. I feel him that way, Mom. I think if I turned around fast enough, I might see him scratching his name on the old plywood lean-to that used to be here. I remember his smile, his laugh, how he used to scoop me up under my arms and spin me around, then flip me over his shoulder and lower me headfirst down his back. You would yell at him to be careful, so he'd do it to you, and Hedley would laugh, and Grampa would tell us all to be quiet. That's a silly memory really, but I can reach out and touch it, and we're all together again. Uncle Del keeps me in stitches about Dad with all his stories and videos of them playing, and that funny record cover with Dad on the little tricycle. He wasn't all that normal as far as I can remember."

"No, dear, he was not." Michelle smiles, her high cheek-boned face momentarily resembling that of a child's.

"But in the end, he connected with you and Hedley, really connected, and I'm resentful of that, Mom. I don't want to be, but I am."

"I wish I could help you with that, but I can't. Do you remember your father's words, that night in the yard? Do you remember what he said to you?"

"Yes. He said that things can get pretty bad sometimes, but as bad as they get, they will always get better if you let them. He said things can only get better if we let them."

"So you see, you have no reason to be jealous, or resentful. Your father somehow convinced the colonel in all his craziness to let that happen. That's a pretty powerful connection from where I'm standing." She pauses. "It's starting, listen."

A soft rustle begins on the pond as hundreds of pairs of wings flutter, testing the air. The first group scurries across the water one by one, propelling themselves forward along the pond's surface with their feet until their wings can lift them up into the crisp morning air. They circle in groups until all are airborne. Heading southwest, they climb, their gentle honking a constant on the air.

"Bye, birdies, bye," Carolyn whispers in a little girl voice she remembers from her childhood. Four years have passed since her kid brother Hedley last said those words in his traditional goodbye chant. Eleven years have passed since she first came here the October after her father's death. She was eight then and still living with the pain of her sudden loneliness. Hedley had been brave, forcing her to see the beauty of the geese through his strength. She never felt closer to him than the moment when he chanted 'bye, birdies, bye' for the first time. It was as though the departing geese stole her pain from her, taking it with them on their journey. And now they are gone again. "Why did Hedley stop coming? Why did he get so angry about—well, everything?"

"I don't know, Carolyn, I wish I did. It was different for him the night of the Newport concert. You were with me, safe on my lap. I'm not saying it wasn't difficult for you, it was, but we were together. Hedley was alone with that madman on the plane. Who can say what scars remain? He has to work this out as best he can. He'll come back with us." Michelle smiles and squeezes her daughter's hand.

"I hope so. I love coming here with you, Mom. I love our life and all the memories that go with it. We'll come again next year."

"We'll come, but right now it's time to go. Breakfast is beckoning, and then we head home to Ada."

◆ ◆ ◆

CHAPTER TWO – WHAT WILL TOMORROW BRING?

SATURDAY, MARCH 13, 2021 – DARKFELLOW

"This better be good, Darwin," Jeff answers on the third ring. As second in command of the ARRCIS Media Group, the lanky man has accustomed himself to twenty-four-hour accessibility.

"Jeff! Tune in Trafalgar quick, channel 733!"

"Come on, man, it's 3 AM. What the hell could be on Trafalgar that's so important it can't wait until morning?"

"Trust me, you're going to want to hear this. Do it, man!"

"Hold." Jeff puts the audio stream in limbo. "Trafalgar H3D," he barks again to the air, "C733." The south wall facing the foot of his bed suddenly glows, and a yellow-orange tri-directional beam illuminates the air with a transparent 3D holograph. A young performer in his late teens materializes, dapper in a light gray pinstriped three-piece suit, the thin crimson lines leading the eye to a dull yellow fedora tilted forward to hide his face. The young man moves effortlessly at the keyboard but the voice blazes in anger as the performance slowly creeps to and around Jeff. "Merge," Jeff commands, bringing Darwin alive again.

"What the hell?" Jeff exclaims as the driving sound assaults his senses.

"Sound familiar?" Darwin asks.

"Ya think?" Jeff replies. "Beginning," he demands, and the image freezes around him briefly, then fades. The beam focuses again, and blackness surrounds him, accompanied by an overpowering, slow rhythm-and-blues vibe from a hidden drum kit. A small circle of backlight places the singer in silhouette as the voice accompanies the invisible drums a cappella.

Who said it's true
Who said it's true
Who told the lie
Who told the lie

The piano enters, powerful in its simplicity.

"Sounds great. We got ourselves a Scott Yonge clone."

"Yeah, and notice the date," Darwin says. "That's got to be more than a coincidence."

"What do you mean? Oh crap, twenty years ago today! What the hell's going on, Darwin?"

"Beats me. I was searching for Scott Yonge and up it came. Maybe Michelle knows something."

"Maybe. Haven't talked to her in a while, but I think it's time I did. I'll get back to you tomorrow after I call her. I don't think I'll sleep much tonight. DarkFellow . . . Do you believe in ghosts, Darwin? I'm beginning to."

Trafalgar

◆ ◆ ◆

ADA

At fifty-six, Michelle Yonge retains much of the aura and beauty that made her an independent film star in the early years of the century. "The girl next door with just the right touch of Hollywood," is how her late husband loved to describe her, and she was all of that. Her compact and fit 5'5" frame and her shoulder-length wavy blonde hair, colored in spots to chase away the approaching gray, gives her the look of a woman much younger than her years.

Still, she has remained unattached since Scott's death in 2009, concentrating instead on giving their children, Hedley and Carolyn, a normal childhood environment. The events leading to the fiery helicopter crash that claimed Scott, and the people and situations involved in those events, are now a part of American music folklore, and the name Colonel Randall is as notorious as that of Benedict Arnold. How to best raise two children in the midst of the tempest surrounding those times presented a perplexing challenge to Michelle, sometimes almost overbearing, but they all came through on the other side, perhaps better for their endeavor. Now, life in Ada, Oklahoma, is good, despite the brewing changes in the world around them.

"I don't know where his head is, I really don't," Michelle replies to Jeff's digital image. "I know he's been dabbling in music, but I'm blindsided by the scope. It hurts that I have to hear this from you. I've given him his space, but he seems so angry these days. No, restless is a better word. Maybe I need to force the issue with him."

"I can't help you there, not my department, but he does seem to have issues to work through. I don't think bearing down on him will help. Just let him know you're there, and I'm sure you've done all of that."

They hadn't spoken in some time—too long—but the sound of her voice and the look of her on the other end of the conversation brought back the same familiar feelings; the sheer thrill of the sum of their experiences shared over the past twenty years: Scott's surprising win at the 2001 Garrett Awards capped the magic night of March 13, 2001, when she met him backstage. Their whirlwind romance, the Scheck incident, the move to Ada, the colonel, all of it came roaring back with one short greeting. They'd exchanged small talk and updated each other, and now they were in the crux of it.

Michelle smiles. "Yes, Jeff, I've done that, but I at least need to prod a bit, maybe try to get inside his head a little more. There is so much of Scott in Hedley, in both of my children, but that restlessness, an almost sweet bitterness, I suspect it lingers from the kidnapping and all that the colonel brought to Hedley's young life. And of course, watching his father die in a fiery crash didn't help—numerous sessions with Brenda notwithstanding. Maybe the music is his outlet. It was for Scott."

"I sympathize, but I don't envy your task, my dear. Don't get in a knot, Michelle, it's not a bad thing. In fact, he's good—really good. I want to talk to him about his future in music. He definitely has one if he wants it, but I wanted to talk to you first."

"You before anyone Jeff. If he tells me that's what he wants, I'll help him get it if I can." She sighs. "My kids are growing up. I'll be a lonely old spinster soon."

"You'll never be lonely. They'll never truly leave you, and neither will I. And there's always Scott. He's floating around somewhere. How about tonight?"

"What about tonight?"

"How about tonight I come out and talk to Hedley while the iron is hot?"

She laughs. "Still the same ol' Jeff, always a deal in the works."

"I'm crushed that you think that of me," he replies innocently. "Seriously, Michelle, if he wants to go that route, it's best to act now. Besides, I could go for some of your apple crisp, big time."

"I'll whip some up. I'm looking forward to seeing you, I really am. It's been too long. Let's treat it like a visit and keep business to a minimum, shall we?"

"You got it."

"Give me a chance to talk to Hedley first. Maybe it's just a phase."

"Either way, I'm coming. I need an excuse to get out of LA for a while. Besides, I want to take our new shuttle for another spin. Feels more like a luxury liner than the beast we used to jet around in. Can't get used to the look of the thing though. It's almost comical. But hey, changing times. It eats about a fifth of the cake the old ARRCIS cruiser devoured and spits out zero emissions. Carolyn would approve. I'll shoot for around five at Oklahoma City. With any luck, I'll be there in time for supper."

"Tell you what, I'll send Hedley to fetch you. You boys can catch up while you assess the situation. He loves to drive, like me. I bought him one of those new two-passenger Pulse electric runabouts that are all the rage right now. Carolyn's had one for about a year. I quite like them, actually. They're safe and fast, if a tad boxy."

"No, I'll take the Mono—forty-five minutes from the Oklahoma City aero-drome. That's wild! Still getting used to these new gadgets. We'll catch up at the kitchen table, everybody in."

"Fair enough, a meeting in the war room. I can't wait. I'm sure we're in for an interesting evening."

"Aye, lass, it'll be all of that. Okay, I'll throw a few things together and slide out your way."

They chat a little more before ending the session, both a little warmer for it. Now the task awaits Michelle. She saunters to the kitchen, a refreshing cup of tea the immediate goal.

"Sounded like Jeff on the other end," Carolyn says.

"Morning, Soup," she smiles. "Yes, it was. Can I fix you some breakfast?"

"No, thanks. I had some juice and a muffin. What's up with Jeff?"

Michelle studies her daughter, twenty and mature beyond her years, her long black hair pinned up in a bun as she lounges in her pajamas at the kitchen table.

"He's coming out later today. A little bit of business to attend to. I'll tell you more when I know more." It's a half lie.

"Dad's stuff?"

"Dad related, yes. Any plans for today?"

"Nothing special, just hanging out. Riki and I are getting together later, maybe going into town for a spell. Ada's finally got an H3D theatre, so we might check that out. You?"

"Well, something's going on with Hedley."

"Something's always going on with Hedley, Mom. Nothing new there. Good luck with that."

Michelle smiles to herself as she crosses the wide planked oak floor to the island counter of the open kitchen, early spring warmth streaming through the large French windows on the eastern wall. "Tea?" she asks Carolyn.

"Please." She doesn't look up from messaging on her new Wombat personal media device. Michelle gathers the ready tea and two cups on a small silver tray and makes her way to the large ash kitchen table set adjacent to the windows, a comfortable chair's width from the eastern wall.

They sit and chat as they do each morning, reaffirming the mother-daughter bond over small talk and the casual passing of the minutes; precious time in the midst of busy lives.

"Hedley should be stirring by now. I'd best get down there before he gets his mind into one of his projects. You know how he gets focused."

"How can you stand it down there, it's just way too neat and clean," Carolyn responds. "What's with that anyway? A room's got to look lived in. Hedley lives in a laboratory."

"Jeff, I suspect. He's the same way, always has been. It drove your dad crazy when he lived with him for a spell. Hedley's time in LA trying to figure out your dad through Jeff and Tom may be the root of it, but who knows really? Maybe it's just the way he is. He was thirteen the last time he went out there—coincidentally the last time he came with us to see the geese. He's lived in the dungeon ever since. And that's when he started keeping everything so immensely clean and organized. Brenda said there's no harm in it."

"Do you think all that shrink stuff helped him? He sure wasn't like that in the old house. I spent half my time picking up after him. I miss that house sometimes."

"I think Brenda helped a lot. Talking to a professional has benefited him, but he may have issues yet. We'll have to see. And yes, I miss the old house, but I couldn't bear to live there with your father gone, and this house was going to waste. I'm glad Michael was able to put it to good use. I hope Sandra and Edward stay with us... Cancer is in our family, Carolyn, always be aware. All the technology of the 'new age' and we still can't fix that."

"They always seem to come up with new ways to *kill* people," Carolyn replies. It's her youthful idealism again. She stands in her full five-foot-eight-inch grace, moving effortlessly as she glides to the split door stainless steel fridge. Looking in, she retrieves an apple and returns.

"They always have, dear, and I suspect 'they' always will. Never stop trying to make a difference. That's all we can do. Anyway, I'd better get down to the dungeon." She loads the same silver tray with a warm buttered bran muffin (no raisins, of course) and a tumbler of milk and sets her mind to the task.

The downstairs living area, fully developed when the house was built back in 2003, has become unofficially off limits to all but Hedley, unless invited. Michelle does her best to honor the tract, allowing Hedley the space he requires (demands), unless a pressing issue forces her hand. Now she questions the validity of that decision. Had she been too lenient, had she not meddled enough? Or did she meddle too much? The age-old question of motherhood: show the children the way, or give them the tools to find their own way? A fine line exists between the two realities.

Michelle turns and walks through the kitchen to the far side of the living room, navigating the wide staircase to Hedley's domain. She stops at the closed double doors and lightly knocks.

◆ ◆ ◆

A gentle wrapping alerts him, followed by the sound of his mother's voice from the far side of the door. "Hang on, Mom. I'll be right with you," Hedley says. He stashes the written lyrics in a drawer on the way to greet her.

Hedley was up early and had heard them walking the floorboards above, but decided not to join them. He wished to finish what he started before breakfast overtook him. He'd already laid down the acoustic guitar tracks and the organ track the day before, but the lyrics plagued him.

No, that's not quite right, he had thought. He crossed through the line of neatly penciled words and quickly scribbled underneath, crowding the new lyrics between the original lines. *There you go. Beauty! 'Text Me,' that's what I'll call it. I hope Marki likes it.*

Satisfied, he stood to full height, running his fingers through his not-yet-combed sandy locks. He fired up his workstation, loaded the Sonar Century Now H3D digital recording studio, and opened the file. He pulled the boom stand up to mouth level, ready for the vocals. He donned a pair of headphones and hit the record key.

Text Me

And when I head out for my ride
I look into my phone mm
I read what's waiting for me there
The words that lay me bare mm
They shine a beauty yet unknown
They shine the way back home
Way back home
Didn't you tell me it was so
Didn't you tell me to let go

I feel you looking in my soul
The words are all I know mm
They help me gently through my day
From a million miles away mm
Never felt so unalone
Never closer to my home
To my home
Didn't you tell me it was so
Didn't you tell me to let go

And when the music dies away
I've nothing left to say mm
Your words will shine on through the years
Take away my pain mm
Didn't you tell me it was so
Didn't you tell me to let go
Didn't you tell me it was so
Didn't you tell me to let go

After several takes, he smiled, knowing he had it. He backed up his work before returning his computer to sleep mode. Perfect timing for Michelle's intrusion.

"Hi, Mom. I was just about to come up."

"I brought you some goodies," Michelle answers as she sets the tray on the small coffee table opposite the brown leather settee. She takes her place beside him as he reaches for the muffin.

"Nice and warm. Thanks." He takes a big bite and a swallow of milk before Michelle jumps in.

"Everything okay with you? You've been a bit distant lately."

"I'm fine, Mom, still adjusting to the new dynamic. I don't think any of us have quite settled in since Marty died."

"I wish you wouldn't call your grandfather that."

"We were pals, he called me Shortstop, I called him Marty. We liked it that way. Marty was a good dude."

Michelle smiles at the word, remembering. "The one thing your father did that absolutely drove me up the bend was his constant use of that word."

"What about his orange shorts?"

"Yes, well, we won't get into that. Stop trying to change the subject. Your dad and your Uncle Del would fall into that rock speak of theirs whenever they got together. I swear they had a twenty-word vocabulary."

"Yeah, but we always knew what they were saying. There was never any BS between them. Dude's a good word. I do not use it lightly."

"I wish you wouldn't use it at all. No, not really. You say it like your father. I actually like to hear you say it, just not in polite company, okay? Choose wisely, Shortstop. There is so much of your father in you – in both of you kids. You wouldn't hear Carolyn call your grandfather dude, or Marty for that matter."

"Well, no, but they had a different setup. Funny, Soup is adopted, yet she was much closer to Marty then I was, at least in that granddad way." Michelle is taken aback. "Don't worry, Mom. I have no resentment about that, she's my sister—case closed. It's just how it was with them. I think Marty saw a lot of you in her. I think he kind of relived watching you grow up all over again through her. And he told Soup about Dad because he couldn't have her hearing it on the news. That's got to bind them. But mostly, I think Soup helped Marty get over the pain of losing Arlene."

"You are wise for one so young. Look at you, almost eighteen. I don't think Arlene would have stood for you calling Marty by his first name. She might have paddled your butt, and mine too for letting you say it. She got to hold you before she died. You wouldn't remember. you were a baby. She was weak, close to the end, but she held you, looked right at you, and smiled her beautiful smile. We were all there, we all saw her through you, even Carolyn. Your grandmother, my mother, was a remarkable human being. I had the best parents in the world, Hedley."

"No, I do. We do. Me and Pipsqueak. We did all right. Thanks to you and Dad. His is a big part of us, here or not."

"I can't deny that. I hope we don't dwell too much."

"I want to go to Saskatchewan. I want to learn more about Duke and Jim Yonge if there's anything to learn."

"So why don't you come with us to see the geese?" Michelle asks. "It's the same, isn't it?" A cloud descends on Hedley for a second, but it's enough for Michelle to see the change.

"There's no point. I get why Dad wants us there. I'm not so sure I buy his logic. That first time, shortly after he died, that was beautiful, absolutely mind blowing. I felt him there with us, but after that first time, I did not. I don't know why I didn't, but I didn't. I guess I should have told you instead of making a scene like I did, but I simply wanted to remember what I found that first time, not what I lost with each visit thereafter. Does that make any sense to you?"

"Not totally, but I can understand how you feel. I think I sensed something along those lines. I could have forced you to come, but there would have been no point. Dad didn't want to come either. I think he loved the alone time with you when Carolyn and I went. Such a place of mystery, that lonely marsh. It means something different to all of us, something magical. Thank you for telling me, Hedley." She smiles with melancholy. They look at each other and laugh suddenly, not really knowing why.

"The past, Mom, I can't say we live in it, but we embrace it. I'm all for moving forward but I can't completely do that until I figure out what it all means, all that we've gone through as a family. There has to be a purpose to it."

"I'm not so sure. Maybe it's random, a part of the unfolding universe."

"You can honestly say that after the Garretts'? There's no way in hell any of that was chance. You and Dad were supposed to meet. There was a purpose in that. I aim to find out what. I don't see that as a complicated situation."

"Nor do I. I've always believed your father and I were destined to meet, but I've never felt there was a greater driving purpose behind it. You obviously do, and I somehow think Carolyn does too. Who am I to say? I certainly do not wish to get in the way of you finding what you think you need to find. Just, trust me, Hedley. Let me help if I can."

"Trust has never been a problem between us, and it never will be. I don't say much until I've figured things out, that's all. And boy, do I have a lot to figure out."

"So tell me about DarkFellow."

"Oh, you know." He looks away. "How?" His eyes greet hers.

"Jeff. He caught your act on Trafalgar. He said you're very good. He wants to talk to you. I'm fine with it if you are."

"I was going to tell you. It's complicated."

"I'm all ears, cutie."

"Aw, don't call me that, Mom. I don't like it any more than Dad did."

"Your dad protested, but he secretly loved it, and so do you," Michelle replies. She ruffles her son's head, his neatly trimmed wavy blonde locks left array. They laugh, breaking the tension.

"I'm not shutting you out, Mom, or Soup, I'm just, well, I'm still figuring this out you know—about dad, who he is, or was. I found lots of neat things in his stuff and I'm still looking. There's something I found last week that I need to show you, something he wanted you to see that I think got lost in the shuffle when we moved into the new house. And the song I did, 'Who Said,' you've doubtless heard it by now, that's Dad's. He's got lots of tunes and ideas on old CDs and files from his Sonar setup. I got his old PC working just fine. He was relentless, always writing. You might have heard a lot of them, but some, I don't know. There's anger in some of his songs. Not anger exactly, but a need to speak out against the way things were going back then. Who's to say he wasn't right? I mean, look at the state of the world now. Things are pretty messed up, you know they are."

"You're much too young to worry about such things, Hedley. Enjoy your youth for at least a little while longer."

"I could be fighting over there in less than a year, Mom. I need to think about all this stuff. I need to think long and hard."

"You go to school. The draft won't be a problem, I'll see to that."

"I don't want to go to school. I want to figure out this music thing. That's what calls me."

"I can't protect you if you don't go to school."

"I don't want to be protected. If they call, I'll go. I don't want to be known as the poor little rich kid hiding behind his mom's skirt. I couldn't live with that."

"What about me? I couldn't bear losing you too, not now."

"You could lose me anytime. Or Soup. What will be will be, but you'll never really lose any of us, just like we've never lost Dad. He was there after he died, wrapped around us like a cocoon."

"Okay, we won't worry about the future right now. Let's live in the present. Show me what you've found."

"Brace yourself. He wrote this note and a song to leave you before he went to meet the colonel. He meant for you to find it if he didn't return. I guess the cleaning crew packed it away when they readied the new house."

"Yes, I thought there would have been something, but when there was not, I assumed he simply did not have the time. Or maybe I didn't look hard enough. Maybe I was scared of what I'd find. That last song, 'The Dream,' the one for the colonel, it scared me. It was so unlike Scott, so dark, so…"

"I remember. I was on the plane with the colonel watching the telecast of the Rockport concert. I'll never forget that moment. Even then, I realized he was completely crazy, a total nut job. I hated what he was doing to Dad. I wanted to hurt him back. That moment changed me. I didn't exactly know how at the time, but I knew something in me was different."

"It changed your sister too. She was sitting on my lap at home. We were watching the insanity of that whole thing live on TV. Maybe because she was with me, maybe because she felt safe, I don't really know, but she did not pick up on your father's darkness. She picked up on the message of the song. Who knows how these things work? The moment disturbed me, you bet it did. To see your father with so much anger, so much pain…" Michelle breaks down, reliving the moment that ultimately started the march to her husband's death.

"It's okay, I've got you," Hedley says, reaching to hold her. "Those times were bad, but we came out okay, all of us, I think even Dad. Things are as they should be. There was a purpose to all that. I believe that to be true."

"And there's your father in you. That's exactly what he would say. Okay, I'm ready, let's look at that note."

Hedley hesitates before rising. He crosses the room with a solemn gait, as though performing a ritual as old as life itself. He bends slightly and then kneels, granting himself easy access to the bottom doors of a nightstand Marty had built for him some years before. He withdraws a thin plastic container and retraces his steps, presenting his mother with his precious cargo. "It's a CD, Mom. Old technology no one uses anymore."

"I know what it is Hedley," she half laughs. "This was cutting edge when I was in my prime, but don't put me out to pasture just yet."

"No, you're done Mom. Time for a walker if you remember these," Hedley teases.

She shoots him a pair of daggers, chased by a wistful chuckle. They grow quiet as Michelle carefully unfolds the note sitting atop the silver circular disk inside the plastic jewel case. A tiny shiver grabs her as she peers down at the loose handwriting. She takes a breath and dives in.

She continues to read, eyes focused on the short note as though breaking the trance would somehow make their impact less relevant. Finished, she looks up, eyes brimming with tears.

"Thank you," she says in a quiet, poignant voice. Hedley reverently says nothing. Michelle rises and draws him to her. They embrace, tears filling both sets of eyes. "It is exactly what I would expect from your father," Michelle says. "His dedication to us was forefront in everything he did. I think it's almost better I read it now than back then. I do not think I could have handled this . . . Do you remember that day, the day we returned home?" Hedley nods. "I remember getting out of the police car feeling delirious joy and bottomless sadness in the same breath. You ran to Carolyn as she ran to you. I was afraid you would collide, but you embraced and laughed as only children can do. Dad was laughing too, but tears streamed down his face as he walked towards me. I clung to him, all of us laughing and crying at once. It was a peculiar moment. I felt guilty for feeling as good as I did, so totally free of any encumbrances. I guess we were all glad the ordeal was finally over. Your father would have loved that moment. Thank you, Hedley."

"There's so much more Mom. Songs and poems, or lyrics that read like poems, and pictures, not of him of course. There don't seem to be any anywhere. Not personal ones anyway. There are letters from his uncle or something. I haven't read them."

"I'd like to. Not now, but soon. That would be his uncle Gord Richter. Scott lived with him after his mother died. He was ten at the time. Your dad was the original Shortstop in this family. Did you know that? He loved to play ball, just like you do, or did."

"The song I did last night, 'Who Said,' did you know that one? I set up his old computer. I had to nurse it back to health, let me tell you. An old Pentium 4 with "XP" on it. But it's been running good since then. Anyway, I found it in his Sonar files. You can't believe how many songs are in there."

"I, ah, actually haven't heard you do the song. I'm not good with the new technology." She blushes.

"What, Trafalgar? That's simple stuff. They were one of the first to put pulse technology to good use. They simply took a laser image and shot it at the pulse particles floating around all of us. All that miniscule junk that the sun has cast our way becomes a natural 360-degree screen for us to play with. There's more to it than that of course, but that's the gist of it."

"I'm sure you've got it all figured out, but I just want to see you play the song."

"Let me show you, Mom. The first thing to remember is that Trafalgar is always on. It's voice activated, like this—Trafalgar H3D," Hedley commands with authority, "C733, beginning." His left bedroom wall suddenly comes to life, the familiar yellow-orange beams filling the air around them with the transparent 3D image of Hedley's performance. He joins his mother on the settee as the drums begin.

Who Said

Who said it's true
Who said it's true
Who told the lie
Who told the lie
Who said it's true
Who said it was it you
Who told the lie
Who told the lie

Who walked the road
Who carried the heavy load
Where are they now
Where are they now

I want to tell you that I am wise
I want to show you that I'll survive
I want to tell you that I'm alive
I want to show you that I'll survive
Oh oh oh oh oh oh
Oh oh oh oh oh oh

Who was the man
Invested in the plan
What did he see
What did he see

Who shone the light
Dividing black from white
Where are they now
Where are they now

I want to tell you that I am wise
I want to show you that I'll survive
I want to tell you that I'm alive
I want to show you that I'll survive
Oh oh oh oh oh oh
Oh oh oh oh oh oh

What was the plan
What was the plan
Where are we now
Where are we now
Oh oh oh oh oh oh
Oh oh oh oh oh oh

"Who are you, really?" Michelle asks. "That was breathtaking. How? Where did that come from?"

"Listening to Dad, where else? I've studied him, how he plays. I've been fiddling around down here since, well, forever."

"Does Carolyn know?"

"I do now," Carolyn says indignantly, walking down the stairs to join them. "You've caused a stir, Hedley. All my friends are talking about this DarkFellow guy. Riki tapped me just a while ago. What do you think you're doing?"

"You can't tell anybody Soup. I'll kill you if you do."

"Nobody's killing anybody around here, and nobody's saying anything about anything until we talk this through. You two settle down."

"Mom, he's been doing this right under our noses. Kind of like lying, isn't it?"

"She's got a point, Hedley. It is a bit deceptive, no matter how you look at it."

"I wasn't hiding anything, you guys just didn't notice."

"Oh come on," Carolyn says. "Who you trying to sell that to?"

"Look, I'm shy, all right? I wasn't intentionally hiding anything from anyone, except maybe myself. This is scary shi—ah, stuff to me, especially at the start of it. I just kinda got used to doing it hush hush, with headphones. Know what I mean?"

"You're actually pretty good, really good. I mean, for a kid." Carolyn smiles. "Why the incognito crap?"

"I...I don't know, it just felt like the thing to do."

"What I'd like to know is where you shot this... this... what do you call it?"

"Halo, Mom, they're called Halos, and I'd like to know the answer to that one too," Carolyn says.

"Promise not to get mad? You've got to promise, Mom." Michelle nods.

"I did it last month on my trip to Calgary."

"That sneaky... Del! I should have figured as much."

"A friend of his actually shot it in Uncle Del's studio."

"And he didn't say a word. I'll—"

"He didn't know either. I thought I'd show him the song, see if he knew it. He didn't, but he was blown away by me doing it. The Halo was his idea, actually. It kind of mushroomed after that. He didn't know about the DarkFellow thing though, that was me, and I put it up there last night, you know, in honor of Dad's Garrett appearance. Del had Dad's old suit, from the 'Thought Away' video way back when."

"I recognized it," Michelle says. "I've often wondered what happened to that suit, and to many of your father's musical trinkets. I think I'm going to have to put Del on the grill about a few things, but not now. The hat wasn't your father's."

Hedley points to the fedora, patiently waiting its call to duty from a recessed shelf running the width of the headboard above his bed.

"Nice touch." Michelle smiles. "Continue."

"I wasn't cutting you out. Marki doesn't know either. I can't begin to know how to tell her. It just kinda happened on a whim. Or more like, one whim after another after another. I didn't expect it would get noticed. Ironic, isn't it? I've tracked it. It's gone viral, over 240,000 plays since I launched it last night."

"Marki doesn't know? Yikes!" Carolyn responds, ignoring Hedley's math. "That won't sit well with her. That sensitivity of hers... I like her, you know I do, but she overreacts to breathing! Right or wrong, the longer you wait, the more she's going to hurt."

"I know. It's not a matter of trust, it's... I don't have a plan, Soup. Like I said, I just put it out there on a whim. I didn't seriously think anything would happen. I just wanted to thank Dad somehow for being who he was. Is."

"And there's your answer," Michelle replies. "Tell her how you told us. She'll understand your honesty."

"We got it, she'll get it," Soup says. "If she doesn't, it's not your fault."

"Why don't you invite her over tonight? She can figure this out with the rest of us and be sworn to secrecy, if that's what the plan calls for. Jeff will know what to do, whichever way you want this to go."

♦ ♦ ♦

"Okay, here's the situation," Jeff starts. He looks around the crowded table at the remnants of the Zoe/Yonge family. They're all present. Michelle, Soup, Michelle's older brother Darren and his lovely wife Marie, their daughter Belinda—twenty-eight and home from Phoenix in honor of the day—the departed brother Michael's third wife and one true love, Sandra (the only one to succeed in bringing Michael out of himself), and her nineteen-year-old son Edward. And of course, along with Hedley is Marquetta 'Marki' Devron, Hedley's shadow.

Shy and sensitive, mature beyond her nineteen years, Marki's plain, almost mousey look fails to hide her inner beauty from the few she allows to truly know her. Hedley is at the top of the list, thanks to a bond formed through their bout of shared childhood cancer therapy. Jeff's eyes fall on her and he smiles, suddenly seeing what Hedley sees. She returns a somewhat nervous grin before looking away.

"The re-release of "One Song, The Scott Yonge Saga" in the new Halo format has been an overwhelming success," Jeff continues. "We've had over 50,000 downloads since its release last week on the pro side of Trafalgar. Your 'DarkFellow' thing is a stroke of genius, Hedley. The way you tied it into your father's legacy is marketing magic." He looks around the room for emphasis. "What I say stays in the room. I'll explain later, but for now, know this: the gods at Trafalgar have moved "Who Said" to the pro side. You're going to get paid, Hedley, and well. Trafalgar assumed, and quite correctly, that the "One Song"

Halo and your foray into the unknown are linked. You indexed DarkFellow as a tribute to Scott Yonge, so people searching him, all those old fans coming out of the woodwork, were getting you first. Why? Who knows? We only know it started in Milwaukee and spread out across the country. My hunch is it's the Kevin Manning crowd linking into Scott via the re-release of Kevin's movie "Twisted Logic," which is where all this started twenty odd years ago. But somewhere along the line, the young crowd latched onto DarkFellow and the hits just keep coming. I say let's keep it that way."

They all look to Jeff at the head of the dining room table, silent at first, until Hedley breaks the ice.

"I'm not sure about the DarkFellow thing, Jeff. That was a lark really, a tribute to Dad for sure, but nothing I expected to pursue. I want to get into music, I want to do some of Dad's unreleased songs and continue writing my own, but not as DarkFellow. That's not me."

"He doesn't have to be you, and you don't have to be DarkFellow. He's a character you've created, and rather successfully I might add. Intentional or not, run with the success. Help me with this, Michelle."

"I don't think you should pressure Hedley," Marki says. "It is his life, after all."

"I agree wholeheartedly," Michelle replies. "But Jeff is merely presenting options. He's a good man. He was Scott's manager for years, and he became a close friend. He's part of the inner circle. I—we—trust his judgment implicitly."

Jeff turns to Marki, sensing her unease. "I've known Hedley since birth. I'm not about to take him down a path he does not want to take. I admit, I hear the cash registers ringing, but they'll never ring louder than Hedley's voice. We have an opportunity here." He turns to address the room again. "DarkFellow has caught on, it's as simple as that. The secrecy, the mystery—I say run with it. Of course, that gets a whole lot more complicated, but that's my bag: solving complications in this crazy business. It almost destroyed your mom and dad with that SAM thing, Hedley. I can assure you I learned my lessons. That will not happen again."

"I gotta admit," Edward adds, "DarkFellow is cool. I had no idea—none—that it was you. Clever."

"I wasn't trying to be clever, it was just something I did," Hedley responds.

"Exactly," Jeff replies, "and that's the key. DarkFellow is honest, raw, and fresh."

"DarkFellow isn't you, but you're DarkFellow," Marki says quietly.

"Marki, that's genius," Jeff says. "I couldn't put it better myself."

Marki beams, happy to contribute. "I like DarkFellow too, now that I've heard him. I just wish you would have told me." She trails off as Hedley softly squeezes her hand under the table. She turns to him and smiles.

"But isn't Hedley a little young for all this?" Marie asks.

"Of course he is," Michelle replies. "That's why we protect him."

"Assuming he wants any of this in the first place."

"Thank you, Belinda," says Michelle. "That is the fact that grounds us all. Ultimately, it is Hedley's decision."

"I'm not giving you a decision now. I've got to think on this. I've got a lot of soul searching to do."

"Great. Talk it over with your honey and—"

"I'm nobody's honey, bucko," Maki says. "We're not . . ."

"Sorry, no disrespect intended," Jeff continues, catching himself. "Think it over, talk it over, but don't take too long. Time waits for no one."

"I will, I promise. Mom, give me a little time."

"Of course, Hedley. I want—we all want—what you want."

"As long as we're soul searching, I'd like to bring another topic to the table," Carolyn says. "Uncle Darren put me in touch with Great Aunt Margret in Pittsburgh last week. She's invited me out. I really want to go."

"Am I the last to know anything around here? Why not ask me?" Michelle says.

"You were busy with the 'One Song' project and—"

"And you know I'm never too busy for either of you."

"Don't get in a knot, Michelle. I was more than happy to help out my only niece," Darren responds. "There's no conspiracy here, she's not running off in the middle of the night on her bike like a certain hot-headed kid I used to know."

"Low blow, big bro," says Michelle. "Okay, give me the goop. What's going on that I should know about?"

"I want to find out more about Grampa, about the Zoe side of the family. Great Aunt Margret wants to show me her personal archives. She has pictures and lots of stories to share with me, with all of us, through me."

"You've got school to think about, Carolyn. The past is not going anywhere, but the future is closing in."

"Aunt Margret's not getting any younger. I might not get another chance. I can take a semester off and not hurt my future any. What would Dad say?"

"That's not fair, Soup. These are different times."

"Didn't you just say?"

"Yes, your father would endorse you wholeheartedly, that was his nature. He was a free spirit. He'd just as soon ask a question as know the answer. The unknown was his friend, but he understood practicality. He was specific in setting aside money for your schooling. He understood the importance of education. You know that."

"Yes, but as you have said many times, he understood the importance of knowing yourself as the key to a happy life, and a happy life, according to Dad and you, is the key to a successful life. I don't know where I'm going. I have no idea what I want to do with my life. I think school is a waste of time at this point. I do know, or I have a strong hunch at least, that Aunt Margret will lead me to a lot of answers about myself, about who I am. I need to know those answers."

"You have your grandfather's way of presenting an argument. You leave me no room to maneuver."

"I seem to remember Grampa saying the same about you."

"Help me out here, people," Michelle says, appealing to the family. "Hedley wants to go to Saskatchewan. Carolyn wants to go to Pittsburgh. Jeff wants Hedley to be a rock star. Michelle wants to cry."

"Are you going away, Hedley?" Marki asks.

"I think *somebody* should go to Pittsburgh," Belinda says. "Aunt Margret obviously wants to see to it that family memories don't get lost. I'd love to go, but I can't. Why not Carolyn? There's nothing like the generations getting together for a hootenanny."

"I agree," says Marie. "There's not a lot out there on the old ones. They're the mystery generation, or will be if no one pays heed."

"And Marki, Hedley will never be far away from you, not after all you two have been through." Sandra's reassuring words settle on Marki, bringing a sweet smile to her usually masked disposition.

"Maybe you can come with me. Mom, can she?" Hedley asks.

"Jeff?"

"Don't ask me, Michelle, I'm here for the apple crisp."

"Okay, one crisis at a time. Carolyn, this is not a blank cheque. Three weeks, and then we focus on school. Do you think you can find yourself in three weeks?"

"I think I can, or get a good start on it."

"And Hedley, you need to give Jeff, and all of us, an answer on DarkFellow. You're almost eighteen. You've started something, and you need to finish it one way or another. Go to Saskatchewan, but come back with an answer. Marki, you're welcome to join Hedley. Honestly, I need a break. I think we all could use some apple crisp."

"Dad's song, Mom, on the CD. I want to play it for you, the one he left. We kind of got distracted earlier. You should all hear this."

"I don't know if I'm ready, but get it and the note. Carolyn, help me please with the apple crisp."

Sandra pitches in with dessert duties while Hedley scoots to the dungeon with Marki in tow.

"Should I do it Marki, this DarkFellow routine?"

They stop their descent, turning eye to eye on the wide hardwood staircase. "I think so. You're good, Hedley, really good. It's you without being you. I think you should."

"I think I should too."

"I'm just worried about the girls."

He smiles, eyes twinkling. "But you said we're not— "

"We're not. I mean, we haven't . . ."

He kisses her then. Really kisses her. Not a just friend's peck; a full-on lip-lock leaving no mistake of its intention. She returns in kind, timidly at first, then passionately, stepping onto the surface of the moon for the first time.

"Now we have, and we are. We're not kids anymore, Marki." They hug.

"We have lots to talk about," she says. "Then again, maybe not. I think we know."

"We know, but we'll talk." He smiles before releasing her. "Let's get that disk."

Returning to the dining room, Hedley places Scott's old battery operated boombox on the table and unfolds the paper.

"I want to read this," Hedley begins. "It's from Dad. He left it before going to meet the colonel."

Still standing, he reads slowly, clinically, almost devoid of emotion.

Michelle,

If you're reading this, I didn't make it. Hopefully Hedley did, but if he did not, live your life for those who remain, and for yourself. That's all you can do in times of war: survive and remember the fallen. Forgive me if I talk in the abstract, but the possibility of the loss of our son in real terms is more than I can bear, though we've walked that road most of his short life. I cannot fathom your grief if you have to face that reality alone, nor can I offer any words that would ease the burden. All I can ask, if the worst should happen, is that you keep his memory alive for Soup. Let her know what her brother would have been. Of course, this letter is only insurance. I have no doubt that come Tuesday we'll all be together, but it feels better from this side of things to leave something, just in case.

But one thing doesn't change, whatever the outcome. You're the best that life has to offer. You are life, and my life began the moment we met. I can't say that enough. Every moment, every ounce of pleasure and pain we shared was worth the ride, regardless of where I am now. I wouldn't trade one second of our life together for an eternity of life without you. Not one second.

Please remember, as I told Soup, no matter how dark life gets, things will get better if you let them. Seek out love again. It will not diminish what we are, or were.

In all probability, we'll make this trip together, but if something should go wrong, promise me you'll take the kids to Tyvan. Show them the geese, Michelle, like we saw them back in '03. Take them to my roots; show them what this ol' prairie boy is about. And tell them about Duke. October, Michelle. Promise me as you read this.

I love you. Always
Scott

Hedley pushes the play button.
They listen, emotion thick in the air.

Desert Nights

A desert night
Lives in beauty in the cold moonlight
Running through me in the open air
There's no one there
In the desert night

Marki weeps silently as Scott's last emotional plea fills the air, tears tracking her cheeks to the floor. Carolyn remembers with honor, squeezing her mother's hand for support. Jeff lends his in like fashion, gently caressing Michelle's free hand as she relives the past, kitty corner close and a world away.

A sea of gold
Covers the trails where the old ones rode
Gone are the stories that they might have told
In days of old in the desert night
With a dream they came bound for glory gonna make a name
So many died alone in the desert night

Don't shed a tear for me
Don't live in fear for me
I'll find my way in the desert night
The old ones tried the old ones died to give us life
Now the desert night is waiting there for me

The strong ones stayed
Finding beauty that the gods had made
Their tools of battle are a pick and spade
They made the grade
In the desert night

The lonely ones
Ride forever in the desert sun
What's their pleasure in the open air
I feel them there in the desert night
The old ones cried the old ones died to give us life
Now the desert night is waiting there for me

Don't shed a tear for me
Don't live in fear for me
I'll find my way in the desert night
The old ones tried the old ones died to give us life
Now the desert night is waiting there for me
Yeah the desert night is waiting there for me
Mm mm

"Wow! That hurts," says Jeff.

"I'm going to do it," Hedley answers quietly. "I'm supposed to."

Nobody argues.

◆ ◆ ◆

Family dramas eradicated, Michelle can now concentrate on executing said plans. But first, she must see Jeff off to LA. Sunday afternoon finds them heading down the escalator to the platform below. They pass through the turnstile of the old converted railway station, modernized to accommodate the new monorail technology, the turnstile granting access to the loading platform.

"Those two are inseparable," Michelle replies to Jeff's question. "I swear they are virtually Siamese twins."

"Are they . . . you know, doing the deed?" Jeff asks.

"You had to ask that. I don't think so. They're close, really tight, but I don't think in that way."

"I don't know. They're into something. I think he's going to marry that girl someday."

"You think so? There certainly was no instant spark between them. We used to travel together for checkups, Maria Devron and myself in the front, Hedley and Marki harnessed side by side in the back. Maria and I became fast friends. Those two . . ." she shakes her head in remembrance. "Not so much. They used to glare at each other, Marki with her oversized round horn-rimmed glasses that made her eyes look like saucers, and Hedley with his blue-eyed stare that usually won everyone over in a flash. Not Marki, at least not at first. Then Hedley relapsed. This is post AFF of course. He had to go for another round of treatments. It was rough on him, and on us all. Marki was particularly upset because she'd been through the hell. She knew all too well Hedley's predicament.

"Maria phoned the day after we returned from a session in Oklahoma City. It was an especially rough day for Hedley. He could tolerate the cramps and the pain, but he hated that his hair was falling out again. I hesitated, but Maria said it was important that Marki see Hedley, so I relented. He was playing Space Invaders when we walked into his room. He scrambled to cover his head when he saw Marki, then realized the folly of it. It was one of the few times I saw Hedley hang his head. He was ashamed, Jeff. I wanted to cry. I'll never forget Marki's words at that moment, a moment as pure as any I've known. 'I think you're beautiful,' she said to Hedley in her soft shy voice. Hedley looked up and smiled. 'Wanna play doubles?' he said. She jumped up on the bed beside him and I don't think she's really left his side since. Hedley was seven, Marki eight.

"Hedley came out of his shell as they grew, but Marki has always remained a shy one, even around us. She is a good soul. I'll never stop thanking her for that moment. I've come to love her like a daughter, but I can't see her as a daughter-in-law. She stuck to Hedley like glue in grade school and high school, maybe a little too clingy. He's a handsome lad and the girls like him, the popular girls, but he mostly ignores them. Yet I never got a sense of those two in a romantic way. I don't think Hedley's ever . . . you know."

"I have a feeling they're gonna, and soon, if they haven't already," Jeff replies. "Love doesn't necessarily happen wham-bam-thank-you-ma'am like it did for you and Scott. Sometimes it's a long, slow burn, waiting for the right moment to announce itself. I myself have not experienced either."

"How have you managed to stay single all these years, with your looks and wit and money?"

You loved her too, didn't you? Scott's words flash through his mind. He brushes the old memory aside and smiles, saying nothing.

"Saved by the bell, Jeff. You dodged the question again."

The Accelerator monorail pulls to a stop in front of them on its cushion of air.

"Amazing how quiet this thing is, I didn't hear it pull up. Makes you wonder why we relied on fossil fuels for so long, doesn't it? These pulse things just might save us from ourselves. Gotta run. It's been an experience. I'll need Hedley out my way soon." He steps into the oval tube-shaped car and turns to face her through the windows of the doors as they close behind him. He holds an imaginary phone to his ear and waves before disappearing into the mid-afternoon light. *Oklahoma City in forty-five minutes,* she thinks. *No wonder they're everywhere.* She shakes her head and chuckles as she makes her way up from the platform.

◆ ◆ ◆

CHAPTER THREE — THE PLANS OF MANY

"It's wild, Michelle, really wild," Jeff says. She can see the excitement written on his lanky face, the still reddish hue of his long hair falling over his eyes as he looks down into his desktop com center, crisp on her Wombat PD screen. "The 'One Song' release, Hedley's DarkFellow thing, they're both going nuts. Ka-ching, Michelle! The estate keeps growing. I look like a genius for an afternoon's work. ARRCIS wants to sign DarkFellow now! They don't know of course that DarkFellow and Hedley are one. What they do know is that DarkFellow is becoming a voice of the new age, a commentary on how things are in this crazy world."

"Scott wouldn't want that for Hedley any more than he wanted it for himself. They tried to make him the new guru with 'MaryAnn Said.' We know how that turned out. Now you want to plan such a scenario for Hedley? Is that wise?"

"That bit with the colonel, no one could have foreseen that. The chances of that happening again . . . there's no chance, Michelle. No chance at all."

"Yes, but does Hedley see himself in that role? I think not."

"Then why did he latch onto 'Who Said'? Not exactly a love song, that."

"Because it was there, it's as simple as that."

"Hedley said there were lots of songs. That particular one is not typical of Scott. Hedley picked it, I'm sure of that."

"Then we need to ask Hedley. Hold on, I'll transfer the call." She makes her way to the dungeon.

"Pick up the call," she says. "Jeff."

"Channel nine," Hedley barks. The 4D wall-mounted screen brings Jeff into view.

"Hedley, my man," Jeff says. "Your mom and I are having a discussion. Why 'Who Said?'"

"I think Dad was looking for answers, just like I am. He's got a lot of those kind of tracks—angry, resentful. Maybe not angry—confrontational is more like it. I'd bet 'MaryAnn Said' came out of the same thinking. He was happy-go-lucky, that's the way I see it. Most of his songs reveal that about him, but I think he became disillusioned with the external world unfolding outside the gentle life we lived. I think he had something to say about those times."

"And?"

"And I want people to know what he was thinking. I want people to know there was more to Scott Yonge than feel-good love songs."

"Thank you. I rest my case. Michelle?"

She winces, not wanting to reply.

"No offence, Mom, I know what his songs mean to you."

"None taken," she replies in a soft voice. "Maybe it's time for a change of perspective."

"Exactly," Jeff says. "That's all it is, and maybe, just maybe it's another way to move forward. I think Scott would approve, and who better than Hedley to be the architect? Hedley, can you come out Friday evening after school? I'll send the ARRCIS shuttle to fetch you from Oklahoma City. My treat."

"Mom?"

"Yes, but I'm coming too. And we're back Monday morning at the latest. School still tops the list."

"Of course," Jeff says. "DarkFellow will rise again. Bring the suit and the fedora."

"Oh God." Michelle terminates the feed, wondering again where the story ends. *Time to call Del*, she thinks. A long-ago conversation with her husband flashes across her consciousness. A melancholy half smile plays on her lips.

"Dudette," Del greets with enthusiasm.

"Just can't drop the rock-speak can you?" Michelle laughs. She embraces her resigned acceptance of Scott and Del's slang talk.

"Hey, I is who I is," he returns in his friendly jocular voice. "How you been Michelle?"

"Good! How's Gloria and the kids?"

"The same, 'cept the kids ain't kids anymore. Melissa's twenty-seven, Daniel's twenty-six, they're all growed up, as Scott would say. Not to Gloria though, they're still babies in her eyes."

She remembers Del's step-children with fondness, having spent many a weekend with them, Scott, and herself, in training for their own adventure. "Same here. Carolyn and Hedley are testing the waters. They won't be underfoot for much longer."

"Danny's still at home 'til he finishes school, but Melissa's out there doing it. She lives just down the block, but it might as well be New York for all we see of her. Oh well, that's the way it goes, I suppose."

"So what are you and Hedley up to?" she asks.

"He's good, really good. He has that thing that Scott had, that concentration, that ability to get totally lost in a song. He's gone when he's playing, really gone."

"I noticed. I saw the DarkFellow Halo."

"He didn't want me to say anything. He said he wanted it to be a surprise."

"Believe me, Del, it was all of that."

"I didn't know about the DarkFellow dude. That was a surprise to me too. Jeff called about the hush-hush."

"What should I do?"

"Hang on, just like you did with Scott. We're in for a ride for sure. DarkFellow is huge out here too. Danny and Melissa are clued in—not about Hedley of course, but about the music. So are their friends. I don't know, Michelle, I think this DarkFellow thing is a stroke of genius, long as Hedley is cool with doin' it."

"That's my concern."

"I've never seen eye to eye with Jeff, but I know he has Hedley's best interests at heart. He's bringing Darwin in. He talked about Tom too. I still want to punch that dude sometimes when I think of what he wrote about you and Scott in '01. Tom led us all to a lot of trouble."

"He did, but in the end, he came through in the Scheck incident. Scott probably survived because of Tom. He changed after Scott died, you know he did, and his pen pal relationship with Hedley went a long way in helping my son understand things a little better than he would have. They helped each other through that period. Tom's okay. We can trust him."

"If you say so. Keep me in the loop."

"I will. Give Gloria a hug."

♦ ♦ ♦

"I've got this," Hedley says. He speaks with authority, but feelings of nervousness and intimidation underlie his tone. It's Saturday, the morning of the twentieth, one short but eventful week after the twentieth anniversary of the Garrett broadcast. He sits in ARRCIS Studio One with Jeff and Darwin Robinson, ARRCIS engineer and Michelle's good friend from her LA days.

"Hedley, you remember Darwin?" Jeff begins.

At six-feet-four-inches and two hundred thirty pounds, Darwin is a hard man to forget. Even at fifty, his curly locks are blonde and plentiful. Though the term fullback comes to mind on first glance, his cheerful demeanor and muscular physique are opposites, downgrading the impression to that of an over-grown teddy bear.

"Sure. Cool, you were around a lot after my dad . . . you know. You helped make the "One Song" documentary."

"Yep, I did. Your dad and I were good friends."

"Mom's got a picture of you and your wife and a bunch of her friends back in Hollywood, posing for a baseball team picture."

"Those games were a whole lot of fun. It was a bunch of film people getting together to blow off steam and goof around a bit. Your dad played, too, though he never made it in any of the pictures. Funny, it's hard to find pictures of Scott. I think he avoided them, or maybe he was a vampire. He sure was a good shortstop though. Nothing got past him. He'd throw you out nine times out of eight! In fact, I met him at one of our baseball parties. Bert Olmstead threw them after every game. Great guy and great producer, Bert was, and he had the bucks, let me tell you. It was back in 2001, five days after your mom and dad met at the Garretts. They were lined up smorgasbord style at the buffet. Michelle called me over to meet your dad. They were horribly in love, those two.

"'Darwin Robinson,' I said as I extended my hand. 'Not a bad spread for roadkill.' Seems like yesterday."

MARCH 17, 2001

"Scott Yonge. It'll do 'til the pizza arrives," Scott replies with a smile.

"So you're the guy who landed Michelle," the woman next to him says in a bubbly voice. "I'm Cindy, I'm married to this big palooka." She runs her fingers through Darwin's curly blonde mop.

"Looks like we both lucked out," Scott replies. "How two ugly guys like us ended up with a couple of babes like you is beyond my comprehension. It must be the sympathy factor."

"You've got a charmer, Michelle. Better leash him," Cindy laughs.

"No problem. A fate worse than death awaits the wandering eye," Michelle jokes. "And the wandering eye knows it."

"Moi? Never! 'Course, the shoestrings some of you California girls pass off as clothing don't exactly help to keep the eyes front and center. But if I look, I look out of curiosity, nothing more."

"Your boy needs a little more training, Zoey," says Cindy.

"It's early. I've got years to mold his molecules," Michelle replies.

"Work me like the pile of putty I really am," Scott pleads. He falls to his knees. "I throw myself at your feet asking forgiveness, and I pray you to strip me of my evil manly ways!" He wraps his arms tightly around her ankles like a slave in the house of the pharaohs.

"Oh get up." She pulls one leg free. "People are looking."

Scott springs to his feet like a cat to a counter. "I'm all right! I'm okay! Nothing to look at here, folks. Everything's under control! It's okay, I'm Canadian!"

People around them chuckle as Scott straightens an imaginary tie, a la Stan Laurel. Michelle leans into him, touching her head to his in affection.

"You're nuts!" she laughs. "What I see in you . . ." she kisses his cheek and ruffles his wavy sandy hair.

The two couples retire to one of the tables with plates piled high, anticipating the meal and the pleasure of each other's company. Michelle bears fond witness to Scott and Darwin's foolish antics with a quiet glee, aware that the two are fast becoming friends. *Anything to solidify his position here,* she thinks with glowing clarity.

MARCH 20, 2021

"Your dad was a nutcase, Hedley. I loved him, we all did," Darwin says. "Sorry, today is your day."

"No, it's nice to talk to people who knew him. Thanks."

"My pleasure. Are you ready to rock?"

"You bet. I've got it on my Wombat. You seen one of these? It's the new professional series. I can run my Sonar Century Now directly off this thing, digital and audio. No more hauling around a laptop and a converter. Heck, it runs mini Halos! Flat, not dimensional, but still, pretty cool!" Hedley manipulates the controls. "I call it 'Between.'

"Dad wrote ferociously in 2009 after he started back at it," Hedley explains. "This is one of those, I think. It's much different from the unreleased songs from the 2001 era. I used Dad's original .wav file as a reference, then built 4D audio around it. The drums are real. That's my friend Kenny Moore. He recorded the drum tracks in his basement studio in Broken Arrow. We send tracks back and forth all the time."

"Does he know about DarkFellow?" Jeff asks.

"He does now. I told him he'd play if we tour or anything. Is that okay? He's cool."

"It is if he's good. If not, we'll deal with it later."

"He's dead on, Jeff. We met at Camp Nakita, before the colonel grabbed me. We stayed in touch, been friends a long time. I added two guitars, bass, and a Hammond organ line. I might like to redo the vocals, but I'm pretty happy with it. It rocks like the old days."

"Spin it," Jeff says.

The sound fills the room, loud and driving with a raw edge. They listen, Hedley on pins and needles.

"It has the attitude," Jeff says. "Darwin?"

"Oh yeah, that'll go. I'll grab the drum tracks and blow them up a bit and give the guitars a little more bite, but we're pretty much good with the tracks. Let's recreate the 'Who Said' set as close as we can and shoot it. We'll do the vocals live, a redo, as you suggested, Hedley."

"Okay, we're on it. By the time interest in 'Who Said' wanes, we'll have 'Between' to pique their imaginations. Come back in two hours, Hedley. Loosen up your voice and rehearse. Oh, and give me a number for Kenny. He's good. We need to talk."

Hedley returns from his makeshift dressing room with suit and fedora in hand and is escorted to Studio Two, a quiet and spacious area in which to rehearse. Darwin readies the set while Jeff retreats to his office with the requested info. He keys in the seven-character alphanumeric code and waits on a response.

"Hello?"

"Kenny? This is Jeff Thompson. I'm a friend of Hedley Yonge. I think you might know what this is about."

The video fades in, revealing a well-built, dark-haired teenager of Jeff's height or a little better—almost a full head taller than Hedley's five-foot-eight-inches. Though rugged and more outgoing than Hedley, Jeff instantly recognizes certain sensitivities in the lad that run through his friend, and he guesses are also the root of Marki's heightened sensitivity.

"Hedley has mentioned you," he replies coolly. "What's up?"

"DarkFellow is up, and I want you to be a part of it. Interested?"

"Why wouldn't I be? Question is, where do I fit in?"

"For starters, your drum track will be on the next Halo, 'Between.' We're shooting it later today for release in the near future. If things go well, there will be a tour. Hedley says you're eighteen, and he soon will be, so legalities are not an issue. There's money to be made, maybe lots. I don't mean to sound hard-edged. Hedley is the closest thing to a son I'll ever have. I managed his father's career, and you can bet I'll have Hedley's—and your—best interests at heart. But I'm a practical man. Strike while the iron is hot, I always say. Can I arrange to fly you out here for tomorrow? I've a hunch adding a second face to the shoot will do us no damage. Not a word to anyone though, not even your parents. The longer the identity of DarkFellow remains a mystery, the greater the advantage for us."

"Geez, can I think this over a bit?"

"Sure, you've got twenty seconds. Oh, and while you're thinking on it, come up with an alter ego for yourself. Can't have people knowing who you are either, can we?"

"Okay, I've got nothing special going on this weekend. Make your arrangements. Later, dude." Kenny terminates the connection.

Jeff smiles at the brash abruptness of the young man, and the familiar use of the almost archaic colloquial term. *Yep, Hedley's buddy to the max,* he thinks. *The Scott and Del show all over again.* He shakes his head and laughs.

◆ ◆ ◆

"I would like you to wear this," Michelle says. She extracts a garment from her overnight bag. Fresh back from a Hollywood shopping spree, she feels the positive tension of the session electrifying the air around her. She holds up a green and white t-shirt, faded somewhat over its years in storage, but still none the worse for wear."

"The Roughriders," Hedley says, almost in awe.

"God knows why, but your father loved this football team."

"Everybody from Saskatchewan does, and everywhere else in Canada. I love them, too. They got something special, mom. I don't know what it is, but they've got it. Dad was nuts about them."

"And that's why I want you to wear it."

"Does everything have to be a shrine? Maybe we go a little too far with this Dad thing sometimes."

"Just try it, see what you think."

Hedley reluctantly dons his father's t-shirt, then buttons the gray with red pinstripe suit coat over top and checks his image in the full-length mirror.

"It does look kind of cool. You can't completely see the logo so there's more mystery, and best of all, I don't have to wear the vest. I didn't like it in the first place. Thanks, Mom."

"I like it. You might want to put on some pants, too."

They make their way to Studio One, where the set and the gear await. Nine H3D cameras are in position instead of the usual five, with one dead center, at front and back, one on each flank, front and back, one on either end of the set, left and right, facing each other, and a wide-angle suspended from above, all carefully aimed to capture the action while remaining out of each other's view. Kenny's mimed performance will be captured tomorrow on the same stage and edited in, with all images merged to form the 3D holographic Halo. Hedley mounts the four-foot-high stage, taking his place behind his single thin keyboard, resting on a simple foldout stand a few feet right of center stage. He wears an almost invisible wireless microphone and earplug monitor setup, as unobtrusive as the new technology will allow.

"We've got a chance to do something new with the extra cameras," Jeff explains. "Darwin's idea is an attempt to thicken the image, make it less transparent, more real. No harm in trying. Trafalgar is new but fast becoming *the* platform, and new means wide open, like MTV in the eighties. We do this right, we can lead the pack. Impact, we want impact. We're gonna give it to them through DarkFellow—so intensity, Hedley. Lots of it."

Hedley awaits the count, nervous and focused, wanting to unleash. He jumps on the hard driving feel, playing along with the track, moving with the music as he does so, while subconsciously preparing to channel the vocal.

Between

One more broken highway
One more battered dream
One more road to nowhere
Left me somewhere in between

One more rusted Chevy
One more angry scream
One more destination
Left me somewhere in between

Catch me I'm falling
I got nowhere I can go
Catch me I'm falling
As to where I don't know
All of my dreams
Left me somewhere in between

It's red on the horizon
And the moon still has its glow
And I can't help but wonder
What a man can do to grow

Grinding out a living
Is burning up my soul
The more I keep climbing
The further down I go

Catch me I'm falling
I got nowhere I can go
Catch me I'm falling
As to where I don't know
All of my dreams
Left me somewhere in between
Oh oh oh oh

"He moves much better than his father did," Michelle says. She and Jeff watch from off stage.

"Doesn't he? Scott was left footed most of the time."

"Tell me about it. Arlene was the only one who could get him dancing with any success."

"What about the 'A Thought Away' video?"

"That was a fluke mostly, but yes, he did look good on that, didn't he?"

"Or maybe everyone was so busy looking at you, they forgot all about Scott. You were sensational." Michelle laughs and turns to watch the action.

Catch me I'm falling
I got nowhere I can go
Catch me I'm falling
As to where I don't know
All of my dreams
All of my dreams
All of my dreams
Left me somewhere in between
Oh from where I am
And where I wanna be yeah

They shoot several takes with the keyboards, then several more with Hedley playing Scott's old light green Fender Stratocaster, reconditioned to factory specs. Two more tracks of Hedley on bass (all tracks accompanied by vocals), and the shoot is complete.

"Looking good," Jeff says. They view the results on the H3D editing screen.

The set is stark white on the playback, but merging colors and patterns will be added at the discretion of the final production edit.

"We'll grab the best vocal track and edit this all together tomorrow after we shoot Kenny," Jeff continues. "This sound, it's retro, but cool. I think that's a big part of it. People don't get 'real' anymore. We're way too processed these days in my opinion. I think DarkFellow is a concept whose time has come. We'll see with 'Between.' If it goes, we've got something. We're done here. Can I take you and Hedley for lunch?" he asks Michelle.

"Let's make it dinner. I want to take Hedley to a boutique I visited today." She turns to Hedley. "I spotted a cute dress I think is perfect for Marki, but I want your opinion. I don't want to overstep."

"She doesn't wear dresses much, Mom."

"Reserve judgment until after you see it. This particular dress is not out of character, trust me."

◆ ◆ ◆

"Dude, you're here!" Hedley bellows as Kenny enters the studio.

"This better be good," Kenny says. He laughs. "I gave up my Hung-gar and an afternoon with Sheila to be here!"

"Trust me, Sheila will see you in a different light after today. But, oh yeah, you can't tell her, can you?" Jeff says.

"Don't worry, Sheila and my parents think I'm hanging with Hedley. They bought that half-truth no sweat. Melanie and Melissa both say hi. Cripes, I don't know what you do, Hedley, but both my dimwit twin sisters are hot for you. Don't even go there."

They laugh, dispense with the small talk and fall into the comfortable camaraderie that started at Camp Nakita back in the summer of 2009.

CAMP NAKITA — JULY 13, 2009

"Hi."

"Hi, I'm Hedley."

"I'm Kenny." The shy dark-haired boy looks up as he dangles his feet from his bottom bunk, GameBox in hand.

"What game are you on?"

"Captain Fantastic," Kenny replies.

"Neat. What are you here for?"

"Melanoma. What are you here for?"

"Leukemia"

"That's gruesome."

"Yeah."

"Yeah."

"But I'm in remission," Hedley says. He sounds almost apologetic.

"That's good. Me too. Dr. Ross?"

"Uh huh. He's cool."

"Yeah. Thought I'd seen you there. Wanna play marbles?" Kenny pulls his small sack of treasure from his pants pocket, hoping the game is on.

"Sure."

"I have to stay out of the sun."

The two boys leave the coolness of the twelve-bed bunkhouse, heading into the warmth of the afternoon sun. They retreat to the shade of a bordering dogwood where they can watch the others in the open field that doubles as a baseball park, soccer ground, and assembly area, which is surrounded by eleven other identical bunkhouses, a row of six on either side of the clearing.

Camp Nakita resembles so many other such summer camps, with green-shingled roofs over white, skid-shack looking wood structures: military and clinical in appearance, yet somehow cozy in their quaintness.

Among about a hundred boys, Hedley and Kenny soon lose themselves in the game, filling the hour and a half of casual time before resuming the structured schedule of the camp. Hedley had been on pins and needles in anticipation, but the second day had replaced the excitement of the new adventure with the unmistakable dull ache of homesickness. He'd never left home before, other than time spent in hospital, but he'd been too sick to notice, and his mom was always there when he woke up. Not today. Hedley woke up alone. He made it through the morning schedule, even ate a solid lunch, but he returned to his bunk at the start of casual time, where the comfort of his comics and few trinkets from home lay waiting. Kenny had similar inclinations, sitting quietly on his bottom bunk two rows over. Now, twenty minutes later, they were playing in the July outdoors, two former struggling six-year-olds with nary a care.

Through each other, they've successfully banished the age-old plague of childhood, moving a step closer to manhood in the process, although to them, it's only a game of marbles.

"Do you like Mr. Johnson?" Kenny asks, referring to the cabin counselor.

"He's okay, but kind of strict," Hedley replies. He draws a freehand circle, two feet in diameter, in the sandy ground.

"Yeah, and he has stinky feet sometimes."

The two boys laugh, and a friendship is struck as the sound of playing children carries on the open air.

"What are you building at craft time?" Kenny asks.

"A balsa wood glider. I hope it flies okay."

"Neat. I'm building a box for my mom to put stuff in."

"My mom has lots of boxes. Did your hair fall out?"

"No, but lots of kids' did, some of them here. See the scarfs on their heads?"

"Yeah, I didn't like losing my hair, but it grew back. Did you hurt?" Hedley asks as he fires one of Kenny's marbles out of the circle.

"No, I just got sick. We playing keepers?"

"Just pretend keepers. We'll give the marbles back at the end."

"That's good. I usually lose. I don't shoot so well, but I'm getting better. What about you, did you hurt?"

"Not so much. But my arms and legs ached, and I threw up sometimes."

"Cool."

"Yeah, and no one got mad like when I ate a whole bunch of chocolates."

"Yeah, we can get away with stuff," Kenny says before nailing Hedley's favorite aggie.

"At first." Hedley pauses. "But my mom's tough. I can't do nothing now."

"Yeah, moms are tough."

"But dad's a pushover."

"My dad doesn't live with us."

"Oh, how come?"

"I don't know. My mom and him fight a lot. They're divorced or something."

"That sucks. Got any brothers?"

"No, but I got two twin sisters."

"Yuck. I got one sister, that's bad enough. She's okay though, for a girl."

"My sisters are okay too. They're ten. That was a good shot, you got two. I think my dad got mad when I was born, I don't know. He doesn't like me, but he likes the girls okay. He seems scared of me or something."

"I wouldn't be."

"Me either. I don't know him much. He's never around. I'm thirsty, wanna get some Kool-Aid?"

"Sure," Hedley replies. They make a quick exchange of their winnings.

"Where do you live?" Kenny asks as they walk to the canteen.

"Ada," Hedley replies.

"Wanna e-mail after camp? I live close to Tulsa."

"Okay. I have my own computer."

"Wish I did. I gotta share with my sisters. My mom doesn't like computers at all."

"Yeah, my mom's pretty dumb with them. I'm always showing her things. My dad has three computers. He plays guitar and drums into his."

"Why?"

"I don't know. He sings too. He's a star or something."

"You mean, like on TV and stuff?"

"Yeah, sometimes. He travels with some other guys who sing."

"Where to?"

"Oh, around. I think he gets paid for that."

"Cool. Ever caught a frog?"

"No, but we had a crow. My grampa caught it. It had a broken wing."

"Still got it?"

"No, it got better and flew away."

"Too bad. I hope we get better."

"I think we will."

"Yeah."

MARCH 21, 2021

"Who are you?" Jeff asks as Kenny climbs behind the classic look of the re-issue Ringo Starr Ludwig Oyster Black Pearl four-piece drum kit. Simplicity at its best, the small kit is all Ringo ("The king of feel", Dave Grohl once said) needed to rule the world of the sixties.

"I'm Bartholomew," Kenny replies with confidence. He wears a black masquerade mask styled after the old Lone Ranger TV show to hide his face from the world. The one-piece black jumpsuit molds to the contours of his lean but muscular physique, sculpted by martial arts, and clings to his every move. A bright red fedora, tilted down over his eyes in Hedley-like fashion adds to the mystique, embracing the DarkFellow idealism as Jeff hoped it would.

"Poifect," Jeff says. "Let's do this. Bring it, Kenny. The microphones are muted, you can pound as hard as you like. Play along with the track as though it's live. Make it you being you."

The count clicks its metallic pulse from the wedge-shaped floor monitor, a preference of Kenny's over headphone monitors, and lends an added touch of realism to the look of the stage. Set back on the drum riser, to the left of Hedley's absent position, Kenny's presence adds a feeling of depth to the set that Jeff hopes will be captured by the extra cameras in use for the 'Between' Halo. Unlike conventional video imagery, the H3D cameras are stationary, catching the movement from all angles simultaneously instead of moving to follow the performer. Camera angles are chosen in the final edit, not at the time of performance. They exist at all times, in holographic 3D imagery.

"Crank the volume," Kenny says, stopping the shoot. "I want it loud and aggressive. I want to feel the tracks in my blood." Darwin ups the levels. "That's got it!" They start again, this time to perfection. Four takes and they have what they need. Jeff is a happy man.

"That's it?" Kenny asks. "I drag my ass out of bed early for half an hour's work?"

"When you got it, you got it. What can I say?" Jeff says. "Why don't you dudes get reacquainted while Darwin and I do a mix and edit? Give us three hours or so. There must be something out there in LA to pique your interest for a spell. Michelle, are you going to hang around and visit?"

"Not on your life. I'll not let these two hooligans loose on the streets. Somebody's got to save Hollywood from their shenanigans."

"We're good, Mom."

She sighs. "Okay, I'll stay where I'm wanted."

"No, join us," Kenny says. "It's been a while since we hung together. I think you're hot, Miss M." Michelle laughs as Kenny lays a quick peck on her cheek. Hedley can only groan.

They return later, the three of them better for the outing, anxious to view the edited Halo.

The extra cameras do their job, making the final image much thicker than the existing five-camera Halo format while maintaining the trademark transparency. Jeff has a hunch they've pulled the production of Halos in a new direction.

They dub the Halo a success and retire to a late lunch, this time on Michelle's dime. Goodbyes are made and all return from whence they came to continue their lives as though the weekend never happened.

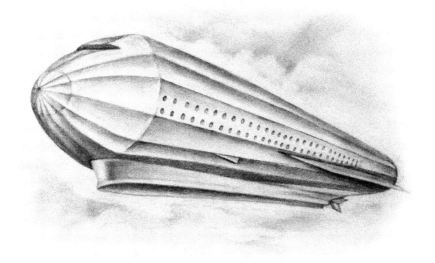

Pulse Air Shuttle

CHAPTER FOUR — PENNSYLVANIA

PITTSBURGH

Michelle and her Aunt Margret were friendly but never close, the distance and the years somehow preventing a solid mesh. Perhaps the tragedies of their singular lives kept them apart. Still, a pleasant time was had by all as they were reacquainted in Pittsburgh. But now, Michelle senses the time has come to depart. Carolyn is settled and safe in her great aunt's guest room at the assisted living complex. It is time to leave Soup to her adventure.

Carolyn and Margret took to each other as the skipped generations often do; renewing the past and the future through each other's widening perspectives. Michelle resented somewhat that she had not been chosen as the protector of the family vault, but she nonetheless relished Carolyn's excitement in the task. Now she worries about both her children as she peers out the window of the air shuttle, gliding silently over the clouds. *I can't believe these things stay in the air,* she thinks. *What does 'floating on an ionized cushion of air' really mean? I'm flying in a flat-bottomed tube is all I see. No wings, no engine noise, and no pollution. All good things, and yet, I can't totally trust this machine. My kids so easily accept what is alien to me.*

As Michelle looks outward, she wonders if she's taken the right directions for her children's future. *What paths would you have chosen?* she quietly asks her departed husband, but of course, he does not answer. She smiles to herself and reclines her seat, resting her eyes.

◆ ◆ ◆

"Why me?" Carolyn asks. "I mean, I've talked to you over the years on the phone and stuff, but we didn't meet until Grandpa's funeral. I miss him."

"And that's a big part of it," Great Aunt Margret replies. "You were close, Martin told me that. He and I were close too, in years and in thinking. He was born in 1935, eight years my senior. Our older siblings were practically strangers to us. Except for Clarence of course, he stayed to run the farm after Robert and Darren were killed in the war. Yes Carolyn, your uncle's namesake. I never liked the name Marty. I always called him Martin, much to his chagrin. He hated that. Did you know that?"

Carolyn nods. "Only Granma could."

"Yes, child, Arlene could do no wrong in his eyes. There's more, Carolyn, so much more we have in common. You see, I was adopted, just like you."

"Wow. I wasn't aware. Would you mind if I recorded our talk? I don't want to miss anything."

"Imagine that, Margret Shaw on tape. Sam was my second husband. Did you know that?"

"Yes," Carolyn nods. She punches up her Wombat's digital recorder. "Not tape, Aunt Margret, not for a long time. There, all set. Thursday April 8, 2021. The Zoe family history by Margret Shaw, née Zoe, as told to Carolyn Yonge-Zoe. I was not aware you were adopted, Aunt Margret." She repeats it for posterity.

"Few are. I'm not convinced your mother knows. Martin certainly did, but he rarely spoke of it. It wasn't an issue to him, or anyone in the family, just as it hasn't been on your side of the fence. Still, we're different. Not outsiders exactly, they've never made us feel that."

"No, not ever," Soup replies. "I forget myself sometimes."

"As I did, dear, but we share a longing, a hole in our lives that no one else can totally understand, just as we could not completely grasp Hedley's predicament when he was sick. My mother and father at least knew the Ashcrofts, my birth parents. They lived close by and were good friends, so it was an easy step to take me in after the fire. I was a baby. My mother got me out but died going back in for my brother. The volunteer squad found me on the ground, safely away from the smoldering remains. I remember none of it, of course."

"That's sad," Carolyn says.

"It's life . . . Michelle knows precious little about your birth parents. She said she wasn't provided much and you never asked, so she never went digging."

"I had no desire to know. I still don't."

"I didn't either, but Violet, my mother, your great-grandmother, kept all she had on the Ashcrofts, which turns out to be plenty. I have a cousin, still living in St. Louis—June Peterson. I've never met her, but I hope you'll take me to see her. She's eighty-seven, the same age Martin would be."

"I'll take you. Mom will help if need be, I know she will. We simply *must* go."

"And we will, very soon. But first, we have business to attend to."

They spend a few days going through various albums and old scrapbooks of pictures and mementos gathered over a lifetime. They have no intrinsic value to speak of, but they are treasures beyond measure to Carolyn. She carefully captures each photo and memento with her Wombat handheld, adding description and commentary to the gathering family history.

"The silly looking fellow with the big ears standing next to me is your grandfather. On that day, we got too close to a skunk. They washed us down with warm milk and lemon juice and made us sleep in the barn until the odor backed off a touch. We were a sorry looking couple my dear, we were indeed.

"This picture is the only image remaining of Graham, your grandfather's grandfather. Your great-great-grandfather, dear. He established the family farm outside Pittsburgh in the early 1880s as the country came out of the depression after the Civil War. Not much is known of him or his reasons for settling where he did, but I'll share what I know." Margret pauses, further gathers her thoughts, and dives in.

"The Zoes were Quakers who first settled in the Philadelphia area. We know they came from England in the early 1680s to escape religious persecution, but specifics of the family history in the old world have been lost over the generations. It is known that Jeremiah Zeeland, the original Zoe, arrived with the second wave of William Penn settlers, and that he married a woman from the Lenni Lenape tribe after his first wife died in childbirth. Your mother's high cheekbones are a product of that union, perhaps."

Carolyn nods in silent agreement.

"It is believed that the Zoe family name came to be at that point, evolving from the combination of the two cultures. Early Lenni Lenape clan membership was inherited from the mother's lineage. It has been reasoned that a compromise was struck when the children arrived. I like to think it was a little more personal. Her name was written down as Nattisoe, an English translation of her Indian name, I would suppose. Jeremiah referred to her as Natty in the family register, what little of it survived. Somewhere in there, he dropped most of his last name, kept the Z, and connected it to the 'oe' of her name. I think he loved her deeply and wanted to honor her, to preserve her heritage. I choose to believe that is the way it was."

"Or maybe he didn't want to be found."

"We'll never know for sure. Record keeping being what it was back then—not the keeping, actually, but the storing. I think the clerks and the family historians kept the records just fine, but so many of those records were lost over the years. The next generation certainly won't share that problem. Just the opposite, I think—they'll spend hours and hours sifting through mountains of pictures and documents to find something of use. The things people keep in their computers."

"I'll say," Carolyn says. "You would not believe the junk on Hedley's Wombat." They laugh, sharing a generational understanding of the growing information overload. "And the files from my dad's old PC. I'd love to see one personal picture, one real snapshot of my mom and dad in a candid moment, instead of the mountains of promotional junk related to their media lives. Why do you think so few real memories exist from their early days? And Duke, my dad's surrogate father, in all that muck there's only one picture of him, emailed by Uncle Del way back when. No, Aunt Margret, I don't think much has changed. The search for something relevant is as hard as ever."

Margret reflects on Soup's soliloquy, a tight-lipped grin accompanying her nod. "Do be a dear and fetch us some tea, Carolyn, I could use a break before we continue."

Carolyn rises to the task, returning to the small, comfortable couch with tray in hand. She pours the tea, serves up two hot buttered croissants (courtesy of the old microwave), and resets the digital recorder. "So, what about the two hundred years between Jeremiah and Graham?"

"You'll have to venture to Philadelphia and the national archives for those blanks, dear." Margret draws from her tea and continues. "What little information we have is from our direct descendants, and most of that was passed on verbally. I've written down what I've been told. The future of this information is in your hands." Margret sees again in the young girl's deep blue eyes an honest and trusting soul, and is better for the knowledge.

"Graham came along in 1853, kicking and screaming, so I was told. He broke away from the Quakers when he left the Kennett Square area, embracing the modern ways of the day. The Civil War changed the way of popular thinking, but he retained much of his Quaker heritage, passing on the values of living a simple and honest life. Truth, honor, and respect for others ran deep in him, beliefs he passed on to his children. Graham married Olivia Jensen in 1887. They had five children in all, starting with Abigail in 1889, followed by Sara in 1891. Sara died two days later of unknown causes. That was a common occurrence in rural America in those days, not at all unexpected. Mary Ann was born in 1894 but died the following year of influenza. It was a harder world then, Carolyn. Tragedy was a part of everyday life."

Carolyn quietly nods in understanding. Margret clears her throat and continues.

"Albert was born in 1897, their first boy, followed by George, my father, your great-grandfather. The surviving girl, Abigail," Margret points to an old sepia photo lying loose in a group spread out on the glass topped coffee table, "married Franklyn Hardy and moved west in 1909. I don't know her story. Albert, the oldest boy, died in the trenches in early 1918. This newspaper article is all I have on our Uncle Albert." Margret draws attention to a scrapbook opened to its proper place in history. Soup examines the narrow two-paragraph article carefully snipped from its home: a grainy sepia photo of a young soldier in dress uniform, the only record of another life lost.

"He looked like Grampa," Carolyn says.

"He did, and like his brother George, our father. George was fifteen when Albert was killed. People mostly call it World War I now, but we called it the Great War in my day. They were back at it twenty years later, not learning a thing from the earlier horrible slaughter. Martin and I lost our oldest brothers in World War II. None of it made any sense to us, but maybe that was the Quaker blood talking."

"Does anybody ever make sense out of war, out of senselessly killing innocent people?" Carolyn asks almost bitterly. "And yet we keep doing it. Taking something as fruitful as the Pulse and turning it into a weapon. That scares me Aunt Margret. What have we learned really?"

"I wish I had an answer. It's the big one, isn't it? Why do we keep doing what history tells us we shouldn't? All we can do is speak out, upset the apple cart a bit. These are dark days, but I've seen darker in my time. Embrace optimism as we did and lead the way. You can do no more."

"We may have to do more—lots more—if things keep going the way they are."

"Each of us is asked to carry the load we can bear. What we carry beyond that is the measure of us. George carried more than his share, I can tell you that. He carried on with the family farm outside of Turtle Creek when Albert shipped out. George married young, falling hard for Violet. Just as well—the farm was too much alone, even for the strapping eighteen-year-old that he was. Robert was born in January of 1922, Darren in the fall of '23. Clarence came along in 1927. Those boys were his pride, Carolyn. He worked hard for Violet and the boys, eking out a living on the farm, growing vegetables mostly, and some wheat and barley, and livestock of course, mostly for personal use. Berries too, lots of berries and even apples for a spell, but they petered out in the depression. Martha was born simple in '31, probably as a result of her troublesome birth. She was wrapped by her umbilical cord and deprived of oxygen for a little longer than she should have. No matter, we were happy to have her with us. She was joyful and honest. A lie never crossed her lips, or so I was told. She died of TB in 1948. I was five, but I remember her well. Your grandfather was born in the middle of the Great Depression. There was no silver spoon in his mouth. Those were tough times for the family and the country."

"I know. Grampa talked about the Depression a lot, with great fondness I might add. He said they always ate well. He told me he never felt poor or deprived of anything. Life was good even then. I'll never forget him saying that."

"Yes, that sounds like Martin. A good man, Carolyn. Martin was a good man. I missed the Depression, of course, being born in 1943, but he told me the same thing. He did well with Arlene, your grandmother. He loved her, and she him, passionately. She was a wonderful girl, full of life, like Martin, but with more discipline. He needed that. He needed her. Your grandmother was a pretty girl. Many of her looks and mannerisms live on in Michelle. I understood Arlene just fine. Your mother, not so much.

"Arlene and Martin married in 1960 and moved to Ada to live their good, simple life. Michael came along in 1962 and your Uncle Darren in 1963. Just when they thought they had it all, your mother arrived in 1966. Martin was smitten. How he used to dote on her. Don't misunderstand, he loved the boys equally, of course he did, but mercy sakes, he doted on Michelle," Margret laughs at some distant memory, kept inward. "She was his princess—that is until you came along. He had a special place in his heart for you, Carolyn. You were Michelle incarnate, and that took nothing from either of you, that's just how it was. You more than anyone brought Martin out of the darkness when Arlene passed on, the one time he lost his zest for life. But you brought him back."

"I didn't do anything, I just loved being with him. He got me through losing Dad. Isn't that what family does?"

Margret grins. "You are a Zoe through and through. I'll always love you for Martin, and for who you are. You delight me, and everyone around you. You are a joy."

Carolyn blushes, her long black hair framing her rosy cheeks. "Thank you, Aunt Margret. I love you too, for sharing the family with me. I'll take care of them, I promise."

"Yes, of course you will. But we're off track." She collects her thoughts once more and continues.

"George struggled with the loss of Robert and Darren, but his struggle was the country's as well. I don't remember the boys. I joined the family in '44 after they shipped out. But I remember a certain look that would come over George from time to time, and when it did, we all knew what was on his mind. No one talked about it, we didn't need to. He would go off by himself for a spell, go fishing or walking, and when he came back, he was usually fine. Everyone was left to deal with it in their own way. That's the way it was, the way of the times. He always wondered about Abigail, where she got to. He was six when she moved away. The last contact was the birth announcement of her first child, Charles. One lonely postcard from Kansas."

The old woman goes to the scrapbook again, a slight tremor in her hand as she extracts the postcard from its archival plastic sheath. "Violet took care of this for years, nursing it along. The picture and this card are all we have of her. She just . . . disappeared. That gnawed at George. He wanted to go out, but he couldn't. People didn't move around as easily as they do now, but he never stopped asking questions. The Hardys fared no better. They hired an investigator, but the trail went cold after Franklyn and Abigail moved to Australia in 1912. No one knows why. Work, maybe? Yes, I think that's the way it was, but we'll probably never know. Eventually George stopped speaking of her, but he never stopped thinking of Abigail."

"Maybe I could try to track her down! There might be more to find online now."

"That was a long time ago, child. Some things are best left undone." Margret's hazel eyes search the air for the proper response. "Knowing or not knowing won't change anything for George, or any of us. And yet, it's out there, isn't it, her legacy? You'll have to search your heart on that one. George died in 1962, just shy of Michael's birth. He never saw any of his grandchildren. Clarence had one child late in life. I never had children. It was up to Martin. He felt he failed somehow, not being able to present his children to George. It's the way of the world, isn't it, the way things happen? Violet, your great-grandmother, went out with the birth of each child. I travelled with her when Michael and Darren were born, but not so with your mother. I was married by then and trying for my own, but it didn't work out. Internal plumbing problems—my one big regret."

"Did you know my dad?"

"Scott? No, I did not. I know he was a good man. What he did to get Hedley back from that awful man . . . I was invited to the wedding, but I was ill. I was out in 1997, but your mother was in Hollywood by then. I never saw much of Michelle, but I followed her. Their story, well, it's legendary, isn't it? But behind it all, I know they loved each other very much. I must profess, I don't understand people like your mother and father, what makes them tick, but I loved them. My heart broke for Michelle, for all of you, when Scott was killed."

"I'm not sure I do either . . . understand them, I mean. Their life together was beautiful and tragic and a whole lot of weird. I miss my dad, but I miss Grampa more."

"Martin was in your life longer, and you were close. He became your father after Scott moved on. It is only natural, dear. It takes nothing away from your father's place in your life."

"Hedley is still tight with Dad. He had the 'experience' you know, at the crash site."

"Do you believe your father came back to Hedley and Michelle?"

"I'm not sure, Aunt Margret. I know they believe it. I want to believe it. I want to feel what they felt. Mom said she can still feel him sometimes. She said she felt his spirit, his essence wrap around her and Hedley. She could feel him telling her that everything was good, that everything was as it was supposed to be."

"The shock of seeing the helicopter hit the ground in a fireball with her husband in it, that's got to have an effect. Maybe . . ."

"Except Hedley felt him too, in exactly the same way Mom did. He was only six, I know, but he swears he could feel Dad touch him. He remembers to this day how that feeling calmed him down. Hedley believes, and when he tells me, I believe. I want to believe."

"There are many things we do not understand. We'll leave that where it lies."

"What about you, Aunt Margret? What's your story?"

"There's not much to tell, really. I go through them, don't I? My first husband Donald was killed in a rollover in '61. Those gravel roads were treacherous sometimes. I probably married too young, but he made me laugh the way Martin used to. I missed Martin when he left. As I said, we were close, the best of friends, but he had the wanderlust. He did what he needed to do, the right thing to do for him. I remarried in '68 when I was twenty-five. We loved each other and had a good but short life together. He died of cancer in '75. That was enough for me. I worked as a pharmacist in Pittsburgh until 2001, when I retired. I ventured out to visit Martin and Arlene several times over the years, but did not leave Pittsburgh much. I tried Philadelphia for a few years, but I prefer Turtle Creek. That's home to me. Clarence died in '83 and left the farm to Roger, his only son. He's still on the farm, living a reclusive life. He wanted to be left alone and I honored that. He had his reasons, I suppose. He's still there if you wish to see him, but he won't give up much."

"What'll happen to the farm when Roger dies?" Carolyn asks.

"It'll pass on to your family, the last of the line. There is a will, but I don't know the particulars. I don't think farming is in anybody's blood out your way. It's sad, but I think we're nearing the end of the line for the Zoe family farm."

"We need to keep in touch, all of us," Carolyn says. "Time is precious."

Zoe Family History

• • •

"Can I call you back, Jeff?" Michelle says. "Carolyn is trying to ring through."

"Oh sure, kick me to the curb." He laughs. "Okay, but get back to me."

Michelle kills the feed.

It's been almost a week and Michelle is missing her daughter more than she wants to admit. She hopes for her return but knows it's too soon for that.

"Hi, Mom," Soup says. "You won't believe what I've learned about us."

"I miss you too, thanks for asking," Michelle says sardonically.

"Don't play the jolted parent with me. You know better."

Michelle laughs at her own foolishness. "Sorry, I really do miss you." She takes in the soft features of the beautiful young woman filling the screen and wonders where the years have gone. "So what's new in Pittsburgh?"

"I'm not in Pittsburgh. I'm in Philadelphia."

"Philadelphia? Why? Who's with you?"

"Mom, I'm twenty. You went to Oklahoma City to live on your own when you were my age."

"Those were different times, Carolyn."

"So?"

"So . . . never mind, we'll talk more about that later. What's in Philadelphia that's got your gander?"

"The National Archives. There is so much to learn about so many people in our family. Aunt Margret said this is a good place to start."

"Well bless her heart. Where are you now?"

"I'm across the street at the Holiday Inn. I had to come. Family history records are by appointment, it was today or not until next week. Aunt Margret paid for the flight."

"You and your independence. There's no holding you back when you put your mind to something. Okay, but phone me, phone me, phone me. How long do you expect to be?"

"A couple of days tops. Then I'm back to Pittsburgh."

"Do you want me to come out?"

"And leave Hedley alone with Marki? There's something going on there, Mom."

"What, you too? What am I missing? Oh, never mind, I'll give you your space. But call, okay?"

"Okay, but I gotta run. Love you."

"I know. I love you too, Carolyn. Call."

The screen is as empty as Michelle feels.

She mulls over the conversation as she heads for the kitchen, bent on a spot of tea.

With teacup in hand, she heads down to the dungeon and takes a vacant spot next to Hedley on the settee.

"Hedley, do we need to talk about Marki?"

Looking, she suddenly sees her son in a different light. The wavy blonde hair is the same, as is the dimpled smile and the cute Roman nose of his father, but Hedley is no longer a child. The tender pain of letting go is upon her as she settles in.

"I don't know. Do we?" It has a touch of sarcasm.

"Have things changed between you? Are you romantic?"

"Well, I love her. I've always loved her. We're not kids anymore. Do you want details?"

"I'm nosing in. I'm sorry. Just . . . be careful."

"Mom, if we are, and I'm not saying we are, but if we are, or if we do, well, we took that in grade eight. We're cool."

"No, no, I mean, be careful with your hearts, with each other's hearts. Marki is a sensitive girl."

"Yes, Mom, she is. No one's more aware of that than I am. Spit it out. What's on your mind?"

"I don't want you to think you need to hide anything from me. You're right, you're not a child any more. If she wants to stay over . . . I mean . . . I love her too . . ."

"Mom, we're good, really. We don't need to have this conversation."

"Okay. But if you are there, or you get there, then, Marki first, in everything you do. That takes nothing away from us. We, Carolyn and I, could not be happier than to see you in love, and you could do no better than Marki."

"Thanks, Mom. I guess I better buy some condoms," Hedley smirks.

"Such a smartass. Just like your dad."

"No, that's me talking."

She stands, feeling lighter for their talk.

"I'll leave you to your thoughts. I'm going to pick up a roast. Do you think you can pull yourself upstairs in time for dinner? I don't know how you can spend so much time down here." She walks the twelve feet to the double dark oak doors sitting almost dead center in the long wall of the open room. "You're slipping, Hedley. You could dust down here a little more."

"I love you too, Mom." His casual sincerity rips through her. She smiles and ascends the stairway.

"Wow, that was embarrassing," Maki says as she exits the adjoining ensuite bathroom.

"Talk about killing the mood. Good thing, though. I didn't know she was home. On the other hand, she'll be gone for at least an hour. Wanna finish what we started?"

"I think so."

Hedley rises, taking her hand. "I love you. You know that." His easy sensuality leaves no doubt. He leads her to the bed.

"Don't be nervous," Hedley says as they undress.

"I'm not," she whispers back.

◆ ◆ ◆

"Let go, Hedley, it's okay," Marki encourages softly as Hedley pauses his movement. He releases and rolls off her with an embarrassed huff.

"What did you expect? It's your first time."

"It's not yours?"

"Gary Wilcox, when I was sixteen. I had to try it. He was moving away, no repercussions. It was awful. That's when I knew it had to be you."

"You should have told me."

"I'm telling you now. I've been waiting for you. Talking about it would have spoiled it. Hedley, I'm happy we did it, I'm really, really happy."

"I forgot to tell you, Hedley," Michelle bursts in, "your sister's—oh—oops! Sorry, the door was open . . . Marki, come out."

"No! Go away!"

"Marki, you obviously heard what I said earlier."

"You're his mother, you're not supposed to see us like this," she replies from under the sheet.

"Okay, I'll go. I don't want you to be uncomfortable."

"For cripes sakes, Marki, come up for air," Hedley says. "She's not going to bite. Mom, you're gonna have to knock from now on."

"I see that."

"Sorry, this is embarrassing," Maki says, head now above water. "How are we supposed to act?"

"No different than you ever have. You two have a deep trust. You've always been comfortable around each other. That doesn't need to change. I need to change. I need to respect your privacy, and I will. Marki, I'm happy for you, for both of you. Hedley, I just wanted to tell you your sister's in Philadelphia. I'll fill you both in later. Welcome to adult love, my children. Tread wisely." She smiles and retreats.

"Now what do we do?" Marki asks in a shy voice.

"We carry on, just like Mom said," Hedley replies.

◆ ◆ ◆

"You were so right, Jeff. They're intimate. I walked in on them a few minutes ago."

"Great. How'd all that go?"

"I hate to say it, but they looked so cute. Marki actually hid under the covers at first."

"And how do you feel about the new reality?" Jeff asks.

"I'm happy for them. I made it clear they don't have to sneak around. I suddenly feel tired though. Everything around me is changing."

"It always does. You more than anyone knows that truth. Speaking of change, I want to talk to Hedley about more Halos and—hold on to your horses, Michelle—touring."

"He's got his mind set on Saskatchewan, you know that."

"He's got time. We're releasing 'Between' tomorrow. That'll keep them happy for a few weeks. Let him get Saskatchewan out of his blood, and then let's get Hedley and Kenny out here. How's Carolyn making out?"

"She's in Philadelphia at the archives. She's having a time of it."

"And how is Michelle?"

"Oh, you know. I'm adjusting to the reality of a future living alone. My kids are in the process of leaving."

"Maybe you and I should finally give it a whirl," he laughs.

"Like that could happen," she says. "I know how you feel about me, Jeff. I've always known. But Scott and I . . . where do I go after that?"

"I know, Michelle. You can't blame a guy for trying."

"If it's any consolation, I know Scott would approve."

"It's small, but I'll take it. I'll win your heart yet," he replies.

She laughs. "Never say never."

◆ ◆ ◆

PHILADELPHIA

"Yes, of course. Your terminal is waiting." The fortyish female clerk hands Carolyn a small rectangular magnetic card. "This temporary passkey will grant you access to any resources needed. Your ID information is encoded, simply swipe and proceed. They're reusable, so please return it when you leave." The clerk turns away from the counter to address a young dark haired male associate inputting data from a workstation behind her. "Brian, could you assist Carolyn in her family search? She'll be with us for most of the day."

The young man rises to his full six feet, tall and slender. Carolyn finds herself attracted to his movement, his graceful fluid demeanor a testament to the respect the old historical building commands. He exits the circular open service area via a sliding half door, presenting himself to Carolyn on her side of the counter.

"Hi, I'm Brian."

"Carolyn," she replies. He smiles and she is smitten, his light brown eyes a sea of wonder to draw her inside.

"Right this way," he says, breaking Carolyn's stare. She follows him to a small rectangular table where a built-in wireless touch terminal and a comfortable, efficient steno chair await.

"You can access all online data through the terminal. It's voice activated, so simply say the family name and the state in which you wish to start your search. You can widen the search from there."

"Zoe," Carolyn commands. "Pennsylvania." Within seconds, data fills the screen, beginning with Jeremiah and Nattisoe in 1683.

"Of course, there's plenty more in the original paper records yet to be digitized. We're about five years away from that goal," Brian says. "I'm here to help. You tell me where to look, and I'll retrieve what you need. I'm here all day, so please feel free."

"There is one area," Carolyn replies. "Alexander and Thomas Zoe were twins born in 1704, near Philadelphia. In 1730, they ventured down south and were lost to the family. Abbot, their brother and my direct descendant, went searching in 1731 but turned up nothing. Do you think there might be something on them in the archives?"

"Possibly," says Brian. "Do you know what state?"

"Virginia, or so my great aunt told me. I'm not much help, I know."

"I'll see what I can find. The records are well indexed, but it might take a while. I'll get back to you." He leaves her to her own search.

Carolyn is fascinated by the history unfolding before her eyes. Data on the family exists going back to the early seventeenth century. Who and when they married, who their children were, when they died. But the data is clinical; nothing is revealed about the people they were. Carolyn can only guess at what was, inspired by tiny clues written down centuries before. The data spreads like a web, extending outward from her core descendants. Suddenly there are many trails to follow, many stories to unravel. Giving up, she inserts her ID card into the slot provided and downloads the data into her Wombat for future study.

"I think I've found something," Brian says on his return. Carolyn looks up from the screen and smiles, bringing a slight blush to Brian's fair-skinned complexion. He stammers as he regains his composure, bringing a nervous chuckle to both as they swim in their shared moment of mutual attraction. "Thomas and Alexander Zoe of Philadelphia were witnesses to a robbery on the Three Notch'd Road outside of what is now Charlottesville. They appeared in court to testify and were duly noted in the court transcripts. It's also noted that their journey west over the Blue Ridge Mountains into the Shenandoah Valley was delayed by three days as a result of their testimony. It's not much, but it's a starting point. The early records of the Shenandoah settlers are sketchy at best, but somebody somewhere wrote down something. Our job is to find out what. I can make digital copies of the transcript if you like."

"Please," Carolyn replies.

"We can scan and download the information directly into your Wombat, but I'll need your ID card to authorize the transfer." Brian accepts the card and passes it over the reader above the screen on Carolyn's terminal, trading places with her to perform the task. "Carolyn Yonge from Ada. You're Soup?" Brian says.

"Yes," she replies. "I'm Soup."

"Sorry, I did not mean to intrude. It's just that your father meant so much to my sister, and more so to my cousin."

"How so?" Carolyn asks.

"The rally back in 2009."

"The rally? What rally?"

"The Washington DC rally, the beginning of the Peace Initiative. It was huge. Your father performed and spoke to the crowd. My sister Karin played 'Do You Hear the Young Girls' for your father. It was a defining moment in my family's history. I was there, I remember it well. I was eight years old, but it seems like yesterday." He smiles at her deer-in-the-headlights expression. "Sorry, I've blindsided you. I'm out of line. I should keep my thoughts to myself."

"No, I'm fascinated. I—It's just that I know nothing of this. How is that possible?"

"That business with the colonel and the AFF started shortly after. I think maybe everything else fell to the wayside. I really shouldn't talk personal on company time. I need this job to pay my way through college in September."

"Yes, of course. Can we meet? After work maybe. I'd like to hear more. I'm staying across the street at the Holiday Inn. How about 4:30 in the coffee shop?"

"Sure, if you don't mind me showing up in my dorky work clothes."

"Like I'm dressed to kill." Carolyn points to her casual blue jeans and cord jacket over a t-shirt.

"You'd look great in a burlap bag. Sorry, that didn't come out quite right." He blushes again, heavily this time.

She laughs, "I'm flattered. The blush says it all. Very cute, that."

"You're not helping," he replies. "Okay, it's a date. Let's finish this scan while I still have some dignity."

◆ ◆ ◆

"Mom, you should come out. I've met a guy who knows a lot about dad, stuff I didn't know about."

Michelle reads the excitement on her daughter's face, even over the cold hard video transmission, and wonders what Carolyn has gotten into. Is she safe? Is she being led down a garden path? A million questions swarm her mind at once. "And where did you meet this guy?"

"Oh, don't worry, Mom. He's cool. He's a dreamboat. He works at the archives. His name is Brian Hamm. Does that name mean anything to you?"

"No, I can't say that it does," she replies, but a hint of recognition plagues her.

"How about Tracy Albright? Does that bring back anything?"

"Tracy?" Michelle replies with growing excitement in her voice. "Oh my god, yes! We met years ago at the Palomino Club in LA."

'She is Brian's cousin. I'm going to meet her on Wednesday, and Brian's sister Karin. They have stories to tell, and you should hear them with me."

"Karin Hamm? Oh yes, this is about the rally, isn't it?" Her senses tingle.

Carolyn picks up the change in her mother's tone and digs in. "Yes, the rally. Why don't I know about any of this?"

"Carolyn, these people, they mean well, but they have a history. They're part of the Peace Initiative. They can be fanatical."

"I like Brian, and I trust him. I want to hear what his family has to share. I thought you would too."

"Do you really want to bring all that back? It might be painful."

"I'm sure it will be, but I think there's something here to open the door to a better understanding of what happened, a better understanding of Dad."

"I'm not sure I'm ready for this, but you're right, I should be there. Thank you for including me. I'm in the middle of getting Hedley and Marki off to Saskatchewan. I'll fill you in when I arrive. Carolyn, tread carefully."

"I will, Mom."

Michelle terminates the transmission, clouds of concern chasing her day to the ground. She recalls the Palomino Club. It was the evening after the 2001 Garrett Awards, the night after the story began. She shakes the feeling and makes her way to the dungeon.

◆ ◆ ◆

"You look smashing, Marki. You should dress up more often," Michelle says. She admires the simple light green and beige dress on Marki's gentle curves, accenting her dark brown locks as they tumble to her shoulders to greet it. "I know you don't think of yourself this way, but you are a very pretty girl. You have a sweet butt, young lady. Don't be afraid to show it."

Marki blushes, enjoying the compliment but pretending not to.

"I wanted to look nice for Hedley."

"Oh, phooey on Hedley. Look nice for yourself. It's okay to be a girl. You don't have to give up anything to go there. This DarkFellow thing, I don't know where it's headed, but sooner or later, they'll figure out it's Hedley, and when they do, everything will change. He'll be out there, like it or not, and you'll be out there with him. Trust me, I know. He's going to need you more than ever. I'll help all I can, but it will be up to you two to see each other through."

"I hope I'm ready. I don't like crowds."

"I know. Scott didn't either at first, but he learned how to handle them, and you will too. Be who you are and they can't touch you." She hugs Marki on impulse, seeing in her the woman she will become. "Don't undersell yourself. There is tremendous strength in you, more than you think, more than Hedley. I love you for him, Marki, what you've done for him, but I love you more for yourself, for who you are. Above all else, you are a good and honest soul, and, as I said, a very pretty girl. Let yourself be that."

"Isn't this sweet," Hedley says, intruding. "My mom and my girlfriend making out?"

"You cad," Michelle says. She and Marki part abruptly. "Must everything be a joke to you? We were having a moment here."

"Obviously," Hedley replies.

"Are you sure you've got everything? One bag for the two of you?"

"I've got my backpack too," says Marki.

"We're only gone a week or so, Mom. We're not moving."

"Okay, I get the picture. I wish I was going with you, but Soup needs me in Philadelphia. She's mixed up in something that involves your father. It's got to do with the Peace Initiative. She thinks there's a link between them and Scott somehow."

"Oh great. They're wing nuts mom. How could Dad be linked to them?"

"They might be a little overboard, but what they stand for isn't," Marki says. "At least they're trying to do something about the stupid war."

"You're beginning to sound like my dingbat sister," Hedley says, to Marki's chagrin.

"Don't start with me, mister. I have my own opinions, thank you very much."

"Good for you, Marki. Give him hell. Maybe he'll learn to think before he speaks. I don't know what's going on in Philadelphia, but I'll fill you in when you call, and you are going to call, every day. Marki, you're the oldest. I'm putting you in charge of the communications department. Look after my boy for me."

"We'll look after each other like we always have," Marki replies.

"Yes, of course you will. I'm counting on it. Call me when you get to Regina. Walter will meet you and get you down to Tyvan. Scott's grandparents' house has been opened and services are up. It will be old and dusty, no doubt, but you can stay there while you nose around. Heck, there's enough of your father's family relics in the attic to keep you busy for a lifetime. I don't know what you expect to find, but I hope you find it. Seeing the streets where your father grew up might be enough, Hedley. It did wonders for me. The mono will take us to the Oklahoma City Aerodrome. You can see me off to Philadelphia and then you'll have two hours before your flight. Do not miss it. I guess we're ready."

◆ ◆ ◆

"Mom, this is Brian Hamm. Brian, meet my mom, Michelle."

"Mrs. Yonge, hello," Brian smiles simply and honestly. Michelle extends her hand and he takes it with a gentle but firm shake. "My cousin Tracy will be thrilled to see you again," he adds.

"And I her. We met briefly twenty years ago, but we connected. I can't help but think of her as a friend."

"She'll be happy to hear that. She definitely feels connected to you and your family."

Michelle listens, but her eyes wonder to Carolyn standing next to Brian; her eyes fixed on him as though nothing else exists. She knows the look well. "I think we're all in for an interesting day," she says warmly. She sizes him up and decides she likes what she sees. "Shall I grab a taxi?"

"I've got my car. It's old style IC, but it's comfortable. I can't afford a Pulse Runabout quite yet," Brian says.

"Internal combustion got us around just fine in the past. I'm sure it'll get us there now," Michelle smiles. "Lead the way, Monsieur."

Brian leads the small parade through the Philadelphia International Aerodrome to his 2014 Chevy waiting patiently in the parkade. "We live across town in Powelton Village, near Lancaster. We share an old Victorian house that's been converted," Brian says as he drives. "My sister Karin and me upstairs, our cousin Tracy on the ground floor. The neighborhood is cool, a self-contained artistic community with all sorts of coffee shops and neat little mom-and-pop restaurants and stores within walking distance. Sometimes I feel like I never want to leave this place. I'll have to someday, I suppose."

"Why?" Carolyn asks from the back seat. "If you love it, why leave?"

"We all have to leave home someday," Michelle says. "It's in our blood. You're in the process now."

They arrive, and Michelle is almost embarrassed by the young man's chivalry as he comes around to open the passenger door. "Thank you," she says with a warm smile. "You don't see that much these days."

The trio crosses the brick sidewalk to the wide but shallow wooden staircase leading to the covered veranda: five ornate wooden posts supporting the second story overhang of the rather large Victorian house. The veranda screen door opens, and there she stands: the thirty-nine-year-old Tracy Albright, looking much like the nineteen-year-old in Michelle's memory banks. They walk to each other and embrace as old friends, saying nothing. Inexplicably, Tracy begins to weep. Michelle clings tighter in response, not totally understanding why. Carolyn and Brian look on, Carolyn unconsciously slipping her hand into Brian's. He squeezes it lightly and smiles.

"I'm sorry," Tracy says, breaking the embrace. "All you've been through over the years. I've followed it all. I can't help but think I'm responsible for a lot of it."

"How could you possibly think that?" Michelle asks.

"Oh, I'm just awful." Tracy apologizes again as she regains her composure. "Please, come inside and sit down. I've put on some tea."

They follow Tracy into a cheery, open, oak-paneled sitting room, its high ornate ceiling dancing with the early afternoon light that streams in through two large stained glass windows on the western wall.

"Hi, I'm Carolyn."

"Yes, of course you are. How rude of me," Tracy responds. "Would you help me with the tea?" They retreat to the kitchen while Michelle and Brian find their seats in the living room, facing each other across a rather large teak coffee table from two high-backed Walnut colored Victorian settees.

"Our place upstairs isn't quite this fancy," Brian says for a lack of anything else.

"It's charming, very comfortable," says Michelle. "I love the wainscoting." She admires the walnut wood paneling along the bottom half of each wall that adds elegance to an otherwise nondescript room.

"I hope you enjoy herbal," Tracy says as she enters with a tray. Carolyn brings up the rear with an assortment of cookies, crackers, and cheeses. After pouring a round, Tracy retrieves a small square artifact from a drawer across the room, presenting Michelle with her treasure. "Remember this?"

"I do," Michelle replies, almost in a whisper. The memory takes her back to LA, back to the Palomino Club a scant twenty-four hours after she met Scott at the Garrett Awards. Jeff had hastily organized a showcase, a chance to introduce Scott to the Hollywood media. A chance to gauge his client under the pressure of a live impromptu performance. Scott dazzled the crowd and the paparazzi alike and was basking in the aftermath of the performance when a young girl approached their table.

"It was a big night for all of us," Michelle remembers. "March 14, 2001. You were timid, and ever so pretty. You politely asked Scott to sign your copy of the *Twisted Logic* soundtrack CD. He was thrilled. Carolyn, I think you should look at this," Michelle says in a reverent voice. She hands the CD across the coffee table where Carolyn sits comfortably beside Brian, their shoulders lightly touching. *They're in it for sure*, Michelle thinks.

Carolyn takes the CD gingerly, not quite grasping its significance to her mother's life. She sees for the first time the casual handwriting on the unfolded inside sleeve, and it hits her.

For Tracy Albright, my first fan in LA. May you find love and happiness in your life.

It is signed Scott Yonge.

"Mom," she stands, crying. Michelle steps around the coffee table to embrace her daughter, quiet tears now filling her own eyes. Brian responds, holding his cousin as she weeps too, then the four of them meld, bound together by a chance meeting some twenty years in the past. They separate and revert to their positions, closer now in perspective.

"See, Mom? This is why I needed you here." Carolyn's hand once again finds Brian's, and the bond continues.

"I was there with friends," Tracy says. "We caught the Garrett Awards the night before. We didn't know the details at the time, but we were pretty sure something was going on with you and Scott."

Michelle is once again propelled backward, memories flooding her mind in tidal waves. "Jeff flew Scott out to LA," she says. "At the time, he was pretty happy with his life back in Calgary. He was playing with Del at the St. Germaine four nights a week and doing part-time computer work and bike couriering during the day. Honestly, he didn't feel he had a place in anything that was going on with the Garrett Awards. He expected nothing to come of it at all. He saw it as a free holiday, nothing more. I knew none of that at the time, of course. I walked into that backstage green room with other things on my mind. Scott was there, waiting to go on. He turned to me as I entered. He stood and stared, and I thought, what a silly man. He was tongue-tied, seemingly incapable of speech. But then he smiled, and he spoke three simple words. 'You look great.'"

TUESDAY, MARCH 13, 2001 — THE GARRETT AWARDS

"Thanks, I guess," Michelle replies. "You have a wonderful stare. It takes me back to high school."

"Sorry, I shouldn't be so forward, but you look enchanting. No—magical is more like it. That sounds silly, I know, but that's what comes to mind. Sorry."

"Not a problem," she answers. "It's nice to be looked at for a change. I usually get the meat market drool. You know that action. Eyes greet the face, eyes down to the chest, eyes dart again to the face before settling on the chest. It's creepy, really. I'd get it all the time waiting tables back in college. I hated it then and I hate it now, but you didn't do that. You looked at *me*."

"Actually, I'm an ass man," he says with a shy grin. "But right now, your eyes give me all I need."

She laughs. "Do you always talk like that?"

"Like what?"

"Like you're shooting from the heart."

"I suppose. I mean, I open my mouth and what comes out comes out. Gets me in trouble sometimes, like now."

"Oh, you're not in trouble with me. I think it's sweet. An honest compliment is gold to a girl, don't you know."

"Is that why you blushed?"

"I take it back, sonny. You are in trouble," she says with mock bravado.

"Who you calling sonny? I'm old enough to be your dad, practically."

"My dad? Hmm, now that would be interesting. You certainly don't look the fatherly type."

"A slight exaggeration perhaps, but I am a product of the sixties, no question."

"That fits. I can picture you with long hair and a headband. No tie-dye I hope. Please tell me I'm right."

"Tie-dye and headbands were for the weekenders. I lived the scene for real, had hair down to my ass at one point. Course, it was a lot thicker up front in those days."

"I bet that was sexy," she replies, rolling her eyes.

"Dangerous would be a better word. It was forever getting caught in car doors."

"So now you go for the young exec look."

"Oh please, no need for politeness. I know I look like a dork. I usually gravitate a little more to the scruffy side of things, but you know how it is. I've got to look like the nice boy for the folks at home. Make no mistake though, I'm a sixties man at heart."

"And here you are hitting on a young seventies babe like me," she says with sparkling eyes. "So now who's blushing?"

"Okay, I asked for that." He feigns a pout. "But sonny? Gimme a break."

"A rose by any other name . . ."

"Huh? Oh, sorry, I'm Scott, Scott Yonge, at your service."

"Well hi, I'm—"

"Michelle Zoe," they say in unison.

Michelle Zoe, art-house talent extraordinaire. Many in circles that know or claim to know say she's poised to break into the mainstream big time, despite her 'too nice' image and her reluctance to go Hollywood. Her previous two projects received raving critical acclaim, and garnered more than modest box office returns. She has become a bankable commodity in the eyes of Hollywood, despite her wish to remain in the independent system.

"I'm flattered," she says. "Small town Oklahoma girls aren't used to being recognized."

"Oklahoma, eh? What part?"

"Central, a small town called Ada. You've never heard of it."

"I've heard of everywhere. I'm a musician. The road never ends for me. I've played Ada. A college campus if I remember correctly."

"East Central," she says.

"Could be, back in '86 or thereabouts. It was quite an eventful night as I recall."

"You're kidding! I was attending then. Maybe I saw you!"

"Maybe. It was a pub night. I don't drink much, and never when I play, but I was hammered that night. We were in the middle of a song when my piano cut out, so I knelt underneath to fiddle with the cords. As I stood up, I caught my head on the underside of the keyboard, knocking it off the stand into the crowd on the dance floor. What a racket. We stopped mid-song. Talk about embarrassing! I jumped from the stage to retrieve the damn thing and—"

"Fell flat on your butt! But you bounced up, skipped around the floor, and then gave a little bow and a pirouette to the crowd," she finishes. "My God, I was there! The audience howled! You scooped up your piano, sat on the edge of the stage with the keyboard across your lap, plugged it back in, looked up with a silly grin on your face, and jumped right back into the song. I'll never forget it. You took what could have been a disaster and turned it into a golden moment. You're right, your hair was quite long—and I remember being impressed by your singing and your cute bopping around. Cool! Small world! You played guitar mostly, didn't you?"

"Bass actually, my first love."

"Yes, that's right. I remember that Zeppelin song you sang with the funky bass part. I enjoyed that, even though I'm not much of a Zeppelin fan."

"Ooh, that's sacrilege my dear. John Paul Jones is one of my heroes. He's up there with the best of the rock bass players."

"Sorry, wrong generation."

"So what brings you here?" he says, changing the subject. "Are you up for an award?"

"I wish." She sighs. "No, I'm a presenter, best supporting actress. I'm window dressing really, but it's good to be seen."

"Don't worry, you'll have one soon enough if your last role is any indication."

"You've seen *Highway of Pain*?"

"You bet, and *The Winds of Forever*, two of my favorites. You gave an absolutely compelling reality to Debra in *Highway*. You tore my heart out with that one."

"That's sweet," she says.

"That's the second time in five minutes you've said that to me. I'm beginning to like hearing it."

"Well, don't get your hopes up." She laughs.

"I suppose marriage is out of the question then? Say, two o'clock tomorrow?"

"You are such a disarming cad," she says, "but of course you know that, don't you? You're so unlike most people I know around here."

"That's stands to reason. I'm not from anywhere around here."

"So where is home?" she asks. "I noticed an accent of sorts."

"I'm Canadian, eh. I live in Calgary. You heard of it?"

"Yes, the oil city, like Houston. I've been there, or at least landed there en route to skiing in the Canadian Rockies."

"Calgary's all right. It's a good place to live."

"There's a lot of movie action there as I recall."

"There is. They call it the Hollywood of the north. That's got a lot to do with how I got here. It's a long story."

"I'm listening, cutie," Michelle replies.

"Ouch! That word. I was shooting for macho. Johnny Depp I ain't, but just once it'd be nice to get by on nothing but a healthy dose of testosterone."

"Why? Macho is a stereotype. I'm sure you know by now that cute guys get lucky too."

"We'll see about that," Scott smiles.

"Aren't you the cheeky one," she laughs.

"No, just being cute. Hey, I got great legs. I'm a god from the waist down. It's the top half that blows it for me. All those years on a courier bike were good for something I guess."

"You're a courier?"

"No, I'm a musician. I courier during the day sometimes for extra bucks, and to keep some semblance of conditioning, but a musician is what I am. Now there's your one-two punch on the lower end of the evolutionary scale."

She smiles. "You are such an enigma. You're constantly poking fun at yourself, yet you radiate such quiet confidence. And that smile of yours. Do you always smile so much?"

"Only when I'm happy."

"Which is most of the time, I take it."

"Pretty much. I also smile when I'm scared."

"So you're scared of me?"

"No, you make me deliriously happy, but I'm sure as hell scared of what I'm about to do."

"Oh yes, back to that. What brought you here?"

"I came in a cab."

"Silly boy," she says. "Seriously."

"In a nutshell, as I said, I'm a musician from Calgary. A film crew from Milwaukee came to town two summers back to shoot an indie movie, a thirties Depression-Lonely-Hearts-Club kind of a love story with some interesting twists. They hung out at the St. Germaine Hotel bar most evenings, shootin' pool and drinkin' beer by the caseload. My best buddy Del and I play the Germaine a lot. It's kind of our second home.

"On one of those nights, a very drunk Kevin Manning, the head honcho of the film troop, took a fancy to some of my originals and asked me if I'd consider writing a few tunes for his movie. I didn't expect anything to come of it, but he used two of my songs on the soundtrack and voila, here I am.

"It's pretty amazing really. In a few minutes, I'm going out to perform a song that somehow managed to get nominated for song of the year. Ain't that a scream? I'd be willing to bet the farm that nobody out there has heard of me or my song. I'm the hick faction of these awards I think, here to prove the fairness of the association or some such rot. I mean, look who I'm up against. How the heck do I fit into this picture?"

"I don't think it works that way, Scott. I really don't. You're here, that means someone obviously thinks you deserve to be. What's the tune?"

"Trust me, you've never heard of it. 'I Call Your Name' from—"

"From *Twisted Logic?* That's you?"

"That's me. Wrote it, arranged it, sang it, and promptly forgot about it. How do you know about it?"

"Everyone knows your song out here! At least everybody I know. You've started a buzz, Scott. The movie's a minor hit, but your song has made quite an impact."

"'I Call Your Name' is not really what I'm about," he says. "I'm a back-door rocker. Trouble is, try as I may, I can't write the R&R. I never could. Everything comes out too damn soft. 'I Call Your Name' doesn't represent my playing style, but it's very representative of my writing style. I find that frustrating sometimes. You're right. I am an enigma, no question there."

"I think it's a really good song. You should be proud of what you write. That's yours, that's what sets you apart."

"Thanks. I definitely need the encouragement. That's what the record dudes keep saying—'go with what's yours.' You know, I feel like my whole world's gone crazy, like I'm having an out-of-body experience. This can't be happening to me. I somehow stepped into someone else's shoes."

"No, they're yours all right," Michelle replies softly, lightly touching his arm. "But you've got to learn how to wear them. You seem relaxed enough."

"Yeah, well, the way I look at it, I've got nothing to lose. I go out there and give it my best shot. The rest is out of my hands. At the very least, I get an eleven-day holiday out of the deal, and some interesting stories to tell back home. I have no right to say this, but frankly, the best part of being here has been meeting you. I mean that. And there you go blushing again. Is that a habit of yours? I find it enchanting."

"Five minutes, Mr. Yonge," says a voice from the door. "I'll wait on you here."

"Oh boy, here we go. What was that you said about me being relaxed? I think I'm about ready to toss my cookies."

"You'll be fine. I can see it in your baby blues. I do know your song, as do a lot of people here. I have a hunch you're in for a surprise tonight."

"Well that makes me feel better. Thanks again, Michelle. Hopefully I'll get a chance to talk to you again before I go."

"There's the party afterwards. Are you on the list?"

"Yeah, the A&R man from ARRCIS Records set it up. He wants me to hobnob a bit. I really don't know why. I'm not much of a party man, but go I must, so say they."

"I know the feeling. Sometimes this Hollywood girl stuff bites, but you've got to play the publicity game in this biz. I'll look for you there?"

"That'd be nice."

"Consider it a date," Michelle says. She leans over and gently kisses his cheek. "Good luck, sonny!"

"Thanks, kid. I'd better get a move on. Hopefully I'll see you later."

Michelle nods as Scott turns and walks briskly away. She stands in the doorway watching as he melts into the backstage maze.

"Good luck, Scott," she whispers softly.

I don't understand, she thinks. *He's not my type, why am I drawn to him? I like my tall California blondes with chiseled chins and pecks that never quit. He's solidly built, I admit, but he's my height, and that wavy brown hair . . . I don't know. He's got a beard, when clean-shaven has always been a must. What am I doing? I like them calm, cool, and hip; he's anything but! And he wears glasses, mamma! Put a pair of wire rims on him and you could drop him right into 1969. How outdated is that? He's everything I never looked for in a man. Definitely cute though, with that Roman nose and those deep blue eyes, and he's full of energy, I like that. I like him. Who am I kidding? I'm infatuated with the guy and I don't know why. He's so boyish in that slightly-too-big jacket of his. I could hug him forever. He makes me laugh, so why do I feel like crying? Why Scott? Who sent you here? Now is not the time.*

She re-enters the holding area and takes a seat in front of a monitor. She settles in to watch.

PRESENT DAY

"And that's how it was that night," Michelle says. "I walk through one door and my life changes—my life and everyone's life around me. Scott touched us all, every single person I knew then."

"You can't stop now, Mom. I've never heard you talk about that night quite like you are now."

"I swear, I close my eyes and I'm right there with him."

"Then close them and take me with you."

MARCH 13, 2001 – THE SONG

"We'll be there soon, Mr. Yonge," says Scott's teenaged escort. "I'm Robert. I've been assigned to you for the next little while. Let me know if I can be of assistance."

"Thanks. And call me Scott. Will you hang on to my phone for me? It's a distraction in my coat pocket. I'll get it soon as I'm done."

"Be happy to."

They walk in silence. Scott wonders how this backstage confusion could have anything to do with the show out front. Born with an insatiable curiosity, he finds the activity intriguing and pines for a second look.

A smile plays on his face as he thinks of Michelle. He feels a surge of confidence and wonders why. It comes to him. It's basic schoolyard stuff really; he's showing off. He's doing this for her. He wants to prove to Michelle he belongs, that he's worthy. The realization brings a chuckle.

"Private joke, Mr. Yonge?" Robert asks.

"No, just thinking 'bout a girl. You know how that goes."

"Yes, Mr. Yonge."

"Scott. Please, call me Scott."

They round a corner and take a short flight of stairs leading to the darkened stage. A small riser holds his amplifier and guitar, flanked by another riser behind and to the left for the featured sax player. The rest of the band is in the orchestra pit. That took some getting used to at rehearsal—hearing, but not seeing, the people you're playing with. Scott wonders how such an insignificant area can appear so big time on the other side of the camera.

A stocky man in headphones approaches Scott as he steps up on the stage riser.

"I'm Paul Bryce, the floor director for your segment," he says in a calm and professional voice. "We've done a preliminary on the equipment. Everything checks out okay, but we'll run another test on your vocal monitors in a few minutes. Watch the green light." He points to a small control console off-camera to the left. "It indicates a line signal. If the light dies, your monitors are gone. If that happens, use these." He hands Scott a lightweight set of wireless headphones. "Let me know via the talkback. Once you give me an all clear, I'll notify control. They'll give you a 'positions' queue, followed shortly by a ten-second warning. The count is vocal, two bars of a six count, prompted by your metronome setting. Everything should sound and feel like yesterday afternoon's rehearsal. No surprises, I hope. Try to watch me. There are three cameras, one straight ahead and one on either side. I'll signal you with one, two, or three fingers, representing cameras one to three from your left to right. Look to the indicated camera if you notice me, but don't let me distract you, camera angle is secondary to the performance. One more thing—be prepared for the lights. Things brighten up considerably when the song starts. Good luck."

"Thanks Paul," Scott says, offering a smile. "I'm sure everything will be fine."

He feels the tension as he straps on his trusted Fender Stratocaster guitar, waiting an eternity for the monitor check. It comes, and everything's peachy. Scott signals the all clear and waits again.

"Positions everyone," a voice prompts over the monitor. Time stands still. "Ten seconds."

Here we go, Scott thinks. A rush of adrenalin ties his stomach in knots. The count comes: one, two, three, four, five, six . . .

Suddenly relaxing, he fingerpicks the guitar intro, playing through the slow blues progression, laying down the groove for the drums and the bass to build on. The rhythm section makes an entrance, erecting a platform for the keyboards and strings, while the sax waits its turn to shine.

The sound is sweet and pure, a combination of the best people in the business running the best available gear. It's the sound of heaven to any musician.

Paul was right: the lights are devastating, but their harsh brilliance soon retreats to the background as the music takes precedence. Scott begins to sing, drifting with the words.

I call your name when I rise up every morning
I see your face when I close my eyes at night
I keep moving as the noonday sun is shining
I call your name that's all right

I've been running from a thousand days of sorrow
I've been running from a ghetto in my mind
I keep moving from the arms that long to hold me
That ain't right
Just ain't right

And suddenly he's back at the St. Germaine in Calgary, back to a rainy night in 1999. It was a simpler time in his life. There's old Mike in his usual spot, waving a greeting to the band as Terry slings beer behind the main bar. Betty-Lu has the floor, serving up the golden elixir with the authority of an inspector general shaking down the troops. Dr. J, the effervescent bar manager, is in position at the shooter bar directly behind the small stage, firing beer caps and insults Scott's way with casual abandon. Such lazy good times they were.

Del and Scott were hot that night, and so was the Germaine. The dance floor was packed and the joint was jumping. Scott noticed a group in the back, rowdy and out of place. *Way too slick,* Scott reflects, *especially for a Wednesday.*

True, all walks of life frequented the Germaine, an old turn-of-the-century character bar in the heart of downtown Calgary, but these guys didn't quite fit somehow.

We get the city hall boys, the oil crowd, the blue collars, the confirmed alkies and slot video junkies, the bikers, and even the odd pimp, Scott thought. *We get it all here, but we don't get the beautiful people, not the uptown dudes and dollies. This group took a wrong turn somewhere.* The thought stayed with Scott that night as they played.

I see your face on every cloud in the sky
Hear your voice in the whispering wind that's no lie
I miss your loving arms but I'm getting by
Then again getting by's just getting by

They were from Milwaukee, in town shooting a movie on a shoestring. It was Kevin Manning's project (young, ambitious, and talented—aren't they all?). He had a dream, like so many before him, of producing a breakthrough independent movie. Ah well, Kevin had a style about him. *He just might do it*, Scott had thought. He liked him, right off.

"I really enjoyed the set," the quiet stranger said with a slightly intoxicated smile. "I'm Kevin Manning."

"Scott Yonge."

"You guys are rocking tonight. You have an interesting sound."

"Thanks. We do it purely for the money, and oh yeah, the fame."

Kevin was producing a thirties depression love story, taking advantage of the natural prairie setting of the area as well as the tax breaks offered to the film industry by the Alberta government.

"We're shooting mostly outside," Kevin said. "The rain is contrary to the theme, so here we are. I like the originals I'm hearing."

"You noticed? Yeah, I like to write. Hell, I love to write."

"That's good. We need music for the soundtrack. I can't pay much, but you might get some exposure. Interested?"

"In what, recording a soundtrack"? Scott asked.

"Or contributing to one," Kevin replied.

"Well yeah, of course I'm interested. Who wouldn't be? It might be fun. I've never done anything along those lines before."

"Tonight I'm off duty. I'm going to drink a bit more, shoot a little pool, basically unwind a touch, but here's my card. Call me tomorrow and we'll talk more."

"Tell you what, I'll give you my number," Scott replies. "If you feel the same tomorrow, you give me a call."

These dirty years rob a man of his pride
Tear his world apart when he can't provide
The empty promise of the road is a lie
Oh lord will I hold that woman of mine

Scott expected nothing to come of it, but Kevin called, so he went. Kevin liked the songs (or maybe they were all he had), so Scott recorded them, and then promptly forgot about the whole thing.

That is until he got another call.

"How do you feel about the nomination?" the reporter asked.

"What nomination?" Scott replied.

"The Garrett Awards' Song of the Year nomination. As if you didn't know!"

Scott didn't know.

And now he's here, and it's over: three and a half minutes of eternity. The applause comes loud and long. Scott thinks it must be for someone else. *Can you believe it? They bought it!* He grins from ear to ear. The director holds up two fingers. Scott looks to camera two, maintaining position. *Okay*, he thinks as the lights die. *Time to move!* He prods himself almost regretfully, eager to hang on to the moment a little longer, but the droning voice of the night's host somewhere in the distance tells him his time is over. Excitement surrounds him as he enters the backstage area with guitar in hand.

"Great job, Mr. Yonge—ah, Scott," Robert says as he returns the cell phone. "That's a good song."

"Thanks," Scott replies. "Have I got time for a quick call? My buddy back in Calgary is probably watching. I want to know what he thinks about all this."

"Sure, but don't be long. I'll stash your guitar, then escort you back to your seat."

"I'd like some privacy on this one, Robert. I know the way back. Don't worry, I'll get there."

"Okay Scott. My ass is on the line if you don't." He turns on a dime. Scott dials as Robert retreats, leaving him alone backstage.

Crap, it's busy. No problem, I've got a few minutes.

♦ ♦ ♦

Michelle watches the monitor from the holding room, waiting for Scott to appear. She stiffens slightly as the announcement comes.

"Please welcome to the stage newcomer Scott Yonge, performing his song of the year nominated 'I Call Your Name' from the motion picture *Twisted Logic*."

Good luck, Scott, she thinks to herself. She resists an urge to cry. *What an odd thing to feel. He's so different. Absolutely no ego, and no sense of where he is, or maybe it doesn't matter to him.*

The music begins. She watches intently. *He's so at home out there,* she thinks. *So in the groove, like it's the only world he knows.* As he sings, the haunting melody draws her in. His voice is high, bluesy, and slightly gruff, chock-full of emotion. She feels familiar stirrings and wonders why now, almost embarrassed to feel the passion rise. *Why does he tug at my heart so?*

It's over. The camera pans the audience, clapping, cheering. *They love it! Good job Scott! Good for you!*

"Yes!" she exclaims to no one in particular.

Scott looks directly into the camera as though somehow responding to her thoughts. He smiles. *How I love that smile!* she thinks, trembling just a little.

"Five minutes, Miss Zoe."

It's Michelle's turn. She walks the same corridor, turning earlier to a different backstage location, barely conscious of her surroundings. She hooks up with the time-honored veteran Shirley Montgomery, a two-time winner of the best actress award. They walk backstage together to their common destination.

"You'll be out there one day," she says to Michelle, "if you continue to follow the path you've chosen for yourself. Pick your roles with your heart and believe in your characters. Become your characters, like you did Debra. That role was brilliant."

"Thank you," Michelle says sincerely. "I'd be happy to become half the actress you are."

"My dear, you're already better than I've ever been. Don't let this town ruin it for you when they realize that fact. Remain true to yourself and trust your instincts. Above all, pay heed to those gut feelings of yours. They're usually right."

Michelle nods as they advance to the podium. Nominees are read, and an envelope is presented. Ms. Montgomery opens the back flap.

"And the winner is . . ." she hands the paper to Michelle, a gesture not lost on the television audience.

"Georgia Braddock from *Williamsburg*!" Michelle says. The audience applauds over the blaring music.

Scott drifts aimlessly amongst the state-of-the-art audio and video equipment tucked neatly away backstage. Cables and computers are everywhere, drawing him like a moth. He spots Michelle on a monitor, smiles, and records the moment as she exits, to be replaced by the evening's host.

I'd better get back to my seat, he thinks, *but first, Del.* He dials. Del answers.

"Hey!" Scott growls.

"Dude! I just saw ya! Nice suit!"

Delbert Gould has been Scott's musical mirror for the past twenty-one years. They've forged a deep bond that comes from sharing the stage together through good times and bad, something only other musicians can truly understand. Although opposites in many ways, their common love for music and their joy of playing together has built a relationship of deep respect and affection. They are brothers in every way.

"Ain't it a beaut?" Scott replies. "Don't blame me, the wardrobe people picked it."

"You must've got a hit from that experience. I bet you were scared shitless."

"Yeah, right up 'til I started singing, then it was like the Germaine with great monitors. The sound was incredible. You'd freak!"

"Sounded good out here too, dude, except you sang the wrong words!"

"I did? Where? I didn't notice."

"You sang 'Getting' by is just getting by,' instead of 'Getting by is no way to live.' Doesn't matter, you did good. I'm proud of you, even if you did look like a dork."

"Man, I wish you were here. You would've loved this."

"No way," Del replies. "We've been over that. It's your gig. LA's not for me, know what I mean? When you coming back?"

"Week from Saturday. Hey Del, I met a girl."

"Naturally."

"No, this is different. I really like her. She's an actress, very nice—"

"Ah, Scott, where are you?" Del says.

"I'm rooting around backstage, why?"

"You'd better move it, dude. You just won!" Del exclaims.

"What?" Scott yells.

"You won, you blockhead, get the hell out there! They've announced you! The cameras are panning for you right now. Hold on, some girl's going out to accept the award. Michelle somebody."

"No! Michelle Zoe?"

"Yeah, that's it. She's a looker."

"Oh oh, I gotta run. I'll call you later."

"Scott! Over here, this way!" yells Robert. "Man, you've got me in hot water! We've got to move!"

Scott chases Robert to the edge of the stage, just as the announcer chimes, "Accepting for Mr. Yonge is *Speed Wagon* actress Michelle Zoe."

People are looking around with that patented blank stare when confusion reigns, wondering what the hell is going on. Scott's mind is in a state of chaos as he watches Michelle cross the stage to the podium.

"No way am I going out there," he says aloud. *Oh man, a camera's picked me up*, he thinks, and panic locks in.

Sure enough, Scott sees himself on a nearby monitor just as a stage manager waves him on. He runs reluctantly across the wide hardwood stage, tripping on the edge of the thick carpet lining the podium area. *Oh shit, I'm going down*, he thinks in a moment of terror. *No, I'm okay. I'm all right*. His heart explodes as he grabs the spotlight next to Michelle, trying to catch his breath. She's laughing, clapping. The audience is cheering. Scott is totally disorientated. *Holy crap! What do I do now?*

"You'd better say something, Scott," Michelle says softly. She gently guides him to the mike. "They're waiting."

He rubs his forehead, takes a deep breath, and dives in. "Wow, sorry everyone," he stammers as the applause trickles. "I got wrapped up backstage . . . I . . . man, it's lonely out here."

The audience laughs and erupts again, sending a warm wave to the stage. Michelle feels it and unconsciously clasps Scott's hand. A camera captures the gesture as Scott looks to her with a heartfelt smile.

"Thank you! Thank you all! This blows me away! I'm totally unprepared for this!" He takes a deep breath before continuing. "I never expected to be here, not in a million years. If I'd known, I'd have worn a better shirt, or at least a pair of new sneaks. Wow." A camera pans to Scott's worn sneakers for the benefit of the at-home audience.

"I want to thank Kevin Manning for coming to the St. Germaine that wet night two years ago, and I'd like to thank the powers that be for sending the rain that drove Kevin and his crew indoors. Go see his movie. It will move you.

"I thank you all for this award, and for making me feel welcome so far from home. I especially thank the lovely Ms. Zoe. She saved the moment and got me through this most trying experience. Angels come in many packages."

Michelle impulsively leans over, brushing his cheek with her lips.

"Now that's *my* idea of an award," laughs Scott. "Thanks again, folks. Have a great night! I'm bringing it home, Del!" he cries, holding the Garrett high in the air.

He backs away from the podium, turns, and walks offstage with Michelle at his side.

"You realize the tabs are going to jump all over this," she says.

"You mad at me?" he asks.

"Do I look mad?"

"No, you look great. Thanks for covering for me. You saved me a lot of embarrassment, and the IFPA, I expect. How'd you get dragged into all that?" Scott asks.

"Just lucky, I guess. Shirley Montgomery and I presented the best supporting actress award a few minutes prior to your no-show. We were standing offstage, right about where we are now, watching. You weren't here, I was. The floor director spotted me, and I got the call. I couldn't believe it when they announced I was accepting for you." She stops, squeezing his arm. "Exactly what were you up to back there? It's only the Garrett Awards. No big deal, right?"

"I'm—I'm sorry, Michelle. I didn't mean for that to happen. I, well, I got lost backstage. I was checking out the activity, then I called my buddy Del in Calgary and I lost track of time. It's a dumb thing. I'm sorry."

"Between you and me, I wouldn't have missed it for the world. The look on your face was worth all of it. Priceless. You had little boy lost written all over you, but your eyes were pure intensity. You looked at me, into me, with those baby blues of yours, and I just melted. No one's ever looked at me quite like that. I felt so warm. Isn't that odd?"

"Not really. That look was a sincere thank you from my heart for not having to face them alone. I was screwing up big time out there."

"Are you serious? They loved you! Couldn't you feel that? You can bet your speech will run on the highlight tapes tomorrow. You're a natural. You have the uncanny ability to make any situation work for you. This is the Garrett Awards. You won song of the year. You performed live for an international audience, and you act like you're home from the drug store. Get with it. This has been one big night in Scott Yonge Land."

"No doubt, it's not every night a guy meets a WCB.

"A what?"

"A WCB, World-Class Babe."

"No silly, I mean the Garrett!"

"Oh, that. What the hell's that all about, anyway?"

"It's your whole world changing, Scott, that's what that's about. Question. What now?"

"Well, I was thinking of asking you out," he says. "Maybe we could go some-place and talk a bit, have a cuppa?"

"I'd love to, Scott, but we've both got to do the after party. You mentioned your guys have plans for you, and I've got people to meet before and during. We'll hook up there, I promise."

"I can't wait. That'll give me a reason to go. I generally hate that kind of thing."

"Oh, me too, but it goes with the territory."

"Yeah, well I didn't ask for any of this. I'm thrilled to win of course, but I never dreamed I would. Never even gave it a thought."

"Not even a little daydream?"

"Nope, 'fraid not. I've got a great life back in Calgary. I love what I do and I make decent money doing it. what more could I ask for? The big event for me was meeting you, not the award. The recognition is great, but if I were to change anything in my life, it would be for someone like you, not for a piece of metal." He clutches the Garrett. "I know I shouldn't say that, but, from the heart, remember? There really is something stirring for me here. The intensity I felt from that first look was riveting, and not because of who you are. It's a sub-conscious thing I think, instinctual. I instantly recognized you as someone . . . someone I could love. Course, I'm sure every guy you meet falls hard for you."

"You really pull your punches, don't you?"

"If I don't say it now, I may never get the chance, and I really need to say it."

"If you were one of the Hollywood vampires, I'd say you're trying to get me into bed, but you? I don't know, I think I can trust you. I can feel your sincerity all around me."

"I hope I haven't freaked you out. I really want to go for that cup of coffee."

"Me too, and we will, but right now, the party." She reaches for his hand. "See you there?"

"Definitely. I'm going with Jeff Thompson from ARRCIS Records. I'm curious to see what's up his sleeve. Let the games begin. By the way Michelle, I am trying to get you in bed."

She laughs, kisses his cheek, and makes her exit.

2021

The room is silent, fixed on Michelle like a crowd on a golfer making a career putt. Carolyn is the first to respond.

"Wow, Mom," she whispers, rising again. "I, oh god—" They embrace again, tears streaking Carolyn's cheeks as she sobs. Michelle is strangely calm, drained by the memories of that night. She says nothing. Carolyn finally composes herself and releases. "Thanks, Mom. I needed that." She laughs.

"The marquee read 'The Palomino Club Proudly Presents Garrett Song of the Year Winner Scott Yonge,'" Tracy continues. "We lived close by. It was the fourteenth, the night after the Garrets. We couldn't believe our luck, though it was tough to figure how Scott would fit with the hip-hop crowd. He didn't. They hated him at first, you could feel it, but by the third song, he had them on his side. He certainly had me. I was enthralled. Do you remember what you said to me that night?" she asks Michelle.

"I remember more what you said to me. You quietly asked if the new love song Scott played that night was written for me. I couldn't say. I left the answer to Scott. He affirmed as much."

"I knew the answer," Tracy says. "I could tell by the way he looked at you when he sang."

"'I hope I find someone who'll look at me the way he looks at you.' That's what I remember you saying." Michelle replies.

"And I'm still looking." Tracy hesitates before continuing. "Don't take this the wrong way, but I think I'm looking for Scott, or someone like him."

Michelle laughs. "I know where you're coming from, believe me. He's a tough one to replace. Don't leave it too long."

"It's getting late," Tracy says, changing the subject. "We should order in. Anyone object to Thai? There's a great restaurant a few blocks over, and they deliver."

"My treat," Michelle says. "It's the least I can do for today." Arrangements are made, and they settle back in.

"Do you believe things happen for a reason?" Carolyn asks. "Take a look around, what do you see? All of us brought together in one room, and what's the common denominator? My dad. This can't be chance."

"I've often wondered the same thing," Tracy responds. "I mean, what are the chances I'd be vacationing in LA with a friend from home the very night of the Garretts, and that we would be watching when Scott came on? And what are the chances that my friend would rent an apartment up the block from the Palomino? Hell, what are the chances of the whole Garrett scenario happening in the first place? It's all linked in more ways than we know."

"Scott believed as much," Michelle says. "I do to an extent, but I don't dwell on it."

"There's more," Tracy continues. "'MaryAnn Said.' Scott was not scheduled to play that song on *Audrey Over America* that day in 2009. Their comeback tour was underway. They were stuck for time and were rehearsing new material when the opportunity presented itself. Audrey heard the song and insisted they play it. Coincidence? Maybe, but I doubt it. I'd just started with Wasserman Insurance, my first real job. I was renting this place at the time, I've since bought it. I set my DVR to record the show, hoping a new Scott Yonge performance would bring me out of the blue funk of losing my aunt to a roadside bomb just outside of Damascus. She was due to come home from her second tour of duty, and just like that, she was gone. My aunt was Brian and Karin's mother. You'll meet Karin later.

"The performance lifted my spirits all too well. We, my friends and I, were sick of the killing. We'd all lost someone in the Middle East and we prayed for an end to the senseless war. When the draft was reinstated, we realized the slaughter would continue. We had to do something. And then, enter Scott Yonge, courtesy of Audrey Waters. More coincidence? You be the judge. I've got a news clip from June 19, 2009, the day they signed the so-called Temporary Measures Act. That was twelve years ago, and the killing still goes on."

Tracy leads them into an adjoining room where an old style 50-inch digital TV monitor sits quietly against the far wall, quaint in its antiquity. "Remember these?" Tracy asks. "Seven years old and obsolete. 'The times they are a-changing.'" She smiles at the old Bob Dylan line, then presses the play button on her DVR remote.

They sit and watch from the small couch and chair provided as a group of twenty to thirty young women fill the screen, singing in a cappella while brandishing signs that say WAR NO MORE and THERE IS A BETTER WAY.

Maryann said Bobby's dead
Maryann said Bobby got angry
Bobby took a gun to the shed
The very one he brought home from the army
Maryann said Bobby's dead
Maryann said Bobby got angry

Other slogans swim before the ever-shifting cameras as they repeat the chorus again. Suddenly they stop as the camera zooms in on the apparent ringleader. She speaks.

"This bill isn't right. All of us here, every one of our group, has lost a family member and a big chunk of our lives over there, and the killing continues. It's too late for our families, but maybe we can stop someone else's son or brother from becoming the next Bobby Johnson."

"And who is Bobby Johnson?" the reporter asks as a new clip plays a portion of 'MaryAnn Said' on the nightly news. "Bobby Johnson is a fictional character from a Scott Yonge song, as performed earlier this week on the *Audrey Over America* show." The camera zooms in on the reporter while the Audrey clip plays in the background. "This is Jerry Bloom reporting from the steps of the Liberty Hall, Philadelphia."

The room goes silent with the click of a remote. Everyone absorbs what they just saw, interpreting the meaning of it.

"That's right, Michelle, Carolyn. I organized the protest that ultimately led to the death of Scott Yonge. I've had to live with that fact for the past twelve years. I'm sorry. I hope you can forgive me." Tracy hangs her head as though ashamed. Carolyn is the first to respond.

"That's just silly. If you believe that was destined to happen, then you did what you were supposed to do. If you believe it was random, then how could you know? Either way, the fault is not yours. It's no one's. It simply is, or was."

"Well put, Carolyn," Michelle says. "Much as I'd like to sit here and blame you, blame anyone for Scott's death, I cannot. I miss him every day, but he died protecting us from that madman. Knowing Scott as you do, do you think he would agree to your blaming yourself? I think not, and neither should you. You dared to speak out against the senseless crap that ultimately killed Scott, but you didn't contribute to his demise. Maybe if someone had taken a stand earlier he'd be with us now, but no one did, and we're still at war fourteen years later. Blame 2001, blame big oil, blame Saddam Husain, blame the colonel's parents if you must blame at all, but please, for my sake as well as your own, do not shoulder one more second of blame for any of it. It's not your call, and it's certainly not mine."

"I think Karin has arrived," Brian says to the squeaky sound of the veranda door.

Karin Hamm enters the room on a wave of silk, moving effortlessly as though a ghost. Tall and thin like her brother, Karin draws eyes to her impressive stature while wielding a calming presence. "Hi everyone, I'm Karin," she says. "Welcome."

"I'm Carolyn Yonge." Soup rises to greet her. "And this is my mother, Michelle." Michelle smiles, taking an eyeful of the striking young woman.

"I'm honored," Karin says. "I met Scott at the rally in 2009. He helped me make sense of all the craziness going on then. We could use him now."

"Yes, we could," Michelle replies. "You say his name like a friend."

"He was a kind man. He had a way about him."

"Our meal has arrived," Tracy says, responding to the buzzer. Michelle rises to the task, presenting her card in payment.

"I suggest we eat in the TV room," Tracy says. "It is a tad informal, I know, but we're beyond small talk, and I have a movie of sorts to run while we're eating. Well, more like a documentary." Karin and Soup assist Tracy in a make-shift smorgasbord setup, gathering plates, glasses, chopsticks, and lap trays for their culinary adventure.

"You do see the way Carolyn looks at you?" Michelle says when she and Brian are left alone.

"I'm aware, yes," Brian says with some discomfort.

"There are powerful emotions on the table with what's going on, and they cannot be excluded from the mix. But I know the signs, she's in for real. Please, don't hurt her. She's new to this, to love."

"Wow, you're direct. I like that."

Michelle smiles to herself. "I'm sorry. I've put you on the spot. Take your time, Brian. She's not going anywhere. You'll figure it out."

"Okay, we're all settled in? Good." Tracy takes charge again as they return. "Michelle, Carolyn, I don't know what you know about the rally, but you're going to know a whole lot more after you see this." Tracy takes her place beside Karin, settling in amongst the hastily rearranged sofa, loveseat, and chair. "I'll skip the political hurrahs and backslapping and cut to the chase. I've book-marked a spot about ten minutes before Scott makes his appearance. Here we go folks, Washington DC, June 27, 2009."

She presses the play button.

The host of the event, well-known civil rights activist Sandra Franklin, takes the stage and thanks democratic Senator Jack Doans, a long-time opponent of the Middle East Strategy, for his words of leadership and inspiration. Sandra turns to Scott and Jeff and smiles their way as they watch from a perch near the edge of the stage stairs. She turns forward again, approaching the microphone to address the audience.

"We have someone special with us today, but of course you know that," Ms. Franklin begins, "but what you do not know is that we have a surprise for our special guest, as well as for all of you. Recently I made the acquaintance of a young girl on the threshold of womanhood, forced there much too soon by events she could not control.

"Karin Hamm lost her mother to a land mine, a much too common occurrence in the daily news these days. Karin's mother was taken during her second tour of duty in the Middle East, but she was not the only victim. That land mine also claimed a big part of Karin's life. It claimed Karin's innocence, her youth, her right to grow up as a normal American teenager should.

"I was instantly struck by Karin. She possesses poise and maturity far beyond what you would expect from one who has been with us a mere seventeen years. I asked her how she copes with the pain of her loss. I found her reply remarkable. Karin told me she must be strong for her nine-year-old brother, whose pain and confusion runs much deeper than her own. 'There's no time to wallow,' she said to me. 'I have to help Brian. I'm all he's got.'

"Karin possesses a remarkable singing voice. When she heard about today's rally, she felt it right to contact me through my dear friend Tracy Albright, Karin's cousin on her mother's side, to ask if she could perform a song that has helped her immensely in dealing with her loss. She hoped that doing so might ease someone else's pain, even if for a little while. I went to visit her in Baltimore. She moved me to tears when she sang the song for me in her aunt's living room. I give you Karin Hamm, my sisters and brothers, performing 'Do You Hear the Young Girls Crying.'"

The pretty, dark-haired teenager, almost ghostly, takes to a stool on the right of the now vacating Sandra Franklin. A stage hand quickly positions a microphone for her acoustic guitar while another adjusts the boom mike already in place for her vocal performance. She nonchalantly checks her tuning and then looks to Scott with a quick nod and a quiet smile before settling in.

She lightly strums the simple open chords of the song's intro, closing her eyes briefly. When they open, she begins to sing with a pure voice untouched by the adult world, bringing a hush to the multitude gathered in the park.

Do You Hear the Young Girls Crying

Do you hear the young girls crying all alone
They cry for their young men who won't make it home
They cry for their brothers lost at sea
They cry for the children who won't be

The eve of the battle approaches the dawn
And many among them won't be with us long
So they look to each other for courage and truth
They look for the meaning of their youth

Who sent them there
Does anybody really care
That they lay down their lives
Wish they were coming home

Do you see the young boy playing in the sand
His pain and confusion he can't understand
What happened to mamma can happen to you
And what is the good boy to do

For the young girls crying in the night
They cry for their young men, lost in the fight
They cry for their brothers lost at sea
They cry for the children who won't be

"Thank you," Karin says when the song ends. She stands, guitar in hand, giving a shy wave and a 'so long' smile to the crowd. The audience is silent at first, but then a warm wave of applause sweeps through the mass, rising to a crescendo that continues as the young girl crosses the stage to the exiting steel stairs. Scott stands to greet her, taking her free hand in both of his. He speaks to Karin, but the words are not heard over the continuing ovation. Tears form in Karin's eyes, but she smiles and gives Scott a quick peck on the cheek. She continues down the steps to the tiny outstretched arms of her brother, while an older woman of remarkable resemblance to Karin looks on, and then joins the embrace.

Sandra Franklin once again advances to the mike. "Well done Karin, well done. We thank you for that. We thank you for your courage." She pauses while the audience acknowledges her again. The applause wanes, then silence. Scott and Jeff look on, absorbing the mass of emotion that soaks the air around them.

"As I said earlier, we have someone special with us today," Sandra continues. "Someone who has taken how we feel and wrapped those feelings around a three-minute song. Every movement needs a focal point, a central icon, a symbol to identify itself to the world. Ours is Bobby Johnson. Please welcome Bobby Johnson's creator, SCOTT YONGE!"

Scott propels himself up the steps and across the vast stage and is floored by the elevated view of the crowd. Hairs he didn't know he had stand to attention on the back of his neck and forearms as the roar continues, but it is nothing compared to the rush he feels when the crowd finally grows quiet in anticipation. A massive wave of calm suddenly chases the knots from his stomach, but the melancholy feeling of sadness remains, a feeling he does not fully understand. He knows the time is now. Full of confidence, he advances to the mike.

"Thank you," Scott begins, "and a heartfelt thanks to Karin Hamm. She does the song more justice than I ever will." He pauses to gather his composure. "I didn't want to come here today. I didn't want any part of this, but I came, because I believe you should know the truth about me.

"I'm flattered that my song has come to mean so much to so many, but I'm not the guru you seek. I'm a simple man—a husband, a father, a writer of songs. What I am not is a politician or a political activist, nor am I an expert on other people's pain. I only know what I feel, and I hurt for the young men and women who come home with shattered lives, limbs, and dreams.

"True, I oppose the war we're embroiled in, but I can't tell you that my opposition is the right path to take. I can only tell you to follow your hearts, and to remember that the path to what is right does not necessarily have to clash with yours or anyone's best interests. Nor is it necessary that it be the most difficult road. If there's an easier way, take it. You'll find plenty of other battles in your lifetime to fill the days.

"I'm fifty-two and I lived the sixties. I look at you now and I see those times looking back at me. Don't make the same mistakes we made. We got a lot of things right, but we screwed with a lot of things we shouldn't have. We lost sight of our ideals and became focused on the battle. We assumed everyone who didn't agree with everything we said or believed was the enemy, and that everything they stood for was wrong. That wasn't true then, and it isn't true now. It's never true.

"The men and women who lead this country want the same things we all do—a safe world for our children and our children's children. But they see the road to that world through different eyes. Believe me, no one here in Washington wants any one of you to be the next Bobby Johnson, but the truth is, history has taught us no other way.

"So make your voices heard, and maybe together we'll find a better road. But don't destroy the good things that have been built by the very men you oppose. Rather, crown them their achievements and help them build a better world. We all make mistakes, but we all need to find a way to live together somehow. Whatever road you take, make sure you add to no one's misery. Be proud to talk of these times with your children, knowing you came here today with peace in your heart.

"Before I go, I want to play the song for you the way I wrote it, just me and my guitar. Maybe you'll come to better understand Bobby Johnson. He doesn't exist, of course, but what he stood for does. See, Bobby wasn't drafted. He joined up, and was proud to do so. He saw the army as an opportunity to add some excitement to his small-town life, and to serve his country in the process.

"Things didn't work out for him. He lost a leg and an equally big chunk of his life, but he wanted no one's pity. All he wanted was a chance to gain back his life. He knew what he was getting into in going over there. But he never figured how it would be when he came back.

"In the end, he couldn't stand the loneliness wrought by social ostracism, but he blamed no one for his lot in life. Not politicians, not generals, not anyone. He simply grew tired of the BS. This song is a soldier's cry for help, nothing more. Pay particular attention to all the words, not just the last verse. Maybe you'll see Bobby Johnson in a different light.

"Listen well, because this will be the last time I perform this song. It's time to put Bobby Johnson to rest. I hope you can hear me at the back."

Scott pauses, reaches back for his guitar, and settles on the same stool Karin Hamm occupied minutes earlier. The sun breaks through the parting clouds. *Great*, he thinks as a warm sunbeam bathes him in a natural spotlight. *Just what I need, more symbolism.* The overhead boom mike is lowered for his voice, and another is set in place for the guitar. He adjusts the angle near the sound hole, moving it slightly to lessen the chances of feedback through the stage monitor, and dives in.

"Here it is folks," he says softly as he fine-tunes the guitar. "The essence of Bobby Johnson, performed as it was written."

Played on a lone guitar, it more resembles a folk song than the studio version, which was built on hugely orchestrated keyboard chords and an avant-garde semi-funky percussion groove, but nothing is lost on the crowd as he begins to sing.

MaryAnn Said

MaryAnn turned twenty-three
She's known Bobby since they were fifteen
Served him coffee with his slice of pie
Don't make much money but she's getting by

One day Bobby came strolling in
Into the diner with a rolling grin
I joined the army she heard him say
Fifteen days from now I'm going away

Twenty months and a week from the day
Bobby Johnson came back to stay
Tried his damndest gonna make the grade
But they sent him home minus a leg

Yesterday Bobby went to her home
Her one day off she wished to be alone
What's doing honey can you lend me an ear
Got something on my mind I want to make clear

He said
Hold me take away the pain
Hold me and show me
Life can be what it was again

Bobby don't MaryAnn replied
Right then and there something in Bobby died
You know I like you I always will
He shook his head and took her bitter pill.

It started as a murmur, mostly feminine in nature, but rapidly spread through the crowd like a ground fire in a high, dry wind. And there it was again, the simple lyrics that have become a mantra. By the time Scott reached the last chorus, the singing was a hundred thousand strong. Scott stopped, but they continued in an almost eerie chant, repeating the last verse again and again. A cooling rush spread over Scott, causing the hair on the back of his neck to stand on end again. *They don't get it; they just don't get it,* he thinks. The cameras roll.

MaryAnn said Bobby's dead
MaryAnn said Bobby got angry
Bobby took a gun to the shed
The very one he brought home from the army
MaryAnn said Bobby's dead
MaryAnn said Bobby got angry

"Thank you," he says softly, but they keep singing. "I've got to go." He smiles and waves. He descends the stairs from the stage, but they continue to sing as he is whisked away.

The screen fades to black.

Silence.

"The future is past and present," Tracy says. "It is one."

More silence.

"I remember him coming home that night," Michelle says. "He was depressed, the first and only time I saw that in Scott. He had such high hopes for that rally. He wanted people to understand that he was not their guru. He wanted them to know that 'MaryAnn Said' was just a song. But they didn't want to. They wanted him to be who they thought he was. They were not prepared to listen to the truth, and it broke his heart for a while."

"That rally was the focal point of the Peace Initiative," Tracy says. "We were a small informal group at the time. We had no idea the rally would become what it did. There were over a hundred thousand people and counting. We had to organize. Don't you see? Scott was the catalyst, or rather, Bobby Johnson was. His song struck a chord with the young people across the country. It really was like the sixties, and how they saw him is what brought them there. Without that rally, there would not have been the Peace Initiative, and without Scott, there wouldn't have been a rally. I firmly believe Scott was placed there for just that purpose."

"Okay, I think that's going too far," Michelle says. "That's way too much to heap on his shoulders. He was what he said he was in his speech—a simple man, a writer of songs, a husband, a father. God, how he was a father, and he was my . . . he was everything to me."

"And he was everything to me, can't you see that? I'm sorry. I'm not trying to tarnish him, I didn't speak to him after the Palomino Club but I've come to love him—who he was, not who I think he was. He was a good, honest man, full of positive light, full of love. He wished harm on no one, not even those who would hurt him most. He was pure, and that's what people saw. That came out somehow in 'MaryAnn Said,' in all his songs. No, Michelle, they came out to see him, to see who they thought he was, and he was who we thought he was. I firmly believe that. We all saw what you saw in Scott the night of the Garrett Awards. A kind, honest man who could take us to a new place."

"What did he say to you, Karin, before you left the stage?" Carolyn asks.

"I was confused, I felt beaten. Our father abandoned us about a year before the rally. I never understood why, I still don't. We went to Baltimore to live with

Aunt Thelma, Tracy's mother. Our mother, Brian's and mine, was killed about a month before the rally. Scott's song 'Do You Hear the Young Girls Crying' gave me comfort and strength when I needed it most. So when I heard your father was appearing at the rally, I begged Tracy to talk to Sandra Franklyn on my behalf. It was imperative that I play for your father, to thank him somehow for that song. He crossed the stage by the stairs to meet me, taking my hand in both of his. He looked right into me. I still see his eyes. I feel them on me sometimes. I remember exactly what he said, and how he said it. 'You're hurting, I could hear it in your voice,' he said. 'That's okay, we all hurt. But no matter how bad things get, they always get better again.'"

"If you let them," Soup finishes. "They always get better again if you let them."

"Yes."

"He said the same words to me just hours before he went to meet the colonel. Remember, Mom, out in the yard?"

Michelle nods.

"It was early Sunday morning. Dad arrived in a cab from the Newport concert, as ordered by the colonel. I so desperately wanted to see him, we all did, but the colonel forbade it. He was to go directly to the vacant 'new' house across the yard from the farmhouse we lived in.

SUNDAY JULY 19, 2009, 2 AM — THE ZOE HOMESTEAD IN ADA

Michelle stands alone in the dark, staring out the window at the approaching headlights. She reaches over, silhouetting herself in the kitchen's warm, incandescent glow. The yellow cab is tinted green by the cooler wash of the fluorescent yard lamp from a centrally located pole. She's had her instructions, but she hopes against hope that the cab will pull up to the old house. Her heart breaks when it does not, though she knew it would not. The cab arcs by, pulling up to the steps of the new house, sterile and threatening somehow in the deep night darkness. A lump forms as she catches a glimpse of his face on traces of the yard light reflecting off the skin of the cab. He gets out, pays the fare, and sends the cab away. He turns to face her. He sees only the outline of her, but it is enough. The sweetness of her gentle curves draws him, beckoning him to cease this madness and run to her, but he does not. He cannot.

"Scott," she coos softly across the one hundred and sixty feet that separate them.

Suddenly the screen door flies open, and a black ponytail blows by Michelle before she can react.

"DADDY, DADDY, DADDY," she cries as she runs.

"Carolyn, NO!" Michelle calls. She takes chase, but she suddenly stops dead in her tracks, halted by a single harsh command in her earpiece.

"Send her back, Mr. Yonge," the same voice commands in his ear. "Send her back now or suffer the consequences."

"Soup, go back!" Scott yells. "Go back for Hedley."

"No, Daddy. I won't. Don't you love me too?"

Her words rip through Scott like a buzz saw, but how does he explain? He aches to hold his daughter, to show her he does love her and to make everything right for her, but he does not dare.

"You know I love you, Soup. You know I do, but you've got to go back. I mean it Carolyn. Turn back now!"

She stops, falling to the ground, her tears mixing with the light drizzle that begins to fall. She cries openly, uncontrollably, her sobs drawing Scott and Michelle involuntarily to her.

"Just this one time, Mr. Yonge. Just this one time," the colonel's voice says, its softness surprising Scott. He runs to her, falling to the ground beside her as the gentle warm rain drifts down.

Marty comes to the porch, holding Michelle as she cries, stopping his daughter from joining the scene in the yard. It is something he instinctively knows she must not do, over and above the colonel's influence. It is Scott and Carolyn's moment.

Scott rocks his daughter in his arms, crying openly with her, feeling strength beyond measure in the feel of her.

"Time's up, Mr. Yonge," the colonel says. "Send her back."

"In a minute," Scott answers. "Please, just one more minute."

"Now, Mr. Yonge. Do not try me!"

"Carolyn, you've got to go back. Your Mom needs you. Tell her I love her, okay?"

"Uh huh, but she knows."

"So do you, but you like to hear it."

"NOW, MR. YONGE!"

"Carolyn, listen to me, remember what I say. Remember that I'll always love you. See this?" He pulls out the plastic toy ring she gave him eons ago. "It's mine now, I'll always have it with me. Carry me with you also, and remember that no matter how bad things may get, they always get better again, if you let them—but you have to let them, Soup." He stands up, pulling the young girl as he rises. "You go now, and remember what I said." He hugs her one more time, then releases her.

"I want to stay with you."

"And I want you to stay, but you can't. That's the way it is right now."

"Bye, Daddy," she whispers. She turns and runs through the now pouring rain into her mother's waiting arms.

"Scott?" Michelle pleads across the ocean between them.

"I'm all right, or will be," he calls back. "You go inside now. Soon, Michelle . . ."

"Enough, Mr. Yonge. How touching, this display of family unity, but now we have a mission to complete. You've weakened me with your sentimental hogwash, but no more. Inside with you, and no further contact with anyone, understood? Wait for further instructions. That is all." Coldness has returned to the colonel's voice, kicking away the trace of humanity that had crept in over the past day.

PRESENT DAY

"I'm sorry," Karin almost weeps the apology. "They're your words, not mine, I had no right."

"That's not true," Carolyn replies. "They're his words. The fact that you heard them first only intensifies their meaning. He didn't just say the words, he believed them, believed *in* them."

"And now we both believe in the words."

"Exactly, Karin. We're family, sisters in a way. Mom, I want to stay in Philadelphia. I want to find out more. More about the Zoes, more about Dad, more about—"

"I don't think that's a good idea, Carolyn. I really don't."

"She could stay with us," Tracy offers. "We'd love to have her."

"I'll be good," Brian adds.

"I know you will. You're not the problem here."

"What's Brian got to do with this?" Carolyn snaps.

"If you don't know, you'd better get in touch with your feelings. Everybody else in the room knows what I'm talking about." Michelle laughs in spite of herself. "Sorry."

"She can stay with me," Tracy says again. "Don't worry, I'll keep them honest. Look what we've accomplished, Michelle, what our movement has done. We've had a right-wing government since 2000. With every election, we've been drawn further and further to the right, but not this time. The Republicans barely squeaked by in 2020 and even then, only because they promised to end the draft and this stupid war. That swing began with the rally. I think Carolyn wants to know more about what's going on."

"I do, Mom. So what's the problem?"

"The problem is, all this political crap killed your father. Oh shit, what did I just say? Sorry, that just came out. I'm all right. You've got your heart set on this, don't you?"

"I do."

"We need to talk, but for now, yes, you can stay, as if I really have any say about it."

"I have the Newport concert if you'd like," Tracy says.

"Oh god no," Michelle replies. "I'm not ready for that. I've had enough for one night. I'm perfectly drained. Besides, I'd like to see it with Hedley."

◆ ◆ ◆

CHAPTER FIVE — SASKATCHEWAN

The Pulse air shuttles came to the smaller cities first; they were the proving grounds. It was in the economics. Converting to the new technology was much cheaper than maintaining the stone-age airports of yesteryear.

Regina was no exception. Upgrading the existing airport to the modern aerodrome was a no-brainer. The wasted land that used to hold miles of concrete runways was easily re-zoned for residential and agricultural use now that noise pollution and the threats of crashes have become distant memories.

Public confidence runs high. In less than half a decade, the old monstrosities are all but gone. The new ways are upon us. Well, almost. Walter Patrick, the family's legal representative in Saskatchewan, met Marki and Hedley at the aerodrome. He had made arrangements for transportation, but it was not what the young couple expected.

"The new electric runabouts haven't quite made their way here yet," Walter had said. "But this gas guzzler will do the trick. It'll be a few years yet before we give up our cars." No matter, Hedley was enjoying the drive to Tyvan, about an hour down Highway 33 through the small prairie towns of Lajord and Sedley.

"Look, Hedley," Marki says. She holds her Wombat up. "Ada is almost a straight line south of Tyvan. It's as though they are invisibly connected by a thin line. According to my online map, if we drove home, we'd be there in about twenty hours. I'm almost tempted."

"Me too. I like this, traveling with you. I think I could get used to the power of these old ICs."

"But they're wasteful and harmful to the air."

They drive on in comfortable silence, taking in the rugged beauty of the prairie countryside.

"So flat and lonesome," Marki comments. "But I like it. I feel free here. There's room to think."

"It gets in your blood," Hedley says. "Mom brought us here every fall after Dad died to see the geese leave on their trip south. I'll show you the spot. We might see some still, though they've been back a while and spread out by now."

"This is an area the electric jobbies haven't improved on," Marki says as she snuggles in. "We couldn't do this in the bucket seats of my runabout."

Hedley smiles. "Change isn't necessarily better." He reaches his right arm snugly around Marki, bringing her close.

"I was getting chilly."

"This is nothing. Dad once told me the winters get down to minus forty sometimes, with four feet of snow."

"I can't imagine that."

"He used to ride his frigging bike in that stuff, here and in Calgary. He was one tough buzzard."

She massages his tummy, casually working her way down.

"Ooh . . . Want me to pull over?" Hedley asks.

"You take care of the driving, I'll take care of you."

Life has changed drastically on the prairies since the 1960s, at least on the surface. Gone are most of the prairie skyscrapers, the local grain elevators that were often the reason for a town's existence. They were the hubs around which commerce revolved and evolved, but were replaced by large, characterless, centrally-located cement monstrosities.

Like the elevators, the small family farms are disappearing, swallowed up by the corporate conglomerates that demand the economy of the bigger unit. Few of the young people stay put, choosing instead to migrate to the cities for the often-empty promises of the blue-eyed sheiks.

But life is good in Saskatchewan; simple and uncomplicated for the most part, at least where it counts. Neighbors help neighbors, and strangers are treated as friends until proven otherwise.

Later, a warm longing tugs at Hedley as they walk the quiet streets of his father's hometown, where fewer than fifty souls dwell. Marki loves the serenity of this quaint village, feeling closer to Hedley than she felt possible. "I love you Hedley, I'm glad we came," she says as they walk hand in hand.

Hedley stops. "What you did in the car was great, Marki, but this, being here with you like this, we needed to come here together. I love you too. I need you here with me."

They walk on again, saying nothing, taking it all in. They enjoy a brisk hike to the graveyard a short distance north of town, bundled in sweaters against the coolness of the early prairie spring. Their laughter grows silent as they walk through the solemn wrought iron gates of the old cemetery, feeling its history wrap around them. They locate the plot where two simple tombstones stand, side-by-side, bearing the names Helen Yonge and Gordon Richter. Hedley hovers at his grandmother's grave, never having known her yet somehow feeling her spirit around them.

"My dad's mom died when he was ten," Hedley begins. "He got pretty screwed up about it. He made up some crazy story about her getting killed in a car accident when they were driving. I guess the thought of her dying suddenly was easier to take than the truth. She suffered in hospital for a long time, wasting to nothing while her mind turned to mush."

"That's sad."

"Yeah. Maybe the car accident thing wasn't so screwed up. It was survival. Dad lived with his Uncle Gordon after that. Dad's dad, my grandfather, and I use the term loosely, ran for the hills when dad was six. I can't imagine my dad leaving us, not on his own accord anyway. Dad's Uncle Gord had a guitar and an amp. He didn't exactly teach Dad to play, but he encouraged him. My dad learned to play a song he thought was on the radio when the imaginary crash occurred. It was called 'Playing Young and in Love.' And therein lies the origin of Scott Yonge and the Zone. He would dance with Grandma Arlene and sing that song to her. I don't know what that was about."

"I do, Michelle told me. Your grandmother taught your dad how to dance to that song. It was one of her favorites."

"Two old tombstones in a pioneer cemetery. There must be more to Dad's family than this."

"We haven't been to the house yet. I'm sure we'll find something more there."

"I don't want things. I want to find people who knew them, people who can tell me what they were like. Sometimes a picture isn't worth a thousand words."

They make their way back to town again, back to the waiting Dodge rental. They quickly find the old two-storey house, though no street signs exist. It is exactly as it has been described, exactly as he remembered. He'd been inside before, when he was eleven, but only for a quick look around.

They walk through the deep backyard, once beautifully sculpted with a forest of flowers and plants, courtesy of Hedley's great grandmother Louise and her exceptional green thumb. But that's long gone. The existing backyard is generically manicured by a lawn care company. Flicks of new green are beginning to show through the winter brown, coaxed upward by the lengthening spring light. They step up onto the small back porch to the beckoning door, granting entrance to the long ago remodeled kitchen. A small bedroom sits directly off the kitchen as they enter, put there for Scott's grandmother in her advancing years when the second storey bedrooms were beyond her. Hedley and Marki deposit their meager bags in the small cozy room and disrobe, saying nothing. They desire each other, brought closer by the history of the house, wishing to be part of its intimacy through their own.

◆ ◆ ◆

"Screwing in my great grandma's house. We're going to hell for sure," Hedley jokes as they lie, spent.

"Don't ruin it," Marki says. "I've never felt closer to you. I feel like I—"

"Belong?"

"Yes, to the family, to all of this, to all that you are."

"Well that's good."

"It is."

◆ ◆ ◆

"Hello?" *Oh crap*, Hedley thinks as he scrambles to disarm the video feed. The incessant gurgling of his ringing Wombat woke him. He regrets answering on instinct. "Hi Mom." He tries to sound nonchalant.

"Hedley, you were supposed to call me from Regina. Put Marki on, please."

"She's out walking."

"No, she's not."

Hedley passes the device.

"Hi, Michelle," Marki says. "You must think I'm awful."

"Not at all. I'm checking in, not checking up. Are you enjoying yourself?" *Obviously*, Michelle thinks.

"Uh huh, it's nice here."

"I figured you two might be hungry right about now, I had Walter stock the place, but you'll have to cook, unless you want to drive to Fillmore. No restaurants or take-outs to be had in Tyvan these days. And please Marki, call, okay? Let me know you're still alive."

"I will, I promise."

"Thank you."

"Mom, do you know anybody we can talk to, somebody that might have known Dad or Duke, or maybe even Jim and Helen? I'd like to hear something firsthand for once, from someone close to home."

"Geez, thanks."

"You know what I mean."

"Talk to Cecil Millar over at the general store. He's had a hand in looking after the house and yard all these years. Cec is an old timer. He's bound to know something of interest."

"Mom, the sex thing . . . I don't want you to think that it's just sex. It's more than that, especially here."

"You don't have to sell me on the power of sex with someone you deeply love, Hedley. I lived it with your father. We were very passionate about each other."

"Ya think? Yuck."

"Oh grow up," Michelle laughs. "Marki, thank you. You're good for my son."

"Bye, Mom," Hedley says.

"All right, I'll leave you to it. Enjoy your time." She chuckles to herself as she hangs up the call. *Too cute*, she thinks. *You'd enjoy them.*

"Hungry?" Hedley asks.

"Nope, I like it where we are."

"Me too, but I think we should get back to where we were."

They spent the rest of the day puttering around, tangling themselves in plenty of sex, relaxation, and hangout time. Marki took a stab at cooking up a simple meal of potatoes, vegetables, and a pork chop each, topped off with two humungous bowls of chocolate ice cream—Hedley's favourite.

"Wow, this is great!" Hedley says on his second spoonful. "Comes from the creamery in Weyburn. My dad used to play there. I think he played all the towns around here when he was young. He lived a crazy life, Marki."

There's no video stream, let alone a TV, as no one has lived in the house for years, but they don't mind. They go upstairs, rummaging around in the dusty attic, accessed through a ceiling-mounted pull-down metal staircase above the second floor. It's full of packed boxes mostly, best left for another day, but they find an old checkers game to while away the time. And of course, they have their Wombats to fill the hours with music and online gossip. They retire early, not necessarily to sleep and wake early—hunger overriding hormones.

◆ ◆ ◆

"Are my glasses on your side?" Marki asks the next morning. She reaches but does not find her large oval horn-rimmed spectacles.

Hedley hands them across and rises to dress.

They grab some toast and cereal, and then head back to the attic. They spend hours carefully examining the contents of the many boxes lining the attic floor. They find mostly trinkets, pictures, old Christmas ornaments, and artifacts from a bygone era kept for no particular reason, though a 33 RPM album by Johnny Noel from 1966 piques Hedley's interest. There it was again, that song, 'Playing Young and in Love,' the title track of the album.

"I don't know what I expected to find, exactly," Hedley says, "but I haven't found it yet."

"I think this is significant," Marki cradles the album two-armed to her chest as though it's a treasure. "We should keep this."

They also finger a small blurry black and white photo, *Helen 10, Gordon 12, 1936* scribbled on the back, as well as an eight-by-ten sepia wedding day photograph of Scott's grandparents from 1922.

"Nothing. Nothing on Jim, nothing on Duke, very little on Helen, we came all this way for this?"

"Maybe being here is enough, Hedley. Here where they lived. I can almost feel them with us in this old attic."

"I'm sorry I'm a suck face. Being here with you . . . I can't describe how good I feel. I don't think I want to leave. I know I'll never leave you."

She smiles like the sun. "Maybe we should go to the store like your mom said and talk to that man?"

"Yeah, Cecil Millar. Let's hope."

Not much remains of Tyvan, Saskatchewan: a scattering of old houses, most in disarray, an old Anglican Church now boarded up, an obsolete gas station slash hardware store slash post office, a haphazard looking bank, and the Tyvan general store. The town once thrived, but the fire of 1931 gutted the downtown core. Now open lots remain where thriving businesses once stood.

The Richter house is on a large corner lot, the front door proudly greeting the rising sun. This rendition of the old 1910 two-storey A-frame is well dressed, with white clapboard siding and an aging dark green, shingled roof to keep out the sometimes harsh prairie elements. Marki and Hedley look back across the alley at the old house before turning to navigate the open lot where the King George Hotel stood in the pre-fire days. They cross what used to be Main Street and head south about half a block down the wooden boardwalk that feels like living history. They stop for a shot of confidence outside the Tyvan General Store, release hands, and walk in. A stocky, white-haired, clean shaven, bespectacled old gent in his mid-seventies (Hedley guesses) looks up as the high-pitched jingling of the small ceiling-mounted, door-activated bell breaks the silence.

The store is a long, narrow affair, the soda fountain counter running lengthwise about four feet south of the north wall as you look west, inviting all inside. Behind the counter are shelves up to the twelve-foot ceiling, neatly piled with dry goods of all types and sizes: the bare necessities required to save the few remaining locals the forty-five mile ride up Highway 33 to Regina. Five stainless steel stools with circular bright red plush vinyl seats spring up from the well-oiled, wide planked floorboards; ancient artifacts of a bygone era. Hedley and Marki move forward in awe as they step into a distant world.

"Mr. Millar?" Hedley asks.

"The same," he says, a half smile playing on the corners of his thin-lipped mouth. "What can I do for you, Mr. Yonge?" he asks.

"What? Who told you?" Hedley feels caught off guard.

"Nobody told me, young feller," he says. He points to the south wall opposite the counter. "You're a dead ringer for Jim. That's him, third row down, five along."

Hedley and Marki turn in sync, following the finger to dozens of framed sepia photos adorning the Tyvan Wall of Heroes.

"You knew him?" Hedley scarcely believes his luck.

"Knew of him. I was about twenty when he disappeared from these parts."

"Yeah, he ran out on my grandmother."

"Could be, but I've got nothing bad to say about our veterans. They faced a hard lot over there in '44 and '45. I expect it was no different for Jim."

"I bet the rest of those guys hanging up there didn't run off on their wives," Hedley's voice holds an edge of bitterness.

"You got a name, young feller?"

"I'm Hedley, and this is Marki."

"I'm Cecil, Cec to my friends." He nods and smiles Marki's way, then continues. "I don't pretend to know what happened between Jim and Helen, but I do know that the war, any war . . . Any time a man is around killing and dying on a daily basis, well, that has to change a man hasn't it? And I expect it changes different men in different ways. Without being there, you have no right to point a finger. Heck, some of those men on the wall did far worse than Jim did, but we buried them all with respect, them that was still around. I heard tell the drinking finally got Jim around '74. Died somewhere in Northern Ontario when his liver went bad. He paid for his trespasses, just as we all do, but that don't make him a bad man. Some people cope with things better than others, that's all it is. Helen had a bad time with Jim, everyone knew that, but she wasn't one to hold a grudge."

"Was she happy?" Marki asks.

"Yes, she was, as far as I could see. She had twenty years on me, but I swear that woman was a looker. She was the town clerk, you know, so everybody knew her, and everybody liked her. A girl like that stuck on Jim, it was a shame. Again, I ain't saying anything bad about Jim, he just couldn't handle responsibility."

"I really don't know much about my grandparents," Hedley says. "I'm trying to fill in the blanks."

"I can only tell you what I know from my view of things. That might not necessarily jive with what you want to hear."

"I think that's exactly what I want to hear, Mr. Millar. They were real to you. Maybe you can make them real to me."

Mr. Millar contemplates Hedley's words, wondering if it is his place to speak. Hedley's yearning wins out.

"When your father came along—that's who we're talking about, right?"

Hedley nods.

"When the boy came along, Jim lit out and it broke Helen's heart clean through. But she was strong. She put on a good face and lived for the boy. Scott. He was a different one, quiet as all get out, but not one to be outdone. He was a hell of a shortstop, even at eight. Course, after Helen died in '68, he clammed up completely. He went to live with Helen's older brother, Gordie. He all but disappeared, and when he came out from hiding, he was quite the guitar player. It wasn't long before he was playing weekends, traveling with the older boys to the towns along Highway 33. I lost track of him after that, up until he died in the helicopter crash. It's just as well Helen wasn't around for that. I'm sorry, I might have overstepped."

"It was a long time ago, I'm okay with it," Hedley says.

"You two pull up a stump," Cec gestures to the idle stools. "Can I get you something, a drink maybe?"

"I would like a root beer, if you have one," Marki asks politely.

"Dr. Pepper for me, please," Hedley says. He pulls out a bill to pay but is waved off.

"On me," Mr. Millar insists. "I don't get a chance to talk to young folk much these days."

"You do look a lot like your grandfather," Marki says. She hops off her stool for another look. "You have his eyes."

"I don't suppose you have another picture around?" Hedley asks.

"No, and that one stays where it is, but tell you what, I'll see to it you get it when I'm done here. You can have them all if you want. It's not as though there's a rush to claim them. It's pretty much the end of the line for Tyvan, I'm afraid."

"That's a shame," Marki says, returning to her perch.

"It's the way of things," Cecil says.

"I hope we're not keeping you from anything," Hedley says.

"I've got nothing pressing. The Saturday rush is three days away," Cecil Millar laughs at his own joke. "No, Helen was a spritely girl, full of laughter. Every available man in town wanted to court her, but she was stuck on Jim. We thought maybe Duke might hit a home run, he was some sweet on Helen, but it wasn't meant to be."

"You knew Duke?" Hedley jumps in.

"I knew Duke. He was older of course, but we got along. I was rooting for him with Helen. He was a good man, but he didn't have Jim's flair. Jim could dance, and he had a way with a joke. He was popular. Ah well. Duke came to town in 1954, in around there. He was an American, from Kansas City I think. He travelled with the carnivals for a long time before he took a hankering to us. I don't know his history. We didn't ask, he didn't tell. He became one of us. That's all we needed to know. He got on at the Massy dealership and settled down. He went home several times, to see his people I guess, but he always came back. Sometimes I think Helen was the attraction. At any rate, he returned for good in '64 with his citizenship in hand and never left again until the early nineties when he moved to Calgary. Why he did that I'll never know. He was long retired by then. Could have stayed here just fine."

"My dad moved to Calgary in 1995. Maybe . . ."

"Could be. He was fond of your dad, took him fishing and hiking and the like. They were tight for a while after Jim left, but you didn't see them together much after Helen died. Duke still kept an eye on the boy though, from afar. Everyone could see your dad was troubled. How could he not be? An only child, no parents. It was hard times for the boy. Your great uncle done his best, but he was a bachelor, and he was not a well man. His heart gave out in '71 when your dad was traveling out east. I always thought fifteen was too young to be out on your own, but your dad done all right. Duke was lost for a while though. Both his hunting buddies were gone, but he kept busy enough."

"There sure are a lot of trees," Marki remarks. "We didn't see many on the drive from Regina."

"No, you wouldn't. It was a tradition started back in 1905 and we kept it up over the years. Poplars mostly. They grow quick on the prairies. We lined the streets with them. Tyvan is a forest in the middle of the flatlands. Same by that old slough northeast of town, we planted trees around it for the geese. They been coming every year for as long as we can remember. They didn't make it this spring though, or last. We don't know what that's about. Long as they keep coming in the fall, that's the big one."

"Yeah, my mom and my sister were here last October for that."

"They've been here every year for the last while, always staying in Fillmore, never at the house. Your mother's been in the store a few times over the years. She's a looker and a nice lady to boot."

Hedley smiles. "I've never heard her referred to as a lady."

"Made quite a ruckus in 2001 when she came with your father, them being famous and all. But they didn't put on airs. People got used to them quick enough. They stayed at the old house then. That's when they brought Walter into the picture, and hence, me. Last time I saw your dad was 2001."

They talked into the afternoon, Hedley and Marki soaking up the history while Cecil Millar relived the past. He told them about Harry Richter and the old hotel, how Harry met Louise Fletcher when she worked there as a clerk. Harry managed the hotel before it was lost in the fire. He spent the rest of his working years with the CPR, the Canadian Pacific Railroad, and was proud of its tradition. The day was everything Hedley and Marki had hoped for.

"Well, it's time to close shop," Mr. Millar announces. "You two are nice folk, I hope I've given you what you need. You know, that picture of Jim . . . Hang on a sec, I'll be right back." He retreats through the twin curtains covering the doorway to the back-storage area and returns with an aluminum stepladder. "Why don't you climb up there and take that picture down? It'll do more good hanging in your home, I expect."

"But it'll leave a gap," Marki protests, not knowing why.

"Yep, and it'll stay that way. And when people ask, I can tell them why the wall is blank. You two will become a part of this town's history, what's left of it."

"Thanks," Hedley replies. "That's cool."

Cecil grins. "You'd better scurry up there. The Leafs are on tonight and I don't want to miss that. They're back in the playoffs this year and we're all glad to see it. Drop in again before you go back home."

Hedley and Marki leave on a high, flushed with the excitement of the day's journey. Pumped with adrenalin, they take a stroll to the old slough not quite a mile northeast of town. It's not much to look at, just a large, tree-lined watering hole really, with cattails and pussy willows lining the edges, revealing their spring heads. It is of great significance to Hedley though. He cries quietly as Marki holds him, standing near the spot where he stood as a young boy. They return to town, sober now and drained. They quickly lose their clothes and tumble into bed, brought ever closer to each other by the magic of the day.

◆ ◆ ◆

"What's up, Mom?" Hedley asks with a slight irritable tinge. Hedley makes no attempt to hide the truth.

"Sorry to wake you." She smiles remembering her own youth. "How'd you make out with Cec? Hello, Marki!"

"Really good, thanks for that." Hedley and Marki give Michelle the details, bubbling with enthusiasm about their adventure.

"There's a slight change in plans. I'd like both of you to come to Philadelphia."

"Philadelphia? What's in Philadelphia that we need to see?"

"I'd really like to stay here for a while," Marki says.

"Me too," Hedley says.

"How about you stay another day and then I fly you out? Marki can room with Carolyn. You can stay with me."

"Get a brain, Mom. Like that's gonna happen."

Michelle laughs loud. "Sorry, I couldn't resist. I'll fix you up with your own room." She laughs again. "Seriously, there are people out here you need to meet."

◆ ◆ ◆

CHAPTER SIX — BACK TO PHILADELPHIA

They're back in Tracy's Philadelphia living room, Hedley and Marki joining the fray. Introductions and alliances have been made over a casual meal at a nearby restaurant. Brian recommended they sit in the new Halo Chamber, a section of the lounge outfitted with the latest technology. There was a lineup for the chamber, but they felt it well worth the wait.

"Cool," Brian had commented when the new DarkFellow Halo was featured. "Doesn't matter where we sit, it feels like we're on the stage with them." Hedley squirmed a little as the ghostly life-sized image of his alter ego swirled around the room, but no one was the wiser.

The impact of the Halo followed them home to Tracy's. Now a heavier vibe dominates the quiet living room as a replay of the 2009 rally fades from their retinas.

"I had no idea Dad was into that," Hedley says.

"He was drawn in against his will. I don't want that for you, or Carolyn," Michelle says.

"But don't you see the significance of that day?" Tracy asks. "The Peace Initiative, all those people drawn together, a lot of them there because of your father, because of Bobby Johnson."

"Yeah, 'MaryAnn Said,'" Hedley says. "Believe me, I know the implications of that song. I spent quality time with the colonel because of those whack jobs using my dad's lyrics to their own end."

"I'm the queen of the whack jobs, Hedley. I'll explain later," Tracy says. "But first, please listen to what I have to say. What your father said to us, what he stood for was in the hearts of all those people. Maybe he didn't intend to be there, but he spoke the words and sang the song that united us. Now we're finally going to see an end to this stupid war, and we can trace it back to that day. Your father was supposed to be there."

"That's a pile of crap," Hedley barks. "Shit happens. Fate had nothing to do with it."

"I don't think so," Carolyn says. "I mean, yes, Dad was there almost against his will, but I can't help but think that all of it is linked, including what happened to you, including all of us being in this room now."

"Exactly, the future is past and present," Tracy says. "There's more, lots more. I've got a video, the concert in Rockport, the last show of Scott Yonge & the Zone."

"What the fuck is with you people? Give it up!" Hedley yells. He rises from his chair. Marki goes to him. Settling him, she leads him back to his spot on the settee.

"I think you should watch it," Marki says in a quiet voice. "I'm right here with you."

"I agree. We all should watch it," says Michelle.

"Sorry, Tracy," Hedley says. "We're obviously touching on a sensitive area of my life, of my family's life."

Tracy nods and smiles empathetically.

"Listen carefully to his words, to what he says," Tracy starts again. "They give root to what drew us to him. Draw your own conclusions."

SATURDAY, JULY 18, 2009 — NEWPORT, RHODE ISLAND

"Mr. Yonge, are you there? Wake up Mr. Yonge."

The gasp of air tells the colonel that Scott is awake, and he smiles, enjoying more and more the power he holds over another man's life.

"You have things to do, Mr. Yonge. No time to dally. There will be a knock at your door very soon. Take the envelope. In it, there is a key to a locker. Go to the bus station and be sure to take the blue case with you. Exchange the blue briefcase for the one in the locker. Return to the hotel. Wait, and speak to no one. That is all."

Scott looks around, trying to ground himself. Oh yes, Newport. It's Saturday, the fourth day of the ordeal. The knock comes as foretold but is no less obtrusive. Scott climbs out of bed fully clothed and stumbles to the door.

"You're the delivery man?"

Del looks down, pointing to the now familiar tie-clip-looking device and the truth of Scott's earlier assumption hits home.

"Del, I—"

Del shakes his head and locks his eyes, pushing the envelope into Scott's half ready hands as he does so. He turns and retraces his steps, leaving a trail of anguish behind him, almost visible in the dimly lit hallway. Scott watches as Del fades away, his heart aching a little more for the misery he has brought down on those closest to him. He doesn't have to ask; he knows all too well the method of control. He resists calling after him, but hopes Del knows that he knows. He closes the door and turns back inside, missing the sound of frustration as Del's fist smashes through the thin drywall of the hallway running at a right angle to the left about thirty feet down from Scott's room.

A head peaks out of a cautiously opening door to see a tall, well-built middle-aged man facing the wall adjacent the door, fist still embedded in the gaping hole as though it belonged. *I'll kill the fucker.* The words scream in Del's mind as the door quickly closes again. *Somehow, some way, I'll get through to the son-of-a-bitch.* Calmer now, with a returning sense of control, he continues through the fire escape door to the street below.

The authorities agree the best route is to cooperate and observe from a safe distance, at least until Monday, the presumed day of the Hedley exchange. What can they do anyway, without more information? The operation is well planned and so far executed in perfect military precision. They still have no clues as to who the man is—a solid indication of the force he commands—or where to strike back. This is urban guerrilla warfare at its finest. At this point, they'll continue to let the colonel play soldier and hope that he will tip his hand. One mistake is all they ask for—one indication, one direction to lead their focus. There is little else they can do.

Scott is thankful for their cooperation but knows that public pressure will soon demand action. He prays he can resolve this as planned before the real war breaks out. The realization that somewhere along the line somebody has to die plays like a reverse mantra in the back of his mind. He turns the key in the lock and walks the hallway with blue briefcase in hand, wondering what surprises lie ahead. Tired and confused, he only wants this to end. He desperately wants to hold his son again.

◆ ◆ ◆

"Mr. Yonge." The image from the provided portable DVD player greets him. "If you're looking at me now, then we've come a long way, and I'm very close to completing my mission."

Scott pauses the image for a moment, taking the time to survey what is happening. *He's showing his face,* he thinks. *Why? That can't be good.* Mesmerized, he takes in the now still image of the insignificant looking man greeting him from behind a nondescript desk in a nondescript office. *Take away the uniform and he's Joe Middle Manager from Anywhere, Ohio. What gives? How can he be doing this to me?* Studying his adversary, he presses the play button again, allowing the familiar, calm and controlled voice to float in the air of the forty-dollar-a-night hotel room.

"We're not that different, you and I," the voice says. "In another time, we might have been friends, but times are what they are, and we must follow our chosen paths. You've done well, Mr. Yonge. Soon we will meet, and soon, we will deliver your son to his mother. But first, I have one more task for you to complete. I want a song, Scott."

Scott cringes at the sound of his given name used in such a fashion, but ignores the urge to throw something through the screen. He stands up and paces, unable to listen for the moment as he tries to wrap his mind around the tone of the colonel's message. *"Soon we'll deliver"?* He thinks as he pauses the player again. *I don't like the sound of that.* Not wanting to listen, but needing answers, he pushes play again, allowing the colonel to continue.

"I want you to write a song, a patriotic song, uplifting and sincere, praising my mission and my country. I've put you on short notice, I know, so I'm not expecting John Phillip Sousa, but a man of your considerable talent should be capable of producing something for the Newport show, which is tonight if all has gone as planned. Keep it simple. Your band mates will need to pick it up fast."

"Christ," Scott mutters to himself. "Will it never end?"

"I know you hate me," the colonel continues in a more human tone. "I don't begrudge you the right, but are we really so different? Do we not want the same thing? Do we not want to live in a country, and ultimately a world, at peace with itself? It will take a strong hand to accomplish that task, a stronger one than mine, but someone has to start the process. My one regret is this business with your son, but fate delivered you to me. I have no choice but to follow my calling. No harm has come to your boy, and in the end, you will see I'm right. The world will see I am right, and will thank me. Don't bother turning this disc or the player over to the authorities. Of course, that's up to you, but it would do you no good. The disc has been rendered electronically useless as it plays, and on the offhand chance that you attempted to make a copy, that file would also be useless. You have better things to do with your time, Mr. Yonge. Until tonight. I eagerly await the fruits of your labor."

The image fades and disappears. Scott attempts a replay, but the screen fills with snow as predicted, white noise greeting him from the small speakers. His mind draws a blank; he can think of nothing or draw any sensible conclusion from what he's seen and heard. A new kind of tiredness settles in, gnawing at him suddenly, incessantly. To write what the colonel wants is alien to the way he is wired. The currents of his thoughts flow in an entirely different direction. Doubt plagues him, but he will try. For Hedley, and for a part of himself he did not know existed, he will try.

♦ ♦ ♦

MAGIC

It was still there, the old three-sided quarter-inch plywood lean-to, standing proud in the early twilight of the brisk autumn morning. Built eons ago by a forgotten observer and quickly annexed as unofficial community property, this monument from the past opens the door to the beckoning future.

Turned gray by countless years of exposure to the harsh Canadian prairie environment, it had somehow stood the test of time, offering its tattered promise of a safe haven from which to watch. Thin layers of wood lift and bubble in spots where the glue has given way over time, but the walls stand firm, extending their arms in silent welcome to all who would venture in. Year after year they came, each generation of wide-eyed kids and curious adults, eager for Mother Nature's annual show.

One look and Scott is again that ten-year-old boy peeking over the rim of the three-foot-deep, twelve-foot-long foxhole, fashioned, he always felt, after a minor league baseball dugout. Fourteen feet across the back, the walls have been lovingly maintained over the years, kept clean and weed free by countless unseen hands in brief caretaking moments spawned by a common sense of community.

You can feel the history of the town in this place, Scott thinks. A wry, sentimental grin plays across his face as he watches his own children gaze over the rim through the gently swaying bull rushes, crisp autumn air filling their lungs with the wonder of the natural world.

"Wow, look at all the boxed lunches staring us down," Hedley says.

"I think they're wonderful," Carolyn whispers in reverence as the hundreds, perhaps thousands of Canada Geese rest comfortably but wearily twenty yards east on the glassy surface of the marsh, silhouetted against the red rising sun. "Listen Daddy! They're singing to us!" She giggles as the geese's persistent soft honking tickles her ears.

"Yeah, like you, Dad," Hedley says. "Only better."

Scott laughs, saying nothing, wondering where the sensitive young boy got his mouth.

"Mom's going to miss it all," Carolyn says. "She'll never find us out here by herself."

"Don't fret, Soup. She's been here before. She'll be along any time now, and she's bringing sandwiches."

"And hot chocolate," Michelle says. She peeks around the south wall of the makeshift shelter. "We're out of coffee."

Scott shivers in delight at the sound of her voice, wrapping around every familiar nuance like a boa. "Hot chocolate's peachy, love. You used whole milk, right?" Scott asks with a twinkle.

"Like you wouldn't drink it if I didn't?"

"Shush, you'll scare them," Carolyn says.

"Yeah, grow up, will ya?" Hedley says. He glides over to help his mom into the shelter. "We came to watch the birds, not give them one."

"I think they're watching us," Carolyn says. Michelle pours hot chocolate with motherly efficiency, doling out the elixir to silent acknowledgements of thanks.

"They know we're here all right, but they don't see us as a threat, or they'd be gone," Scott replies.

They sip in silence, the four of them brought together in a moment for the memory banks, staring in awe at the flock before them.

One of God's better creations, Michelle thinks, squeezing a hand on either side of her. Warmth courses through her veins, stealing the chill from the early autumn Saskatchewan morning.

"Oh Daddy, they're so beautiful," Carolyn whispers, delighting in the thrill of discovery only a child can know.

Scott leans down involuntarily, lightly kissing the top of her head in a show of agreement.

And beautiful they are, as Carolyn said, from the distinctive white-on-black cheek markings to the soft pastel brown-gray shades of the body, melding to the brilliant white of the undercarriage. Slender black necks gracefully float regal black heads, held proud against the elements in the ultimate statement of freedom.

"Magic, Soup, that's what they are," Hedley says. "Better than anything Merlin can make up."

"Look! Oh look at them! What are they doing?" Carolyn asks.

"They're getting ready to go," Scott answers. The flock almost simultaneously ruffles and fluffs its feathers, testing their wings on the air.

Slowly at first, then with a fury, the flock ascends, leaping off the surface of the marsh in pursuit of an unknown leader, taking to the sky in waves. They circle and break into natural flying *V* formations, climbing as they go, looking south-southwest, taking a piece of eternity with them.

"Bye birdies, bye," whispers Hedley.

Carolyn waves sadly, wishing her new friends could stay, but knowing they cannot or must not. Thoughts of well wishes chase them as they move steadily from sight.

Then they're gone, and silence wraps around the four beating hearts like a blanket as they stare after the black dots in the distance.

"Show's over, gang. Let's go home," Scott says. He slips his uneaten sandwich into the front pouch of his purple kangaroo pullover.

Michelle smiles as she steps up and out into the brilliant new sunlight, disappearing in its golden glow.

She's gone, and a wave of panic hits Scott as he loses sight of her in the harsh new light. He wakes with a start, heart pounding and breaking simultaneously as he reaches for her. It's 2:30 PM, time to move. He stumbles from the bed to the tiny bathroom, throwing cool water on his face in an effort to reach full consciousness. Exhaustion is ever present, but the need to proceed fights to the foreground, taking charge of necessary motor functions until the mind fully engages.

It's a hot day, too hot for the old window air conditioning to be effective, so he remains in his favorite trademark orange shorts, but changes into a fresh dark blue t-shirt. He wishes for his clip-ons, lost somewhere in his travels. *Left at the bus depot*, he thinks. He'll have to brave the sunlight through his prescription specs. Hungry, but with no desire to eat, he compromises, stopping at the lobby late-night dispenser, lonely now in the light of day, grabbing a couple of chocolate bars. A different machine offers a can of another diet soda. Not his desired choice, but cold and wet anyway, and available. A quick swig, a rinse and swallow, another long draw, and he heads out the front door to a waiting cab.

He dozes again during the twenty-minute ride to the stadium, passing through security without a hitch. The driver recognizes him and is surprised, but says nothing, though he wants to. He knows. Everybody knows. Scott is amazed at how easy he can move about, but then it's always been that way with him. His has a forgettable face, even at the height of his popularity. Not so with

Michelle. She is still the recognizable one, though she left the limelight years ago. Her looks, her beauty, and her aura are of the ages.

By tonight, the stadium will be crawling with the curious and the sympathetic, led by the charge of the paparazzi brigade, flanked by a barrage of flashing cameras, still and otherwise. Scott doubts that anyone much cares about the music tonight, but he does. The feeling that this will be the last performance in a long time, maybe the last performance ever from Scott Yonge, weighs heavily on him like the ocean, not crushing him, but buoying him up. The knot in his stomach is as tight as it's ever been, and there are still over six hours to show time. He does not wonder—he knows—he will be at his best. The musician and performer in him guarantees the fact. It is the key to who he is. The exhaustion, the frustration of the past week, and the pressure of the moment will be pushed aside when the lights go up, and the essence of what is Scott Yonge will shine through. He will offer himself. He will face the court and answer the charges, and the world will judge him. His work will be done.

But first, this afternoon's sound-check and unscheduled rehearsal. Or is it? He doesn't know what to expect from his band mates. He does not know what they know, but he suspects they know a lot. He won't be surprised to see them all wearing the familiar tie-clip device, though he hopes otherwise. He hopes the level of control exercised on their lives is minimal, but doubts it. How will it be with them? He's been instructed to interact as little as possible, and assumes those instructions have also been communicated to them. *Should be interesting*, he thinks. He sighs. *Michelle . . .*

◆ ◆ ◆

JEFF

"Get in!"

"What? Michael?"

"Yeah, get in."

Jeff opens the back seat of the older model Chevy sedan, struggling with the oversized backpack and the two medium-sized suitcases neatly stuffed to the brim with thousand-dollar bills. *People have no idea how much fifteen million weighs*, he thinks. *But most would gladly make the sacrifice to feel the weight on their backs.* The sight of him on the street in full business suit with a backpack and two suitcases handcuffed to his wrists on this overly hot day draws more than a casual look from passers-by, but nervousness has never been one of Jeff's traits. He correctly assumes that the colonel has his people watching him, and that he is probably as safe as he's ever been in his life.

"He got to you too," Jeff states with resignation. He reaches into his coat pocket, pulling out a key. He unlocks one, then the other of the cuffs.

"Big time," Michael replies.

"You being followed?" Jeff asks as he slides into the passenger side of the front seat.

"I don't think so, but maybe. It doesn't matter apparently. You?"

"Same. The authorities are cooperating, but I can't help but think we're being watched from both sides of the fence."

Michael says nothing as he pulls away from the curb. He hates the feel of the stocks around him, but the colonel has placed the future of his niece Belinda directly on Michael's shoulders, curiously leaving Michelle's other brother Darren and his wife out of the plan. Or so it would appear.

The silence between the two men in the car is uncomfortable but welcome, as neither much cares for or understands the other, though there is no bad blood between them.

"So," Jeff says, finally breaking the deadlock as they head out of town. "We headed any place special?"

"Out of state. I've got instructions. We'll be driving awhile."

"I take it I won't be back for the show."

"Nope, that's part of it, I think," Michael replies.

"So it would seem. Isolate Scott. That's been the plan from the beginning. How's Michelle holding up?"

"Okay, I guess. She's tough. I haven't talked to her in a while. I don't think she knows about this."

"Probably not, though she knows about the money. I had papers for her to sign. This colonel guy told the world yesterday on Audrey."

"I missed that. It's a long drive from Oklahoma."

"That it is Michael, but there's no place far enough away from this mess."

◆ ◆ ◆

They are waiting at the far side of the stage, huddled together like a would-be band of thieves planning their first heist. Obvious in their nervousness, they fall short of the nonchalant stance they wish to attain, growing quiet and looking away as Scott approaches. Except Del. He meets Scott's gaze as his friend crosses the sixty feet between them. What he needs to say has to be said now, but how? What would be the medium? He has his own set of instructions to follow and is tongue-tied by the tracking and communication device clipped to his t-shirt. There is no room to maneuver. Suddenly, he smiles as a familiar scene floods his mind. He has his answer. He raises his hands and brings them together, slowly at first, then rapidly as the gesture becomes real to him. Randy is next, smiling as he grabs the meaning of the moment. The others rapidly follow suit, surrounding Scott as he reaches them, except Frank, who claps over the talkback mike from his position behind the sound counsel mid-floor. Never has applause sounded sweeter, rich as it was with ripples of support beyond that of any audience he has known. Scott's eyes water at the feel of it.

"I want to thank you guys for sticking with me," Scott begins. "I've had my instructions, and I'm sure you've had yours, but he can't begrudge us at least a little appreciation for the moment. I've got a new song."

"We know," Randy interrupts. "We're ready. Sound check is done, Frank can fine-tune as we rehearse. Let's get to the song."

Scott searches involuntarily for the tie-clip devices but sees only one, on Del, and is hopeful that the involvement of the others has been kept to a minimum. "Where's Jeff?" he asks as he completes his survey.

"He won't be back anytime soon," Ian says. "He's got a job of his own."

"That's the word," Del adds. "We haven't seen him."

Scott turns to Del and smiles, locking eyes again. *Thank you*, he mouths, feeling it is the thing to do.

Del nods, returning an easy smile.

"Right, let's do it." Scott looks at them a second or two, then continues. "Tonight could be the last time we play together for a while, so let's leave them remembering who we are." They nod, pledging their agreement as they take their places.

They're good at what they do. It takes less than two hours to translate the sound in Scott's head into a living, breathing song, painting the notes on the canvas of the air as though it were the ceiling of the Sistine Chapel. They don't have to be told; they know when a song is happening. Frank likes what he hears as he twists the knobs and moves the faders, tightening the sound while security people and arena staff trade their tasks of the moment for a listen. Satisfied, he gives the all clear, and they're done.

Tired beyond words, Scott chooses to remain in the backstage dressing room, hoping to get some rest before the show, now less than three-and-a-half hours away. There is no reason to return to the hotel; the commute would only eat up valuable sack time, and sleep is the priority. There is fresh fruit and sandwiches available should he desire food, and enough Diet Pepsi to fill a swimming pool, thanks to the fulfillment of the not-too-demanding rider. No, he'll stay put and prepare here. A large part of him wishes for a dark hole in which to hide, but another side, the performer in him, bristles with anticipation, the knot in his stomach already gathering and channeling energy for tonight's event.

And it is an event, a drama to be played out on the international stage. The day crews run, testing cameras and equipment and adjusting lights for the broadcast. They were chased out, as per the colonel's wishes (and the band's) for the rehearsal and sound check, but they begin to drift back into the arena. Security is busy cordoning off a twelve-foot by twenty-foot area directly in front of the stage, hanging *Press – Keep Out* signs on the bright orange crossbars running between the inverted *V* end pieces of the temporary barriers. The standard *No Access* blockades are more symbolic than functional, but most people tend to respect them. Security personnel placed at strategic points will handle those who do not. Something in the stance of the men, an air of professionalism earned through experience far beyond that of an average for-hire security force, tells Scott the authorities are present and accounted for. The realization neither calms nor alarms him; it is simply a fact of the moment. He does not expect trouble, at least not from the colonel. His instincts tell him that's not part of the picture. Tonight is about publicity: capturing a wide audience and keeping the colonel's mission in front of the people's short attention span. *Everything is in place*, Scott thinks, surveying the playing field one last time. Satisfied and exhausted, he heads backstage and down a cement corridor to the temporary dressing room where a makeshift cot beckons.

◆ ◆ ◆

The dream wakes him, the same one. Hedley's whispered words "Bye birdies, bye" still ring in his ears as he achieves consciousness. Sound of a different source soon intrudes: that of music playing through the PA system. It's late, he realizes, and jumps to his feet. He can feel more than hear the rustle of people filing into the arena, bringing with them a sense of tension that will build until show time, then burst like a stick dam before a raging river with the first note. It's 7:10 PM; an hour and twenty to go. A shrill knock comes to the door, followed by Del's voice.

"You in there, dude?"

"Si," Scott replies. All the years of the road, sharing the stage, and the music are audible in Del's simple words. They don't have to speak to talk; they're on the same wavelength. The show, the focus is the show. Whatever lies with tomorrow lives with tomorrow; they live for tonight. "I need a shower, I stink. I'll be along soon."

"Cool, dude, don't forget your pants."

He hears cowboy booted footsteps receding on the concrete floor.

A new, unidentifiable tension floats to the surface as Scott showers, rising from the dark side. It has an ominous feel about it, winding like a creeping vine around Scott's confidence, bringing with it a sense of fear, and worse, a sense of defeat. The wariness settles on him again, draining his energy and his will. He shivers uncontrollably as coldness sets in, and he wonders if he can go on. Then it occurs to him as he cranks the hot water that this is all part of it. The plan all along was to isolate him, weaken him bit by bit, reducing him to a shell of what he is. By show time, they would see Scott as the colonel wants them to see him, a weak and ineffective fool incapable of sustaining a mission of any substance.

"You will not break me," Scott whispers. He leans his head against the cool tiles of the shower stall. "I will not give you that."

♦ ♦ ♦

"Come in, Mr. Carlson." Bill Mueller stands casually in the doorway of a neat, small office. He beckons to a regulation stackable straight-backed chair, then takes his place behind the desk nestled in the heart of the Washington, DC, Federal Bureau building. Captain Mueller is a high-profile man, a twenty-year man assigned to those 'politically sensitive' cases requiring a delicate touch. He reports directly to the man at the top, who reports directly to the president.

Kidnapping cases don't usually fall in his hands, but then, most kidnapping cases do not involve an ultra-right wing, homegrown terrorist with an undetermined amount of military might at his disposal. Most kidnapping cases do not directly threaten the internal security of the nation, or capture the imagination of the public the way this one has. All eyes are upon him, yet he is no closer now than he was three days ago to solving the mystery of this colonel and the organization he calls the AFF. Bill has slept little since Wednesday, going over every known detail again and again, drawing nothing but blanks. There is simply not enough information available. Hell, there is virtually no information beyond what is commonly known through the press. He is no more in the know than the man on the street, or so he felt, until now. When word came up from the nerve center, his gut literally climbed into his mouth as he was briefed on the development. So he called in the expert, the man at the top of the field, to interpret the data. No one else would conduct this interview. Call it luck or divine intervention, but he would not squander the opportunity. He is quick to the point.

"Something new has developed," Captain Mueller begins. "We're not sure what it means, or if it means anything at all, but seeing as you're in town anyway, I thought I'd put it to you directly."

"Of course, anything to help," Robert Carlson replies. He tips his sunglasses up, anchoring them atop his head. He scrutinizes the well-built six-footer pushing fifty (or is it the stress of his job?) for clues to what he really knows. The eyes are cool, revealing nothing.

Dressed in khaki shorts and a light green t-shirt, Robert's attire is the antithesis of Bill Mueller's no-nonsense dark suit, white shirt, and tie ensemble. *Not the picture his reputation paints*, Mueller thinks. *But hey, everyone's allowed the occasional casual moment, even an iron-clad business exec like this guy.*

"We know the colonel has Scott wired," Captain Mueller says. "He monitors his movement and is capable of listening as well as speaking to Scott. There has been an electromagnetic field surrounding Scott since this began. The field is beyond our understanding. It seems fairly weak, but constant, and impossible to trace to a source. It's just there somehow, everywhere, but going nowhere. The field has weakened steadily since early yesterday, and disappeared completely this morning, but we feel Scott is still under surveillance. We've picked up another similar signal, weaker but constant and omnidirectional, with an almost imperceptible peak in strength from a northwesterly bearing. It's not much, but it's something."

"Interesting." Robert pauses, deciding what to surrender. "My guess is the power source of the original field was portable, something Scott was carrying with him or near him. That's what you're getting now. That means the mother source and Scott have moved closer to each other, or they are indeed out of contact." It was a lie, but he couldn't give everything away. "Keep scanning for another portable source to kick in. These people are good, real good. I think they've developed a wireless protocol that piggybacks on any other broadcast feed it finds. I believe this protocol can adapt to any feed that is available and jump across frequencies and bandwidths at will until it reaches its destination. It can hook onto available phone transmissions, TV or radio broadcasts, and wireless internet transmissions, anything out there really, and become part of that feed. That is why it seems to be everywhere. It is. You're correct in assuming that the slight bump in the frequency response is significant. Find that source, and you find your man, or some mighty fine clues to his whereabouts. That mother signal allows transmission and reception to occur, but it would still need a decoder on Scott's end. The mother signal has to have something to lock onto, some sort of recognition that this is home. That's what you locked on to originally, the decoder. That field does not have to go anywhere, it simply radiates out from the source. The mother signal searches until it locates that field, then becomes part of it. And the whole process is untraceable. That's my theory.

We're on our way to becoming a virtual nation. There are millions of wireless signals floating around out there for the mother feed to exploit. The decoder, or homing field, whatever you want to call it, doesn't need a lot of power, but it needs to be sustained. My guess is the source is small and battery powered—it will need to be replaced. Where is Mr. Yonge now?"

"Newport. The show is tonight."

"Oh yes, the concert. Newport is on everyone's mind. Strange, isn't it?" Robert seems to reflect. "Check the equipment, and search the vicinity of the Yonge house when the opportunity is presented. I'm sure you'll find something."

"We'll do that. Right now, we watch, and hopefully learn, but we'll not intervene until after the exchange. We really have nothing to act on anyway."

"My people are working on it, but likewise, not much has surfaced. They're impressed, I can tell you that. It is very sound technology."

"Yes, the whole operation is sound. We still have no clue to his identity, his whereabouts, or the size of his force, but he'll make a mistake somewhere. We've got to believe that."

Maybe he already has, Robert thinks. *A small, almost imperceptible blip in strength from the northwest—better fix that.*

Mueller smiles wistfully and rises, indicating the meeting's end. "I appreciate your coming in on the spur," he says. "You have definitely shed some new light on the matter."

"My pleasure, Captain," Carlson replies. They move to the door. "Anything to help." They shake hands in the hallway. *What are the chances?* Robert thinks. He draws the sunglasses down over his eyes just as a dark-haired woman exits the adjacent office. He walks past her. The attractive brunette turns to the sound of his footsteps as he recedes. Janis Isley had returned to the DC offices at the request of Agent Barry Glover. They'd been over it, but he felt that her direct interaction with the colonel at the kidnapping scene could stand another look.

"If you think of anything at all, please contact me at any time," Bill Mueller calls.

"I'll do that," the colonel replies. He turns and waves from the far side of Janis Isley.

She stiffens at the sound of the man's voice but softens again as he walks away. Still, the director of Camp Nakita wears a puzzled look that grates on Barry Glover as she turns to him. He stands curious in the door of his office.

"Something there, Ms. Isley?" Agent Glover asks.

"His voice. Who is that man?"

"That's Robert Carlson, the E-Lok Security software developer. He's aiding us in the investigation," Bill Mueller says.

"It's nothing, really," Janis says. "Jitters, I guess. I thought I caught something in his voice, but there's nothing in the look of the man."

Barry Glover smiles and thanks her for coming to Washington. He turns to Bill Mueller, still standing in the open doorway of his office. Hours of reviewing every lead and viewing every possible mug shot turned up nothing, but significant answers sometimes present themselves at the most insignificant moment. "You heard?" Glover asks.

"Yeah, I heard. He has the smarts, and the resources. Wouldn't that be something?" Mueller replies. "Doubtful, but we'd better check him out one more time. I'll run another background, you see if you can dig up any more tapes on this guy." Mueller walks the short distance to his desk and returns with a mini-tape in his hand. "Take this down to the lab. Have them run this through a phone and re-record. I want Mrs. Yonge to hear what they come up with. Ms. Isley caught something. Sometimes the gut leads you where the mind won't go."

◆ ◆ ◆

Four hours later found Jeff and Michael are on Mishaum Point, a small peninsula jutting into Buzzards Bay near the southern tip of the greater Massachusetts shoreline. They arrived at their remote destination fifteen minutes earlier and now watch from their position outside the car at the crest of a sizeable hill. Two men approach from a bluff to the north, their camouflage uniforms blending with the surrounding bushy countryside.

"We got action," Jeff says.

"Hope they've got gas, or we're walking out of here," Michael replies.

"What, a twenty-mile hike in the ninety-four-degree humidity not appealing to you just now?" Jeff says.

Michael says nothing as the men draw near. They are armed, but not drawn, and they are masked. They move with an effortless stealth that only years of specialized precision military training can instill in a man. They make no sound but they scream of authority— and danger. No words are spoken as they approach. One stands guard, with hand on sidearm in a now opened holster, while the other silently scans the car, retrieving the suitcases and the backpack from the rear seat. He nudges the door shut with his boot, then hands one case to his partner, and turns to Michael and Jeff, still leaning against the driver's side front fender.

If it comes, it comes now, Michael thinks. Jeff entertains similar thoughts as the two pairs of men face each other, eight feet apart.

"Gentlemen, proceed," says the guard. They turn back the way they came.

"Guess we're walking," Jeff says. He shrugs off the tension.

"Guess so," Michael replies. "We might make a few miles on fumes. It's part of the plan, Jeff. They don't want you at the show."

Michael tries the ignition, but to no avail. The engine sputters and fake fires a bit, then dies.

"Great. We walk," Jeff says. "At least you're dressed for it."

"Yeah, but my legs are a mosquito feast. Oh well, no time like the present."

"I don't suppose you thought to bring any water."

"In the glovie. Warm as hell by now, but wet. One each, so ration."

Ten minutes in they hear the unmistakable sound of a helicopter engine sputtering to life. They turn at the sound as the revs peak, to see an older model militarily-painted dragonfly-looking chopper with a heavily tinted plexi-glass bubble canopy rise up and head east, out to sea.

"Thanks for nothing, you bastards," Jeff yells.

They continue walking in the afternoon heat as the chopper disappears from sight.

◆ ◆ ◆

Michelle sits quietly in the twilight of Ada, wanting desperately to talk to Scott, needing so much more to hold him. *Will it never end, this life apart?* She slips to the floor, careful not to wake the sleeping Carolyn, curled up in a ball at the other end of the couch. Michelle leans back against the sturdy wooden frame of the chesterfield, wrapping her arms around her legs for support as she draws her knees to her chest. Time is meaningless. Lately, their routine is nonexistent. They eat when they're hungry, sleep when they're tired, and breathe when they need air. It all seems meaningless, each task requiring a gargantuan effort. *This has got to stop. We've got to take back our lives. Scott, please call, if only for a moment.*

She hears the door in the distance, then Marty's voice. Two sets of footsteps, and they appear, Marty and FBI tech Danny Livermore. The agent smiles and hands Michelle his cell, scrambled on a discreet FBI frequency, while raising an index finger to his lips in the universal signal for 'don't talk'. Michelle rises to her feet to accept, placing the receiver to the ear opposite the tie-clip device.

"This is Captain Mueller from Washington," the voice begins, responding to her breathing. "Listen, and do not talk. I'm going to play a tape over the phone. Let Livermore know what you think, what you feel, okay? Here it comes."

Michelle listens as an edited tape of the afternoon meeting plays, a touch muffled in places and somewhat echoey, but distinguishable. It's not the man, she's sure, yet the hair bristles on her arms, and a peculiar feeling pinches her spine. Still, there's nothing concrete, nothing that tells her for sure one way or the other.

"We'll courier a copy of this to you," Mueller says as the tape ends. "As well as a version that was played back over a phone and recorded. You'll have them tomorrow. Listen to them closely. Let us know if you pick up on anything. Thank you, Mrs. Yonge. Please put Livermore on."

She hands the phone to Danny Livermore. He talks briefly before turning to her.

Anything? Livermore writes before passing the pad to Michelle.

No, she scribbles in her neat hand. *Well, maybe. I can't say for sure, a feeling mostly, but there is something familiar about it.*

Livermore nods, then retreats to the kitchen, chatting with Marty along the way. The hall phone rings, calling them quickly back. Carolyn stirs but does not wake as Livermore beckons Michelle to answer. She moves to the staircase phone, praying it is Scott, but knowing whose voice she will hear.

"Ms. Yonge, our business is near completion," the familiar voice begins. A chill runs down her back. "Your husband returns home later tonight. You must not speak to him, understood? You must not."

"Please," she begs. "Five minutes. Give me five minutes. Let me hold him, let his daughter hold him."

"You will not!" he says. "He is under house arrest, Mrs. Yonge. You'd do well to remember that. It will be over soon." His tone softens. "Your son will be back with you, and all will be well."

"And my husband?"

"You catch a flight tomorrow from Oklahoma City," he says, ignoring her question. "Be at the JetsWest counter at 2:30 PM. A ticket waits. Pack an overnight bag. You're driving back with your son. Your car waits at LA International, so take your keys. You do have a spare?"

"Yes, of course."

"Good. Wear your communicator at all times, your father and daughter also. I want no cheating. I'll instruct you further tomorrow. That is all."

She explodes into the kitchen where Marty, the now awake Carolyn, and Agent Livermore are gathered. "Your father comes home tonight," she says to Carolyn as she hurriedly searches a drawer for a pad of paper and a pen. *THE TAPE, IT'S HIM!* she scribbles as she continues to talk. She holds up the sheet for Danny. He nods in understanding and leaves the room.

"Soup, your dad will stay in the new house for a while. We must not talk to him or hug him. None of us. Understood?"

"But Mom, I want to," she whines.

"We all want to, but we cannot," Michelle says. "Not for a while anyway. Dad, you and Carolyn are to leave your clips on while Scott is here. Those are the instructions. Let's settle in for the show, it's near time."

"This could be hard to watch," Marty says in a tender voice.

"I know, but there's no way I'm not going to. It's going to be a long night."

"I wish your mother were here, Michelle," Marty says. "She'd know what to do about this mess."

◆ ◆ ◆

TOM SEES

It felt good. The fact that his investigative nose was being used for the benefit of someone other than himself had not registered with his conscious mind, but Tom's subconscious self took note and wrapped him in a feeling he hadn't felt in a long, long time. He decided he liked the feeling even though he didn't quite understand why he was feeling it; it felt good just the same. It brought him out of the hollow hole he'd been in since the early days of his 'recruitment.'

Recruitment, that's a laugh. He'd been involuntarily drafted into the army of the AFF, like it or not. At first, that loss of control had driven him into a deep depression that forced him to confront the total uselessness of his life up to that point. That was quickly replaced by a steely determination to do something about it. He isolated himself from everyone, partly out of necessity, and partly out of not wanting inadvertently to drag some other unsuspecting soul into the firestorm that has become his life. He would do the colonel's bidding and report the story as instructed, but he would also use the considerable skills he'd developed over his years on the sleazier side to unearth the man. He'd almost begun to look forward to the intruding, intimidating voice in his earpiece, so taunting in its calculated way, for in it lay valuable clues. He listened to that voice, really listened, and particular nuances were beginning to let themselves be known. So when a file photo of Robert Carlson showed up on a television screen along with the news that he was in Washington for the signing of a new government contract with E-Lok, journalistic bells rang. Tom played on it, and what a hunch it turned out to be.

This has got to be more than a coincidence, he thought as he stumbled across Travis Brewer's name on the micro disk. *Way more than a coincidence. Shit, time to go. Don't you worry, baby, I'll be back to address this further.* He made note of his position, patted the monitor of the data disk reader for luck, and returned the disk to the librarian, wishing like hell he could stay.

◆ ◆ ◆

SATURDAY NIGHT

People go to the stock car races anticipating a crash. Most hope none will occur, but everyone knows it is inevitable, that's what draws them. So it is tonight. Scott can feel that new tension, the sense of possible disaster thick on the air as he walks the concrete corridor to the stage. It emits from everywhere, from the rustle of the crowd as they take their places, from the quiet clinking of the band as they prepare themselves on stage, from the very walls of the hallway he walks, and from the depths of his own self. It is ever-present. *Anticipation wrapped around a sense of history is what it is*, he thinks as he ambles forward.

Somewhere out front, close to the stage in the cordoned-off press area, Tom Brascoe entertains similar thoughts as the house lights dim. He likes a good story as much as the next fellow. Hell, a good story, true or false, is his business, but if given the choice, he'd just as soon avoid the whole situation. This time, he was not granted that luxury. He hopes everything works out, but he can't help but feel otherwise. *You lucked through the Scheck thing intact*, he thinks. *How you did that, we'll never know, but you can't count on that kind of luck too often in a lifetime. I fear for you buddy, I fear for you big time.* He hopes everyone can soon get back to the lives they led, but history tells Tom there is no going back, even though the road that winds through these times offers little to pull us forward. *But go we must, for out there lies our salvation.* He shakes his head sarcastically, chasing the thought away as a roar of approval accompanies a single spotlight, tracing Scott as he steps across the stage. The last show of the Scott Yonge & the Zone Revival Tour has begun. Scott intends to make it a memorable one.

The ovation continues long after Scott reaches his central position, surrounded by his band mates who join in the show of support. He stops behind his boom mike stand, shyly acknowledging the crowd with raised hands, and still it grows. Even some members of the press surrounding Tom join in as the whirring video cameras record the scene from their respective positions on and along the stage.

Signs are held up in the audience flaunting slogans like *Free Hedley, Let Our People Go*, and *Freedom – No Price Too High*, as well as a great abundance of American flags on shirts and jeans, or carried aloft as the forefathers carried Old

Glory many times in the past. *Feels more like a revival than a concert*, Tom thinks as Scott approaches the mike.

"Thank you," Scott begins simply, bidding the applause to wane. "Lovely to see you all. I expect you know what tonight is about. One word: Hedley!"

Again the crowd roars, sparking another ovation, and again Scott holds up his hands to quiet them.

"Kick ass Scott," a lone male voice rings out over the finally stilled audience.

"We will do that," Scott says. "That is our purpose tonight." He reaches back for his light green Fender Strat, draping the strap over his shoulder as he's done a thousand times on a thousand stages.

"This one started it all," he says. "The process that brought all of us here tonight." He begins the familiar guitar intro that Del usually plays, but tonight it is played exactly as it was back in March of 2001, or as close as memory will allow. Unbeknownst to Scott, the home audience sees a split screen image of now and that night as he plays, merging into the present as he begins to sing.

I Call Your Name

I call your name when I rise up every morning
I see your face when I close my eyes at night
I keep moving as the noonday sun is shining
I call your name that's all right

I've been running from a thousand days of sorrow
I've been running from a ghetto in my mind
I keep moving from the arms that long to hold me
That ain't right
Just ain't right

Michelle holds her daughter on her knee, snuggled tightly against her chest as they watch. She sobs openly as Scott sings, letting Carolyn console her as Marty sits helplessly by, dangerously close to his own tears.

I see your face on every cloud in the sky
Hear your voice on the whispering wind that's no lie
I miss your loving arms but I'm getting by
Then again getting by's just getting by

Bob Martin's sax solo could not be more haunting, each note a wailing banshee moaning from the depths of loneliness as it glimpses the last light of day before plunging into the eternal darkness. It is almost more than Scott can bear; the sound of his fellow band mate saying goodbye the best way he knows how. The emotion is not lost on the audience, those present, or at home watching.

These dirty years rob a man of his pride
Tear his world apart when he can't provide
The empty promise of the road is a lie
Oh lord can I hold that woman of mine

I call your name when I rise up every morning
I see your face when I close my eyes at night
I keep moving as the noonday sun is shining
I call your name that's all right
I call your name that's all right
That's all right
That's all right

"Something here, Bill," Agent Glover says to Bill Mueller, "and it's big. Carlson's uncle, Travis Brewer, was the other man in the Scheck incident, at least at the start of it. He was an aimless drifter really, but he did spend some time with Carlson as a boy. And get this, Brewer is the man that Scott killed, or at least injured, leading to his death."

Captain Mueller says nothing while digesting the information, his eyes locked to the same telecast Michelle watches half a continent away. "So there's a personal angle," he replies, looking up from the screen. "That changes everything. Where's Carlson now?"

"He flew home to Portland. After that, we don't know. His people say he's unavailable."

"What a surprise. Get our Oregon people on it. Of course, if it is him, we won't find him, will we?"

"I called his cell and left a message to call. He did. He claims he's on his way to South America on business. He'll be back Tuesday. How convenient. A private jet registered to the company did leave the Portland airport earlier this afternoon for Santiago, but there's nothing saying he's on it."

"Can we get someone on the ground to see who gets off?"

"The State Department is looking after it, but it's doubtful we'll get more than a body count. They'll get as close as they can with a telephoto."

"Good. If nothing else, we'll know where he isn't. We wait a little longer."

Both heads turn to the brisk double rap, followed by the rapid opening of Bill's office door.

"This just in from the nerve center, sir," the messenger begins. "Mama has made a positive ID. Our man phoned shortly after you called. Perfect timing, she made the link."

A satisfying rush of adrenaline settles on Mueller, like an experienced hunter spotting the trophy kill of a lifetime. The finger gently caresses the trigger, waiting for the optimal squeeze time to approach.

"So it's settled. Robert Carlson is our man. Mr. All-America himself. The knowledge in itself does us little good at this point, but it's a big start. We sit tight a little longer, observe and learn. We need to know where his people are, his key people anyway, before we strike. He wanted us to know what's going on, that's why he phoned Mrs. Yonge. I'm sure of it. But why? Still more questions than answers, but we're in the game at least."

◆ ◆ ◆

Tom's mind races back as the applause surrounds him. He remembers a scene from an old black and white movie he watched on TV with his mother when he was a kid, one of the old *Titanic* movies. It was near the end, when the ship was going down. In it, a small string section plays serenely on the deck of the doomed ship, surrounded on all sides by pandemonium. As they finish, the conductor bids them farewell, and they part with their instruments, except one, the cellist. He remains seated and continues to play. One by one they return, joining in. Their job done, they now play for themselves. Whatever happens, they leave doing what they love. *A Night to Remember,* Tom thinks. *That was the name. How fitting.* He is drawn to the present as he watches Scott pick up his bass, but the feeling of the memory remains as the count comes.

Two, three. The clicks of Randy's sticks ring out and Del's powerful slide guitar settles on the opening shots of 'Don't Make Me Late.' The straight-ahead blues shuffle kicks ass, raising the already high energy level of the room to a new peak. Everyone lives in the moment, like those musicians on the deck of the Titanic. The immediate future is certain in its uncertainty, so the mind embraces now and rides the wave. It is not so much the ostrich burying his head in the sand as it is the kid living the last day of freedom before the new school year, or two lovers sharing precious time before a long separation. The moment is all there is.

The band plays with an intensity and purity far beyond what they've previously known, surpassing even the glory days of '01 and '02 and the early part of this tour. They are screaming "This is who we are, remember us." A review of the audio and video tapes captured perfectly the feeling of desperate cohesion and would produce what would become a classic live album, but they think of none of that now. They tie their thoughts to the next note, and the one after that, and the one after that, each its own universe, created, growing, and dying in its brief vibrating time on the air.

A scuffle breaks out as two obvious supporters of the colonel unravel a banner that read *MANY ARE THE SINS OF THE FATHER. GO AND SIN NO MORE.* It seems oddly fitting in this night of torrid lunacy, part of the three-ring media circus the entire event has become. It would not have been Scott's choice to be here, but here he is, so the moment will be all it should be, all that it is.

Jeff and Michael straggle in, having made their way back in time for the last part of the show. They stand just off stage as Ian's synthesizer solo in 'Don't You Think About Me' fills the air. Scott sees them and waves. They wave back. The moment is oddly warm to Jeff, insignificant as it is, but everything they've been through over the years seems wrapped around that wave, and his eyes water. To Michael, it's just a wave, but he is glad to be there to wave back.

Scott joins the band again for the last verses featuring Del, Randy, and Bob in three parts behind Scott's lead, the harmonies weaving in and out in a round as the song builds to the last large a cappella chord where the fadeout begins on the recorded version. The audience is caught in the magic that was the first hit off the new CD. It is a huge moment for Scott, to be recognized and supported for something other than 'Bobby Johnson.' He finally feels he has re-arrived, for what the feeling is worth.

"Thanks for that," Scott says warmly. "I'm glad other songs from the CD have reached you. Now I'd like to indulge myself a little bit, so please bear with me. This is new to the tour, the first and only performance of this song. It is very personal, a statement of my mantra in life, which is to never give up hope. This is for my family, all of them, my children, my in-laws, Del and Jeff, the Zone, some good people back in LA I have lost contact with over the years, but this is especially for Michelle, my . . ." he stammers, choked with emotion, unable to continue.

"We're with you, Scott!" a voice yells from the deathly quiet audience. Everyone hears, and everyone responds, clapping and cheering as though the war had finally ended. The thunder continues for several minutes before dying out, giving Scott the time he needs to compose himself.

"Michelle is everything. She has given me life. She has given me two beautiful children who have warmed me beyond reason. Carolyn, I know you're out there right now, sitting on your mom's knee listening. Soup, I want you to know that you are precious to me and you always will be. You have brought your own special brand of joy to my life, and I cannot thank you enough for that, ever.

"And I want you to know that you have not been lost in all this, though the focus these past few days has rightfully been on Hedley. I love you, Soup, I always will, and I'll always be with you. These are only words, Carolyn, but words are all I have right now, when what I desperately want to do is hold you close. So take my words and hold them until we are all together again.

"Michelle, this is the very first song I wrote for you. How could I know that it would lead us to this day? What can I say to you that I haven't already said? Your courage back in '01 saved us in our darkest hour. You made us what we are. This song is my thank you for that." Scott breaks down again, but quickly composes himself.

"You risked everything to save us, Michelle. You had the courage to do what I could not. You are the key to what we are. This song is for you, as is my heart, as are my thoughts, as is everything I am. I love you. It is as simple as that."

The crowd is riveted as Del begins, strumming the chords of the intro with a soft R&B feel. The band enters, pushed by Randy's pounding kit and Robin's subtle percussive Latin overlay. It is a typical Scott Yonge song, melodic and moody over a sophisticated bed.

Beginnings

The silver lining 'round a photograph is all that remains
A faded image two young lovers
Forever laughing in the pouring rain
So far away so many days have gone
Between now and then
Still the memory lives before my eyes
Oh here I go again

Don't walk away from me
That's not our destiny
You said these words to me

Never give up never give in
It's not us it's the age we live in
Never give up never give in
Dare I be so very bold
As to suggest that we could mold
A new beginning

"I want my dad," Carolyn sobs. Michelle gently rocks her. "I need him to come home now. When, Mommy?"

"Soon Carolyn, very soon," is all Michelle can reply through her own wet tears. "Soon we'll all be together, I promise." Michelle continues to rock her crying daughter, silently praying the promise can be fulfilled. Her heart breaks as she listens.

Here we are again we face the world
Clinging to visions that we held so dear
We were younger then but truth lives on
Truth is forever it's crystal on the air
We found it then and we will find it now
We'll see it to the end

I won't walk away from you
That's something I can't do
I say your words to you

Never give up never give in
It's not us it's the age we live in
Never give up never give in
Dare I be so very bold
As to suggest that we could mold
A new beginning

Never give up never give in
It's not us it's the age we live in
Never give up never give in
Dare I be so very bold
As to suggest that we could mold
Dare I be so very bold
As to suggest that we could mold
A new beginning

The applause washes over Scott Yonge & the Zone in wave after wave of warmth and support as tears streak Scott's face. First Del, then Randy, quickly followed by Bob, Robin, and Ian, gather around Scott. Jeff and Michael rush out to join in, forming a circle of support for Scott to lean against. They shake hands and embrace as best they can before returning to their positions while the applause goes on and on. Except Del; he remains, wanting to say something beyond what has already been said.

"Dude," he begins, and then stops.

"You don't have to say nothing, dude. You're here. That's enough. That has always been enough."

"I'll look out for them, dude."

"I know, Del. I know. We all will."

"Now, Mr. Yonge," the voice says in his ear. Scott places his hand over his ear to better hear the colonel's voice. The crowd senses something in Scott, as does the band. He backs away from the mike. He trades his bass for position behind the Roland keyboard, a change that is not scheduled to occur for another five songs. Ian takes the cue and moves from piano to his own bank of electronic keyboards as Scott settles in.

"This is a new one. I wrote this song today for . . . for someone who lately has had a big impact on my life. It might not be exactly what the person in question had in mind, but I hope I make the grade. In a way, it is fitting. My son is missing and I'm not happy about that. I'm very scared about that, furious about that, furious in my helplessness. My heart aches for Hedley, but I know that, scared as he must be, he knows he is not alone. None of us are, if we choose not to be, and together, we can make a difference.

"There's been much talk of loyalty and patriotism in the past week, but isn't the desire to want to make things better not for one town, or one state, or one country, but for the entire world, the highest form of patriotism there is? We need to be patriots of each other, patriots of the human race. I think that is what Colonel Randall wants. While I can't condone the methods of the colonel, who can argue with the message? He wants to take the best of what we were and reapply it to now, and so make a better future for all of us. As I look around the world I become angry and believe me, I don't like being angry. But I see what we've done as a race and I've got to ask the question, what the hell are we doing to ourselves? What kind of world are we leaving for our children? All of us—me, you, the guy sitting next to you—we're the ones that have to change things. Not the colonel, not the generals, certainly not the politicians. Us. Let's not lose sight of the dream."

Scott turns to a crouching cameraman aiming a video camera at his face three feet to his left. "I hope you like it," he whispers. "I hope this fits the bill."

Somewhere in his intro, the crowd and the band come to realize that Scott is no longer talking to them, but to someone far away on another stage.

A deathly silence befalls the stadium as they wait in anticipation. Scott looks to Randy and nods. Four clicks of the drumsticks later the song explodes in their faces, the powerful thunder of Scott's keyboard bass and piano right hand locking together with Ian's huge orchestral string chords and Del's guitar power chords while Bob mimics Ian's string line melody in perfect unison on his Les Paul electric. The sound is huge as Randy and Robin's twin kits drive the band forward, a sound unlike any other Scott Yonge song yet heard. All the anger and frustration of the past week scream out through Scott's voice as he sings at the top end of his vocal range, clear and piercing and ever so forlorn.

The Dream

The rain is falling down on me
The taste is bitter my face is burning cold
I remember long ago
I loved the rain I loved the falling snow
But somewhere in the in between
We sold ourselves a false prophet's dream
We filled the sky with dollar signs
We filled the air with anything unclean
And now the question on my mind is
What have we done to the rain

It is all Michelle can do to hold her composure as she watches and listens, seeing a side of her husband previously unknown to her. Carolyn, watching from her mother's lap, is too young to grasp the situation fully, but she is moved by the song in ways she does not understand.

We're turning shades of green to gray to build a path
But no one knows the way
We sold out the butterflies now concrete lairs
Poison our eyes
And in the air the doves do cry for all of those
Who died for the lie
The mothers know they wonder why
They dare not speak their freedom is
A sigh in the wind
And now the question on my mind is
What have we done to the dream

Del and Bob anchor a dual guitar harmony part set to stun as the song moves into its final set of movements. Del joins Scott in a moody vocal harmony in the choruses to come while continuing the guitar harmonies throughout.

See
See what we've done living in fear afraid of the sun
See
See what we've done living in fear can't be undone

Suddenly, a powerful bolero breaks out, the Spanish themed shots almost military in precision and mood, pounding the senses of everyone present. The vocals and dual guitar harmonies fight to the surface of the driving fury of this band on fire.

See
See what we've done living in fear afraid of the sun
See
See what we've done living in fear can't be undone

See
See what we've done living in fear afraid of the sun
See
See what we've done living in fear can't be undone

The vocals cease but the band continues its incessant hammering of the Spanish theme, driving the energy up and up, and then, nothing. It is over. A stunned gasp fills the silence before the crowd erupts as one, on their feet, filling the air with their clapping and cheering and whistling while the band looks on in drained silence.

◆ ◆ ◆

"Bring the boy," the colonel orders over the intercom. A few minutes pass before the door to his private cabin swings open, allowing Hedley a view of the sophisticated equipment inside.

"Sit." The colonel beckons to an adjacent first-class-style seat to his right, parked in front of the cutting-edge control console. "I have a treat for you."

The colonel adjusts a pair of faders, allowing the music to come through loud and pure, synced to the video image now appearing on the console monitor.

"That's my dad!" Hedley says proudly.

"It is," the colonel replies. "A song he is performing for me."

Hedley looks inquisitively at his captor, taking in the queer, distant look on the man's face, thinking it best to say nothing. As he listens, Hedley Yonge senses something in his father's voice that raises the taste of anger in his blood, bringing forth for the first time in his young life a glimpse of the adult world. He does not understand the feeling, he barely acknowledges its existence, but it is there, and a seed has been planted. They sit in silence as the jet flies stealthily westward in the evening sky, invisible to the electronic world.

"Acceptable, Mr. Yonge," the colonel says over the dying applause. The moment would be immortalized later on the news channels, the close-up of Scott as his hand jumps involuntarily to his ear to hear the colonel's transient voice. Something in the look of Scott's face captured the imagination of the public, to know the exact moment when contact between two players in a major game was made.

"Can I talk too?" Hedley pleads, but the colonel's silent stare and the brief shake of his head crushes any hopes the boy had. The colonel stands and opens the door. Hedley leaves quietly, knowing better than to ask again. He is escorted back to his seat up front by the soldier standing guard outside.

The colonel turns his attention again to the concert, zooming in on Scott as though he were present in the room. "Time to go, Mr. Yonge," he commands. He allows himself to feel a wave of excitement as the last phase of the operation begins.

What? Scott almost mouths the word, and confusion abounds as the crowd stares into the uncomfortable silence.

"Tell them you'll be back. The band plays without you, but you leave now through the right stage door."

Scott advances to the mike, trying to vocalize the command. He turns to Del, staring into him before mouthing the word goodbye. He breaks away and faces the crowd.

"We're going to feature the band on this one while I take a pee break," he says, trying to lighten the mood. "Just kidding, this is a bit of a jam, an instrumental I wrote a while back that allows Bob a chance to stretch out a bit on the sax. Folks, 'Fair Game.' Stay tuned, I'll be back."

Fair Game

He turns to Del once more, recording the sadness that's there in his eyes. Suddenly the tiredness creeps back, but he smiles and gives the count, forcing the band to action. He waves to the crowd then sprints past Ian, descending a short flight of metal stairs at the right of the stage to the exit a half floor below. A push of the dividing metal horizontal bar and he is outside, standing next to a surprised security guard.

"Mr. Yonge?" the guard asks, knowing the answer.

"Yes. Stretching my legs a bit, getting some air, you know?"

"Okay, I guess. It's not in the agenda."

"Many things aren't, but we move on," Scott says. "I'll be back."

Scott jogs around to the front of the building, hailing one of the cabs waiting for a juicy after-concert fare.

"To the airport," Scott says, following the colonel's bidding. "There's an extra fiver in it if you make it by midnight."

"Gotcha," the cabbie replies. "Like I haven't heard that one before."

A pair of headlights light up from across the street. *The Feds,* Scott thinks. He smiles.

Jeff tries to catch Del's eye, hoping for a clue to what's happening, but he knows. It's begun. Everyone knows, or senses it. The crowd has gone flat, listening but not listening, aware that the night as they've known it is over. *Elvis has left the building and he ain't coming back*, Jeff thinks with a heavy heart. He finally locks eyes with Del, and sees that he sees. He nods and gives the thumbs up, but both men wonder when they'll see Scott again.

"God help you," Jeff whispers. "Good luck, Scott."

2021 — THE PRESENT

The room is silent until Carolyn breaks down, as Brian suspected she would. Michelle consoles her, holding her as everyone looks on. Marki grasps Hedley's hand as tears well in his eyes. She says nothing. Karin and Tracy rise and embrace, the mood in the room overwhelming them also.

"Brian?" Carolyn pleads. Michelle releases her as he comes to them. *Good,* Michelle thinks, *they know.* Carolyn rises to his arms, clinging now, vulnerable in her melancholy hurt, trusting the safety of her new sanctuary.

They return to previous positions in pairs: settee, loveseat, and couch now hastily re-arranged from their straight line facing the LCD screen into an intimate face-to-face grouping, allowing them to talk. Michelle holds court from the wraparound armchair, the anchor point of the small grouping.

"Scott said it himself," Tracy says, breaking the silence of the darkening room. "With his introduction to 'I Call Your Name,' and I quote, 'This one started it all, the process that brought all of us here tonight.' Do I need to say more? Like it or not, Scott Yonge is a big part of the Peace Initiative."

"I think we can trace this back further," Michelle says. "The key to Scott Yonge the man is Scott Yonge the ten-year-old boy. The real beginning of this journey we're on is 1968, I see that now. We were in Calgary, about two weeks after the Garrett Awards. He had loose ends to tie up and a weekend booking to play out at the St. Germane Hotel. It was the night before we returned to LA, the night I met that ten-year-old boy in all his anguish. Carolyn, Hedley, I'm about to take you far beyond what you know of this. It will be hard, but you need to hear it. All of us in this room need to hear it, including me. The night had wrapped up at the St. Germane, the end of an era for Scott and Del at that charming old hotel bar. We returned to Scott's condo, both a little tipsy. I woke up alone. I could hear Scott playing the piano in the living room."

MARCH 30, 2001 – CALGARY

The melancholy sound of lonesome piano blues wakes Michelle from a restless sleep. She throws on Scott's old faded black and white striped cotton robe and makes her way through the darkness to the living room. She takes her place beside him on the piano bench, his face partially lit by a solitary low wattage lamp sitting to the left, on the mantle of the old antique acoustic piano. He shows her a sad smile and continues playing an old blues tune she can't place, but knows she's heard somewhere before.

"Scott, are you okay?" she asks.

He stops and turns to face her, patting her bare leg. "I've been better," he replies with a wry grin.

"You've been crying," she says softly. "What's wrong?"

"The dream woke me again, same one. I remember more this time. A little, anyway. I'm a kid outside a blonde wooden door in a long white hallway. The door has number 519 stenciled in black on its surface. I don't want to open that door, Michelle."

So it's come to this, she thinks. *No time like the present.* Her stomach knots, but she proceeds. "I think you should open that door, Scott. As much as you don't want to, I think you should. It's the last hurdle to clear. Remember that I'm ready to jump with you, and I'll be there when you land."

"What's wrong with me, Michelle? Why do I hurt so bad? Why now? Help me understand this, this—what? What is this? Am I going crazy, what?"

"The answer lies behind door number 519. Open it and see what's there. You know what's there, don't you?"

"I wish I did. I wish I had the courage to find out, but I don't, not yet."

"Sure you do. Whatever hurt you then can't hurt you now. Do you hear me? I won't let it. It might be bigger than you, but it's not bigger then both of us, so trust me one more time and go through that door. You have to, for both of us. I need you to go there too. I've got something I want you to see, probably something you've seen before. I'll be right back."

He plays again as Michelle hurries to the bedroom to retrieve the paper from the pocket of her shorts. She rushes back to his side with the results of her afternoon's microfiche search at the library.

"You keep playing if that's easier, or stop and listen, but either way you need to hear this. She reads in a soft, firm voice from the paper.

"It is with great regret that we announce the passing of Helen Louise Yonge, taken too soon from us on the morning of March 2, 1968, at the age of forty-two. Helen passed away quietly at the Grey Nuns Hospital in Regina after losing her battle to illness. She is survived by her son, Scott Hamilton Yonge, age ten, and her brother, Gordon Robert Richter, age forty-eight. A private service for friends and family will be held at the Anglican church in Tyvan, Saskatchewan, on Friday, March 8, 1968, at 2:30 PM. In lieu of flowers, donations to the ALS Society of Canada c/o the Grey Nuns Hospital in Regina, Saskatchewan would be greatly appreciated."

The piano grows quiet as Michelle sets the paper before him.

"There was no accident, Scott. She was sick. She died in room 519. She died in hospital Scott."

He sits quietly, his face ashen, his eyes fixed on a distant memory ahead. The shaking starts slowly at first, barely perceptible to Michelle, but she feels his anguish arch between them. She braces herself for what's coming, not knowing what.

The force of the words free some long forgotten memory in Scott, a memory wrapped in the desperate pain of a lonely, scared ten-year-old boy. A memory left unacknowledged too long. He feels the pain as though he were a third-party observer trying to comfort an accident victim, but his attempt to dodge the truth fails him. Panic seizes him as rational thought makes its escape, replaced by fragments of swirling memories pulling him down into their vortex. He pounds the piano keyboard with closed fists in an attempt to drive the confusion from his mind, but he slips further back.

"No, no," he sobs. "It couldn't have been that way, it can't be that way, Michelle. She didn't remember me. She called my father's name, she wanted him. She didn't want me. I . . . was . . . nothing to her!" He rocks slowly back and forth, cradling his head in his hands, fighting for control, gasping irregularly for the air that has abandoned him.

Michelle reaches out, trying to stem the flow, knowing she'd have better luck with a monsoon. She cradles his head to her chest, softly stroking his hair.

"Scott, listen to me, it wasn't that way. Her mind was gone. His name happened to be in there at the time, that's all. It didn't mean anything, it was only a reflex. She was already dead to the world."

"Then why make me remember? Why pull this from me now? I was fine with this, I had it beat. I was in control! God how it hurts, even after all these years." He sobs uncontrollably as Michelle gently rocks him, her tears joining his in a barrage. Finally, when he can cry no more, he continues.

"I remember it all," he says in a shaky voice. The accident was the night she told me she was sick, very sick, and she had to go away for a long time. That was a Friday, just like I said. She left the following Monday for Regina. I went to my uncle's. She never came back. She died the following spring." He gasps for air and courage, and then continues.

"They wouldn't let me see her, it wasn't allowed. The best I could do was wave to her in a fifth-floor window. I hated them all for that. The loneliness impaled me. I withdrew into myself that winter, never setting foot outside the house, other than school. I don't know how I passed, but I did. On reflex, I guess. I couldn't stand the other kids looking at me with pity in their eyes, and all the girls talking in that soft, phony caring voice they do when they sense tragedy. I guess they meant well, but it was a terrible time.

"One morning, close to the end, Uncle Gord woke me, telling me to get dressed. It was time to go to Regina. We stayed with friends of my uncle up the street from the hospital. I sensed the worst, but said nothing.

"That night, I snuck out of the house. I made it to the fifth floor of the hospital, sneaking around the nurse's desk. I remember my young hands pressed against the stark white tiles of the corridor outside room 519, wanting to go in, but fearing what I might see. It took a while to work up my courage.

"She was by herself, tubes and wires attached to her like an octopus. I barely recognized her, that's how thin she was, and drawn. She used to be such a beautiful woman, that's how I remember her, but I had to fight to stay in that room. There was enough of her left for me to hang on to for a little while longer.

"I shook her hand gently to wake her. Selfish, I know, but I didn't know what else to do. She moaned and opened her eyes. I found myself staring into the biggest pit of nothing you could imagine. I became frightened—beyond frightened, terrified, even beyond that. 'Mom, Mom, talk to me. It's me mommy, please talk to me,' I remember saying.

"'Jim,' she answered. 'Jim is that you? I need you, Jim.' That's what she said. She wanted him, the loser, the drunk, the betrayer.

"'Mom, please, it's me. I love you, Mom. Please see me,' I said.

"She looked at me then and smiled, but I don't know if she knew I was there. I'll never know. I'll never know the answer to that. She died later that night.

"I ran from there crying, screaming. They caught me in the hallway and sedated me. When I woke my uncle was there, and the vision of the accident was in my mind. I never spoke of that to my uncle, he must have assumed I was dealing with it in my own way. That's how it was back then. People didn't talk about stuff.

"Honest to God, Michelle, I did not lie to you. What I told you is the way I remembered things. The rest, the times with my uncle, the so-called healing process, that happened, I know it did. It's the six months of her hospital stay that I wiped away."

"But you're okay, Scott. You're still here with me, and everything's all right. Everything will be better for you, for both of us. You know what I think? I think she did know you when she smiled. I think you were what she needed to let go. Painful as that is, you must believe you helped her to get to the other side. She could finally go in peace."

"No! No sympathy! I beat this once, and I'll beat it now! I think I already have, we have. You are right in doing this, you're always right in these matters, and I'm going to be fine, I know that, as long as you're with me to help. I feel awful, but I don't feel desperate. I can face this, finally."

"I'm going to stay another day. I'll move the screen test to Monday. This is where I need to be."

"No, you go. I'm okay, or I will be. Thank you, Michelle. This must have been awful for you, to see me so weak."

"Weak? You're not weak. You're the strongest man I know, and this only makes you stronger. It makes both of us stronger. Don't you see? This is all part of that plan you speak of. I'm supposed to do this for you, for both of us. I love you so much, and this only adds fuel to that fire. I love you and that strong, lonely little ten-year-old you were. Again, I want to hold that little boy and rock him gently to sleep."

"You are. I think ten is about all I can muster up right now. I am ten and I do feel like sleeping right here in your arms."

"Then hush, my sweet, and sleep."

She leads him gently to the couch, laying his head in her lap, allowing her to look into his now gentle eyes. She slowly tickles his face and neck, giving comfort to Scott and herself.

"You go, Michelle. I'm going to sleep all day anyway. I hope this is the end of it. There can't be any more out there, can there?" He tries a lame smile. "I'll be fine, and I'll be home Sunday night. You go do what you have to, and I'll sleep. That's the best thing for me right now."

She contemplates his proposition before answering. "Okay," she replies, "but I'll phone. Promise me you'll be here at three-thirty your time. You'd better pick up. Promise me you'll be here for that call."

"I promise. I won't be going anywhere, you can bet on that. Let's go to bed and grab a couple. Six AM comes early. I'll buy you breakfast at the airport."

She nods. "Remember, 3:30. Promise?"

"Have I ever let you down?"

"No."

"All right then. Let's cuddle up and grab some shut eye, I'm drained."

◆ ◆ ◆

Six AM does come early, and it comes rough, for both of them. They grab a shower together, quickly dress, and cab it to the airport.

"Are you absolutely certain you're all right, Scott?" Michelle asks over a quick breakfast. "I feel guilty leaving you just now."

"I'm fine, really. A little rough around the edges perhaps, but I think I'll live." He sips his coffee.

"You look pretty beat up."

"No offense, but you've looked better your own self. We could both use a good eight hours. Unfortunately, you don't have that luxury. Hopefully you can grab some shuteye on the plane. Don't worry, Mitch, I'm okay. I'll be home tomorrow night. Home—the word never sounded better."

She clasps his free hand between hers, taking him in from across the table.

"I'd kill for that look, Michelle. Nothing says you love me more than that expression. That look is you all the way. I can never thank you enough."

"You thank me by coming back to me, that's all the thanks I need. Keep coming back to me, Scott. Just keep coming back. Don't ever give up on me."

"Like that could happen. I'd just as soon jump into a meat grinder as to do that. No kid, you're stuck with me, until you throw me out on my ass. We'd better get you to your gate, boarding time looms."

They discard their paper cups and silently make their way to the US Departures loading area.

"Three-thirty, you hear me? You be there."

"Relax, Mitch, I'm fine. See?" He does a bad rendition of a soft shoe followed by a mock curtsy, bringing a smile to her face. "Could I do that if I was all screwed up? Or at least, more screwed up than usual? I think not. Go with an easy mind, I'll be back tomorrow night, and then the fun really begins for us." He grabs her and gregariously dips her, planting a full wet one on her lips. "Here's looking at you, sweetheart," he says in his best Bogart voice. "You're tops!"

She smiles uneasily, trying to be nonchalant. "Okay, I'll pick you up tomorrow night. You be a good boy 'til you get home."

"Always. You know that. See you tomorrow."

"Bye," She kisses his cheek in that affectionate way lovers do, then walks toward the departure area, only to come running back to his arms with frightened tears in her eyes. "Are you sure? No fooling around, just tell me you're all right." She shakes slightly as she clings to him.

He releases her, gently cupping her face in his hands, kissing her tears away. "Michelle, look at me. I'm fine. Now go, or you'll miss your plane." He hugs her again, spins her around, and gives her splendid derriere a gentle pat. "On your way, lass."

She turns to him one more time. "I love you, Scott."

"I know Michelle. I'll be home soon." He smiles deeply.

"Bye."

"See you, kid."

She disappears into the departure lounge.

◆ ◆ ◆

Scott wakes yet again with the dream on his mind as his head pounds. The clock yells 2 PM as he pulls himself up by the bootstraps. He curses himself as the medicine cabinet yields no headache remedies. *Why should it?* he thinks. *When was the last time I had a headache?*

Coffee brings little relief, but the habit itself brings comfort to his disordered mind. *Business as usual, yeah, right! This will be one tough night, buddy boy. Who you kidding?* Grabbing his coffee, he parks on the couch by the phone and dials.

"Gloria! How's it going?"

"Hi Scott, fine. Hold on, he's in the studio. I'll patch you through."

"Hey, dude. What's up? Michelle got off okay?"

"Yeah, fine. She got away clean. Got a little time to talk, Del?"

"Always, dude. What's on your mind?"

"Tonight."

"I know what you're gonna say, but it's time to hang up the guns."

I know. Still . . ."

"Still nothing, man. No regrets, no tears. Hey, we had the world, dude. We still do, in a different way, that's all. The times they are a' changing. Time for us to change too. It's all for the good, Scott."

"Yeah, I guess. I feel pretty lonely right now."

"Once you're back in LA and she's got those sweet legs of hers wrapped around your body you'll lose that lonesome feeling real quick."

Scott laughs. "You have such a way with words."

"Not delicately put perhaps, but you get the drift."

"I do, and you're right. She's my life, and hopefully soon, my wife."

"Atta boy!"

"Del, there's something else, something I've been meaning to tell you for a long time now. A little family history, shall we say. Are you up to it?"

"Sure buddy, enlighten me!"

Scott spends the better part of an hour telling Del his story, ignoring the irritating beep of the seemingly constant call waiting signal in his ear.

"Wow dude, that's a lot of baggage to be lugging around," Del says. "You okay with all this?"

"Pretty much. I've got Michelle to thank. She dragged it out of me and I'm better for it. She's an amazing woman. I think she came pretty close to saving my life in all this."

"She pulled you out of the fire, period, dude, a fire you didn't even know you were in."

"I agree. I guess you never know how hollow your life is until you have something better to compare it to. Pretty deep huh?"

"Deep dude, real deep."

"Now you know my story. I guess that completes the puzzle for us all."

"You sure you're okay? You sound a little weird."

"Yeah. Tired, that's all. Didn't sleep much last night. I think I'll grab some zees now. Catch you tonight for one more time around the mulberry bush."

"Catch you dude. Rock on!"

Scott returns to his bed ignoring the now ringing phone. *4:10,* he thinks. *Been on the phone a while. I'd better grab a few hours.*

◆ ◆ ◆

"Pick up the phone, Scott," she whispers. "Pick up the damn phone!" She slams the receiver down in frustration and fear, craving relief from the dread growing in her. *Why are you doing this? I know you're there—the message comes on after three rings.*

She grabs the phone again, dialing a different number.

"Hello."

"Del, it's Michelle. Something's wrong, I can't reach Scott. We agreed this morning to hook up at 3:30, but I can't get through. That's not like him."

"Sorry Michelle, my fault. I rang him up to chat and I guess we lost track of time. He's fine. He told me the most amazing story about his mom, and how you coaxed it out of him. He feels real good about talking about it."

"He told you? That's good, I think," she replies, relaxing a little.

"I think so too. He credits you for the whole thing. It's a ton off his mind, I'm sure. He said he needed more sleep, so he's probably a little foggy and forgot about your call. That's not unlike him sometimes."

"True, he can be forgetful. His mind works in mysterious ways." She laughs nervously. "Okay, I'll let him sleep. I'll call him later, or if you talk to him, tell him to call me. Thanks Del."

"My pleasure. No wonder Scott hates drunks with such a passion. He's packed a lot of resentment around for a lot of years."

"What? What do you mean?" The pit of her stomach turns.

"The drunk that killed his mom, that's got to eat at a guy."

"I don't understand. That's not the way . . . that's not—" She stammers. "What did he tell you?"

Del relates the story as told, sensing the growing tension over the miles of wire.

"I knew I should have stayed. He just didn't seem right, I felt it. Damn. Del, listen to me. Something's very wrong with Scott. That's not the way it happened."

The sense of urgency in her voice slams home as the true story unfolds, causing alarm bells to clang in his head.

"I'm heading over there right now, Michelle. Give me your number and I'll call you from the apartment. I've got a set of keys to his place. Don't worry too much. It's a relapse, that's all. I'm sure he's fine. I'll call you in twenty minutes."

Del heads the van into the core with a growing sense of dread tugging at his gut. *What's going on in your head, buddy?*

• • •

Dell called. Scott is missing in action.

"Frank, I have to go," Michelle says, fighting the tears. "Family emergency. I'll be back for Monday, I promise."

"Michelle, we're in the middle of a screen test. Can't this wait a few hours?"

"No Frank, it can't. I'm going."

"Okay," he says, seeing her anguished look, "I'll cover for you, but this better be important."

"Thanks. It is. Nothing could be more important to me. I owe you big time."

"Just get back here, okay?"

She runs for her car, dialing as she flees.

"Jeff? Big problems, I've got to get back to Calgary, Scott needs me. I don't have time to explain, but I want to charter that plane of yours."

"Are you nuts? Do you have any idea what that'll cost? What could be that urgent?"

"Maybe nothing, but maybe everything. You'll have to trust me. Can you swing it?"

"I must be crazy, but yeah, I can swing it. Meet me at the airport in an hour in front of the rental car booths. Try and relax a little, you sound delirious."

"I'm out of my fucking mind, Jeff."

• • •

Michelle throws two twenties at the cabbie and runs inside the Germaine in search of a familiar face. It's late, and the lineup has dissipated. All who wished to participate are inside below or have gone home. *Must be on a break*, she thinks as she descends the stairs, emerging at the staff table. She spots Del on his way to the stage, but no Scott. Then she sees him, bent over the keyboard, preparing for the final set. She wants to run to him, but stops. *No, not yet,* she thinks. She turns her attention to Del, feeling a weird tension in the buzzing room.

"Michelle!" Del says, pulling her out of Scott's line of vision. "Christ, what a strange night. He seems okay, but he's mad as hell at something and at the same time extremely distant, and he's shrugging off today like nothing happened.

Even these guys are picking up on the buzz." His eyes sweep the crowd. "They're drinking like crazy. You need a machete to cut the tension in here. I don't know if I should hug him or punch his lights out, and I've never been big on hugging."

"I'm going to stay back here out of sight 'til you're done. I don't know what to do, but at least I feel better seeing him. Is Duke on tonight?"

"No, he didn't want to be here. We said our goodbyes last night and left it at that. It's his way of dealing with goodbye."

"I guess. Too bad, I think he could help."

"Don't know. I'd better go. Good luck to us both."

She sits while they play on, oblivious to the zoo around her, thinking only of what to do, what to say, what course of action is available to her. Suddenly it hits her with astonishing clarity. *Of course*, she thinks. *Why didn't I see it earlier?* She rises from her chair and approaches the dance floor, waiting for an opportunity. It comes with the change from keyboards to bass. She bolts to the front of the stage with fire in her eyes.

"I have a request!" she says sternly to the astonished Scott.

Her eyes burn through him as she looks up from the dance floor. Scott struggles to find words.

"What did you have in mind?" he asks coolly. Some untouched emotion seems to surface in him.

Time slows to a crawl as the crowd on the floor parts, giving room for the scene to unfold.

"I don't know, how about something old, something mellow, a song your mother could love?" she says in a subdued but angry tone.

Del stiffens at her words. Scott turns to ashes.

"I can't," Scott replies. "Not here. Not now. You should know better."

"So should you, buddy boy! Play the song, Scott. Now!"

"And the voice of betrayal rears her ugly head," he fires back.

Michelle shrugs off the words, but she can't hold the tears. "Scott, please. If I mean anything to you, anything at all, you'll play me the song."

He cradles his head in his hands as he realizes what he said, breaking his sacred promise to her. Dazed and confused, he stands alone, not knowing what to do, how to undo the pain of his last words.

Michelle pulls the last weapon from her arsenal, even as fear grips her at the implications of what she's about to say. The moment of truth has arrived. She realizes she must follow through on her words, regardless of the outcome. She takes a deep breath and explodes.

"Play the fucking song, Scott, or I'm out of here right now. You hear me? Out of here and out of your life! I mean it. The song or me! It's in your hands."

Scott recoils, unable to move, unable to speak, unable to breathe in or out, stunned by the force of her words.

She stares him down as beads of perspiration form on his face, and ultimate fear grips her. Pain stabs her repeatedly as she backs away in defeat, already feeling a loss beyond words. Dead to the world, she turns with head held high and walks slowly to the stairway as the crowd looks on.

"Wait, Michelle, please," he says. "Come back. You win. You always win, I'll play it, just don't go!" The pleading in his voice grips her heart, and a trickle of hope plays across her mind. She returns to the dance floor steely eyed, barely in control, hoping her ace will turn the trick.

He sets down his bass, parks at the piano, adjusts his mike, and starts to play. "I'm sorry," he mouths to her with a sincerity that reaches to the bone. She nods.

Scott takes his deepest breath and dives in over his head.

Playing Young and In Love

Girl we gotta get away
From the life we've been living these days
We need a little time together to play
Young and in love again

You and I together alone
Far away from ringing telephones
No one's ever gonna know we're home
Playing young and in love again

And we won't answer the door
Seeing anybody else would be just a bore
We're here all alone in a world of our own
Playing young and in love again

Del stands silently by, sensing Scott's need to go it alone, though wishing to find some other way to lend support.

Michelle looks on from the dance floor, lost in the melody and meaning behind the lyrics that only she understands. Her tears flow as she quietly absorbs the hurt in his voice.

Entranced, the audience watches as the scene plays out, not understanding why, but knowing something important hangs in the balance. No one moves, it seems no one breathes as Scott sings through his tears.

Del jumps in, sensing the time is right, lending support the best way he knows how. He lays down a beautifully simple solo, so Scott can take an emotional break, thanking Del with a silent nod before continuing through the last chorus.

And we won't answer the door
Seeing anybody else would be just a bore
We're here all alone in a world of our own
Playing young and in love again

He continues after the lyric, breaking Michelle's heart with an emotional falsetto cooing, allowing the pent-up pain to release his past.

Scott's confusion ends with the song, and the truth is finally home. Once again, Michelle has worked her magic. Once again, her love has taken him to the brink and returned him, unscathed.

Del approaches the smaller man, wrapping his long arms around him unabashedly. "Let it go, dude," he says softly.

The audience, silent to this point, erupts as if on cue, clapping and whistling for their musical heroes as the famous friends embrace. Michelle climbs under the spindle railing onto the stage to join them, needing to hold Scott near. Del senses her need and backs away, taking the opportunity to announce a break.

"Hey dudes, relax for a while, will ya? We got some serious emotions that need to be addressed up here. We'll be back to finish the night."

Michelle clings to Scott as if trying to force their molecules to merge. "Thank you, Scott, thank you. I love you for that, for everything we are."

"I'm okay Mitch. I'm really okay this time. Weak maybe, very drained, but I'm okay. It's over. I see the truth for what it is. The ten-year-old I was can't hurt me anymore. I'm sorry for what I said. I meant none of it. I'm sorry for everything this ordeal has put you through."

He looks at her with that special tenderness in his eyes, an expression of need that reduces Michelle to a new round of tears.

"No Scott, don't you see? There's nothing to be sorry for. For the first time in my life, I made a difference to someone. For the first time, I feel important to someone other than my immediate family. You've made me a complete woman through your trust in me. I want you to see somebody when we get back home, okay? Brenda's a good friend who helped me through some rough times after Jeremy. Will you do that?"

He nods. "I will for you. I don't think it's necessary, but I will, if you want it. It can't hurt I guess."

She kisses him with unabashed passion, drawing applause from the crowd. A dark cloud dissipates as she realizes they can finally move on with their lives. The purpose of their love has played out; now the purpose of their life together can be written in the book for all to see.

The final moments of the night play like a melodrama, ending in an anticlimactic celebration of what was. They rock the crowd with an electrifying final set of classic rock, thank everyone for their patronage over the years, drink a toast to the future, and shed more than a few tears for the past as it sinks into the sea of memories like a great ocean liner of yesteryear.

"I'll look after the gear, dude," Del says. "You guys get the hell out of here while the getting's good. No looking back, Scott. We had ours." He smiles, but his voice breaks. "Michelle, I turn him over to you. Look after him for me. I know he's in good hands, the best there is."

She hugs Del and they both lose it, crying like children in the middle of the dance floor of the now deserted bar. After promises of undying friendship, they part, bound to each other through Scott in a unique pact, a common kinship.

Scott watches the tender scene as Del says goodbye through her. The sweet pain chokes in his throat, burning his eyes.

"Del," Scott cries, "this is not goodbye, do you hear me? Not goodbye. I love you, man. There can—there can never be goodbye between us." He longs to hold his tall friend, but doesn't. They stand and face each other, bridging the distance between them once again, and suddenly it's a cold Winnipeg winter day in 1981. Del tilts his head, looks down at his little buddy, and smiles.

"Course you know we got to hook up."

"Absolutely!" Scott replies with a heartfelt grin.

"Dude!"

"Dude!"

They embrace with their eyes, saying all that needs to be said. The new world begins now, for all of them.

"We'd better go," Michelle says. "The taxi is waiting."

She links arms with Scott, gently parting him from the past, her heart at once aching for yesterday's pain, while rejoicing for tomorrow's promise. He lends her a knowing smile as she leads him to the wide stairway and the beckoning world above.

She looks back one more time before climbing the stairs to see Del's head bowed, his shoulders slumped the way only shoulders can when left with their loneliness.

The torch will pass to a new generation of players as Del and Scott's time in the old bar comes to an end. They will join the ranks of the 'remember when' gang, inductees to the 'Legion of Memories' who write the growing legend of the St. Germaine Hotel.

Outside, the waiting taxi whisks them away, first to the apartment for Scott's bag and a hasty lockdown, then off to the airport where the ARRCIS jet patiently waits.

Old worlds end, new worlds begin, such is the way of life. And so it is for Scott and Michelle. The dawn of their twentieth day together waits on the horizon, ready to beckon them into its baptizing light. Hand in hand they climb the steps leading to the plane's cabin, knowing whatever they face, they face together, believing it is their destiny to do so.

As they lay motionless on a couch, six miles above the ground, Scott basks in a feeling of stability nearly lost in the avalanche, quickly restored by the sheer force of their love for each other. He kisses her glistening hair as her sleeping head rests on his chest. *Never again*, he thinks. *Never again will I come so close to losing you.* He smiles to himself as the jet engines drone on, lulling him into a deep, restful sleep.

2021 — THE PRESENT

"If we're to accept what you say as true," Michelle says to Tracy, "then those two days were the purpose of my role, to bring Scott out of himself."

"Holy crap mom," Hedley exclaims. "That song—remember Marki, the album?"

"We found a Johnny Noel album from 1966 in the attic of the old house in Tyvan," Marki explains. "The title of the album is 'Playing Young and In Love.' It was like it was sitting there waiting for us, on top of the rest of the records packed away in a box underneath. I said it was important, I didn't realize how much. I brought it back with us."

"I was gonna tell you, Mom, you too, Soup," Hedley says. "No time like now."

Hedley and Marki replay the trip to Tyvan for the group in the room, binding them all ever closer to each other.

"I get it, Mom, or I'm beginning to," Hedley says. "This DarkFellow thing, I'm supposed to do it."

"You're DarkFellow?" Brian exclaims. "I guess I shouldn't be surprised under the circumstances. It makes sense actually."

"It does, doesn't it?" Hedley replies. "I had no idea what I was doing or why, I just did it, almost unconsciously. That's what I was trying to tell you and Soup, Mom, and you, Marki. I wasn't hiding anything from anyone, I hardly knew I was doing it myself until I was doing it. Does *that* make any sense?"

"It does now," Carolyn says.

"Exactly," Tracy replies. "Everything we've talked about, everything that's happened makes sense if you connect the dots. Scott Yonge was meant to be at that rally in 2009. Intentionally or otherwise, Scott Yonge is a big part of the Peace Initiative."

"And I want to be," Carolyn replies. "I feel him, Mom, I feel closer to Dad now than I ever have. Every memory, every word, everything about him, I feel right now in this room. I feel . . ."

"Alive? You feel alive, Carolyn, is that it?"

"That's exactly it, Mom. Alive. I want to stay."

"And you shall. I see this is where you need to be right now. Karin, you've been quiet."

"I don't think it's my place to say."

"We're in this together, whatever it is we're into," Michelle says. "You need to speak your mind."

"Okay. Please don't take this the wrong way, but ever since we met at the rally, the way he talked to me, I have no right to say this, but I've always felt him around me. I've always felt him as a guiding light, like a . . ."

"A father, is that what you're trying to say?" Carolyn says.

"Yes, I'm sorry," Karin replies.

"Why would you be sorry that he touched you in your moment of pain? Dad reached out to you, feeling what he once felt through your hurt. I think it's beautiful. You can't help how you feel. I say it again, Karin, we're kin sisters, brought together over all these years."

"Yeah, Karin. Dad gets to people. It's not your fault, if you can call it a fault," Hedley adds sincerely. "I think it's great."

"Thank you. I love DarkFellow. 'Who Said' grabs me in a big way," Karin says. "I'd love to play with you sometime. I've continued since the rally. I play a lot in the coffee shops around here."

"At this point, I'm supposed to guard my 'secret identity.'" Hedley chuckles. "That doesn't mean we can't sit down with our guitars and have at it in the living room sometime. You have a great voice."

"I'd like that," Karin replies.

"I'm serious about DarkFellow though, it stays in this room, at least for the immediate future," Hedley says. "I kind of let that slip out, but I'm glad of it."

They all agree to the pact.

"I'm the only one in this room with no link to Hedley's dad," Marki says. "I barely remember him. I don't see how I fit into this preordained plan."

"I don't have an answer for you, Marki. But it feels right that you are here," Michelle says. "I know there's no Hedley without you by his side, especially now. That speaks volumes in itself."

"Yes, my baby," Hedley says. "You is DarkFellow's main squeeze, you ain't goin' nowheres." He laughs.

"I'm nobody's main squeeze, and don't call me baby," Marki says. She smiles and playfully love slaps Hedley's shoulder.

"DarkFellow and Marki. They used to call mom and dad SAM, they'll probably call you Darki," Carolyn jests with a chuckle.

"And then they were seven. We're all part of the inner circle after tonight," Michelle says. "Question is, to what purpose? What happens now?"

"I was hoping you had the answer to that one," Tracy replies. They laugh, breaking the tension.

"I guess we sit tight and do what we do. I'm perfectly famished. Anyone for Thai?"

◆ ◆ ◆

CHAPTER SEVEN — THE CONNECTION

"I really think we should say something, Hedley. You know how your mom is about you telling her stuff."

"Na, she'll be too busy getting Carolyn settled in Philadelphia. Why bother her with this now? She doesn't need to be involved with everything we do. If we find out anything we can fill her in when she gets back. If we don't, we have a nice trip together. Our own thing, know what I mean?"

"If you say so."

Hedley had done a little digging of his own, using his considerable computer skills to search and cross-reference. He came up with a name. "She's Duke's sister-in-law, I'm sure of it," he said. "We've got to check it out." Now they're in the yard readying the Runabout for their journey. "This is cool, Marki. The highway is totally wired. I won't have to touch the controls hardly at all. We could make out all the way in one of these, if such a thing were possible."

"I think we could swing it. Get in the passenger seat."

"What? Now?"

"No silly, a trial run. Keep your clothes on, bucko. Sit up straight, don't slouch. That's it. Good. Okay, I'm going to straddle you. Don't move." Marki climbs in facing Hedley, closing the door in the process. She leans back against the dash, her eyes looking up and out the curved front canopy as she raises her legs, one ankle resting on either side of Hedley's head.

"Oh, this is good," Hedley says.

"I see that you're up for it, you naughty boy." Marki giggles with sparkling eyes, happy to have garnered the desired reaction. "Oh cripes—"

"Marki, what are you doing?" Michelle exclaims through the now open Plexiglass half canopy.

"We were just, I mean . . . wow."

"Can you pull yourself apart long enough to come in for lunch? Oh, and be careful. You wouldn't want to hurt yourself when you try that for real."

"Mom," Hedley protests, not at all impressed, "you gotta stop sneaking up on us."

"I'm sorry. Luck of the draw. Lunch is getting cold."

Michelle laughs and turns away, a light bounce in her step accompanying her return to the kitchen.

"That settles it," Hedley says. "We leave for St. Louis the day after tomorrow. Soon as I'm done with Jeff."

◆ ◆ ◆

They were up bright and early, wide-eyed and ready for their adventure. Now they are in the midst of enjoying the hands-free ride on the open highway. They had contemplated the idea of their earlier wild endeavor, but saner heads prevailed.

Hedley programmed the coordinates into his Wombat, which in turn linked to the built-in navigation console of the Runabout, allowing the Runabout to triangulate with special sensors built into the road surface and one of many GPS satellites in the outer limits, guiding the vehicle safely to its destination.

The Pulse-driven Runabouts offer little in the style department, not like the still sought-after muscle cars of the sixties and early seventies, but they are relatively fast, efficient, and cheap to operate. Their clear, high-tech, half-car, forward tilting canopy and the tapered rear end of the specially engineered graphite body give the Runabouts the appearance of a streamlined bumblebee as it moves through the air. The technology is extremely safe and popular, so it is only a matter of time before larger multi-passenger models hit the market. The rapid pace of change in the new Pulse age has become the norm.

Hedley takes the controls again, lightly gripping the aviation-style guide wheel as they approach city limits.

"This is it," Hedley says, "576 Ashbury Street." He guides the Runabout to the curb, taking in the old post-World War II neighborhood. Though built in the early 1950s, the old houses are mostly well maintained, pride of ownership evident in the pristine yards and manicured boulevards of the old street. Row after row of similar one-and-a-half story square boxes with A-frame rooflines prevail, their individuality well marked by various exterior paint schemes, added porches, and window canopies. They find the neighborhood enchanting.

"I still think we should've phoned ahead," says Marki as they traipse their way up the sidewalk.

"Maybe," Hedley replies, suddenly doubting his plan of attack, "but we're here now." Undaunted, they climb the three-step wrought iron adorned and concrete stairway to the front door. Taking a breath, he pushes the doorbell button. Nothing. He tries again. The inside door opens. An elderly woman's inquiring eyes look out through the small exterior door widow, taking them in.

"Hello," she says. "I was expecting someone else. Can I help you?" She raises her eyebrows.

"Sorry to intrude," Hedley says. "My mom knew Duke Peterson, and I—we would like to know more about him. My search led us here."

"Duke Peterson? For heaven's sake, do come in. I've often thought of Duke over the years. He's my brother-in-law, you know. We fell out of touch when he moved to Canada. He was a good man."

"He was practically a father to my dad, and I want to know more about him. He's family to us."

She leads them to her small but cheerfully cozy living room, its quaint 1970s décor wrapping around them like a comfortable memory. "Please sit. I've got lemonade prepared for company, but you're welcome to a glass. We haven't a lot of time." The white haired, elegantly dressed woman retreats to the kitchen. *In her eighties I'd guess, and still mobile,* Hedley thinks as she returns.

"Here, let me help with that." Hedley rises from his seat on the overstuffed antique couch to assist.

"Thank you," she says in a musical tone as Hedley takes control of the small wooden serving cart. "I didn't catch your name."

"This is my friend Marki Devon, and I'm Hedley Yonge."

A shadow of recognition crosses her face, quickly followed by a dark cloud of deepening despair.

"Is this your idea of a cruel joke?" she replies in a hoarse whisper. "Who sent you here?"

"I don't understand." Hedley says. "Nobody sent me. My father was close to Duke. I want to know more about him, about Duke. That's why we're here."

"I'm well aware of your father, Hedley, of what happened to him, and what happened to you. I say again, who sent you?" There's a buzz at the door. "My company is here. You and your friend should leave. Now!"

"We're sorry we've upset you," Marki says. "We meant you no harm, honest we didn't. We don't know why you're upset with us."

"I don't wish to discuss the matter. I must get the door." She leaves them to attend to her task. The door opens. They hear voices. Hedley rises and darts to the front foyer.

"Mom?" he exclaims. Marki bounds to Hedley's side at the sound of his voice.

"Marki?" Carolyn says. "What are you doing here?"

"I was about to ask the same question," Hedley says. "What the hell is going on here?"

"No need for profanity, young man," his aunt Margret, standing beside Michelle, takes charge. She turns to the elderly host, extending her hand. "I'm Margret Zoe, born Ashcroft. I'm your cousin. I'm sorry we're meeting under such confusing circumstances."

"I'm June Peterson," she replies, regaining a semblance of her composure. "I'm so glad to finally meet you. I think we'd *all* best return to the living room," she looks at Hedley and Marki. "Hedley, lead the way, I need a moment to compose myself."

Mrs. Peterson returns with more glasses and sits, asking her guests to help themselves to the lemonade and biscuits provided.

"So where do we start?" Hedley asks.

"We can start with you explaining yourself. I expected more of you," Michelle replies with obvious hurt.

"Yes, but that can wait," Aunt Margret says. "Hedley, I don't know if you know, but I was adopted, long ago. My family perished in a fire in 1944 when I was barely one year old. Violet and George, your great grandparents, immediately took me in as one of their own. I was as much a sister to Marty as Carolyn is to you. I am and always will be a Zoe. But I'm an Ashcroft too. That's where June comes in. June's father was my biological father's older brother, Robert

Ashcroft. I was not aware of June until recently, nor her of me. I contacted June a few days ago to arrange this meeting."

"Mom, I guess you've been holding out on me too." Hedley says.

"We simply need to talk more," replies Michelle.

"Well everybody, hold on to your horses, the story's about to get way more interesting." The hairs on the nape of Hedley's neck bristle at the implications of what he is about to tell them, wondering how many more twists and turns lay waiting. "Mrs. Peterson, I've alarmed you, and I'm sorry. I did not wish that in coming here. Please understand, Duke was important to our family. That's why I came. Mom, Carolyn, you're not going to believe this, but June Peterson is Duke's sister-in-law."

"Hedley is correct," June says. "If indeed we are talking about the same man."

"I have no doubt we are," Hedley says. "How many Duke Peterson's do you know who came from Kansas City, worked the carnies, and settled in Tyvan, Saskatchewan, in 1953?"

"Yes, that would be him," June says. She is still somewhat shaken by the events of the day. "How does he connect to your family?"

"I think I can best answer that," Michelle says. "My late husband was from Tyvan."

"That would be Scott Yonge," June says.

"You are aware?"

"Not of the link to your family, but I am aware of the name Scott Yonge. I'll explain in due time. Please continue."

Michelle dives in, telling the story of Scott's childhood days in Tyvan. She explains the drama of his mother's illness, the entanglement of Duke and Scott's mother Helen, and the watchful eyes of Duke from afar after Helen died. Michelle laid it on the table for all to examine, lives unfolding before their eyes in a small St. Louis living room.

"I first met Duke in 2001. Jeff Thompson, my husband's manager at the time, arranged an impromptu jaunt from Los Angeles to Calgary on business and invited me along. Scott and I were early in our relationship and I was dying to surprise him. We did all of that with the help of Duke."

THURSDAY, MARCH 29, 2001 — CALGARY

"Thirty-eight bucks! That's ridiculous!" Jeff complains to the cabbie. "We wanted a lift from the airport, not the pink slip to your cab. Oh, what's the use! Don't expect a tip out of me!" He throws two bills on the seat and slams the door. Michelle slips the cabbie a fiver and an apologetic look as Jeff grabs their overnight bags from the trunk.

The flight passed quickly as did the queue through customs. The two now find themselves outside the St. Germaine Hotel smack in downtown Calgary, confronted by a lineup extending up the stairs and out the door from the bar below.

"Try calling him on his cell," Michelle suggests. "We could be stuck out here for hours. I never expected this."

"My fault. I should've remembered. I'll try the lobby." Jeff raps on the old glass and metal-framed door to the west of the north-facing bar entrance, hoping to attract the night man's attention. The elderly, well-built man, on the tall side, looks up at the sound. He places his open paperback pages-face-down on the check-in counter and rises to unlock the door.

"Howdy folks," he says. "What can I do you for?"

"Hi, I'm Jeff Thompson, Scott Yonge's manager. It's important that I see Scott."

"I'm Duke Peterson, Scott's friend. He usually tells me if he's expecting someone." Duke ponders for a bit. "What was your name again? I'll phone down and have Dr. J. check with him."

"We wanted to surprise Scott, Mr. Peterson," Michelle says, stepping forward.

"Holy smokes! You're the girl he's been talking about all week! I'd recognize you anywhere. Pardon my French ma'am, but he just won't shut up about you. 'Course now I can see why. He's got it bad for you, little lady."

They all laugh.

"That's our Scotty all right," Jeff says.

"That's why I flew twenty-five-hundred miles on the spur of the moment to see him," Michelle replies.

"Glad to hear it, ma'am. We want him in good hands. It's quite an adventure he's having out your way. You will look after him out there, won't you? He's our guy, and he really does need someone to look out for him."

"You needn't worry, Duke. We're looking out for each other. We're both better off."

"That's good. You know, through all the years, and even now, he's still the same guy, the same Scott. That counts for something around here. He'll always be welcome, and you too, Ms. Zoe."

"Michelle, please. That is so sweet. Thank you, Duke." She leans and kisses him on the cheek. "I just bet you could tell me stories about Scott and this place. The Germaine is home to him."

"I go back a lot further than the Germaine. I knew Scott as a young boy, and his mother. He doesn't remember me from then, and I haven't said anything. It was a painful time, what with his mother's illness and all. Still, I like to keep an eye on the lad. He was a good kid, if a trifle different. You two come with me, I'll show you an elevator like you've never seen."

"You've certainly piqued my curiosity," Michelle replies. Duke escorts the two out the lobby door to the narrow side of the building, away from the lineup. Crouching, the limber old timer unlocks a padlock, withdrawing the liberated upside-down *u* from a half-inch hole drilled in a metal bar that passes through steel rings on either side of a four-foot-square split metal grate embedded in the sidewalk. The rusty metal hinges scream in protest as Duke swings open one, then the other of the grate's halves to reveal an old wooden platform riding just below the surface of the open cavity.

"Good, it's up here," Duke says. "I don't have to go down and get the sucker. You won't see another one like this anytime soon. This baby was built in the olden days to load goods into the cold storage room that runs out under the sidewalk about eight feet or so. Course it's a beer cooler now, but this old hand-operated lift still comes in handy. Sure beats lugging case after case down the stairs! We've got to go one at a time. I'll go first so's I can winch her back up from the bottom. You're next ma'am. Step on this brake release when you're ready and you'll descend to the room below. Watch your head getting off, the room's ill-lit and the ceiling is low."

Duke demonstrates the technique with a touch of glee and a semblance of pride for the old contraption as he steps on the metal lever and glides eight feet down to the room below. He scrambles off the platform, pulls the string of the single overhead light, and winches the lift back to street level via an old rope-and-pulley mechanism.

"You clear down there?" Michelle yells.

"Go!" Duke replies.

She mounts the platform and releases the brake. She enjoys the quick ride to the depths.

"Welcome aboard ma'am," Duke teases. "Shall we leave the hotshot stranded for a bit?"

"No," she laughs. "Behind those sunglasses shine the eyes of a sensitive man. We'd better get him down here. He's okay for a west coast man," she smiles.

"If you say so, ma'am. Up she goes."

Duke works the rope-and-pulley mechanism one more time, maneuvering the platform to the surface. He unlocks the beer room door from the inside and peers out as Jeff makes his descent. Duke leads them out through the chicken prep room (where thousands of the famous Germaine deep-fried chicken and chips orders have been prepared over the years), and into the boisterous tavern to the right of the main serving bar. An atmosphere of noisy, rowdy fun surrounds them, bringing an involuntary smile to Michelle's lips. Duke presents an empty table below a pool cue rack fastened to the wall next to the jukebox, across the room from and slightly behind the stage. A paper sign folded like a pup tent gives the designation *STAFF TABLE,* explaining its idleness in the crowded tavern.

"Not a good view from here, I'm afraid," Duke says over the music and bar hubbub. "But it's the best I can do under the circumstances. At least you can see most of Scott from here. We knew it would be lively, but we didn't expect this kind of pandemonium. You'd think it was Stampede Week. The Germaine is like this damn near twenty-four hours a day during the Calgary Stampede. These people are going to miss the boys. It's an end of an era around here, I'm sad to say, but it's been a good run. Anybody gives you a hassle or tries to take the table you grab the big fellow with the curly black hair at the shooter bar behind the stage. That's Dr. J., the night manager. I'll tell him you're here. He'll look out for you."

"Thanks, Duke," Jeff says, shaking the older man's hand. "We appreciate your concern."

"Yes, thank you so much, Mr. Peterson," Michelle adds. "Maybe we could grab a coffee sometime. I'd like to hear your stories." She gives Duke a genuine smile.

"Thank you, ma'am. Anytime. I'd like that. You know where to find me." He reciprocates her warm smile and returns to his post.

"That's how it was," Michelle relates quietly. "It seems like yesterday. I came to love Duke like a father over the years. I did indeed take him up on his offer, joining him for a cup the next day in the St. Germane coffee shop."

FRIDAY, MARCH 30, 2001

Right on time, Duke thinks with a smile as he spots Michelle locking Scott's spare bike to a parking meter out front. He greets her and escorts her to the St. Germaine coffee shop on the second floor of the rustic old hotel.

"Frankly ma'am—ah, Michelle, I was expecting your call." Duke says over a steaming cup. "And since you called, I assume this concerns Scott and his mom. Correct?"

She nods.

"I thought so. I guess I'd better start from the beginning, but before I do, I must tell you that some of what I say may disturb you. Scott is a great guy, and none of what I say today changes that fact, but he has a sizeable blip in his life that needs facing up to on his account, and he's going to need help doing that. I can see you care for him deeply, and that's good, because the info I'm trusting to you today could hurt him bad if dealt with in the wrong way. Do you see where I'm going with this?"

She nods again.

"I'm talking trust, Michelle, serious amounts of trust. Trust in you, and trust in my decision to pass this info on to you. That's why I put a bug in your ear last night."

"Duke, the last thing in the world I want to do is hurt Scott. Know that in your heart. I'll do whatever it takes to deal with what you tell me. Scott has talked a lot with me about his mother, so I know some of his history, including the night of the accident."

"Good, then the healing has already begun. The accident you say? I know nothing of that, but I have an inkling. More on that later, but first, I'm going to take you back a few years.

"I'm from Tyvan, Scott's hometown. I knew his mother well, and his father. Helen was a wonderful woman, warm and witty with a refreshing natural look about her. She was a free-spirited lass born before her time. We're talking a mid-fifties timeframe, when life was good, but free-thinking was frowned upon—especially by women.

"She was the town clerk, the best we ever had. She loved her job, and she loved life. I don't know, I guess a small town was just about the worse place for her, but she done okay—until she met Jim. Oh, he was a dashing figure all right, and he could dance a mean streak, but there was no depth to the man. I don't know what she saw in him, but the rest of the town saw the man for what he was. I'd a hurt him bad if I would've known the pain he'd cause her.

"When Scott was born, Jim lit out for the hills, leaving Helen holding the bag. Oh sure, he came back a couple of times when the money run out, but he never stayed around long. Responsibility was his greatest enemy—that and the bottle. Finally got him too. I heard he died years later in Ontario minus a liver. I feel no sorrow for his kind.

"She threw him out for good when he beat the boy in a drunken rage, but not before she took a broom handle to the man. Broke his nose, I heard. I say good on her.

"She made Scott her life. She loved the boy, maybe too much. Then again, is there such a thing?"

"I don't know. I don't think so. I hope not."

He gives Michelle a knowing glance. "Scott was always a loner. Some kids are that way naturally. He inherited his mother's sensitivity and his father's looks. That's all there was of Jim in him, thank God. He knew nothing of the man. I don't think he existed to the boy. He was a non-issue in his life.

"Scott had a close friend get killed in front of him when he was seven. Damn fool kids played chicken with the trains. How that started, I don't know, but all the kids done it. Must've drove the engineers crazy. They'd hide in the bushes and see who would let the train get the closest before jumping across the tracks. The Marshall kid didn't make it once, a real tragedy. Scott kept to himself after that, except for the pickup baseball games. He was a hell of a shortstop, even then."

"Still is." She shares a sad smile.

"He was a happy lad, or so it seemed. Nothing got to him, ever. He was open and friendly with a weird slant on things. He had quite a sense of humor, and he was crazy about his mom. So was I, but that's another story. Another time, perhaps?"

Michelle nods.

"The boy was a whippersnapper in school. You know the type . . . good grades with little effort. He liked to write stories, and he loved to sing. He was always singing, like his mom."

Another knowing smile escapes Michelle.

"He was starting to come out of his shell when Helen got sick. I don't know exactly what it was, but it was bad, and it was fast. She had one of those nervous diseases. You know what I mean, the type that eat away at your mind, leaving empty black spaces where memories used to be? What a terrible way to go. Scott was devastated. He had no inkling. One minute he's a happy ten-year-old, the next his world is ripped from under him. She entered hospital in Regina in the late summer of '67. She never came out. She died the following spring."

The words put a strangle-hold on Michelle. *This can't be*, she thinks, *he's an old man, he's mistaken, he's got it wrong, or . . .*

"Ma'am? Michelle, you with me? You look like you've seen a ghost. I take it the story is somewhat different then the version you've heard. That's okay. This will all make sense, just bear with me a bit. I think I can shed a little light on the matter."

She nods, tears welling in her eyes. Her heart aches as her thoughts reach for that ten-year-old boy she's come to love.

"Scott moved in with his uncle in the grandparents' house, both deceased. His uncle Gordon was a good man, a middle-aged bachelor with a sterling heart. He did his best for Scott, and I guess that's all anyone can ask.

"It was tough for the boy, real tough. It might have been better if death came sooner for his mom. As it was, he wasn't allowed to see her. Stupid rules of the day, no kids under fourteen allowed for hospital visiting hours. Cruel, very cruel to separate a boy from his mom, don't you think?"

She nods again.

"When she died, Scott clammed up for good. He managed school all right, but no involvement, no outside activities."

"Except ball," Michelle says. She feels her composure slipping away.

"There you go," he says tenderly. He hands her a fresh napkin. "That's good to let go. I could see the dam ready to burst for a while now. Don't worry, Scott's okay. He'll only be better once we help him through this. Do you get what I'm saying? Don't be frightened for him, or yourself. This can make both of you stronger."

"It will, Duke. I promise you that." She fights back the tears as determination grips her heart.

"Good. He's lucky to have you. I heard it in his voice the second he started telling me about you, and I spotted it in yourself last night. He has a very deep love for you, Michelle."

"And I for him Duke. He is my life."

"And so it should be, especially these days." He paused and then continued. "Yes, baseball was his savior, and later, music. We'd never see the boy in the winter months, seldom in the summer for that matter. That can't be good for anyone, but that's how it was. He never talked about his mother's death. Never spoke about her at all. People of the town didn't like that much, but small towns have their own codes. Everyone knows about everyone's business, but no one speaks about the things they instinctually know will cause people hurt, at least not to their face. Except for the children—they can be piranhas sometimes, going in for the kill with their teasing. Maybe if we'd confronted the boy things would be different, but that's not the way things were done then. He completely shut out that part of his life as a result.

"The accident theory you spoke of, I heard tell of it once in some gossip, but I paid it no never mind. Looking back, it makes sense. He had to deal with her death somehow. The mind of a child might deal with a quick death better than a long drawn out affair, don't you think? I'm no expert, but I think whatever story he told you is real in his mind, so however you break this to him, do it gentle like, and pick your time wisely. I sense you're a strong woman, and that's good. You'll have to be strong for the both of you when the truth comes out. Are you up to the task?"

"Duke, I was born for this. Hard as this may be to understand, I feel this is the purpose of my life. Scott and I were destined to be. Do you believe that? How else can I explain two different people from two different worlds coming together with such passion, such intensity? We knew each other from the first moment backstage at the Garrett Awards. It was magic, there's no other word for it. We bonded instantly and have been together ever since. I've never known such love, such blind, unalterable, intense love. It frankly scares the hell out of both of us sometimes, but we're in head first, and we face the world together. Don't worry, one day we'll tell our grandchildren this story and laugh about how silly life can get sometimes. Scott is in good hands, and so am I."

"I had a feeling you'd see it that way. I won't wish you luck, because I know you won't need it. I envy the love you feel for him. I loved someone that way once. Ah well, no regrets, life is what it is. We all make do with what's given. I'm going to leave you with your thoughts now, Michelle. Try not to worry. If you follow your heart and your gut, then you'll be fine. Coffee's on me, it's a small price to pay to unburden my heart."

He stops, recalling something else he wants to say. "One more thing. Please don't tell him about me. He remembers nothing of my involvement in his early life. I think it's best to let sleeping dogs lie, at least for now. I'd like to keep things the way they are as far as he's concerned. He's the closest thing to a son I'll ever have."

He rises from his seat, signaling an end to their meeting. "Perhaps you could call from time to time, or maybe drop me a note. I'd like to know how things are, for both of you. Could you do that?"

"Of course. You're part of us now, you're family." She rises and embraces him with a sincerity that cuts to the core of the old man. "I can't thank you enough.

You've given me the last piece of the Scott Yonge puzzle. I'll always love you for this."

He releases Michelle and surveys her through watery eyes, then chuckles. "Of this particular puzzle maybe, but that man is multi-layered. He'll keep you on your toes for years to come. You've made an old man very happy. Life still dishes out its sweet surprises, even at my age. Remember that. See you tonight?"

"Tonight." She smiles. "What a night it's going to be."

He returns the smile and then backs away before turning, leaving Michelle alone.

"Duke, wait." She chases him through the second-floor hallway. "Was there a local paper in Tyvan? I'd like to get a copy of the obituary, if one exists."

"No, we were too small. Your best bet would be the *Regina Leader-Post*. They ran a local news section for a lot of small towns around there. It was a big deal to get your name printed in the *Leader-Post* back then."

"Do you remember the date?"

"I do. March 2, 1968. The main library's right up the street. Go out the back door over to Seventh Ave and follow the tracks about two blocks west. The library's the big silver-gray glass building on your right."

"Thanks, Duke. You're a regular sweetheart. If you were twenty years younger and I was twenty years older, I'd scoop you up myself."

He laughs heartily. "You do know the way to an old man's heart. Good luck, Michelle."

"Thanks. See you later."

2021

"I went to the library as he suggested, printed a copy of the obituary, and confronted Scott later that night in his condo. Now you can see why Duke came to mean so much to me. And there's more. We went to Tyvan in the fall of 2001. Those were terrible times, what went on that September. It was the beginning of where we are now. We went to Tyvan to escape all that for a while.

"It was a cool day. We went for a walk, strolling hand in hand through the gravel roads out to the graveyard. We stood right where you and Marki stood last week," Michelle says to Hedley. "We stared down at the graves of his mother and his uncle, Scott close in, me reverently behind, saying nothing. 'It was Duke,' Scott said to me."

LATE SEPTEMBER, 2001 — TYVAN

"It was Duke, that last Christmas with my mom. He was there, the other one I couldn't remember until now. He brought me a metal fire truck, the one back at the house. He was around a lot, for a while. Why didn't I remember?"

They'd spent the morning going through Scott's grandparents' house, his childhood home, unlocked for the first time since his uncle's funeral. They treasured each artifact, alternately laughing and crying as Scott recalled memory after golden memory.

The dusty attic room where his mother's things were kept neatly locked away became a vast vault of buried treasure for these pirates of frozen time. Scott experienced a quiet joy at touching again the familiar artifacts without being ripped apart by the pain of his mother's passing. Michelle wept openly at the pictures they found there: the pretty woman and her adorable son with the searching eyes, staring back at her in black and white. She gathered many of the photos, leaving the rest of the things behind.

Scott took a ballerina music box and a chainless locket with a small photo of Helen and Jim in happier times, the only vision of his biological father he wished to carry. He contemplated the red metal fire truck, rusty patches showing through the peeling paint as it pleaded to him from its stash amongst his mother's things. But in the end, he left it in its place, the safe haven it has known for so many years.

Michelle stands in reverence at his side, unable to answer his question, then realizing he doesn't expect one.

"I want to go back and get the fire truck," he says. "We're done here. Time to sell the place. I could keep the stuff in storage, but why? We've got the pictures, we've got the locket, what else do we need? It's all in here." He taps his heart. "The furniture stays. The rest is hauled off, or given away."

"No Scott, don't. Not yet. Our kids . . . they should see this place."

"Our kids? Those little bastards are becoming more real by the day, aren't they?"

She laughs and nods.

"Okay, we'll keep it, but we're going back to Calgary, to Duke. I've got to let him know I know. I think that's important."

And they do that, stopping first in Regina to continue arrangements for the care of the house and property. That being done, they set on their way again, stopping for the night in Gull Lake. They let Duke know they are coming before turning in.

"So you remember," Duke says with a laugh. It's edged with just a tinge of bitterness. His reaction was immediate as Scott placed the fire truck on the table between them, brought forth from its new home in Scott's overnight bag. "It's all come back to you, hasn't it?"

Scott nods across the small booth in the St Germaine coffee shop as the waitress departs with an order of soup and sandwiches to go around. Michelle had offered to treat Duke to a nice steak dinner, but he declined. "Too fancy," he said. "That's not my world." So the Germaine it was, as always, and as it should be.

"That was some Christmas," Duke began. "It was freezing—forty below and high winds whipping the snow into a frenzy. That winter was brutal, but we were cozy in that big old house of your grandparents'. What a day that was! Christmas 1966 . . . you were in your ninth year, and that fire truck was a big hit."

"I remember. I played with it for hours. I never got my electric train, too expensive, but the truck was a great replacement!"

Duke smiles fondly, echoed by Michelle, as a vision of the boy playing under the tree with his treasured truck warms both hearts.

"Helen had laid out quite a spread. Cooking wasn't her thing, but she went all out that day. Turkey and all its fixings—sweet potatoes, cranberries, green vegetables, and a pumpkin pie. What a feast! Your Uncle Gord mixed up a batch of his famous eggnog, just right with a spot of rum. Not for you, of course, but the rest of us were feeling no pain. Later, as you slept, Helen and I had quite a conversation. I loved your mother, but always from a distance. I told her that night. She told me she loved me too, but in a different way. She couldn't get Jim out of her mind, she never could. I never hated the man more. She kissed me, the one and only time that happened, and it changed my life. I hung on to that kiss, never allowing anyone else in. I stopped coming around. There was no use, but I couldn't forget her. When she died, a big part of me died with her. That was my mistake, I allowed it. We make our own beds in this life. But I kept my eye on you. I cared for you too, Scott, always, but I think my memory was too tied up with your pain. I was buried along with the rest of those times. You don't know how often I wanted to comfort you, but I couldn't stop the pain any more than your uncle could, so I stood silently by, helpless. I contemplated leaving town, but where would I go? Tyvan was all I had.

"I lost track of you over the years, but I knew you were okay out there, I could feel it. When you showed up here six years ago, something alive was reborn in me. I realized I wasn't going to die alone, and my life hadn't been a waste. Michelle, your videos, they mean the world to me. They are golden treasure to this ornery old time-thief."

She reaches across the table, clasping his forearm with both hands, smiling through tear-soaked eyes.

"You two go out there and give them hell! I live through your adventures. You've brought great happiness to this crotchety old man, and I love you for it."

"We love you too, Duke." Michelle replies in a shaky voice. "You're a big part of us. You're family."

"I'm so lucky to have you," Scott says quietly. "I've always felt you, all those years out there. I've never been alone, you've always been there, like now. I always knew there was someone else, I just couldn't remember whom exactly, but I felt you. It came to me at my mother's grave. You're my father. You've been that to me, and I think my mother knows it to be true, wherever she is."

Duke loses control, sobbing uncharacteristically as a few lonely patrons look on, lost souls in a lost world. Scott slides in beside him, embracing him. Not for long, but long enough. Everything that needed to be said has been said. Scott Yonge finally knows who he is, but it has taken a lot of help from some very special people to get him here. Always alone but never lonely, he has found his place in the world. Home is all around him.

PRESENT DAY

"I was with Duke when he died," Michelle says solemnly as she looks around June's living room, taking in the faces looking back at her. She realizes the story she is about to tell needs to be told, for her sake as well as theirs. She risks coming off shallow, uncaring, but nothing could be further from the truth. She takes a breath, and dives in.

"I was the last person to see him. He'd been sick for some time, but his orneriness made him hide it from us until the coughing gave it away. Even in his dying, he was focused on our troubles. Carolyn, Hedley, what I say now is painful for me, but it needs to be said. At that time in our lives, your father and I were apart. This is going to be hard, but I think now is the time. We need to go back again to December of 2001. Scott and I hadn't talked in weeks. It was a very hard time. It still is for me.

"Scott called, but I did not pick up. His message froze me in my tracks. 'Michelle, it's Duke, Del says it's time. He's in Foothills Hospital in the private room you so thoughtfully suggested. Good call, kid. I'm on my way there. Bye.'

"Duke was dying of lung cancer. I was not prepared, and the message laid me to waste. I knew I had to reach him first. I had to make him understand what had happened between Scott and I. Problem is, I did not understand myself.

"I was able to secure a charter, arriving late in the day near the end of visiting hours. The sterile smell of the Calgary Foothills Hospital jolted the grogginess from me as I walked through the almost silent swoosh of the automatic sliding front doors into the entrance hallway. I asked directions, and then made my way to the third floor of the west wing. I hesitated outside his hospital room, afraid to go in, more afraid not to. I collected myself before pushing down on the levered doorknob."

THURSDAY, DECEMBER 13, 2001

"Hi, Duke, how they hanging, you old geezer?" she grins.

"To the left, Michelle, where they always are these days," he replies weakly.

They make eye contact, share a laugh, and for a brief moment, they're back in the St. Germaine coffee shop. It was a happier time for them both.

"Rough deal," she says sadly while clasping his hand. "I wish I could do something for you." She grabs the armless, regulation hospital guest chair, pulling it close to Duke between the bed and the wall, tucking in tight against the generic hospital night table, where she can be close to his eyes.

"A visit from a pretty girl is more than this old fool deserves," he says with a grin. He pats her hand as a tear forms in her eye.

"Now, now, Michelle. None of that. Shed no tears for an old man who's lived his life. I done all right. How did Sinatra put it? 'Regrets, I've had a few, but then again, too few to mention.' Those are true words, Michelle. Never look back with regret. Hold your head up and live with your decisions, whichever way they may turn."

She seizes the moment, recognizing the opening. "Duke, I want to explain about Scott and me. I . . . I don't know if I can make you understand, because I'm not sure I understand myself, but I'll try."

"You don't owe me an explanation. You have your reasons, and that's good enough for me."

"I know, and I love you for that. You never judged me. Neither did Scott, for that matter. I want to talk to you about it, but I just don't know where to begin."

"Begin at the beginning, where it all started," he says in a wheezy voice. He tries an encouraging grin, but a dry hacking cough chases the expression from his face.

Michelle pours him a fresh glass from a pitcher of ice water on the night table and begins.

She goes back to that pivotal night at the Garretts, reliving the story in all its emotional glory. *I felt so young then,* she thinks. *Was that really only nine months ago?*

A warm, melancholy blanket wraps around her as the story unfolds, and the sweet memory of that meeting comes alive in her again.

Duke listens intently, watching as her eyes light up with the emotional peaks and valleys that render her face.

"I'm supposed to make *you* feel better," she laughs. "Here I am blubbering like an idiot." She sniffs and wipes her nose as the tears flow.

"But you are making me feel better, child, in ways you can't understand. To be looked to this close to death without pity and remorse, why, that validates my whole life, doesn't it? You give relevance to my time on this planet. No, girl, you're giving me just what the doctor ordered. Not my doctor, of course, he's as useless as tits on a rooster, but he means well."

Michelle laughs like the little girl she feels she is, grateful for the understanding of one wiser then herself. She takes a good breath of air and relaxes, enjoying the warm intimacy of the moment.

"You still love him," Duke states calmly. "Anybody can see that. You would not feel the way you do now if you didn't."

"I still love who he was, and what we had, that beautiful moment in the sun when nothing could touch us. Yes, I'm in love with that Scott Yonge, and that life we had, but I despise what we became. I try to find a fault in him to blame, but I can't. It's not his fault, it's not mine, it just is. We're both responsible for not seeing what was coming until it was too late. We should've stayed in Calgary, then everything would be different."

"Would it? I think that's a pipe dream, a world of pretend. You're living with ghosts, and ghosts have a habit of not helping with the rent. You two belonged where you were, and you belonged together. Circumstances changed, but you're still the same people, the way I see it. Two people pining for each other, I might add. What does that tell you?"

"I tried, damn it I tried, but I couldn't rekindle the magic. I want him so much sometimes. It would be so good to feel his arms around me again and make the hurt go away like he always could. I wanted to be his wife, I wanted to have his children, but I can't bring kids into that insane world we created in Hollywood. What happened to us, Duke? What happened to all that sweet promise? How did we let it get away?" She looks at him with pleading eyes, hoping for an answer she knows he can't give.

"I don't know, maybe nothing. Maybe the changes are perceived, not real. What happened outside the zone you created for each other happened, but what happened inside, well, maybe it bent a little, but I don't think it broke. Maybe you just think it did. Take a hard look and see what you really see, and if it did break, maybe you can mend it. Magic is a fleeting thing, Michelle, that's what makes it magic. Sure, something is lost between you, but magic has a way of recreating itself. Things can never be the same, so don't try to make them so, but that doesn't mean things can't be just as good, or better. Find a new magic if you can, and maybe base it on a stronger foundation. Look inside again, and then look to each other. Either way you need closure. You both need to find an answer to your questions. Say hello, or say goodbye, anything in between will lead to more pain for you both. Have courage, my child, whichever road you follow, and know that you carry my heart with you."

Michelle can hold the tears no more. She breaks down, resting her head on his chest as he gestures his hand to her. He strokes her hair as she sobs uncontrollably, the dam of emotion breaking loose.

"There now. Get it out, don't bottle it up. Tell me all there is to tell, and you'll feel better for it."

She gasps for air as she cries, wondering whom it is she cries for. The thought strikes her as funny somehow, and she laughs at herself and her situation, but finds composure enough to continue. She sits up again, wipes her eyes and nose, and dives in.

"That last night, the night of the TV concert at the Bowl, I went down there because I desperately needed to see him. I was scared out of my mind and I wanted him to hold me and chase away the fear, like always. I haven't told anyone, not Scott, not my family or friends, no one, but I think you'll understand. I hope so. I hope I don't come off sounding like a shallow teenager. Duke, I didn't go down to break up with him, I went to shore things up again. We were so tight, so close, with no distance between us, and in many ways, I still feel that. What a horrible day that was for me, and for Scott too. The pressure had been building for weeks. At the height of our Hollywood days, the media attention was unfathomable, what with that SAM acronym they concocted. The paparazzi were all over us. But we had those silly baseball games we played with our friends in the business. We loved those games. They were ours, far from the maddening crowd. It was such a relief to think about that island of sanity in the sea of madness around us. When Bert called to cancel because the media discovered the location of the final seasonal game, something died in me. Again, not Scott's fault, nor mine, just the way of the world that day. I felt ill. I had to lie down with the shades drawn. No light, no sound, I needed darkness to escape to, and for the first time, Scott could not comfort me. He sensed that, finally leaving me alone to sit by himself on the couch. It was a very strange feeling of utter helplessness and hopelessness, yet I somehow felt comfort in that. I didn't understand, and I still don't. Maybe it's a defense thing, to help me face the end, or maybe I was going crazy. The mind has its own set of protocols, doesn't it?

"Scott came up later to lie with me, but it did no good. We made love, but on a physical level only, the emotional exchange wasn't there. I didn't know him, and I didn't know myself. I felt like a third party watching two strangers enact some sort of a pornographic exchange."

The tears start again, but she fights them back and continues.

"Understand, we had no problems to this point. Everything we were was there, right up to Bert's phone call. I wanted desperately to get it back, and I thought making love would help. I kissed him, but I couldn't continue. I just couldn't. I never felt so scared in my life. 'It's okay, Michelle, I'm right here,' he said. 'You'll feel better tomorrow, and we'll work on fixing this.' but his words were hollow. He knew. He tried to hide it, but I knew he had been crying, and was starting to again. He held me and it felt good, despite the missing ingredients, but I could feel doors slamming shut inside me, and Scott had lost the keys somewhere, or I did.

"We both slept, and I remember dreaming I was a young girl again, on my bike in the hills around Ada, and life was good. I woke to the sound of gentle breathing. I looked down on him and was filled again with the love I've always felt for him, but the panic was still there. I wrapped around him, escaping into sleep again. When I awoke, he was gone. He left a note telling me he loved me, and begged me to come down to the concert, but the words lay flat on the paper. Maybe if he would've quit at that moment and stayed with me, we could've forged a new beginning. He didn't, but again, I'm not blaming him, I'm only stating what happened, and how I felt.

"I thought about it throughout the day, and I reasoned that what was happening simply couldn't be if what we had was as strong as we thought it was. I thought it was a bump in the road, not the road itself, and desire for him began to rise in me again as I watched him on TV. I felt the magic, at least physically, and I wanted to be with him, so I jumped in my car and rushed down to the concert with my hopes in the clouds. I wanted to feel that special feeling I feel when I watch him perform, that feeling that the world exists only for us.

"I could hear the music louder and clearer as security ushered me through to the backstage area, stage left, where I could see him. My heart pounded with anticipation as I approached. And there he was, thirty feet straight ahead of me in full profile. I stood and watched, feeling nothing. He didn't sense me there, but why should he? Still, I thought he might somehow. 'Dry Your Eyes' came to an end, not one of my favorites, so I blamed the song. He picked up his guitar and the crowd roared. I knew what was coming. *This is it*, I thought, as he played the familiar intro to 'I Call Your Name,' the feeling will come, and everything will be okay. I felt a rush of excitement overtake me.

"He sang with such beauty, such emotion, as he always does, but not for me, not this time. He was a stranger out there, any singer on any stage. That's when I knew, that moment. I broke down, crying uncontrollably as the song ended to a huge ovation. He saw me then, and fear filled his eyes, I could feel it over the distance. He ran to me, reeking of anguish and concern. He was so full of hurt. So much of that lost little ten-year-old was there in his face. I wanted to hold him and make the pain go away for both of us, like I did in Calgary, but I couldn't. We fell apart right there, and I couldn't connect the pieces again. I wish I could. More than life, I wish I could, but I can't. I don't think anyone can." She stops and looks to him with pleading eyes, expecting no answers.

"No, Michelle, no one else can. Not me, not Scott, not your friends or family. But *you* can, if you want to bad enough. Listen to me, girl, he'll take you back in a blink, I know that, but only if he thinks you want him, or at least are willing to try. You do hold the key, but you have to have it clear in your mind what you want before you can unlock the lock."

"I'm so sorry, Duke, I'm so sorry. This visit is supposed to be about you, not me. I promise, I will get on with my life, and I'll always carry you in my heart." She squeezes his hand tight. "You'll always be a part of me, regardless of what happens."

"To be remembered is all anyone can ask, and if that memory brings a smile to your face from time to time, so much the better." He pauses, contemplating his next words. "Child, listen to me. I once gave up the love of my life, and I wound up alone. Are the two situations related? Maybe not, but they might be.

Whatever you choose, don't give up on love somewhere. We're not meant to be alone. It's a harsh way of living.

"Promise me something before you leave. Promise you'll think this thing through one more time. Satisfy yourself that you've done everything you can, let your head lead your heart for a little while. Ultimately, the answer will come from the heart, but sometimes the heart needs a little help getting its rhythm straight. If you feel anything for him at all, then you owe it to yourself to give those feelings a good hard look and find some answers you can live with. It may mean taking some risks, maybe the chance of more short-term pain, but the greater the risk, the greater the reward. If you succeed, you can build a new life together. If you fail, well, it can't be any worse that what you're going through now, and at least you'll know. You'll be able to walk away with your head high, and your heart free."

"I love you," she says. The tears roll silently down both cheeks. "Know that I'll carry you with me always. If I do have his children, or any children, they will know you, I promise that." She cries again, bringing her hands to her face in an attempt to cover her tears.

"There now, child," he whispers, himself close to tears. "Don't cry for me or yourself. I've lived my life, and you've got most of yours ahead of you."

"I have no right to cry for myself. I live the dream. I have the career I've always wanted, I'm rich in family and friends, and I've got more money than I'll possibly ever need, but my heart is empty, and I'm afraid to fill it. I'd give it all to be back at the Garretts again, back with the knowledge I have now."

She laughs at the image in her mind. She looks down to the old man's eyes and smiles. "We'd be together right now, sharing the news of our pregnancy with you, and isn't that a happy thought? And I'd be a drama teacher, and he'd be a computer nerd playing in a weekend band with Del. A simpler life. Somehow I think that would be better."

"That is a happy thought, but you can't look back. You can only learn from where you've been. You're strong. You'll do what you need to do." He pats the back of the hand holding his, signaling time. "I thank you so much for making a sick old man very happy. I'll leave this world on a high note. My body may be ravaged, but my mind will drift to a higher plane. We will meet again some-where, I'm sure, but now you better go, I need my beauty rest. I love you too, you're a daughter to me. I'll be out there somewhere, looking out for you. Look for me on a star some clear winter night, or high in the northern lights. There I'll be, looking down. You'll feel me around you, as will Scott."

She stands, refusing to release his hand. She hurts still, but she feels comforting warmth around her, and a buoyancy of the heart she hasn't felt in weeks. She looks deep into the old man's eyes, and sees he sees what she feels. She returns the warm grin playing on his face, lighting up like a young girl on her first pony ride.

"I'll be all right, Duke, whatever happens, and I promise I'll try. I know you love him and want us together. I'll try to make that happen, for all of us. If we fail, we fail, but either way, we'll be happy again. I see that now. Thank you for everything."

He nods as she releases his hand.

"So long, old timer. Til we meet again."

"So long, Michelle," he replies with his craggy grin. "I count the days."

She walks slowly to the door, stops, and turns. "Give Scott my best when you see him, and you will."

He nods.

She closes the door quietly behind her.

◆ ◆ ◆

SCOTT

"Hey Duke," Scott says. "You don't look so hot."

"And I feel worse than I look. I'm not long for this world, son."

"So they tell me," Scott replies, not knowing what else to say.

"Good, an honest sentiment. I am sick to death of their patronizing ways and their high falootin' words. Some of them young nurses still get a rise out of me though. I ain't dead yet!" He laughs, and then coughs as the cancer tightens its grip. "Ironic, isn't it? I never touched a cigarette, and I get this. Just shows to go ya, don't it?"

"Aah, you're too ornery to die, Papa. You'll be around for a while yet."

"I'm tired. Not of living, tired of not dying. This disease has a way of making you appreciate the end. No, it's time to hang 'em up."

"I'll miss you, Duke. Hell, I miss you now. You're a big part of my life."

"And no finer tribute a man could have than to be missed. I could ask for nothing more. I have no complaints. I had my ups and downs, but I got my due and more in the bargain. Promise me one thing, son, promise me you'll leave no stone unturned to get Michelle back in your life. I don't understand what happened, and I offer no advice, but I do know you belong together. There's a lot of your mother in that woman. Did you know that?"

"I sensed it, yes. I can only relate to her through the eyes of a child. You've got that over me. You've known them both from an adult point of view."

"I loved your mother, from a distance. We almost could have been, 'cept for Jim. I couldn't compete with his flair."

"But you never told her. She never knew."

"Yes, I put it off too long, and by then it was too late. Helen was a remarkable woman, but I guess I don't have to tell you that, even with your ten-year-old view of her."

"What could have been, Duke?"

"There are no 'what could have beens' in this world, only what was and what is."

"You're right, I've always believed that myself. No point in speculating now. I'll tell you what, things would've been better for all three of us had it gone your way. You are the only father I've had in my life, the only one who's fit the bill, other than Uncle Gord. But that was different. We were more friends than anything. He did his best, but he was not prepared for me. No one else was there. I told you that. I've always felt you looking out for me, even though I lost track of who exactly you were. There are no ways of thanking you for that, only remembrance. I think we may make it yet, Michelle and me. Maybe, if we do, our children will know you as their grandfather, I promise you that." He squeezes the old man's hand, hoping the gesture will go beyond the words.

Duke smiles with eyes still full of the defining fire. "I'm fading, Scott. I need my sleep. Can you stay 'til I nod off? That would be nice." Scott nods, saying nothing.

"She was here yesterday, and Del later. I'm getting a good send off. She looked well, but she's troubled, I can tell. No stone unturned, you hear? So long, Scotty."

Scott pats his hand gently, still holding on to the dying man. "So long, Duke," he whispers to the irregular sound of Duke's wheezing. "I'll see you some time." He gently places the frail arm on the bed by his side and slips into the other world of the hospital hallway. Tears fill his eyes as a weight bears down on his heart. He leans against the wall, staggering under the load. *Michelle, where are you? I need you now. God how I need you now. Fuck it, she's gone! Get used to it, bucko!*

He beats the feeling back, shrugs his shoulders, and steps into the cool December air, feeling refreshed again as he accepts yet another new phase in his life.

• • •

"Let's do it! It's the right thing to do, I feel it!"

"I don't know, dude, he's weak. Besides, I doubt the hospital will let us."

"He's not weak, Del, he's dying. He's dead already, essentially. If it kills him, he dies a happy man, the way I see it."

The plan was hatched the night before, after Scott's return from the hospital. A few rums may have clouded the judgment a touch, but Scott is thinking clearly this morning, and last night's decision is screaming at him, loud and clear.

"He loves the mountains," Scott says. "What better view to hold in his mind as he drifts away from us? If it were you, you'd be hip to it."

"Okay, let's ask him." Del nods slowly. "Yeah, I think maybe you're right, dude. It's on."

"What about Michelle?" Gloria asks. "She should be involved. Nothing would light up Duke more than to see you two together. Don't give me that look, Scott. Let's cut through the bullshit here. I don't pretend to know what happened, and I'm not sure I want to know, but you two have to talk, it's that simple. You're both dying to, but pride is getting in the way. Here's your opportunity. I'm not saying you lie to Duke, quite the contrary, but let him see you together. I think it'll do all of us a world of good. We're all on death watch here.

She is our friend, and I'm sure she's at least that to you. I've got her number. She's staying at the Palace. Do you call her, or shall I?"

"Don't look at me, little buddy," Del says, ever the innocent. "I'm clear of this issue. No. Gloria's right. Just call her, Scott. Ask her if she wants to come help us make an old man very happy."

"Right, I'll do it. Thanks, Gloria," Scott says. "It's such a simple thing, isn't it? This talking. So why am I so scared?"

"Because you've put it off too long, so get on with it!" Gloria says. She hands him a hastily scribbled note. "Use the phone in the den. Ask for room 1242."

He smiles rather uncomfortably, determined to forge ahead with the task, his stomach full of the butterflies of a thirteen-year-old. Gingerly, he dials.

"Yes, hello. Room 1242 please."

"I'm sorry sir, that room is accepting no calls. May I take a message?"

"Please, if you can, ring her. Tell her it's Scott Yonge."

"One moment please."

"Hi, Scott." The familiar, sweet voice freezes him. His heart beats in his ears as blood rushes to the extremities, carrying its precious cargo of adrenalin to his hungry cells.

"Hi, kid." He smiles at the ease with which he addresses her. "How you been?"

"Okay. Better. How about you."

"Oh, I don't know. Getting by I guess. I . . . I miss you."

"I know. Me too. But I don't think we should get into this on the phone."

"Right. Listen, we want to take Duke to the mountains this afternoon. It's a nice day, not too cold, and he'll get a kick out of it. What do you think?"

"Sure, I guess. If it's okay with Duke. He tires easily. Oh Scott, my heart breaks for him. I love that old man."

"I know you do. If nothing else, we've got that in common."

"I'd like to think we came through what we did with a little more to show for our efforts."

"Of course we did, but not on the phone, okay?"

"Touché."

"No, sorry Mitch, I didn't mean it the way it came out."

"Mmm, I haven't heard that in a while," she says softly. "No one else calls me Mitch. Funny how we miss the little things."

"I miss everything about you, everything. What can I say?"

Michelle feels the knot beginning in her chest, working its way to her throat. She wants terribly to say the right thing, but what is that? She doesn't know.

"Scott, I . . . I have issues. Not with you, with myself. I'm working on them. I have no right, but if you could give me some time. I can't promise—"

"Take all the time you need, kid. I'll be here. I'm not asking for promises, I'm asking for a chance. That's where it sits. You decide you want me, I'm yours."

"It's not a matter of want. I do want you, you must know that."

"Then why are we apart? What gives with that? No, I'm sorry. Let's not get into it now. You work out what you need to work out at your own speed. No pressure."

Silence.

"So back to Duke," he continues. "Meet us at the Foothills Hospital at one o'clock. Let's give the ol' guy a hell of a sendoff, okay?"

"I'll be there. Scott?"

"Yes?"

"Thanks."

"No thanks needed, Mitch. My motives are purely selfish."

"No, they're not, you're trying to save both our drowning lives."

◆ ◆ ◆

Duke's doctor agreed the trip could do no harm, especially after the enthusiasm shown by Duke himself.

"I feel sixty-three again!" he jokes as they load him into the Handi-Bus rented for the trip. The bus is really a customized van, complete with a wheelchair ramp for the back doors, and a shallow lift granting access via the side cargo door. There is a cot provided, but Duke chooses to sit upright on the rear bench seat for the hour-and-a-half ride to Banff, not wishing to miss any of the action. Though visibly drawn, his spirits soar with every bend in the road.

"God knows when I'll get out this way again," he says.

It was a beautiful trip, and not just because of the scenery, the four of them laughed like old times. Del played the wisecracking chauffer while Duke anchored himself between Scott and Michelle, the three of them arm in arm. The pair could feel each other through Duke: so close, yet so far, yet together.

Scott and Michelle hugged briefly but sincerely when they met outside the Foothills, not at all feeling uncomfortable as they strolled into Duke's room hand in hand.

If anything, comfort came too easy, Del thought as he too hugged Michelle. *Still, it's great to see them together. How could two supposedly uncomplicated people become so complicated? This is all too weird for me.*

Gloria was right, the sight of them lifted a great burden from Duke's heart, and he told them so. Never one to over blow a situation, he nevertheless realized the possibility of reconciliation did exist. *That's all any of us can ask of life, a chance. We're owed nothing more than that. I go to my grave knowing there's a chance for them.*

Now Duke sits between them, feeling as perplexed as Del as to the plight of the not-so-golden couple. He knows damn well they love each other. Hell, they're crazy for each other! And yet he sits between them. Go figure.

The town of Banff grows small in the rearview as Del maneuvers the van up the winding road to the bottom of the gondola lift on Mount Norquay. They're suddenly silent as they begin the fifteen-minute gondola ride to the top, each awed in their own way by the majestic beauty around them.

"It's God's gift," Duke says quietly as they disembark at the top.

Scott pushes while Del and Michelle walk on either side, advancing as far as they are allowed to the edge of the precipice. They look down on the town of Banff, nestled in the valley below, surrounded on all sides by the rugged beauty of the Canadian Rockies.

"There isn't a view anywhere to rival it," Duke says. "You see this, and you know anything's possible. Anything!" He rises to his feet, steadied now by Michelle and Del, surveying the beauty before him. "I'M NOT DEAD YET, YOU HEAR ME! THERE'S LIFE IN MY VEINS STILL!"

He smiles and sits down again, drained by his protest, but happy for it. They remain silent for some minutes, taking it all in, freeing the mind of all thoughts save what lies before their eyes. How could it not move anyone who sees?

"Okay, children, time to go. I've about soaked it all up. I'll remember this day as long as I live." Duke laughs before coughing. They laugh together in one of life's uncomplicated moments. Everything's laid on the table for the four of them to see, and they all see it. Life, under any circumstances, is the key.

◆ ◆ ◆

Scott and Del didn't make it in time. Michelle was there waiting when they arrived.

"He died a few minutes ago," she says quietly. "He smiled at me and simply stopped living."

Scott holds her then, and they cry. Del joins them in an embrace as they remember Duke as he was, a good man and a great friend, one of God's guiding lights. They separate and walk quietly to the waiting room while Duke's body is whisked away.

"It seems fitting somehow that you're the last person he saw," Scott says. "I don't know why exactly, but I know that's the way it's supposed to be. You brought him great happiness, Mitch, apart from our connection. You came to mean so much to him, and maybe that's the purpose of 'us.' There's a bond between you and Duke that transcends any I formed with him, and that takes nothing away from what he means to me, or I to you."

She kisses his cheek before they sit, with silent tears in her eyes. Sadness, sure, but great joy too, for a life lived with dignity and compassion. She never analyzed the bond between them; she simply accepted it for what it was. She realizes that fact now. *So why can't I do so again with Scott?*

There is no funeral, as requested. Scott scatters Duke's ashes to the wind from the spot where they stood four days earlier, while the snow gently falls around him. The ashes float in the air, blending in with the overcast skies, becoming again a part of nature. *Ashes to ashes,* Scott thinks. He pulls his coat around him against the cold and starts his journey back.

2021 — THE PRESENT

"That's what Duke did for us," Michelle says.

The group is solemn around her.

"He's as much a part of our family as breathing. We had a way to go yet before we got back together. It took the Scheck incident and all that that entailed to really seal the deal, but that's a story for another time. The important thing is that Duke's passing was the catalyst that started us on the road to our getting back together, the road to where we are now."

"I wish Brian could have come with us," Carolyn says. "Mom, how could this be? How could we have not known about the interconnections all these years?"

"We were not supposed to know," Margret says. "The links run long and deep, too deep for coincidence. It's beyond me, but we're learning what we need to know when we need to know it."

"But why St. Louis?" Marki asks. "What brings us all together on this day in this living room?"

"I believe I have the answer," June says. "It pains me to tell my story, but I understand now that it needs to be told.

"I grew up in Kansas City, in a house not far from the Petersons'. I've known Duke and Harold all my life. We went to school together, played together. Harold was the younger, a most serious young man, but I could always make him laugh. Maybe that's why he married me. Duke was quite the opposite, more my type in many ways. He had a wild streak, what we used to call a free spirit. They were both too young to fight, but Harold felt he was part of the war while Duke despised everything about it. Harold loved Duke, but they never quite saw eye to eye on anything. Everything, all the kind things you said about Duke, are true. Take it from me, I know, I dated Duke back around 1952, long before I married Harold, God bless his soul.

"I loved Duke, but I was eighteen and impatient. He had the wanderlust. He joined up with the carnivals when times were tight, and I hardly saw him. I ended it before we got started really, and he settled in Canada a few years later. I moved to St. Louis chasing work, that's when I again crossed trails with Harold, back in '62. Duke was out in 1964 for the wedding; that was the last I saw of him. Harold and Duke came to blows over something and Duke just disappeared from our life. That's a shame. His influence might have changed things for our Hughie, but who can say for sure.

"Hugh was born in 1968. I was getting on in years, so we thought we'd best do it while we still could. He was an only child, so naturally, we spoiled him. If

I could go back and do things over, I would, but that's not the way of the world is it? I'm so sorry about what happened to you, Hedley, that awful business with Robert Carlson—Colonel Randall to most of the world. You and your sister lost your father. Your mother lost her husband. I don't know if I could have changed any of that, but I would have tried if I'd known how. You see . . . Hughie was AFF."

The room goes cold at the words, a light gasp involuntarily escaping Michelle's lips as she fights for air.

"Let me get this straight," Michelle says. "You're saying your son, essentially related to us, was involved in that mess?" She tries to suppress her fury.

"Hughie was a good boy for most of his life," June says. "But he never quite found himself, never quite figured himself out. I was ecstatic when he was offered a high paying job with E-Lok. Finally, he would settle down and get his life together. But that man, Robert Carlson, he fed on people like my Hughie, people unsure of themselves, directionless people ripe for the plucking. How could I have known? How could any of us have known?" She breaks down then, sobbing uncontrollably as the others look on.

Michelle walks to her, crouching down to her level in the wraparound arm chair. She hands the elderly lady some tissues from a small box sitting idly on a nearby end table. "You are as much a victim of the AFF as the rest of us in this room," Michelle says. "I have no idea the level of involvement your son had in the scheme of things, nor do I wish to know. But the knowledge would change nothing. I have no misgivings towards you. You're one of us, not one of them."

"My mom's right, Mrs. Peterson. You share no blame in any of that mess. Those people, they were all gooned out, brainwashed by the colonel's crap. I know that to be true, I was there. Hugh has to take responsibility for his actions, yes, but don't you shoulder any blame, you have no right to it."

"Hughie disappeared in the cleanup raids," June says. "He is presumed dead, though his body was never found. If he was alive, I think I would feel him somehow, but I don't. Harold was never the same after that. He died a year later. Cancer they said, but I know different. He died of a broken heart. He had such hopes for Hughie, we both did."

"That's water under the bridge now, June. What is important is that we've found each other. We need to stay in touch," Margret says. "We're family, all of us in this room."

"Yes, we are, Mrs. Peterson," Carolyn adds. "May I call you Aunt June? I don't know what other title I should use. Mrs. Peterson is too formal. I feel closer to you than that."

"I would be honored," June smiles to Carolyn. "So few of my people remain. I'm glad Duke didn't live to see it, if he knew about Hughie at all. I have a picture from just before he left us. Hedley, would you . . . could you have a look, tell me if you saw him?"

"I guess I could," Hedley says. "I was young. I might not be of any help."

June Peterson rises from her chair, leaving the room. She returns a few minutes later with a shiny, hastily snapped four-by-six color portrait of a trim, smiling man in his mid-thirties, his short cropped blond hair and his stylishly tailored dark suit coat over light dress shirt screaming middle management.

"I think he was there, in the mountains of California, where they took me," Hedley says. "He worked at one of the consoles, communications I think. I wish I could tell you more."

"May I take a copy of that?" Carolyn asks. "I'm putting together a family history. Hugh is part of what brought us here. I think it's important we tell the story of who Hughie was, not who he became. I think it's important we do that."

"Thank you, child, thank all of you." They rally round when June breaks down again, giving support and comfort as best they can.

"Mom, we have to go. There are seven hours on the highway waiting."

"Stay the night, Hedley. I'll put you up."

"We can't, Marki's got a swim class to teach. We'll be fine. It's wired all the way.

"Okay, but be careful. Stay at the wheel, and don't fall asleep."

"I'll keep him awake," Marki says.

"Yes, I'm sure you will," Michelle says. She goes to Marki then, realizing her tone was much too flippant. "I love you, Marki. You know that, don't you?"

Marki smiles and nods in her shy way. They embrace.

"Margret's staying for a few days with June," Michelle says. "Carolyn will help her settle in and gather more information for her family project. I have a flight booked for tomorrow, but maybe I should ride back with you."

"Mom, it's my Runabout, you'd be mighty cramped in the back. We'll be fine, stop with the worrying."

"Never, my sweet." She gives her son a quick hug and breaks away. Hedley and Marki cross the room to the two elderly ladies, making their goodbyes before heading to the door.

"When you coming home, Pipsqueak?" Hedley asks his sister.

"Never would be too soon with that attitude hanging around," Soup smiles and skips across the room, hugging her brother and Marki. "Now scoot. Don't want you out on the highway too long after dark."

◆ ◆ ◆

CHAPTER EIGHT — THE TIES THAT BIND

"No, Hedley, you're not going to drop out," Jeff says. "Your mom would have my nuts if you did, you know that. We'll do it long distance, just like we're talking now. We're coming into May. Let's look at Monday the tenth as our goal. You got a place on the homestead where we can set up a studio, something big enough for a sound stage? We don't need huge, but we need private."

"We've got Marty's puttering shed. His old Model A is in there, but we can move it to the new garage."

"Good, I'll send Darwin out to hire a crew and renovate the space. He'll bring H3D cameras and any gear you'll need. We'll set Kenny up in Broken Arrow too, on ARRCIS. Their dime, kiddo. Nothing to worry about there. How are you fixed for tunes?"

"I've got a lot of dad's old material that I can rework. I found a stash of pre-2001 songs that put him in a different perspective. I've also got a couple of my own."

"Okay, you work on them while we get the studios together. Work the tunes as you always have with Kenny. Darwin's going to run the cameras remotely from the ARRCIS studio when we shoot the Halos, then mix and convert them here. You've got no excuse not to finish your school year. We'll discuss college later."

"Marki's going to ECU in the fall."

"You two are tight."

"Yeah, we're into it. She figures in everything I do from here on in."

"I kind of gathered that. What's she taking?"

"Phys ed. She wants to keep up with her swimming. She teaches classes now."

"What about you?"

"I don't know. I think I might like to get in on the ground floor of the Pulse technology, after I'm done with DarkFellow."

"I got to tell you Hedley, I think DarkFellow is going to be around a while. Touring is inevitable."

"How we gonna swing all the secret identity crap with that?"

"That's my department. I'll sweat the details."

◆ ◆ ◆

Carolyn and Brian lay together on Brian's bed, the softness of the afternoon light playing gently on their naked bodies.

"Do you think Tracy knows?" Carolyn asks.

"I don't know what she knows, but for now we should at least keep the illusion that you're living downstairs with her." Brian unconsciously tickles the small of her back.

She turns to him. "I don't want to sneak around. We're adults after all, and I think she knows."

"She doesn't know about this. We didn't know ourselves until about an hour ago."

"Don't be silly, Brian. We knew we'd end up here the second we met. I did, anyway."

"Well, yeah, but she's my cousin."

A timid knock comes from the door. "Can I come in? It's important." Karin's voice comes from the other side.

"Hold on," Brian replies. They scramble under the covers. "Okay, but brace yourself."

"I've been home for a while. You guys were a tad noisy." She smiles, slightly embarrassed. "I'm happy for you, but Tracy's on her way home," Karin says. "She wants us to meet downstairs in ten minutes. Something's brewing, so dress yourselves or each other and let's get down there."

They quickly dress and make their way, arriving downstairs just as Tracy walks in.

"This is big!" Tracy says. "Barker has called a news conference. I think it's what we've been waiting for. I think the troops are coming home."

They gather around the sixty-inch wall mount, watching as the image from the Oval Office is beamed in. President Leo Barker is seated. The vice president, the speaker of the house, and the president pro tempore of the senate stand behind him in a show of bipartisan support.

"Good evening," President Barker begins. "Today, I signed into law the repeal of the Temporary Measures Act of June 19, 2009. Effective June 19, 2021, the military draft will be no more. Inductees in training at this time, and those called between now and June 19, will serve their required tour of duties as outlined by the law. Military personnel nearing the completion of their obligations can remain in service, enlist in the reserve, or return to civilian life if they so choose.

"No new troops beyond those slated for relief duties will leave our shores for the Middle East. No new military duties will be undertaken by our forces that could escalate the situation that now exists. It is our hope that the much-anticipated peace process will proceed as planned, and we may soon bring all our people home. Until such time, we will remain steadfast in our mission to secure the integrity of the region. Until such time, we will work towards a settlement to bring peace to America, and the world. My fellow Americans, the march towards peace has begun."

"Well, that's a start," says Tracy. "They fell short of our objectives, but the ball is rolling. I think it is significant that Sam Meade was present—more indication that the Peace Initiative has made a difference."

"Why?" Carolyn asks, genuinely curious.

"Because he's a democrat," Karin says.

"What's more, as of January 1, he became the third man in the line of succession. The Republicans barely squeaked in this time, and they lost the Senate. As the longest running senator of the majority party, Samuel Meade was elected president pro tempore. So, the possibility remains, however remote, that a Democrat could serve out the remainder of the term if an unforeseen event should happen. Nothing will, of course, but it is further indication that the political situation that has existed for most of this century is finally moving towards center. Our movement has played a big role in that, and so has Scott Yonge. Carolyn, your dad was, and is, a big part of the Peace Initiative."

◆ ◆ ◆

HART BUILDING — SENATE OFFICES WASHINGTON DC

"That went well." The aging southern senator speaks in a soft but authoritative manner.

"It did, sir. An historic day for us all."

"I hope we look back on it as that," the senator replies. "He may be president, but he's still Leo Barker, and the Leo Barker I know usually has something up his sleeve."

"The bill is signed, what can he do?"

"June 19 bothers me, Allan. I don't buy the anniversary date as a good one to close on. There will be problems that could be avoided by an immediate cessation of activity. Why create unnecessary problems unless . . ."

"Unless what, sir?" Allan Bruce replies.

"Unless it's a stall tactic. We know his actions are reluctant. If Leo had his way, we'd escalate, not deescalate. He's got almost two months. Allan, keep a close watch on the Draft Board. I have a hunch we're going to see a steep rise in the number of inductees in the next few weeks. If we do, I want to know about it. If we do, I'm going to tip Leo's hand. I've got that finance meeting in front of me. Will you finish up here?"

"Certainly, sir. I'll have things in order before your return. The renovations were worth the wait."

"The place does look good. I feel like an old fart surrounded by this new-fangled technology. Sometimes I feel I've been in the game too long. Allan, you've been with me almost eight years, I can say these things to you. I'm growing tired of the fight. I'm not well. I'm seventy-six. Funny, back in the day I would've been considered young for the job. Ah well, times change. I'm going to count on you more than ever, going forward."

"Thank you, sir. I won't fail you." Allan smiles. "Your meeting, sir."

"Yes, my meeting," Samuel Meade takes his leave.

At precisely 5:10 PM, Allan Bruce places a secure call on his private line. "Everything in order?" he asks. His voice tells the caller they'd better be.

"Yes."

"Proceed."

We tried your way, Colonel. It was a gallant effort, but people need a bold, concrete demonstration of political leadership. This time, we shall give them that.

◆ ◆ ◆

May 10 has come and gone, and several new DarkFellow tunes are in the can, as Jeff would say, ready for Trafalgar. But this time, the songs will premiere live on *Audrey Over America*. Audrey Waters owns the national 3:30 to 4:30 PM weekday time slot, broadcast live from New York for the past twelve years. It was on her show that 'MaryAnn Said' first premiered during the Scott Yonge & The Zone comeback tour in 2009. But Scott and Michelle go back even further with Audrey, back to 2001 when she had her *LA Afternoon* daily slot. Their meteoric rise as a celebrity couple can be traced to their first appearance with Audrey shortly after the 2001 Garrett Awards. Now it will be Hedley's turn. Audrey does not know the story, of course, but as a DarkFellow fan, she is tickled to premiere the mysterious young performer on her show.

"Nervous?" Kenny asks.

"I'm beyond nervous," Hedley replies. "I'm scared shitless. Riding around in this limo all day is no help. I could use a run to release some of this tension. I wish Marki were here."

"Chill out, dude. Have a hit on this," Kenny passes a joint.

"No, I'm good."

"Thought you might cave this time, but no, always a cleanie, just like your old man." Kenny chuckles.

"He didn't need any help in the crazy department. He was there on his own behalf."

"Yeah, dude. He was a complicated guy."

"Not really. Everybody says that, but I think he was real simple. Not dumb simple, but uncomplicated. He loved to play, that's what drove him."

"And he was crazy 'bout Mitch."

"You're the only guy other than Del who can call her that and not lose your balls. Mom really *got* Dad, she saw who he was."

"They totally got each other, dude. I've seen the clips, the documentaries, the Audrey re-runs. People dug SAM."

"I just wish there was more of *them* around, and less media images. I sometimes wonder if it was my mom's doing . . . keep the legend alive and all that rot."

"Maybe, or maybe it was easier for her. She was the biggest loser in all that AFF crap. She's a beautiful gal, Michelle is. I wouldn't mind—"

Whack goes Hedley's right arm across Kenny's chest.

"Oh, easy dude, I'm kidding."

"I know, just keeping you honest."

"Point is, she never remarried."

"You had to be there to really understand. When he died, I mean, he came to us, me and mom huddled on the ground. He was there. Sounds weird I know, but it was real. I'll go to my grave believing that. It's hard for my mom, living with a ghost."

"And a legendary ghost at that. Your mom's okay, dude."

"Switch on the screen, boys," Darwin says. "Jeff's online."

Hedley reacts, quickly switching the monitor embedded in the back of the seat facing them to the live video stream.

"Hey gang," Jeff says. "This is big, you know it is. The important thing is to go out and have fun. Give them the show. Get into being DarkFellow and Bartholomew. Damn, I wish I was there, but Audrey would put two and two together."

"Somebody's gonna sooner or later."

"I know, Hedley, but until they do, well, you know the drill. And don't worry. I've got a contingency plan once the cat's out. For now, you do the tunes and leave the way you came. You'll have company in the car. Darwin will whisk you to the ARRCIS jet, and your passengers, dressed like you, will board the shuttle. The shuttle flies west while Darwin drives you to Philadelphia. Tracy's got things set up for you there. Nail it, boys! We'll talk!"

It was Jeff's idea. Selling Audrey was easy; keeping up the incognito was not. ARRCIS Media purchased and registered the jet-black stretch limo, keeping all records under the company name. Darwin, also in masked disguise, was flown in to chauffer. They would not enter the studio until announced, and only then directly from the waiting limo, not from a backstage green room. They would proceed directly to their performance positions on the stage, perform two songs, and leave as they came. No interview, no talking, just DarkFellow and Bartholomew coming and going on the air. It seemed like a good plan at the time, but now Hedley begins to doubt the whole procedure.

"I feel like Bruce Wayne," Hedley says.

"It was your idea," Kenny says. "And a brilliant one at that. I think you planned it this way, no comparisons to the legend, only DarkFellow."

"Nope, none of that. Just did it, that's all."

"Come on, dude, I know you. You overthink everything."

"Not this, not the music. I just do it. I guess I'm simple too. When you telling your mom and sisters?"

"I don't know. These one-day out and back appearances are easy to cover, but a tour? I guess I'll spill the beans then."

Darwin glides the limo to the curb, the gas-guzzler responding like a clipper ship to his touch. "Loosen up, boys," he barks over the intercom. "Time to pounce." He piles out, opens the rear curbside door adjacent to the temporary jet-black vinyl accordion tunnel connected to the studio side entrance. DarkFellow exits first, then Bartholomew, sliding over and out into the rainy New York afternoon. They scramble through the makeshift tunnel, past security, to the open door, quickly darting up the backstage staircase and deftly taking their positions on the darkened stage. The scene is destined to become a net staple, running on millions of devices over the coming days and weeks.

I hope they got it right, Hedley thinks as he checks the gear. The rehearsal was run remotely, the equipment and camera setup done with stand-ins. Now they're about a minute away from the real deal.

"Are you ready for this?" Audrey rouses the crowd. "Please welcome, on their debut national telecast, the mystery music sensation sweeping the nation, DARKFELLOW AND BARTHOLOMEW!"

The stage and backdrop is of trademark DarkFellow aesthetic: sparse, bold, and uncomplicated. The sunburst orange backdrop draws the viewer to the simple lime green stage and its two occupants, fully lit now by the exploding lights. They're dressed as they were in the Halos, Hedley in his light gray with red pinstriped suit and yellow fedora, Kenny in his black one-piece jumpsuit and bright red fedora. The one difference is Hedley too wears a masquerade-style mask. There's no editing out accidental full-face shots when you're live.

Kenny begins the R&B drum intro over the roar of the crowd as Hedley looks on, waiting for his queue. Hedley takes the breath, and DarkFellow sings with all his youthful angst.

Who said it's true
Who said it's true
Who told the lie
Who told the lie

Hedley attacks the piano, joined with guitar and bass from the studio band. The angry young man that is DarkFellow grabs the vocal again, belting the lyrics as though it were his last chance to speak.

Who said it's true
Who said it was it you
Who told the lie
Who told the lie
Who walked the road
Who carried the heavy load . . .

The song ends to a rising rumble from the studio audience, clapping, pounding, and whistling its approval.

Audrey waits for the applause to die, taking advantage of a moment of silence to build the tension. Sensing the time at hand, she speaks.

"DarkFellow and Bartholomew have captured the imagination of young and old, daring to challenge us with their music, daring us to feel what they feel when they perform. Their message is universal, appealing to the times. I give you once again, DarkFellow and Bartholomew and their brand-new song, 'Something There.'"

They begin together, Kenny's pounding kick drum anchoring Hedley's acoustic guitar, low E tuned down to D to suit the song's mystical feel. DarkFellow comes to life once more as the vocals take over.

Something There

Some days give some days take
Some days leave your mind half baked
I know there's something there for me
Whatever it is it's waiting patiently yeah yeah

Same old story same old song
Gettin' nowhere just gettin' along
I know there's something there for me
Whatever it is it's waiting patiently yeah yeah

Bartholomew adds his low voice to the dreamy effect of the bridge, the two-part harmony twisting through the melody like a snake.

Daylight shining through
Leading me to you
Whatever it is whatever will be
I know it's waiting there for me

Daylight shining through
Leading me to you
Whatever it is whatever will be
I know it's waiting there for me

Nothing's easy nothing's free
Nothing's written in stone to be
But I know there's something there for me
Whatever it is it's waiting patiently

Yeah I know there's something there for me yeah yeah
Whatever it is it's waiting patiently

Waiting there for me
There for me

The stage goes dark with the abrupt closing shot, leaving only silence. The audience reacts as one to the song's sudden end, exploding like a bomb. They beckon the objects of their adulation to show themselves, but the lights come up on an empty stage. Hedley and Kenny are down the stairs and in the tunnel as the ovation continues.

They are gone.

"What a blast!" Kenny yells as they pile into the waiting limo. "I definitely want a whole lot more of that!"

"Yeah, neat!" Hedley says. "We nailed that bitch, didn't we?"

"Whoa dude, that Hedley or DarkFellow talkin'?"

"I got my hat off, it's gotta be me," Hedley says.

"Settle in boys, we're off to the airport—except we're not," Darwin says. He puts the limo in glide and continues. "The airport is a diversion. We pull into the hangar, the ARRCIS shuttle leaves about twenty minutes later for LA, with your stand-in partners in crime on it, and we exit out the back way in a four-passenger Runabout en route to Philadelphia. Marki is there, at Tracy's. We should be there in a couple of hours. That's right. It's actually good having some people in the know, makes it easier to move you around. Kenny, you'll be back in Broken Arrow tomorrow, and no one will be the wiser. Another day in Ada with your buddy Hedley Yonge is how that script will read."

"We won't sell them for long in this day and age," Hedley says. "People are gonna want to know."

"We've got Tom working on it, using his old tabloid skills in reverse to conjure up cloak and dagger scenarios for you two budding young pop stars. You're right though, sooner or later someone will slip up."

"How is Tom these days?" Hedley asks with genuine curiosity. "We used to be pen pals in my younger days, but we've fallen out of touch."

"I think he's hanging in okay, but it wouldn't hurt to ring him up sometime. You two went through a lot together after your dad died. Hell, it was your idea to get him into TV news. Pretty good thinking for a seven-year-old."

"Mom told me about his tabloid wars with Dad, but I don't know that Tom."

"Just goes to show you how a man can change," Kenny says.

"I guess," Hedley replies. "But if you believe my sister and Tracy the wing nut, Tom was just doing what he was supposed to do. If you believe that sort of thing."

◆ ◆ ◆

AUDREY WATERS

Audrey Waters came up the hard way in show business. A child of the American Heartland, she clawed her way to the top while remaining true to her convictions, refusing to compromise her solid values for tabloid-inspired ratings. Though not a typical Hollywood beauty, she nevertheless compensated for her average looks with intelligence and a wit that has captured the American afternoon audience. She defined the timeslot with honesty and integrity, and a warm downhome brand of common sense. She is living proof that real beauty comes from within.

Her humble beginnings on a weekly, half-hour, local afternoon talk show in Indianapolis are long gone, replaced by the nationally televised hour-long daily program, *LA Afternoon*. Her move to New York and the *Audrey Over America* show in January 2002 has only served to solidify her presence to the national audience. Now, seventeen years later, Audrey Waters and *Audrey Over America* are American institutions, best served with a slice of apple pie.

"Audrey, good to see your smiling face," Jeff says. "What's on your mind?"

"There's the Jeff I know, straight to the heart of the matter." She laughs, and they fill a few minutes with small talk before diving in. "I don't know the relationship between DarkFellow and ARRCIS, but I have a hunch you're into it up to your knees. No need to confirm or deny, I know the drill, but I think the time is right for an interview. It can be done any way DarkFellow would wish, incognito of course, no close-ups, just the two of them and myself in a dimly lit studio with voices thoroughly disguised. If you can get that message to their entourage, I'd be eternally grateful." She laughs again. "You might possibly owe me one, Jeff, although the events entwining us over the years make it impossible to ascertain for certain who owes what to whom."

"It's been a journey hasn't it, that whole SAM thing and all? Why do I get the feeling it ain't over? Okay, I'm not making any promises, but I'll put in a good word or two."

"Thanks, Jeff. That's all I can ask."

◆ ◆ ◆

Marki was indeed waiting in Philadelphia, dying for some hot alone time with Hedley, but the situation insisted that cooler heads prevail. Still, she was glad to see Hedley, though she didn't mind avoiding the spotlight engulfing him in the least. No, she was quite content to watch from afar, the quiet and unassuming significant other of one Hedley Martin Yonge.

They were all there in Tracy's media room, re-watching the Audrey performance of a few hours earlier. Kenny and Karin were hitting it off—could something be brewing? Marki seemed to think so, but Hedley had his doubts.

"Are you shooting a Halo for the new song?" Brian asks from his natural position beside Carolyn.

"Already done, dude," Kenny responds.

"And three others," Hedley adds, "and three more yet to do. It's cool. Kenny and I send the tracks back and forth, multi layering the instruments. Darwin dials in remotely and controls the cameras when it's time to shoot."

"Yeah, we never actually appear together, but you'd never know it," Kenny says. "Darwin's a flipping genius."

"Is the new song yours?" Marki asks. "You don't tell me these things."

"Yes, Hedley, illuminate us all," Michelle says.

"I'm sorry, to both of you. You know how I am." Marki lightly squeezes his hand in understanding. "The song is Dad's, from the early days in Calgary, before you met. Even then, it was like he was waiting for you to come along. I don't read as much into this stuff as some of you here, but it's eerie, how it all fits together. I kind of hope this DarkFellow thing gets out in the open soon. I won't spill the beans, but I'd like people to know about Dad, the other side of him. There was so much more. And touring, I don't want to be away from Marki. Things are different for us now, but beyond that," he turns to face her, "Marki, you've been my best friend for years. Now, when I need you most, you can't be there because of a mythical character I invented. I want you to know I do not like the situation."

"Me either, quite honestly. But I encouraged you. We'll get through it. It's temporary." She hugs Hedley, clinging and lending support. "I want you in me," she whispers, then lightly kisses his cheek. Hedley smiles.

◆ ◆ ◆

May turns to June, and life goes on. Carolyn remains in Philadelphia, almost against Michelle's wishes, but the mom in her knows she cannot keep her from Brian. *I'll give them the summer*, Michelle thinks, *then we'll have to see about them making their own way.* She smiles to herself, reaping joy from both her children's happiness, though somewhat saddened at her own loneliness. She brushes the thought aside as she prepares to drive Hedley and Kenny to the monorail, another DarkFellow performance looming. The duo desired to do the tracks for their next couple of songs together, bringing Kenny to Ada for a few days. It would also serve as cover while they went to LA for the next TV performance of DarkFellow and Bartholomew.

Tour dates were fast to take shape, coinciding with the beginning of summer. The idea was put forth of hiring two sidemen, but in the end the plan was to pre-record the needed tracks and keep it simple. They would play live to their own backing tracks, the two of them as they appear in the Halos. Kenny's mother and sisters are beginning to suspect, although of what, they have no idea. Still, they're aware that something is up. Kenny caved under the constant barrage of Sheila Baines, his girlfriend of two years, swearing her to secrecy. They're tight, and she can be trusted. That's the way Kenny sees it anyway. The circle of knowledge grows.

After much deliberation, it was felt that an interview with Audrey would do well for the situation. Thursday, August 5, was set aside for that purpose, coinciding with their New York concert that night. All twenty-two shows throughout the country are sold out, theatres and concert venues mostly; no arenas as of yet, but Jeff suspects they might get there by summer's end. There is no sign of the DarkFellow infatuation slowing down any time soon. The Fillmore appearance and the interview will cap off the first leg of the tour quite nicely. The DarkFellow mystique will be preserved by the now routine procedure of their TV appearances, applying the techniques learned to the aspect of touring. They will live quite comfortably on the ARRCIS shuttle, too busy over the fifty-six-day tour to miss anything as they transfer from shuttle to limo to concert hall and back again. That is Jeff's hope, though in reality, he knows there will be logistics to cover on the fly. Everything is in place, and as Michelle watches the mono disappear, she wonders what that future holds for them all.

◆ ◆ ◆

"Hedley, can you come out?" The tone in Carolyn's voice rekindles an unconscious distant memory, and an accompanying cool shiver courses through him.

"What's up? You sound, I don't know, almost scared."

"Not scared exactly, I'm not sure what. Just come out, okay?"

"I'm on it. Is Mom clued in?"

"No, not yet, not until I know for sure. I don't want her to worry. Tell her you're going to Kenny's for a couple of days."

"I don't like to lie to her."

"You should this time. Trust me on this, Hedley. Please come out. We'll clue mom in later if my suspicions are correct."

"Okay. I'll bring Marki. I'll tell mom I'm lonely for my big sister. She'll buy that. We'll be there tonight."

Brian and Carolyn could not appear more serious as they greet them at the aerodrome, and a heightened nervousness is present on the ride back to Tracy's house. They settle in upstairs, cool beers in hand to counter the exceedingly warm early June evening.

"Brian and I popped down to Pittsburgh last weekend. June was in to spend a week with Aunt Margret. We thought it a good time to catch up. June asked me how the family project was going. I told her that following the legs of the brothers and sisters has led to confusion and many dead ends, and that I'm not sure if any of it can be called progress. Aunt Margret stated that I should concentrate on our direct lineage and follow those trails to their conclusion. I said I would do that, and I have. June asked me if I'd gotten around to fitting Hugh into the picture. I told her I have not, but I would do so once I got back."

Carolyn rises from her seat on the sofa next to Brian and crosses to her laptop, open on an old wooden table. "Have a look at this, Hedley. Tell me what you see." They stand in a half circle facing the screen. The somewhat blurry torso shot of a youngish man in his mid-thirties stares up at them, a steadfast seriousness written on his demeanor.

"I would say that's Hugh Peterson, much as he appeared to me in California," Hedley replies.

"Exactly, except it's not. Follow me through on this. I was doing some digging. I had Hughie's picture up on my screen, the one June gave me in St. Louis. That TV was on." She points to a now black screen hanging from a wall, up and forward from where they stand. "A replay of the Temporary Measures repeal signing was on the news. I caught something that made my blood run cold." She approaches the keyboard and brings another image to the screen. "The picture on the left is the picture June gave me. The picture on the right, the one I just showed you, was captured from an internet replay of the news telecast. I doctored it somewhat, made him look younger, but that's Allan Bruce."

"Holy cripes, they're the same guy!" Hedley exclaims.

"Exactly," Carolyn says. "I think Allan Bruce is AFF. I think they're still around." She pauses, letting what she's said sink in. "There's more. I searched from the archives using Brian's security credentials. The story of Allan Bruce reads like an American fairy tale. He was born in Wisconsin in 1969. His parents moved to Chicago in the early seventies. He was a straight A student, never made any waves, and nobody seems to remember much about him. There is absolutely nothing out of place about this guy according to the records. His life reads like a script until 2010. Then things begin to happen. He gets involved, he gets hired, he does things, he develops a track record. Allan Bruce starts to live about the time Hugh Peterson disappears. I think that's more than coincidence. Question is, what's he up to?"

"You'd have to be very sure before you made any accusations," Marki says.

"And that's why I didn't want to bring Mom in just yet."

"It would take a lot of resources to make a falsified record hold up," Marki says.

"Fifteen million ought to cover it," Hedley says coldly. "The ransom money never did turn up. But really, it doesn't take money, it takes knowhow, and Hugh's got plenty of that. The online database is not as secure as you would think. Not anywhere near where it should be, I can tell you that. Once a record is in there, who's gonna know? People see it on a screen, they believe it. Case closed. You've got to dig real deep to verify, so unless they have a reason to dig, they're not going to. Hugh was part of the inner circle with the colonel. They're one and the same, I'm sure of it. I feel it, and now we have to prove it. We've got to give them a reason to dig."

"Exactly," Soup says. "That's why you're here. I want you to use your own considerable skills to try to hack into Allan Bruce's records."

"Wow, the web you weave."

"Hedley, is that advisable?" Marki asks.

"I was there. Those AFF guys are crazy. If they're back and organized, we need to know about it. Chances are that Hughie has gone legit. He may well have seen the error of his ways and is living a new productive life under an alias to protect June, and good on him if that is so. But if that isn't the case . . ."

"I can reach Danny Livermore once we have more. Do you remember him? He was one of the FBI field agents at the house during the kidnapping."

"We can do the digging from the archives." Brian offers. "I could lose my job, but really, if we're smart, who's going to know? I'll log you in, Hedley, you do the deed."

"That might be the leg up I'll need to get in. Once I find a path, I can access from any computer. We won't have to use your archive login for long. No point in needlessly rocking the boat."

◆ ◆ ◆

CHAPTER NINE — CHICKEN STEW

"Nothing, absolutely nothing!" Hedley cries in frustration. "Three days of digging and nothing. We need to get into his personal files—that's where we would find something, if there is something to find. I have no idea how to locate his personal stash, let alone penetrate it. You can continue the search from here, Carolyn, using the path I bookmarked on your PC. I doubt that his official senate records will reveal much. We need to get home before Mom comes out. I'll keep digging from there. Kenny and I start rehearsals soon, the tour is looming. I don't know how much we'll be in contact once that's underway."

"Frustrating, to say the least," Carolyn says.

"Really, what did you expect to find?" Marki asks.

"Something that would indicate nothing is going on," Hedley says. "It's all too clean and perfect, but it smells like a smoke screen. Maybe it's the past screaming at me, but it has that feel about it. Wait a minute, I got it! We have an in to the senator's office, we know the layout. There are two computers, the senator's and Allan's, probably official work stations. They'd be on twenty-four-seven for network monitoring, so odds are the IP addresses won't change."

"So?" Brian asks.

"So we go fishing. It will take some patience, but I have a hunch that sooner or later Allan will be there working, and he'll need to access something on his personal PC. He'll either hop on the wireless, which I doubt, connect to a third outlet, or unplug his official workstation and plug in. Don't search, monitor. If a new IP address pops up, follow it. We can't go to him, so let him come to us."

JUNE 17— WASHINGTON, DC

"I don't wish to alarm you, sir, but it appears as though someone is attempting to reach Allan's inner files," the senate security officer informs Sam Meade.

"Is there anything in there that could hurt us?" the senator asks.

"No, not at all. Allan is as clean as they come. He's been with you since 2010 without a ripple. Probably nothing, but I thought you should be informed."

"Thanks, Richard. We'll look into it." Samuel Meade stares into the blank screen of his desktop communication console, pushes some buttons, and places a call.

◆ ◆ ◆

THE AFF

They lacked the resources Robert Carlson had brought to the table, and they were no longer an armed force to be reckoned with. But they were there, splintered off into small groups, waiting for the man and the moment to unite them once again. The man was Allan Bruce, née Hugh Peterson, reaching out over the years to reconnect the web. Allan realized the American Freedom Force needed to infiltrate the politics of the nation; seek power at its base. The colonel's plan of gaining power through a grass roots army was doomed to fail, Allan realizes that now, but he believed in the colonel at the time. And just as he believed, so do Allan's followers believe in him now. As head of communications and the third in line in that power structure, he knows the former identities of the then-AFF members, and how to reach them. The plan is far reaching; perhaps another ten years in the making, but the result will place a plethora of AFF believers directly in the path of power. Not as politicians themselves, not all of them anyway—a near impossibility that. No, the plan is to build more like himself, the righthand men of the people holding power. With trust comes confidence, and with confidence comes knowledge—knowledge to use against the very men they pretend to serve. Everyone is dirty, Allan believes. There are many ways to open their eyes to the AFF's point of view.

Already, dozens of AFF members have done just that, infiltrating the structure by gaining the confidence of the power elite. Allan has painstakingly schooled his disciples, teaching them the required tools. When the time comes, the AFF network will be firmly entrenched, and a transfer of power will occur without firing a shot. The trick is to have people of influence on both sides of the political structure, and eventually in the Oval Office itself. The American Freedom Force will realize its objectives through the very institutions it serves to protect, the vote on the floors of the Senate and the Congress of the United States. Allan Bruce firmly believes he will live to see that objective. There is simply too much at stake to let an insolent little brat from the past throw a monkey wrench into the machine.

It was assumed that the fateful helicopter crash put an end to the AFF for good, and indeed, eleven years have passed with nary a whisper. But Carolyn's spider senses are tingling, and Hedley lies awake at night, wondering if the end was merely the beginning.

◆ ◆ ◆

"Hedley!" Marki gently shakes him, hoping to wake him from his dream. "Hedley, wake up."

"Wha . . . Marki? Oh, not again?"

"I thought you were past this." She draws him to her, rocking him gently as he pulls himself together.

"I am, or I thought I was, but Allan Bruce is bringing it all back. We can't let them—"

"Hedley, Marki, is everything all right?" a pajama-clad Michelle asks in a concerned voice.

"Mom, the lights—"

Marki reaches to a small lamp on the night table, allowing Michelle to kill the overheads.

"I was back at the colonel's California base with Dad," Hedley begins. "He was sleeping… they'd brought him in earlier by helicopter. The colonel sent me in with a breakfast tray."

JULY 20, 2009

Scott is woken by the light touch of a finger to the cheek and the unmistakable smell of cooked bacon tickling his nostrils.

"Hedley?" he asks, believing he is dreaming.

"Yeah, dad." Hedley stands over Scott with a tray and an impatient demeanor. "I knew you would come. You gonna sleep all day?"

Ever a disciple of discipline, the colonel assigned a task to the reunification of son and father in an effort to defuse the emotional impact of the moment. It does not work. Scott relieves Hedley of the tray, setting the diversion device on the bunk beside him. "Come here," he says, opening his arms. Hedley dives in, tucking into his father as naturally as a baby kangaroo in a pouch. Scott can no more hold back the flood than a stick could hold a raging river, and tears flow as he unabashedly breaks down, slowly rocking his boy in his arms. Pure relief and joy at the feel of his son, safe for the moment, washes over him in a surfer's wave, the smell of Hedley the sweet perfume of ecstasy.

"Aw Dad, I'm okay. Are we going home soon?"

"Very soon, son," says a deep voice from the doorway. "But first, I wish to talk to your father alone. You will wash up and make yourself presentable for your mother before we leave."

Hedley obeys, silently trading his father for the escort waiting behind the colonel, though he does not wish to do so. Instinct and his short stay in the military environment warn him it is the thing to do.

"So we meet," Scott says.

"It is customary when an officer enters a room to stand and salute, but I'll overlook your civilian manners for now. As you can see, I am a man, not a monster."

Scott is flooded with a battalion of emotions and briefly contemplates jumping the man while they are alone, but he remains where he sits, saying nothing.

"I see hatred in your eyes, and a desire for murder, but I assure you as I have all along, no harm has come to your boy, and none will. He has seen my face, as you do now. It matters not. I believe they know who I am. Sooner than expected, I must admit, but it is of no consequence. The person I was no longer exists. I am, from this moment on, Colonel Randall, Commander in Chief of the American Freedom Force. We are a small, well-equipped force, but we grow by the day. We are ready to mobilize from various strategic posts throughout the nation. Our mission is to point America back in the direction that made us great. Every one of us has sacrificed our identities and our previous lives for this moment. We go to our graves as soldiers, proud of and dedicated to our cause. From this day forward, we shed our dress uniforms, honoring the brave fighting men of WWII, and don combat fatigues. We will wear our dress uniforms again when our mission is complete.

"Seven hundred and fifty million, Mr. Yonge. That's how much of my personal fortune is invested in this project. Most of the rest has been liquidated, converted to easily accessible cash. We will conduct a guerrilla war the likes of which this country has never known, at least not on domestic soil. When the conflict begins, I believe many of the Armed Forces will lay down their arms and join us in our cause. When the conflict begins, my troops will hold on long enough to wake the angry beast in the American people, and our direction as a nation will once again be on track. We will win, Mr. Yonge. We will win because we are right!"

"Do you always talk like you're rallying the troops, or can we talk as we are, one on one?" Scott asks. He sounds sarcastic, despite his efforts to control his emotions.

"Very well. Man to man, as you wish. I've given my life to this. I believe I was chosen. I befriended no one, trusted no one, left no portal unattended where weakness can slip in and undermine my mission. I've known great loneliness in my time, but it is a price worth paying. I sense in you also the knowledge of loneliness, and an appreciation of the inner strength that loneliness can bring. We as a race have come to fear the meaning of the word, but I embrace it as you have done at times in your life. I can feel its presence in you, written on every gesture. We are alike, Mr. Yonge. We might have been friends in a different time."

Both men contemplate the words, saying nothing, but a binding recognition of the truth passes between them. They see themselves in each other.

"We leave here soon to deliver Hedley to your wife." The colonel's voice is tinged with a hint of sadness. "You will return with me. There is the matter of your court martial. You've conducted yourself well, and that will be taken into account, but you must pay for your crimes."

"I don't care what you do with me as long as I have your word my son will be safe."

"You have it. You will not be executed, but you will serve hard time. How much is yet to be determined by the tribunal, but you must serve as an example. The trial will be televised. You're more valuable alive, Mr. Yonge. Eat and wash up, we leave in fifteen minutes."

The colonel returns, gathering Scott for the last leg of the journey. The bright California sunshine is at odds with the cool mountain breeze, assaulting the senses as they step into the open air.

"There are many such bases, Mr. Yonge," the Colonel explains, with obvious pride. "Some larger, some smaller, each capable of autonomous operation should the line of command be broken. Each camp is well armed and well supplied and has a list of prepared missions to complete in a given timetable. My men, all of them, believe as I do, and as untold millions out there do, that we will only get stronger, and we will win."

Scott is contemplative as they walk, trying to digest the logic of this man who has taken charge of his life. It's like searching from the shore for a ship in a thick fog.

"Colonel, may I speak candidly?" Scott asks.

"Yes, of course, Mr. Yonge. Speak your mind." The colonel stops walking.

"This cannot succeed. It is not our way. Even I admit that your purpose is a good one, maybe even a great one, but Americans won't buy into the method. It simply is not the way of this nation."

"It was the way of the nation in 1776 and again in 1861, and in every other campaign we've taken upon ourselves. It is but another battle of the ongoing

American Revolution. We do not wish to shed blood, but as in any battle, people will die. As commander, that knowledge weighs heavily on me as it did Eisenhower on D-Day, but our mission is every bit as urgent as his was. And like General Eisenhower, I will succeed."

"Why not politics?" Scott asks. "You're an obviously gifted man, why not that route?"

"Politics?" The colonel stiffens slightly before continuing, his answer cool and calculated, tinged with anger. "The political process is the problem, Mr. Yonge. The system is corrupt, too corrupt to be cleansed from the inside. Many of them are the enemy. Many of them will surely die in the conflict."

What a waste, Scott thinks, saying nothing. The colonel's words reaffirm what he suspected he had heard in Janis Isley's voice: this man is as mad as a hatter.

They walk again in silence as around them, men prepare for missions known only to themselves.

Up ahead, Hedley waits with another man by the smaller four-man helicopter, now pulled out of its cozy hangar and ready for action.

Hedley breaks away, running toward Scott and the colonel the second he spots them, hitting his stride quickly. "We're gonna ride in the chopper again!" he exclaims, turning and slowing his pace to match the stroll of the two men. They stop to receive him, Scott involuntarily stretching out an arm. He relishes the feel of Hedley's trusting hand as his small fingers entwine with his. The meaning of fatherhood could not be clearer to Scott, illuminated by the warm innocent smile Hedley gives him. The silent emotional exchange is not lost on the colonel, weakened for the moment by the bonding of father and son.

"I envy you, Mr. Yonge. I shall never know your joy. Ready to go home, son?" he says to Hedley.

"Hell yeah!" the lad replies, bringing a smirk to Scott's drawn face.

The colonel also smiles briefly and continues again, closing the forty-yard gap between them and the craft where the other man waits.

These two do not salute, Scott thinks. *They're equal, or almost. Second in command. Spock. Obviously cocky in their success, they've put the president and the vice-president on the same mission.*

"After you," the colonel says with an extended hand. Scott shrugs off his thought and climbs in the back, followed by the colonel. The pilot buckles Hedley in and closes the clear Plexiglass door, then circles around the front of the chopper to the other side.

"It's time," the colonel says. The pilot nods at the end of their brief eye contact and climbs aboard. He straps himself in before manipulating the controls that make the engine come alive. The roar of the engine is soon joined by the familiar *thunka-thunka* sound of the blade chopping the air, and in seconds, they are airborne.

They are in the air for perhaps an hour, maybe a little longer, whisking over and through the rugged mountain terrain of south central California. The high air is cool despite the hot day, bringing Scott alive as it streams in through an adjustable side vent. Very little is said. Even the colonel seems mesmerized by the beauty around them.

They bank left through a steep pass and begin their descent to an open meadow below. An unfamiliar vehicle waits with a lone figure leaning against the front fender, looking up.

"Mom! Look, Dad, she's there!"

Scott smiles as a strange new calm eradicates any void he may have felt in his life. A feeling of well-being is all there is, and he sees the complete beauty of living. "You bet, Hedley," he says quietly. "She's there."

"A fitting place, don't you think?" the colonel asks as he spies recognition in Scott's eyes. "This location has meaning to you."

"It does," Scott replies. "It truly does."

"Strategic, also. There's no way for unseen observers to break the perimeter."

The craft circles and settles to the ground, tail in direct line with Michelle's tunnel of sight, canopy away from her view. The engine slows to an idle but does not die as Hedley struggles excitedly with his harness.

"Out you go, son," the colonel commands.

"You go ahead, Hedley," Scott says to his son's backward glance. "I'll be right behind you." Hedley breathes excitement, quivering like a puppy as he unlatches the door and steps down.

Scott's heart breaks as he follows his son's progress through the open hatch and along the ground, but a calmness born of relief floods through him as the boy bounds free.

The relentless tension of the past week is simultaneously lifted from Michelle and Scott as Hedley's tiny feet race across the open ground.

"Mom!" Hedley cries as he runs to her, and tears break the surface of Michelle's eyes. She looks up momentarily for Scott, but only sees a uniformed man step down from the helicopter, then back in again. A downward gust of wind forces dust into her eyes as the engine accelerates, and the small craft heads skyward again.

She's in disbelief at first, then panic as the realization hits her, followed by a deepening sadness. She watches in slow motion as Hedley turns in his tracks to the sound of the craft, yelling inaudibly. She catches the briefest glimpse of Scott as the chopper turns slightly, feeling his eyes long after his image disappears from sight. Trembling, she falls to her knees, emotionally spent but already adjusting to the new reality.

Hedley's voice is lost to Scott in the revving rotors as the chopper lifts skyward again. Hedley turns to the sound, allowing Scott to see the anguish written on his son's face. Scott cranks his head sharply left, peering out the back of the Plexiglass canopy, following Hedley as Hedley does a one-eighty, running away from the forward progress of the rising craft. He catches a quick glimpse of Michelle before the craft veers hard right, replacing her image with empty blue sky. He burns that faint glimpse into his memory, knowing it may be the last he'll see of her. His heart breaks for the time they may not have.

Hedley runs to his mother, great joy tarnished by the realization he has traded one parent for another. He feels himself age with every step as he advances to her arms, collapsing into them again as a six-year-old. Michelle wraps him up, throwing a protective blanket over Hedley, shielding him from the world and the realization of her loss. One hole in her heart opens as another closed, and a before unknown loneliness flows through her. Scott would not be coming home.

The colonel turns and looks directly into Scott, his eyes as cold as an Arctic wind. "You don't know who I am, do you?" he asks.

"Should I?" Scott replies.

"No, I suppose not." The colonel smiles.

Maybe it was the presence of his most trusted lieutenant that made him do it. Maybe he felt he needed to demonstrate to his second in command his ability to make the tough decision when it needed to be made. Or maybe he simply despised the moment of weakness he felt at the sight of Hedley's reunion with his father, and felt he could eradicate it by an act of what he envisioned to be a show of overpowering strength. Or maybe it was the most primitive of human emotions, the need to avenge the death of his uncle. Whatever it was, Scott never knew. They all make mistakes, these despots of the world. Sooner or later they bring themselves down. Hitler's grave error was Russia. The colonel's was to make it personal.

"Circle back," he commands, tapping the pilot's shoulder.

"What?"

"Circle back over them. Come in low," the colonel orders again. The pilot nods, sending the chopper in a hard-left bank following the arc of a semi-circle back to where Michelle and Hedley still huddle on the ground. Scott can see them again, distant, but close enough to see their heads react to the sound of the returning helicopter. Hope surges in Scott's veins, and for a moment, he can believe he will feel his wife in his arms again, he will hold his daughter as he held his son a few hours before. His golden moment of sunshine is interrupted by the cool voice of the colonel, taunting Scott with an inhuman tone.

"Someone has to pay for Butch," he says coldly. He reaches into his coat. "After all, he was family. I will keep my word, Mr. Yonge, your son will not be harmed."

"NOOOO!" Scott screams as the realization hits him like a tractor in a hurricane. He lunges up and forward on instinct, unaware yet of his own goal. The colonel's gun responds involuntarily to the movement, sending a bullet through Scott's kidney, but it is too late. The chopper is doomed.

Searing pain, then a fireball as Scott's forward momentum against the control stick slams the helicopter into the ground. *There, you're safe*, Scott thinks. *Why am I so cold?* Then nothing.

The heat hits Michelle before the sound of the explosion, or maybe she refuses to accept the sound, but the heat cannot be denied.

"Dad!" Hedley yells. He knows that Scott Yonge, the father, the husband, the man, is no more.

Timeless darkness, followed by a brilliant light and the soothing sound of a feminine voice compel Scott.

"Come home, son. Your work is done. They'll join us, they'll all join us, and we'll be together. Come."

Scott rises up, high above the burning copter, warmth and comfort wrapping him in a golden silence as he ascends. He looks down again, drawn to the two figures huddled together on the ground, their torment evident over the great distance between them. He plunges down, wrapping the remaining grams of his existence around them as they shake and cry, and they cry no more.

"He's here, Mom! I feel Dad!" Hedley says.

"Yes, Hedley, I feel him, too." She smiles and wipes the tears from her eyes and rises to her feet. Hedley rises with her, holding her hand with a tender ferocity inspired by a new and greater reality.

A soothing calm descends on them, pushing away the despair. They hear the sirens in the distance, not quite drowning out the popping metal in the crackling flames.

"Let's go home, Hedley." Michelle says. "Your sister needs us."

Bye my love, she thinks. *Go where you need to go.*

Scott reaches out one more time, lightly brushing her cheek as she flickers and fades in the bright light. She is gone from him.

2021 — THE PRESENT

"What did you yell at the chopper when they took off, Hedley?" Michelle says in a gentle voice. "I never asked you that." She longs to hold her son, but realizes it is no longer her place. Still, her heart breaks at the anguished look of him.

"I yelled, 'It's supposed to be me, it's supposed to be me!' That's what I said, and I meant it. I still mean it." He breaks down, clinging to Marki. Michelle can stand it no longer. She joins them on the bed, taking them both into her arms. They cry, the three of them, brought together by the bittersweet memory of the past, the moment they lost, and found.

"We've got to stop them, Mom," Hedley says. "Whatever they're up to, we need to stop them."

"Stop who? What's got you so upset?"

He takes a deep breath and looks to Marki. She nods, clasping his hand.

"The AFF. They're back. They never really went away."

He tells her all that he knows as she sits and listens, panic rising in her like vomit.

"If what you say is true, it's beyond us. We need to go the authorities. How could you and Carolyn get dragged into this?" She sounds surprisingly calm.

"How could we not? I don't buy all the fate crap, I never have, but all of us ending up in the same living room in St. Louis on the same day, looking for the same person for entirely different reasons, where do we file that? Carolyn's got Danny what's his name, the FBI guy—"

"Livermore?"

"Yeah, Danny Livermore. Carolyn wants to call him, but not now. All we've got is a sliver. You think they're going to believe a bunch of punk kids?"

"I think that particular agent would take this particular group of punk kids very seriously. He was there, remember? He knows what those people can do, maybe as much as we do. We can't do anything about it tonight, but tomorrow first thing, we get online with Carolyn. I don't know about you, but sleep is the farthest thing from my mind. Anyone for tea?"

They join her.

◆ ◆ ◆

"Oh, you're up. I'll throw breakfast together."

"Juice is all, Mom. I'm not hungry. I'll wait for Marki."

Hedley, half asleep walks to the fridge. Settling on apple, he joins Michelle at the table.

"Are the dreams bad, honey? Tell me what's going on."

"Not bad, just constant. Since last week. I'm not freaked or anything, just tired, and right now, I can't be tired. We've got the tour, and I'm in knots about that."

"Scott used to knot up before every performance, but he looked forward to it. He said it was his way of channeling the energy to the music. I think it is a necessary part of the process."

"I'm not Dad. I do things differently."

"I know, but maybe some things are universal. Marki loves you, you know that."

"Yes."

"So share things with her, the songs. Your father used to play his songs for me, right from the beginning. It was maybe the most intimate part of our relationship. His songs were deeply personal to him. Your father lived with a lot of emotional pain all his life, but he wouldn't let it beat him. He was the most positive man I knew. Scott and your grandfather both had that. Scott told me he could be that way because he was able to shovel away the pain through the music. Sharing his music with me was a big part of our attachment, I think it's why we bonded so quickly."

"Right, but they were his songs, and they're still his songs. People out there think they're DarkFellow songs, and I can't tell them they're not."

"So write your own songs."

"I have, they're just—"

"Not as good as your dad's?"

"No."

"How do you know? Have you shown them to anyone?"

Hedley shakes his head.

"Well you should, starting with Marki. 'I Call Your Name,' the Garrett Awards, all of that was a happy accident. Scott expected nothing to come of it. It was a holiday to him, a lark, a diversion. He expected to return to Calgary and continue with his life, and he would've been content with that. He didn't bank on us meeting. Neither did I. Our meeting changed everything. He didn't believe in his own songs, Hedley. They were a hobby for him. I'm not taking credit for anything beyond just being there, but sometimes, that's all it takes. He told me time and again that my belief in his songs gave him the courage to show them to the world. Scott Yonge & The Zone began in my condo the morning after the Garretts. That's when your father opened up to me."

"So he spent the night?"

Michelle blushes at the memory.

"Wow, didn't waste any time, did you?"

"No, we did not. Most people thought we were fools, and maybe we were, but we're sitting here twenty years later talking about it. I don't think anybody's laughing now. I miss your father, every minute of my life, but in a good way. My life would've been different had he lived, but it can't be any better than it is right now, right here at this table. I've had and still have everything. Missing your dad is a sweet and good part of my life, but it is not my focus. Life is the focus of life. Scott believed in that above all else. It is as simple as that—live your life. I will go on missing your dad, and I will live my life. Open up to Marki, show her your songs. It will bring you closer. Make her miss you the way I miss your dad."

"I already do," Marki says, entering. "More than you know. Even when we're together I miss him sometimes. I don't know what that's about, I just do."

She turns to Hedley. "I don't say it, you know how I am, but I've loved you forever, Hedley, I always will. And I'm scared about last night." She shakes, fighting the tears, but they come. Hedley rises to her.

"I'm here, I'm here. I'll always be here."

Michelle takes her cue and rises to quietly exit.

"Michelle don't . . . don't go."

Michelle moves to them, wrapping around them as best she can, the three of them in tears, not really knowing why.

"I think we could use some breakfast," Michelle says. "My treat."

"No, let's stay home. We'll help," Marki says.

"And after breakfast, I've got some songs to show Marki."

Michelle smiles and fetches the eggs.

An enjoyable breakfast was had by all. Michelle takes the opportunity to pick up a few things in town. Hedley leads Marki to the dungeon, bristling with anticipation.

"It seemed like a good idea upstairs, but now I feel like I'm sitting on a hotplate." Hedley looks up from his stool with guitar in hand, not quite knowing how to start. "Maybe I should join you on the bed for a romp first?"

"Not on your life, buster. You're going to do this. You need to do this. Hedley, it's me. Why won't you trust me?"

"It's not that, not at all. I'm . . . well . . . scared."

"Scared? Scared of what, that I won't like them?"

"Yeah."

"If I don't, I'll tell you. So what?"

"What do you mean so what? You're killing me here."

"Look, I have no idea what's good or bad. Okay, that's not entirely true. Hedley, I'm not here to judge you, I'm here to listen. You talk, I listen. Only you're singing to me. I'm here to listen. It's as simple as that."

"Simple to you maybe."

She looks at him, saying nothing.

"Okay, okay, I'm ready." He pauses. "The lyrics aren't necessarily me talking. I mean, they are, but they're not necessarily literal, they simply fit the melody in places. It's all about the mood, capturing the mood of the song. Here goes."

After a moment of contemplation, he begins, finger picking the slightly jazzy 6/8 downward moving progression of the song's intro, drawing Marki into his circle of light. Softly, he sings.

Time after time
I got out with nothing more
Than one thin dime
Into this world of mine

As I look around
I tell you what I found . . .

"That's very cool, Hedley. That's something." She smiles.

Hedley beams.

"Do it as DarkFellow. It's good, really good. I love it! You need to do your songs Hedley. That was me, right? A woman to help you along?"

He nods.

"You've never referred to me as a woman before. I quite like it. Now, about that romp you referred to earlier . . ." she removes the guitar from his hands.

◆ ◆ ◆

"Carolyn, look at me."

Carolyn turns her Wombat inward again, bringing both participants back in focus.

"We need to deal with this, honey, the right way. Hedley did not squeal on you, it came out by accident. He's dreaming again. He's back in 2009."

"Oh shit."

"We don't even know for sure that it is Hughie. True, he looks like him, but you're basing it on a twelve-year-old memory from the perspective of a six-year-old."

"Really, Mom. You're trying to sell that to me?"

"Okay, it's probably true. There, I said it. Are you happy now? There's no winning on this. If he is Hughie, that does not mean he's AFF. And what about June?"

"Exactly. What about June? Don't you think I've thought about that one? She's been through enough."

"But if he is AFF, then you're in way over your head. You need to go to Dan Livermore."

"With what?"

"With your story. Let him be the judge."

"We've got nothing."

"Then leave it alone, at least for now. You want me to call him?"

"No, I don't. I wish you knew none of this."

"Thanks for that." Michelle cannot hide the hurt in her voice.

"Sorry. Actually, I'm glad you know. Maybe you can help make some sense of it all. So what now?"

"My vote is to call Livermore, but I'll meet you half way. I'll say nothing if you do nothing. Hedley starts his tour in less than two weeks. I'll tell him we've laid it to rest for now. Deal?"

"Sure, whatever Hedley needs, as usual."

"Carolyn—"

"I'm okay with it, Mom. I know it has to be that way sometimes. He is my little brother, after all."

"Speaking of which, can you ask Tracy if Marki could come out while Hedley's on tour? Maybe you could invite her. She'd do much better around you than hanging out with an old babe like me. The separation will be hard on them both. I know how she's going to feel. No, not exactly, she's got the added weight of the incognito crap to pull her down."

"Good idea mom, I like having Marki around. They all like her here too. I'll make the call—but then you'll be alone."

"I'll survive. I'm planning on a week in Calgary with Del and Gloria, then some time on the coast. I've got business with Jeff. I can catch up with the baseball crowd, and maybe get Tom's perspective on this AFF situation. I'm sure he'll have some suggestions."

◆ ◆ ◆

CHAPTER TEN — THE TOUR

FRIDAY, JULY 2, 2021

"This is it, boys," Jeff says. He leads Hedley and Kenny up the steps of the brand-new bus. "Home for the next two months. Learn to love it. You will eat, sleep, and suck air aboard this beauty. It's the first of its kind, lads, a fully functional, Pulse-powered luxury tour bus, courtesy of the ARRCIS Media Group. You'll be flying on the ground in a jet-black cabin cruiser with all the comforts of home. And get this, coupled with the Pulse limo and the ARRCIS air shuttle, we are officially the first touring act to go totally Pulse green, and that's huge in the public eye, folks, huge."

Kenny moves past Jeff to the state rooms, the private bedrooms designed for Hedley and himself, suitcase and drumsticks in hand. Jeff and Hedley follow suit.

"You don't need to sell me, Jeff. I dig it," Kenny says. "This is the ultimate shaggin' wagon in my books."

"Yeah, well keep your mask and your glove on for those duties, Kenny. We don't want nothing given away on this tour if we can help ourselves. Why do I bother?"

Hedley and Marki spent last night trying to squeeze every ounce of each other into the few remaining hours before the dreaded separation, as did Kenny and Shelia in Broken Arrow.

"Stop your whining," Jeff had said. "You'll see each other in four days. I'm sure you can reel in your hormones until then. Tracy's co-operation and assistance in using Philadelphia as a stop off point will go a long way in helping us maintain the DarkFellow mystique and give you guys a break from the close quarters of the tour, so buck up, buckos. We got a job to do. Man, I wish I was going with you, I really do, but that would give away too much. Not to worry, Darwin stands on guard for thee. You're in good hands. Look, I know you're nervous, and that's okay, that's good actually, it keeps the edge on. This is new to both of you, but trust me, Hedley, it's in your blood, and Kenny, you'll take to touring like breathing. You open in Sandusky, Ohio, tomorrow night. You'll enjoy the outside setting, a great tune-up for Dayton on the fourth. Jessie and his two-man crew will have everything waiting. I'm not saying you have to, but after the show, don't be afraid to pitch in and help. Believe me, that'll go a long way to earning their respect. Remember, nothing happens without those guys, so don't go rock star on them. It's a long walk to Dayton."

"Can you define help?" Kenny asks.

"I don't want you humping gear, but anything else—wrapping cords, holding doors, any little thing to help. Get to know them. They've got your back. Let them know you've got theirs, know what I mean? You leave in fifteen minutes, with eight hundred and ninety miles to go, so Hedley, you'd best say goodbye to your mom. She's standing in the yard as we speak, and she looks as though the dam is gonna burst."

"Yeah, dude, be gentle," Kenny says. "Her little boy is leaving home." He laughs, slapping Hedley on the shoulder as he passes.

"Are you ready for this?" Michelle asks in an over composed voice.

"I don't know, Mom, I guess I'll find out tomorrow night. Are you?"

"I'm trying, Hedley. I have to let go. Please call me."

He moves to her, holding her as her composure goes south. "I will. Mom, I'm scared."

"Yes, of course you are. Who wouldn't be? Your dad was, all the time. He needed to be."

"I'm not Dad, Mom."

"No, but you can't escape being his son. There is a lot of him in you. Learn to embrace that."

"I wish he was here."

She laughs, suddenly feeling better. "You and me both, honey. I'm sure he is in one form or another." She hugs Hedley again, then releases. "Now scoot, you know how Jeff is with his schedule. Speak of the devil." The lanky man approaches them. "I know, Jeff. Time to go."

Jeff says nothing as he trades places with Hedley.

"Bye, Mom. I love you."

"I know. Me too." She smiles through the coming loneliness as Hedley walks heavily back to the bus.

Jeff senses her emotion and moves in, offering an outstretched arm. She accepts the shelter, each watching Hedley disappear up the steps.

"They'll be fine, Michelle."

"I know." She smiles, and then embraces Jeff fully, feeling a chill.

◆ ◆ ◆

OHIO

Hedley stares out at the seven thousand faces staring back at him in the warmth of the afternoon sun, adrenaline coursing through his veins like a dam bursting through a mountain valley, and suddenly DarkFellow is as real to him as the air he breathes. Nothing exists but the next two hours; the universe shrunk down to the real estate visible from the stage in Dayton, Ohio. It is July 4, 2021, but time and space are meaningless. Only the music matters.

They break into it. Kenny pounds the drum kit, setting the foundation for Hedley's keyboards as they accompany their own recorded backing bass and guitar tracks. Hedley had anxiety about the format, but the overwhelming acceptance at last night's Sandusky show had laid to rest any doubts, at least for now. Still, he pines for the experience of playing with a five-piece band, a subject he was determined to raise with Jeff. But for now, the mystery and pure fun of the two-man outfit is just fine. He looks quickly to the drum riser, smiles, and dives into the vocals.

One more broken highway
One more battered dream
One more road to nowhere
Left me somewhere in between

One more rusty Chevy
One more angry scream
One more destination
Left me somewhere in between . . .

The crowd is instantly with them, clapping and whistling, capturing the energy of the moment like the atmosphere around a meteorite. Kenny waits for the applause to subside, then pounds out the drum intro of 'Who Said.' The audience roars in recognition as Hedley jumps on the a capalla vocal.

Who said it's true . . .

"How you doing?" Hedley asks the crowd at song's end. "Good to see you all on this hot Independence Day bash! I'm DarkFellow. Over to my right is my good friend Bartholomew! There's a rising tide out there, folks, asking you all to join. This is a new one, our next Halo, soon to be released on Trafalgar. I try not to get political. Life should be fun, after all, but it seems every time I sit down to write, I cannot help but comment on the state of things around us. The world cannot be ignored, my friends. Dig it!"

They launch into 'Rising Tide,' Hedley switching to his Gibson jumbo acoustic for the driving folk-rock tune.

Rising Tide

Everybody's waiting on the rising tide
We all look out we never look inside
There's an answer that we can use
It's in all of us we have the right to choose

Look around there's something we all feel
It's moving in there's no denying it's real
Feel the hunger feel the time to feed
Give ourselves the very thing we all need

Gather round and feel the coming breeze
We ain't the first to live in times like these

The world around us is a murky haze
We've got the bill we've earned the right to pay
Here's something that we all know
Gotta shed the old ways
But we just can't let go

Gather round and feel the coming breeze
We ain't the first to live in times like these

Everybody waiting on the rising tide
We all look out we never look inside
There's an answer that we can use
It's in all of us we have the right to choose

The crowd is drawn further into the web, fully grabbing the message. Hedley feels the gap between the audience and the stage dwindle to nothing as he reaches out and they reach back. He is visibly moved by the aura of it all, by the realization that DarkFellow and Bartholomew are real in the eyes of the people staring back at them. The experience is humbling.

Hedley remains on acoustic, tuning the low E string down to D for the tune 'Something There.' He's back to standard tuning for 'Walk to Jerusalem,' the rockers 'Primitive' and 'Dirty Water,' and the effervescent 'Text Me.'

"Thanks folks, appreciate it. Something different coming your way. A new one in a new style for us. Bartholomew is gonna accompany me in the chorus. He's a little sensitive about his singing, so please give him a hand to help him along."

The crowd warmly responds to Hedley's plea, helping to settle Kenny.

"'A Distant Lie,' folks. I hope you like it."

The moody, slightly jazzy intro with a heavy synth-rock bottom end takes the crowd in a new direction as they quietly anticipate the duo vocal.

A Distant Lie

Building a world on a distant lie
Whatever gets you high
Whatever gets you home

Running it all from a mobile throne
Scanning the world for a hollow bone
But will it get you home

You try so hard to be the one
Tell yourself it's all good fun
But will it get you home
One more text won't get you by
You are smiling but it is a lie
A distant lie

Nine hundred faces on an empty page
One of them happy 'cause she got engaged
You don't know her name

Another pop-up can I be your friend
Sure why not let's just pretend
We give a damn in the end

You try so hard to be the one
Tell yourself it's all good fun
But will it get you home
One more text won't get you by
You are smiling but it is a lie
A distant lie

You are smiling but it is a lie
Yes it is a distant lie

Hedley's ode to social media finds a home, everyone in the audience identifying with the cold feel of dealing with the virtual world they live in. It is a new sound for DarkFellow. With the help of Del, sitting in on lead guitar, the recorded backing tracks are deeper, more mature. Hedley is spreading his wings. Once again, he is hit with the reality of the DarkFellow and Bartholomew mystique. It is a sobering moment for the young man, not yet nineteen. They lead the crowd through many more twists and turns, performing another ten songs before coming back for two encores. And as quickly as it started, it is over. Already Hedley is thinking about tomorrow's show in Cleveland as he and Kenny help Jessie's crew strike the stage.

After Cleveland, they have three days in Philadelphia with Marki to look forward to. Then, who can say? All Hedley knows is that he is exactly where he should be, doing exactly what he should be doing. He glides into dreamland as the bus rolls down the highway into the darkness.

◆ ◆ ◆

The first three dates of the tour are behind them. They're off until Friday the ninth, when Minneapolis beckons. Tracy has graciously consented to harbor Hedley from the rigors of the tour, giving him the spare room next to Carolyn and Marki's roost. "I'm on the other side of the house," Tracy says. "You can't hear me, and I can't hear you, so come and go as you please." She chuckled and walked away from Hedley and Marki, allowing them their needed together time.

"That's fine for her," Hedley says to Marki, "but I'm a little freaked out about us right next door to my sister. That's got to cramp our style."

"Not to worry," Marki says, "Soup spends most of her time upstairs with Brian. We all pretend, but we all know what's going on, Tracy included."

"Great, so I have to worry about my big sister."

"I'll leave you little time to worry about anything, sweetie."

◆ ◆ ◆

"What do you make of this, Hedley?" Soup asks. She held back, giving Marki and Hedley time to reacquaint, but now she is busting at the seams to share her findings.

"I kept monitoring, like you said. Nothing happened for days but then, look, this IP address shows up, the one ending in .1624. The .1439 address disappeared, so I'm guessing it happened as you said it would: he unplugged his senate PC to hook up his personal. I didn't go in. I was scared he was on it. Would he know if he was and I did?"

"I don't know, probably. He's a high-level geek, after all."

"Isn't it risky for him? I mean, wouldn't the senate IT crew pick up the change?"

"You would think so," Hedley surmises, "but I just wonder . . . E-Lok."

"E-Lok?"

"E-Lok, the colonel's invention, as Robert Carlson I mean. The colonel used a variation of E-Lok, a modification, to communicate with and track Dad without being detected. E-Lok was banned in '09 after the AFF fiasco, but Hughie was party to the code. So it stands to reason that he would apply it to his personal rig to hide himself from the rest of the senate network."

"Wouldn't he pick up on me snooping around?"

"Not necessarily. He'd use E-Lok to hide the outgoing, and count on his cronies to be hidden from their outgoing. I've done some digging over the years. I planted a rudimentary version of the E-Lok modification on your system. Keep that to yourself. Mom would freak. The colonel was a smart guy. Too bad he was a deranged orangutan."

"So I should go in the next time that number pops up?"

"It might be a different address, dynamically assigned as a new PC, but I'm pretty sure the official senate rigs are static, so look for any number ending in anything other than .1438 and .1439. If you don't go in, we can't learn much. You'll figure it out. Good job, Pipsqueak, I'm proud of you."

"I'm proud of you, Hedley. DarkFellow, I don't know, it feels right somehow. I don't know why, it just does."

"Yeah, well it still freaks me out, this pretending to be somebody else, but I'm beginning to like it."

Marki bursts into Carolyn's room with attitude. "I don't think you should do any of this!"

"I thought you liked DarkFellow. What gives Marki?"

"Not you. Carolyn. I don't think you should get into this AFF stuff any deeper than you are. You were dreaming again last night, Hedley, tossing and turning and—"

"And what?"

"You were crying Hedley, really crying. You know what they can do. I wish you'd leave it alone. I'm scared for you and terrified for Carolyn." She turns to face Soup, almost in tears. "Please, Carolyn, go to the authorities. You're in way over your head."

"I just need something, one little thing to prove it is Hughie, and that he's AFF. Then I'll go to Livermore, I promise. Look, even if he thinks someone is snooping around, he won't know who. I have no intention of putting myself anywhere near the senate offices anytime soon. I'm safe."

Marki shakes her head, saying nothing.

◆ ◆ ◆

The tour continues into July. Minneapolis, Milwaukee, Chicago, Indianapolis, and Cincinnati lay behind them, all successful dates. The DarkFellow legend continues as new favorites emerge out of the live shows. One song in particular has become an audience favorite everywhere. 'Text Me,' an early Hedley song, prevails.

Sunday, July 18, finds the boys at an outdoor show in Philadelphia, headlining an all-day event. It has been grueling for Hedley, sitting in costume aboard the tour bus while Marki (along with the rest of the Philadelphia gang) sit out front waiting for the show to begin. He can feel her presence, almost reach out and touch her, but he will have to wait a few more hours to achieve that blissful high. The past ten days without her have been agony, but they are off until the twenty-second, when the tour resumes in Pittsburgh. Three-and-a-half days to immerse themselves in each other. Meantime, he has a surprise for Marki. She will hear 'All of These Things,' the first song he shared with her. It seems now so long ago.

Marki waits in anticipation. Hedley introduced the song and is in the middle of the guitar intro, finger picking the strings of his favorite Gibson acoustic large body guitar in beautiful 6/8 time, readying himself to sing.

All Of These Things

Time after time
I got out with nothing more
Than one thin dime
Into this world of mine

As I look around
I tell you what I found
Many people
In a strange state of mind

They fight and they die
Not knowing the reason why
If you ask them
They got nothing to say

But I swear I will find
A place to give me peace of mind
And a woman to help me along
And we'll sing us a song
Keep us high keep us strong
We'll build a world where we belong
All of these things
All of these things

Marki is lost in the melody and lyrics, lost in the significance of the shared moment between them as she sits cross legged on the ground not more than fifty feet in direct line of DarkFellow.

Day after day
I hope that I do more than pray
That the future holds something
For us all

Of that I have no doubt
I will scream and I will shout
If you pay me
You can listen for free

And we will dance in the street
Burn up our poor feet
On the promise
Of the new elite

Until then I will find
A place to give me peace of mind
And a woman to help me along
And we'll sing us a song
Keep us high keep us strong
We'll build a world where we belong
All of these things
All of these things
All of these things
All of these things

The concert would continue from there, eleven more songs performed, an hour and ten minutes of time, but for Marki, time stood still. She realized as their eyes locked at song's end that she too was exactly where she was supposed to be, doing exactly what she was supposed to do. She never loved Hedley more than she did at that moment. She would hold on to that.

◆ ◆ ◆

"I don't like it Michelle, I don't like it at all," Tom Brascoe says across his home office desk. "The AFF has been on my mind since 2009. An organization like that doesn't go away easily. If Allan Bruce is indeed Hugh Peterson, well, that's a hornet's nest, isn't it? Do you want your kids in this?"

"Of course not, but there's no avoiding it, not now. I'm going up to Philadelphia to see Carolyn. I'll take this to Dan Livermore, despite Carolyn and Hedley's objections."

"Good." Tom relaxes. "This DarkFellow thing, that's something isn't it? Scott would be proud."

"Scott would be proud, yes."

"I'll dig into this AFF connection more without raising alarm bells. My years with the tabloids living life on the sleazier side of things taught me how to dig up the dirt, if nothing else. I only wish, Michelle—"

"That's in the past, Tom. Who you are and who you were are different people. You were there when Scott needed you most. You were there for Hedley when he needed answers. Your trespasses are long since forgotten. You are inner circle."

"I know you and the family has forgiven me, but I haven't quite forgiven myself."

"Enough of that. The past is the past. Time for lunch. Jeff is holding a table at Barclay's, and then I'm doing a little bit of west coast shopping before I embark. Shall we?"

◆ ◆ ◆

This is beginning to irritate me, Allan Bruce thinks. *Not that the intrusion of a twenty-year-old upstart alarms me, but why that particular girl from that particular family?*

Allan Bruce extracts a phone from a locked drawer in his Washington, DC, apartment. After several rings a cool professional voice answers. "I need you to handle the Philadelphia situation. Discreetly."

"Understood."

◆ ◆ ◆

"I can't explain it exactly. Who knows these things, really," Jeff says to Hedley and Kenny via a conference call hookup. "I expect the link started with the 'Who Said' Halo. From the onset, Scott Yonge and the Zone searches brought up DarkFellow. Listing the song as a tribute to the 2001 Garrett performance was a stroke of genius, intentional or otherwise. Scott Yonge fans are tuning in on Trafalgar and showing up at the live shows."

"There's no denying that DarkFellow has a sound reminiscent of Scott Yonge," Michelle says from Jeff's side. "The fact takes nothing away from your own creativity, Hedley, but, let's face it, it's in your genes. It cannot be denied."

"I'm painfully aware of who I am, Mom," Hedley says. "Sorry. I'm still figuring this stuff out."

"And that's why Milwaukee wants you back," Jeff says. "Kevin Manning's hometown and all that rot. I don't know, they might be wising up. Somebody's putting the connection together, maybe? We'll have to be on our toes. This kills

Philadelphia for the twenty-fifth, but Milwaukee is huge. They want us for the twenty-sixth and seventh. We should take it. You'll still have August sixth to the tenth in Philadelphia before we head out west."

"It might be a little much, Jeff," Michelle says.

"No, Mom. That's why we're out here. I'm in. Kenny?"

"You know it, dude. As you say, that's why we're out here."

"And Marki?" Michelle asks.

"I know, but it's Milwaukee. I'd bring her with me if I could."

"Too risky. Okay, I'll take the dates. Great job, boys. You're making me proud. Slay them in Pittsburgh tonight."

◆ ◆ ◆

"I want to go home, Hedley," Marki says over the transmission. "I want *us* to go home. Why didn't you talk to me about this? Don't I count?"

"Marki, it's two weeks. It'll pass quickly, and the tour will be done on the twenty-ninth in Oklahoma City, done for good. What's the big deal?"

"I guess I have no choice, do I? You should have at least talked to me first. It's my life too. I thought we were in this together. If we're not, then I need to look at you through different eyes. I trusted you, Hedley. This is not what I signed up for."

"Marki, please . . . I'm sorry."

"Don't be sorry, be Hedley." She terminates the call.

"Kenny, what have I done?" Hedley says as they pull away from Rochester. The decision now weighs heavily on Hedley's mind as they roll west. He can't recall when he has felt more alone.

◆ ◆ ◆

Rochester, New York, on the twenty-fourth followed by four days with Marki in Philadelphia; that seemed so easy and so right, but no, instead they'd bought themselves a ten-hour drive to Milwaukee to do two hastily booked shows in Kevin Manning's hometown. Milwaukee has had a fascination with the Kevin Manning–Scott Yonge connection since the release of Kevin's independent movie *Twisted Logic* in the summer of 2000. Scott's song 'I Call Your Name' from the soundtrack was nominated for 'Song of the Year' at the Garrett Awards and led to Scott's legendary performance and acceptance speech in 2001. Milwaukee remembered, and the promoters responded. Two sold-out shows on July 26 and 27 prove that the momentum of DarkFellow and Bartholomew continues to build.

Hedley stands at the door, hesitant to ring the bell, not quite sure what to expect from the meeting. Still, it was the prime directive for accepting the Milwaukee shows—a chance to talk to Kevin Manning, one on one. The door suddenly opens, startling Hedley. A vibrant middle-aged man of medium stature greets him with a warm smile, casual in faded jeans and a light brown t-shirt.

"Come in, Hedley. I'm glad you could make it." Kevin Manning extends his hand. Intense brown eyes burn into Hedley's, inquisitive but non-threatening, imparting a feeling of kinship.

"Hi. Sorry, I'm a bit nervous, I don't know why," Hedley responds.

"Don't be. I'm happy to talk to you. Let's step into my office."

They proceed into a mahogany-paneled den to the right of the foyer. The room reeks of casual comfort, its effect instantly relaxing Hedley. After preliminary small talk, they get down to business.

"I can guess why you're here," Kevin begins. "Your father."

"Yes."

Kevin reflects briefly, a warm grin working his face. "I did not know him well, but well enough to call him a friend. More than a friend. We've been connected since we met in Calgary back in 1999. We clicked, right from the start. Our meeting at the St. Germane is pretty well documented, but what happened the next day is not. I booked time in a studio in the west end of the city, high on a hill, giving a fantastic view of the sprawling city looking east. It was a fabulous studio for its time, well equipped and staffed. I'll never forget your dad straggling in, sleepy eyed, his hair sticking every which way. It was a hot day, he was wearing a black t-shirt with the word 'rethink' emblazoned across it in large white letters, but the letters were upstaged by a pair of bright orange shorts he was wearing. He had a guitar case in each hand, his Fender bass and a light green six-string Stratocaster. You know the one."

Hedley nods and smiles. "I still have it, the guitar. Del has the bass."

"Yes, Del. How is he?"

"Good, real good. I went to Calgary in the spring." He stops, catching himself.

"It was early for both of us. I took his bass, handed him a coffee, and started laughing. He looked silly, actually, and vulnerable. You couldn't help but love the guy." Kevin smiles again, remembering the moment. "'Let's get to it,' he said in his friendly manner. He took a swig, smiled, and followed me into the control room. There was an acoustic guitar sitting on a guitar stand next to the mixing console. He wheeled one of the armless chairs close to it, picked up the guitar, sat down, and started to play. It was 'I Call Your Name' pretty much as it is now, minus the sax solo of course, but complete. 'Will that do it?' he asked quietly when he was done. I was standing. I hadn't moved since he started to play. I was mesmerized, speechless. 'I guess not,' he replied to my silence. It was a fact to him, no disappointment in his voice at all. I grabbed another chair and wheeled it over. 'It's perfect,' I said. 'Let's get some guys together and lay it down.'

'We got everything we need right here, right now,' he replied, indicating the drum kit and the piano on the studio floor. 'I can play all the parts and have her done this afternoon if you like.' 'Well yeah,' I replied, and he did just that. We had 'I Call Your Name' and 'Give It Up' ready for mixing in a matter of hours. I was blown away. He delivered what he said he would as though it was nothing to him, as easy as breathing. A local sax player from a band waiting on their booked time heard 'I Call Your Name' and practically begged to play on the song. The other parts are your dad. And the rest, as they say, is history. Your history, Hedley. Yours and mine. We never found the time to hang out much over the years, different cities at different times, but we always had a good time when we hooked up. Jeff and I go way back, I almost know your dad more through him. I feel close to Scott."

"People who knew him say that a lot," Hedley says. "I really like talking like this, seeing him through his friends' eyes."

"He was a peculiar fellow, and I mean that in the best of ways. You're right, everybody loved him, but he was close to no one, excluding your mother of course. What a story SAM was. We won't see another saga like that anytime soon."

"It's still going on, I think. My mom, she never got over him. I'm not saying that's a good thing or a bad thing, just stating the fact. Del and dad were tight."

"They were crazy together. Their story is unique in itself. Jeff got in, to a point anyway, the only outsider to do so. Always alone, but never lonely, that was your dad."

"Except I think he *was* lonely. He was searching for something he never quite found. He found strength in his loneliness, found strength in his breaking heart, but it's a good thing my mom found him when she did. I don't know from what, but she saved him from something. Himself, maybe? I don't know."

"He was the easiest guy to talk to, totally approachable, yet he was the mystery man incarnate, always on the outside looking in, even though everyone tried to invite him inside. I'm sorry, that's presumptuous."

"No, I think you're right. I felt that when I was young. I still feel that. It doesn't make me sad, it's just the way it is—or was."

"Speaking of mystery, I can't help but notice that the green Strat DarkFellow plays is suspiciously like your dad's."

"I noticed that too," Hedley says. "I think DarkFellow is a fan. I'm actually here to catch tonight's show. I'm on my way to Philadelphia to visit my sister and my great aunt."

They talked into the afternoon, filling gaps where they could, the better to strengthen each other's perception of Scott Yonge. Hedley left a little lighter than he came, his enlightenment somewhat overshadowed by the realization that Kevin knew the truth about DarkFellow, though they left it unspoken. Still, Hedley feels no threat in the knowledge. *He's one of us*, he thinks as he steps into the waiting taxi. He turns to the open door one last time, returning Kevin's wave as they pull away. He can feel the beating of his heart as he leans his head against the rear side window.

◆ ◆ ◆

Scott Yonge is perceived in the public eye to be the muse of DarkFellow. The circle is tightening; people sense a connection and want to know the truth. A 'Reveal Yourself' faction has appeared at the shows, a totally unanticipated concept, and it is growing. The chanting before the encore in Rochester made the local news and was picked up by the news network. The first Milwaukee show expanded on the theme, taking the boys by surprise at the show's end. The second show on the twenty-seventh was positively deafening, more than 14,000 voices chanting 'Reveal yourself! Reveal yourself' after the second encore. The movement had become a phenomenon, unexplainable in its growth, but fast becoming a vital factor of the DarkFellow experience.

"I guess we'll know for sure in Baltimore," Jeff said. "If it happens again, we play it up."

And it did happen in Baltimore, only this time the chanting started before they came on. It had become part of the fun, part of the show, and soon became a huge distraction from the music. It was no longer fun for Hedley and Kenny, but what could they do?

"Hold her steady, boys," Jeff advised. "There's nothing to be gained by revealing yourselves at this point. The interview with Audrey takes on new proportions. New York shall prove to be interesting indeed."

♦ ♦ ♦

"It's very weird, Hedley," Soup says on the call. "There's no sign of a break in, no disturbance at all. I had twenty bucks sitting on the desk. It stayed, but my computer is gone. Not the monitor, not the keyboard, nothing but the computer. What's that tell you?"

"I don't think it's a coincidence. We've hit a nerve. Someone's sending you a message, and we'd better listen. Shut it down, Soup. No more snooping. Did you report it?"

"Nope, only Brian knows, and now you. We can't tell Mom."

"What about Marki?"

"She noticed the computer is gone, she doesn't know why. I lied. I told her it was out for repairs. I hate lying to her."

"Then don't. Trust her, I think that's important."

"Okay. There's more. I got in. I didn't find much, but I came across a directory called Rose. All the other directories are called things like Senate Documents or Spreadsheets, or Information videos, typical business labels. Then, Rose. I thought that odd. I was going to download the directory, but the computer shut down. How could he trace it back to me?"

"I don't know. Look, tell Marki, and never be alone. Have her or Brian with you all the time. When I get back, we go to Livermore. I think the missing computer is the proof we need. It's out of our hands, Soup. It's bigger than us."

"Marki just walked in, I'll put her on." She hands her Wombat to Marki, bringing her into focus on Hedley's portable screen.

"Hi baby, what's happening?" Hedley says. His laugh is nervous.

"Hi, Mr. DarkFellow. How's the rock star business these days?" Her tone is icy.

"Wow, we obviously need to talk, but right now, Carolyn needs your help." Hedley and Soup explain the circumstances to her over speaker, galvanizing the seriousness of the situation.

"I knew it. I knew you were in over your head. Yes, Hedley, we need to talk, but you're right, Carolyn needs my help, and that takes precedence. I'm stuck to her like glue until we talk to this Livermore guy." She hugs Soup. "We're strictly Siamese until you get here, Hedley. Then I'll deal with you."

• • •

Tuesday, August 3, and Hartford beckons. The mood is heavy, as is the rain, beating down around them in a torrent. The news of a strong counter-offensive in the Middle East has done nothing to lift the spirits of the crowd, and a restless vibe dominates the concert hall. Hedley has been riding the wave all day, and by late afternoon decides the situation perfect to introduce new material into the show. Now the tightness grips his stomach as they prepare to go on, opening with the heavily Arabic themed 'Who Among Us,' the story of an ancient village recovering from the attack of an invading horde. In reality, the song is Hedley's tribute to Robert the Bruce, the original DarkFellow, a Scottish warrior who led the Scots to independence in the early 1300s.

"Dude, I thought you were a man of peace," Kenny says. "Why the hero worship?"

"I am. I hate violence, but those were different times. Robert the Bruce did what he had to with the circumstances presented him. There is something intrinsically noble about a man who risks it all for a cause that he knows, going in, he has no chance of winning. And yet he wins."

"You're too deep for me dude," Kenny replies with a snicker. "Good tune though. I'll have tons of fun with the drums."

Hedley opens on guitar, mimicking the accompanying pre-recorded bass lick while Kenny subtly pounds out a repetitive percussive pattern, using soft mallets to obtain the desired sound from the various percussion instruments used. The vocals begin with an eerie chant, Bartholomew harmonizing below DarkFellow's droning lead.

Who Among Us

Who among us will throw the first stone cast the first stone
Who among us will stand alone against the throne
And show us the way to paradise
To freedom we've never known
To rise up our flag in no man's land
To take what was once our own

Who among us will spread the word
Will dare to be heard
Who among us will dare to rise up dare to rise up
And carry the torch of our fathers
To lands we have never known
To drive out the forces upon us
Drive them away from our home

Who among us will carry the pain of a nation's domain
Who among us will lay down their lives lay down their lives
And live on forever in legend
The story will never die
The victory is surely upon us
The women will wail and cry
Who among us
Who among us
Who among us

The mood of the tune matches the crowd's demeanor, quickly locking them in, setting them up for the DarkFellow experience. The chant "Reveal yourself, reveal yourself!" begins but is cut off by the energetic opening shots of the almost punk rock 'Primitive,' followed by 'Who Said' and 'Between.' Several more songs in, DarkFellow approaches the mike to introduce yet another new song.

"I've learned a lot on this tour. The back alleys behind many a concert hall in many a town have revealed a new world to me, one I've been aware of all along, but like most of us, have chosen to ignore. I'm talking about the homeless faces that pass us on the streets every day, invisible to us as though they exist in a different dimension. I don't know what I can do to help, but I can at least acknowledge that they are there. I can't pretend to know them or understand their world, but I can salute their right to life. I hope this song brings attention to their plight because after all, very little separates us from their world. One wrong turn of events could put any one of us in their shoes. One batch of bad luck could land anyone of us in the middle of their nightmare. I don't want to bring anybody down, but I hope you listen to the words and maybe think about a solution. That's the only way we can fix it folks, by putting our heads together, all our heads. Like this."

The song begins with power chord shots driven by Kenny's relentless tom-tom jungle rhythm, inviting the crowd into the energy.

Out on the Streets

Out on the streets everything will remind you
The only thing real is the pain that you feel
The pain that you feel is a gun set to paralyze
That's how you deal with pain that is real

Out on the streets you don't know your own name
Who you once were isn't part of the game

Out on the streets you can feel the disease
Crawling on you feeding on you
The sickness you feel is a constant refrain
Of nothing to lose nothing to gain

Out on the streets you can't trust your own soul
You live in a dream an invisible hole

Don't let me fade I don't think I can take one more day
Show me the way cannot help that I don't make the grade

Out on the streets you can float in the air
No one will see you no one will care
Though millions of people will pass where you lay
You are not real but you won't go away

Out on the streets you will live by the rule
No one's a friend won't be nobody's fool
Out on the streets you don't know your own name
Who you once were isn't part of the game
Who you once were isn't part of the game
Who you once were isn't part of the game

The Hartford show weighs heavily on Hedley as the bus rolls on, every bit as successful as the previous shows on the tour, but different somehow in its cool rigidity. He begins to sense a bigger purpose for himself, apart from DarkFellow, but what it is he cannot quite ascertain. Hollowness prevails, and anxiety-fueled doubt about the coming days grips his stability. *Dad, where are you?* The loneliness plagues him, keeping him from sleep.

◆ ◆ ◆

Thursday, August 5 brings the hot summer sunshine to New York. The hype around the live appearance of DarkFellow and Bartholomew on that afternoon's national broadcast of *Audrey Over America* shines brighter. People of all ages are tuned in, hoping to get an up-close look at the duo that has captured the imagination of the country.

Michelle is in LA with Jeff and Tom, clinging to the excitement of the moment while Carolyn, Marki, and Karin tune in from Philadelphia. Brian has to work, but Tracy will soon join them, having booked off early for the event.

"We have a first," Audrey begins as the cameras roll. "A special half-hour segment, featuring DarkFellow and Bartholomew. The studio audience will join the show later. Right now, the three of us will have a sit-down chat, beamed straight into your homes." She sits across from the mystery duo, separated by the familiar glass coffee table dividing the twin loveseats of America's living room, as Audrey's New York set has come to be known. The lights are dimmed and the boy's voices electronically altered, leaving nothing to chance. Settling in, Audrey begins.

"Since the release of the 'Who Said' Halo this past March, the phenomenon of DarkFellow and Bartholomew has mushroomed across the country. You have the top three viewed Halos on Trafalgar, the top music download count in the nation, and you're playing to sellout shows in every town on your current tour. The lyrics to your songs are on the lips of people everywhere as they take the DarkFellow experience to heart. Does your success surprise you?"

"Nothing surprises us anymore," Bartholomew says.

"But of course, we had no idea it would become what it has," DarkFellow adds. "How could we?"

"How indeed," Audrey replies. "The question I have to ask, what everyone wants to know, is, why the mystery? Why not show yourselves?"

"We want to be a voice, not a face. We want our message to be heard," DarkFellow says.

"And that message is . . ." Audrey leaves it hanging.

"That things need to change, and only we, the little guys on the street, can make that change happen," Bartholomew says.

"Yes," says DarkFellow. "We all need to work together to make a kinder, gentler world. Is that too much to ask?"

"It shouldn't be," Audrey says. "It seems a simple thing really, something we all want, but politics, small or large P, manage to alter the road there. It's been our story."

"We need to change the story," says DarkFellow. "A new age requires new thinking, new approaches to the reoccurring challenges of our history. That's what our song 'Rising Tide' is all about."

"We instinctively know how to hurt each other," says Bartholomew, "but it seems we have to learn how to help each other. Why can't we flip that around?"

"Don't get us wrong," DarkFellow says. "Life is good, but we all need to strive to make it better, that's all. That's our simple message. Bottom line, we want people to come to our shows to have fun, and so much the better if we can raise consciousness levels while doing that. We can't sit still, we need to stay positive and rise to the call of our troubled times. The environment, the war, our indifference to the forces of poverty, our indifference to each other . . . these things have to change. We need to find a way to humanize the digital world we live in. We live on our Wombats and our gadgets and that's cool, the freedom to move around and communicate is awesome, but in our virtual connections, we've somehow managed to put a greater distance between our personal selves. We need to close that gap and find a way to look into each other's eyes again when we talk. We need to bring the good things from the past forward, not bury them in a digital landslide."

"The nineteen sixties preached a similar message," Audrey says.

"They lit the torch, but they dropped it somewhere along the way. We need to pick it up again," says Bartholomew.

"March 13, 2001, and the Garrett Awards, what does that date mean to DarkFellow and Bartholomew?"

"Well, it was the beginning of the legend, wasn't it? We all know the story of Scott Yonge and the colonel." Anger grips Hedley briefly before settling into a dull gripping despair. "Scott Yonge got drawn into something he wanted no part of. He was the last of the innocents, the last to believe in the music for the music alone. They took his music and turned it into something it wasn't meant to be. That whole thing with 'MaryAnn Said,' that was crap. He was tried and convicted and hung out to dry long before the colonel was dragged into the picture. The colonel was a nutcase, but the rest of them should have known better." Hedley pauses, not knowing how to continue.

"You have obviously strong feelings on the matter," Audrey says, searching for a way to defuse the mood. "How could one so young be drawn to those times?"

"Kenny, I'm sorry," he says to Bartholomew. "I can't do this anymore." He turns to Audrey before Bartholomew can reply.

"I'm Hedley Yonge. Scott Yonge was my dad, and yes, I have strong feelings about the matter."

He turns to the camera then, faces the nation, and removes his mask. Kenny follows suit, not quite knowing what else to do, but feeling good about doing it. Audrey remains steadfast, letting the story unfold on its own.

"Oh man." Jeff sighs from his living room couch. "Wow, I'm not ready for this." He turns to Michelle and Tom with a smile. "Just like his old man, never the easy way."

"I'm not surprised," Michelle replies. "What does this mean?"

"It means they'll come at him big time," Tom says. "I guess the two of you will be heading east." They sit open-mouthed as the broadcast continues.

"Audrey, can we turn off the voice diffuser and turn up the lights? Let them see and hear who we are. Much better. Folks, meet my best friend, Kenny Moore. We met at Camp Nakita in 2009, the same camp the colonel grabbed me from. Kenny was there, and he knows all about those times. Mom, Jeff, I'm sorry. I need to tell people the truth about Dad. Tracy, your family, they've been great. You've shown Soup and me things about our dad we couldn't possibly have known without you coming into our lives. You're a part of us. Audrey, I know about your relationship with my mom and dad, what your role has been in our lives. I want to talk to you about those things. I can't do that as DarkFellow."

"My door is open to you, Hedley. I'm here to talk anytime you want about anything you want to know."

"Thank you. All you people out there who support us, I hope you still come to see us, to hear our music. This changes things, I know, but I think for the better. See, my dad has lots of songs that nobody's heard. 'Who Said' is one of them, so are 'Between,' and 'Something There.' I want everyone to hear them, to come to understand what he was really about. He had a reputation as a light-weight, a singer of love songs and romantic fluff, but there is so much more to him that I want to share with all of you. And now that you know who we are, we can play with a full band. We can play the music live the way it was meant to be played. And there's more, Audrey, much more. My girlfriend Marki . . . she's more than my girlfriend, she's everything to me. DarkFellow is coming between us. None of this means anything to me if she's not by my side. Mom, I know now why Dad wrote so many songs for you. Just as Marki is my life, you were his. I understand all of that because I've written a song for Marki. See, we had a fight, our first real fight, because I made a decision about our life, a decision that impacts her as much as it does me, but I didn't talk to her about it. I didn't think it was a big deal, but it was, and it is. Audrey, we were set to play 'Who Said,' but I'd like to do the new one, our first song as . . . I don't know who the hell we'll be, really. We'll have to figure that one out."

"Masked or unmasked, you're still DarkFellow and Bartholomew," Audrey encourages. "Fred," she looks to her producer. "Are we good?" Fred Murphy nods from offstage, the camera catching him.

"I'd like your alto sax man to join in," says Hedley. "It's easy. Pick up the solo after the first chorus, and then carry on through to the end."

Hedley and Kenny leave their roost for the studio stage twenty-five feet to the left of the living room. Kenny picks up Hedley's bass while Hedley takes his place on the piano bench. Hedley gives the count and they're in, the moody melodic ballad defining itself on the air around them.

Shoot for Twice

It's funny but I don't recall ever seeing you mad before
I don't wanna see it again 'cause the feeling's in our way
So maybe now I'll think a bit about the things I say
I know you got a lot on your mind but you really ought to know

That I'm sorry for all the things I said
The crazy ideas going through my head
I was reaching out for something gone
But it's over lord it's over
I'll never do those things again
I won't shoot for twice

Yes I'm sorry for all the things I said
The crazy ideas going through my head
I was reaching out for something gone
But it's over lord it's over
I'll never do those things again
I won't shoot for twice

It's funny but I don't recall ever seeing you cry in that way
I guess I might've tried too hard to bring my feeling your way
But can't you see I need it girl but you keep it all inside
I only wanna know what's mine but you keep me on the line
Yeah you keep me on the line
Oh these sad and lonely days
Ooh oh ooh yeah

"Marki, I'm sorry," Hedley whispers, almost lost but still audible. "Thank you, Audrey, for letting me do that. Now I can tell you and everyone about our next release. It's not mine. It's from my dad, written some time before he met Kevin Manning and my mom. Before all of this began. This song is more typical of Scott Yonge, or at least the general view of what my dad is about. There is no particular deep meaning to this song, it's universal and simply fun. It's called 'I Don't Know You.' I like it. I hope you do too."

Hedley switches to guitar and waits on the count to sync to their pre-recorded bass and keyboard tracks. They break into the early sixties feel, driving the opening shots home.

Taking a breath, Hedley dives in.

I Don't Know You

I don't know why you love me
I don't know why you make me blue
But you do
I don't know why you kiss me
Your lips will never miss me maybe
I don't know you

Walking alone after midnight
Can't help thinking about you
I close my eyes my heart is sinking
Into the mystery of all that you do

I don't know why you love me
I don't know why you make me blue
But you do
I don't know why you kiss me
Your lips will never miss me maybe
I don't know you

Maybe tomorrow when I'm holding you
I'll see clearly what to do
Your eyes are cold my heart is lonely
You don't see me the way I see you

I don't know why you love me
I don't know why you make me blue
But you do
I don't know why you kiss me
Your lips will never miss me maybe
I don't know you
Yeah maybe
I don't know you

◆ ◆ ◆

The boys left the studio on a high, laughing and smiling, free of the encumbrances of their alter egos.

"Dude, you're crazy, but I love you, man," Kenny says. They run to the waiting limo. Darwin is there, a huge grin playing across his face. "Quickly boys, quickly." He waves them on to the open door.

As they pull up to the newly restored and reopened Fillmore East Concert Hall, they are greeted by an informed crowd of well-wishers, stomping and clapping their approval from behind the hastily prepared barricades lining the wide walkway to the entrance of the historic music hall. "Reveal yourself, reveal yourself!" cries the chant as they exit the Pulse limo. They stop and wave before bounding up the steps en route to the sound check.

High on the energy of the day, they launch into the driving 'Primitive' as the dress rehearsal for the evening's telecast show.

Primitive

Primitive is what we are nature didn't mean for us to die in a car
Going ninety-five against the grain
Down a one-way street in the driving rain

Primitive is what we feel when we strap ourselves behind the wheel
Civilized in a dignified way
'til the pedal goes down then it's time to play
We're primitive
So primitive
Yeah primitive
So primitive

Primitive is what we see when we watch ourselves in H3D
Killing dying crime in the air
We shake our heads but we don't really care

Primitive is what we do we are ape in the head we belong in a zoo
With the orangutan and the chimpanzee
For a greater thinking thing to come and see
We're primitive
So primitive
Yeah primitive
So primitive

Primitive is what we cry when we waste ourselves on a chemical high
Losing our minds in a crimson haze
Got a gun to our heads and our eyes are glazed
We're primitive
Yeah primitive
So primitive
So primitive

"Well Hedley, it's a fine mess you've got us into," Jeff says. He and Michelle had grabbed the first shuttle out of LA, arriving just in time to catch the last half hour of the show. The broadcast was a huge success, chants of "Reveal yourself, reveal yourself" still breaking out, despite the obvious. The mood in the restored historic concert hall was loud and boisterous, the approving crowd embracing their heroes in the new light of things. They sang and clapped along, swaying to the familiar lyrics firmly ingrained in their heads. A splendid time was had by all, including Michelle and Jeff.

"I'm proud of you, honey," Michelle says over the hum of the backstage activity. "It looks as though we're none the worse for wear because of it."

"For now maybe," Jeff says. "Once the aura wears off, we'll have to see. You've humanized DarkFellow and Bartholomew. How much the loss of mystery will play in this, I can only guess. What the hell, it had to come out sooner or later. You did it in the family tradition, with Audrey, just like your wacky parents."

"I don't think it had quite the impact Mom's kiss did back in 2001."

"Yes, well, we won't get into that. I take it you planned it then?" Michelle asks.

"No, I didn't plan any of this. It just happened."

"Marki will be pleased."

And indeed she was. She ran to Hedley as he stepped out of the taxi. It was late. He left shortly after the show, but the two-hour drive and the aftermath of the concert had left him exhausted. No matter, Maki had plans for her man and they were not to be denied. "Don't say anything," she commanded. "I'm in charge tonight." She led him to his room, undressing him while softly cooing in his ear. Now Hedley lies in her arms, gentle sleep playing on his breath. She feels for the first time like the woman she will be.

♦ ♦ ♦

They spent a euphoric four and a half days together in Philadelphia, embracing the break from the tour with reverent passion and a pure dose of adolescent fun. Michelle journeyed there the following day, correctly giving Hedley and Marki their alone time. After reacquainting with the kids, she made arrangements for Aunt Margret and her visiting cousin June to come to Philadelphia for a few days, as both were keen on seeing Carolyn and Hedley before Hedley left on the tenth for Austin.

June was quick to question Carolyn on her research into her son Hugh's disappearance. Carolyn has not voiced her suspicions to June and she does not wish to do so now. She has come to love and admire the old woman, considering her family. June has been through enough, and Carolyn has no wish to hurt her if she can avoid doing so. She tells June that she has learned nothing new, but that she will keep on searching. She is sure something will turn up. June smiles and pats her hand.

Now, as she lies awake in her bed, she once again thinks about Allan Bruce, wanting a definitive answer for June.

I'll try one more time, she thinks, reaching for her Wombat.

◆ ◆ ◆

CHAPTER ELEVEN — THE FUTURE IS PAST AND PRESENT

True to his word, Jeff arranged to have Bob Martin and Ian Drucker join the tour in Austin, rehearsing with Hedley and Kenny on the afternoon of the show. Sheila had journeyed with Kenny from Broken Arrow, glad as Marki about the turn of events in all their lives.

Bob and Ian are seasoned west coast players, both veterans of the Scott Yonge & the Zone projects of the past. Aside from their considerable talents as musicians, they bring to the tour a historical connection Jeff feels will help attract a whole new legion of Scott Yonge fans. He is beginning to realize that the mystery may be gone, but the curiosity and the almost mystic connotations surrounding Scott Yonge have heightened, not lessened expectations towards Hedley. DarkFellow has not gone away; he has become a dual personality in the public eye, a complex and enigmatic character of the new age. The media attention since the revelation on Audrey's show has reached a new furor.

But for Hedley, it is business as usual, and in his eyes, business is great. He and Kenny are in awe of the level of musicianship brought to the band by Bob and Ian. It is a beautiful blend of their precision and experience coupled with Hedley and Kenny's drive and purity of youth. "Dudes, this band rocks," Kenny said during rehearsal, and he was right. With Bob Martin switching from guitar to sax, and Ian Drucker doing likewise on keyboards and bass, the flexibility is there for Hedley to shine on whatever instrument is featured on a particular song. The foursome, now known simply as DarkFellow, has clicked. They have become a live band.

Hedley is pumped. He originally envisioned a five-piece band—but the sound is everything he has hoped for: rich, thick, rhythmic, and pure fun. And now he can give credit where credit is due. He can finally explain the origins of songs like 'Who Said,' 'Something There,' and 'Between.' The unknown and unreleased songs of Scott Yonge and the history behind them will become public knowledge through DarkFellow and, Hedley hopes, a better under-standing of Scott Yonge the man will be realized.

Now, tight as ever as he waits to go on, Hedley can hear the rustling of the crowd, almost feel the sweet tension of their positive anticipation of the new sound and look. Hedley and Kenny will remain in character as DarkFellow and Bartholomew. Jeff feels the masks should remain, at least for the close-in shows. As the chant of "Reveal yourself, reveal yourself," builds out front, Hedley sees the logic in the decision, though he was not in agreement at the time. *It is show business, after all*, he thinks.

The introduction by a popular local DJ quickly ends, and they're into it. They open with Kenny on drums, Ian on bass, Bob on sax, and Hedley on piano, banging out the rhythm to his latest composition.

"Howdy folks," he says while continuing to play. "Get up and move your feet if you feel like dancing. Hope you like it. I think you'll figure out the title."

Walk to Jerusalem

I would walk to Jerusalem if you wanted it to be
For you or with you it's all the same to me
The road would be easy the payload would be free
I would walk to Jerusalem if you wanted it to be

I would walk to Jerusalem it doesn't seem that far
It's the only way to get there even if I had a car
The feel of the road would be good beneath my feet
I would walk to Jerusalem to see who I might meet

I would walk to Jerusalem what I'll find is not in doubt
Though my legs may be heavy my heart would scream and shout
The air would be sweetness the water pure and cold
I would walk to Jerusalem the Jerusalem of old

I would walk to Jerusalem hope my brothers understand
I would walk to Jerusalem hope they take me by the hand
I would walk to Jerusalem to escape the mother lode
I would walk to Jerusalem nothing bought, nothing sold

I would walk to Jerusalem if it's all the same to me
With you or for you that's the way it's gotta be
I would walk to Jerusalem I would swim across the sea
I would walk to Jerusalem to get to Galilee

Walk to Jerusalem
I would walk to Jerusalem
Walk to Jerusalem

Bob moves to guitar over the applause. Poised, they wait for the eventual silence, but for now, the applause continues. The band anticipates the launch of 'All of You,' an early Scott Yonge song recently discovered by Hedley. The song is curiously an ode from Scott to a family he did not have. It's as though he was looking into the future from the eighties to see what was coming. That's how Hedley sees it anyway. He built the song on a rhythmic bottom end with stacked keyboards and guitar power chords floating on the solid foundation.

Hedley begins on the Hammond organ, to be joined by the band pounding out the half-time shots. The power of the full band grabs them all, instantly propelling them to a locked in groove on which to fly. Hedley advances to the mike, building on the moment.

All of You

So many years away from you all
So many years living off the wall
I'd be here you'd be there
You might think that I didn't care
Oh, oh it just ain't so
Just ain't so

So many years out on my own
You shine a light to bring me home
I'm not worthy of this thing you do
But I feel again I'm a part of you

Oh oh yes it's true
It's so true

To all of you from all of me
I was blind but now I see
You took my hand now I understand
I belong to you
You belong to me

Oh oh yes it's true
It's so true

Oh oh yes it's true
It's so true
Yes it's true

"Oh my, yeah, thank you! Do you like the new band?" DarkFellow asks the crowd, already knowing the answer. They respond again, clapping and cheering in response to his query. "My father wrote that back in the eighties. It's nice to finally be able to tell you that. He believed in the words he wrote, but he also believed we should not take ourselves too seriously, and above all we should enjoy our lives, have some fun while we're here."

"Reveal yourself, reveal yourself!" seventeen thousand voices chant. It started small but quickly spread through the audience. Bartholomew was the first to react, standing with arms raised in the air in a giant *V*, drumsticks firmly clasped in his right hand. He rips his mask free with his left, tossing it to the floor in an act of defiance. Hedley turns to Kenny in response to the crowd's reaction.

"YEAH KENNY!" he yells, and smiles. He turns again to the crowd and follows suit, laughing as he removes the dark mask from his eyes. On impulse, he flicks his yellow fedora into the crowd like a Frisbee, letting it soar on the vibrating, deafening roar directed his way. Hedley has never been higher.

◆ ◆ ◆

Marki has just got off a call with Hedley, the Austin concert now behind him. They've spent an hour cooing with each other and talking about the show. Now she is hungry and restless, with the cool Wednesday night beckoning. "Let's go grab a burger," she says. "I could use some air."

"I didn't think burgers were your thing," Soup replies. She rises from her prone reading position on the bed.

"I crave meat," Marki replies in a silly voice. "And some greasy fries. And I need to move. I'm far too cranked to sleep anytime soon."

"Let's go," Carolyn says. "Wanna come?" she asks Brian.

"No, you go ahead. I've got to study up on the new security requirements for work but, bring me back an iced coffee."

◆ ◆ ◆

"They left over three hours ago. How could they just disappear?" Brian asks the officer. The Philadelphia Police had responded out of courtesy, but persons missing for three hours could hardly be reason enough to launch an APB. They explained that to Brian, and now Tracy, who was brought into the mix of things.

"I know her, I know them both. They were going for burgers."

"And they will probably do that," the officer says. "It's a beautiful summer night. Odds are they decided to take a joy ride before hitting the drive-in. I'm not telling you not to be concerned, but trust me, I've seen it a thousand times on a thousand summer nights just like this. I can't officially start a missing persons alert, but the guys around the area have a description of the girls and the car. They'll show up."

◆ ◆ ◆

They never made it to the Old-Fashioned Drive-In; a gloved hand over each mouth saw to that. Carolyn is pushed into the passenger seat of her Runabout while Marki is forced into the back seat of an old-style gas guzzling sedan. "You guys watch too many old movies," Marki says to the men on either side of her. She appears calm, but the panic rises in her as they pull away, following the Runabout. She looks ahead, concentrating on Carolyn's plight in an attempt to sidestep, at least for the moment, her own. She sees a dark figure in the driver's seat, controlling the Runabout in a totally law-abiding manner grossly at odds with the predicament they are in. She wonders about Carolyn's state of mind, unaware that Soup is now handcuffed.

Neither of them had noticed the dark sedan pulling up behind them as they talked and laughed at an empty intersection, nor had they noticed the doors quickly opening, or the three rather intimidating looking men approach the Runabout from behind. It was over before the light changed; they yanked the Runabout's canopy up, snipped Marki's shoulder restraint, and dragged her from the vehicle. Carolyn was yanked from the driver's side, handcuffs applied before she had time to react. Now she sits, trembling, painfully aware of the situation she has brought about for Marki and herself.

"Marki doesn't know anything," she says to her captor.

"She does now," the voice replies.

"Where are you taking us?"

"You'll know soon enough. There's no need to talk."

Soup reflects back to last night and curses herself for not heeding Hedley's words, and Michelle's. *Mom, I'm sorry*, she thinks, and fights back the tears. It was late. She was wide awake and in a somber mood. She too had enjoyed having her kid brother about. The foursome had become hanging buddies, often expanding to six with the addition of Karin and Tracy. Five suddenly seemed a lonely number. Her restlessness led to thoughts of June, which led to thoughts of Hughie, which led to thoughts of Alan—which led to the trouble they were in now.

The temptation was too great, and as it happened, Allan had just finished updating information on his growing army of conspirators. He was distracted momentarily by an incoming call on the AFF hidden line. When he returned to his task, his anger almost caused him to sweep the laptop to the floor, but sanity prevailed. He simply switched the PC off, stashing it away for safe keeping.

But it was enough. The Rose directory was open. On a hunch, Soup downloaded a file called The Rose Garden. She didn't know what exactly, but she knew she had something. Tired and content, she could finally sleep. That was less then twenty-four hours ago, but it seems like a lifetime. How much of a lifetime she has remaining haunts her now as they head northwest into the wooded terrain of the rolling hills surrounding Philadelphia.

After an eternity of an hour or so, they pull off the main road onto a small lane you'd have to look for to notice from the highway. A few minutes beyond that and they're navigating a narrow bridge spanning a steep embankment to a flowing river below, beautiful in the soft moonlight of the night. They proceed up a shallow hill into an open yard, a nineteenth century, two-and-a-half storey, rectangular whitewashed farmhouse parked lengthwise ahead of them on the crest. The vehicles stop directly in front of what would normally be an inviting looking door, but it looms threateningly now. Freedom never felt more distant.

◆ ◆ ◆

It is now 6:34 AM and the girls have been missing for more than five hours. A patrol officer had spotted the Runabout before the alert and registered it in his subconscious. He remembered he felt that the car behind the Runabout was following a tad too close, but not enough to justify a pull-over. When the alert came, something tickled his street senses. The silhouette of the driver in the Runabout was not that of a young adult female, and they were quite a distance from the expected area of containment. He called in his suspicions. Now the originating officer has returned with cap in hand.

"I'm calling Michelle," Tracy says.

Michelle terminates the call and places another, fighting the panic as she punches in the code. "Jeff, Carolyn and Marki are in trouble, maybe great danger. It might be AFF."

"What? What the hell is going on?" he says. The effects of early arousal quickly leave him. Michelle explains the situation and what has led them to the situation.

"Have you called the authorities?"

"I'm going to call Danny Livermore."

"Do that. Who better?"

"What have I done, Jeff? I knew the dangers and did nothing. Now my children are wrapped up in this shit again."

"This is no time to beat yourself up. You need to stay focused. Does Hedley know?"

"Not yet."

"Call him. Tell him to get to the aerodrome. I'll pick him up. We'll meet in Philadelphia as quickly as we can."

"I'm scared. Really, really scared."

◆ ◆ ◆

Danny Livermore was as close to the story as anyone, having been assigned to the Yonge household when the case broke in 2009. He stuck to the family like glue, monitoring the conversations between Colonel Randall and Michelle, with the understanding that the colonel knew and accepted his presence. Danny was an FBI field technician reporting directly to Bill Mueller in Washington. Mueller went on to form a special task force to deal with the cleanup of the mess left by the American Freedom Force. One of Bill Mueller's first recommendations was to bring Livermore in to the fold. Now Livermore holds the seat of command, his upon the retirement of Mueller two years previous. The AFF had been considered enough of a threat to warrant keeping the commission open. Livermore had learned much over the years, but this turn of events surprised even him.

"I wish you would have come forward sooner, Mrs. Yonge," Livermore says.

"Me too. And please, call me Michelle. We've been through too much together over the years."

"Of course, Michelle, I remember all too well."

They met at Tracy's. They were all there—Jeff, Brian, Karin, Kenny and Shelia, Michelle and Livermore, and of course, Hedley. He was sick with worry, leaning on and offering a leaning post for Michelle.

Hedley had said nothing at first, just clung to Michelle when she greeted him at the door. They embraced and cried, everyone giving them space to do what they needed to do. When they finally let go, Hedley responded to the anguish in his mother's eyes.

"This is my fault, Mom, not yours. Who better to have known?"

"There is no time for the blame game," Livermore says. "We need to put our heads together and think. We beat them once, we can beat them again."

Scott beat them, and he died doing it. That can't happen again. Michelle settles in on the living room loveseat next to Hedley and takes in Agent Livermore's directives.

◆ ◆ ◆

ALLAN AND SOUP

Soup and Marki were directed to adjoining windowless rooms down an internal hallway in the old structure. They were treated well enough, ignored mostly, except for their needs of water and sustenance. After unlocking Soup's hand-cuffs, they were served meat sandwiches of some kind, quite tasty actually, and coffee, generic but warm. They were not spoken to, or allowed to speak to each other, but the situation did not feel overly threatening; at least, not at the moment. Marki heard a car start and drive away, and she heard muffled voices from the direction of the front entrance, and correctly assumed there were two men remaining.

Later that night, another car approached, internal combustion the timbre of its engine. Moments later she heard voices of greeting from the front door, quickly followed by a set of footsteps growing ever louder down the hallway to the adjoining room where they had stashed Carolyn. Marki heard the deadbolt turn with a clunk, nodding her head at the familiarity of the sound. She heard Carolyn's muffled voice, calm and confident as she faced her captor. Marki hoped the ensuing conversation would be enough to distract the man while she put her plan into effect. She also hoped the man had come alone. *One crisis at a time*, she thinks as she begins her work.

"I'm well aware of the connection, Carolyn, long before you were. I'm well aware of you and the great Scott Yonge, the philosopher Scott Yonge, the asshole Scott Yonge. Believe me, I'm well aware."

"He was great, but not for any of the reasons people say. He simply lived his life doing what he loved, taking care not to hurt anyone else. He believed in people, Hughie, believed in the good in all of us. He didn't judge people."

"Then take a lesson and don't judge me."

"I'm not. You're doing a fine job of judging yourself."

"I know your type. You holier-than-thou do-gooders go through life preaching to everyone, never risking a damn thing. I, all of us, the AFF, we're trying to change things."

"To what end, Hughie, or whoever you are?"

"Hugh Peterson is dead. Why didn't you leave him dead and walk away?"

"He's not dead to your mother, Hugh. Allan's the dead one—dead wrong in what he's doing."

"My mother? You bring my mother into this? Believe me, she's as dead to me as I am to her. She never once took the time to understand me, to see me for who I am."

"She doesn't need to understand you to love you. She still does you know. Love you."

"You won't let this go, will you? What am I supposed to do with you?"

"What can you do? There are more than me who know the truth."

"About me maybe, but not the list. I can disappear, just like that. I did it once, I can do it again, but the cause will go on. No, I think I've contained you just fine. You stole from me, Carolyn. I'm just taking back what is mine."

For the first time, Carolyn shows fear. She realizes being right guarantees nothing. An avalanche cares not about the things it bowls over.

"You don't know what people know. That list is in many people's hands as we speak."

"I don't see any sent indications on your precious little Wombat. No, what happens in Vegas stays in Vegas. You are hooped, to say the least, you and your snot-nosed friend in the next room, the goon-eyed, freckle-faced bitch I believe you call Marki."

"Look, she's got nothing to do with this. You're right, no one but me has the list. You've got my Wombat, so let us go. Who'd believe us anyway?"

"I can't risk that. You may think that now, but as soon as you're out there, as soon as you feel safe, you'll spill the beans. I need to disappear, and unfortunately, so do you and your friend. I regret that."

"Come on! I'm twenty. I'm just beginning to live. Marki is younger."

"You're old enough to understand consequences. Have you no sense of history?"

Allan was out before he hit the ground, before he could let out much more than a whimpered grunt.

"Did I tell you I was good at picking locks?" Marki replies to Soup's questioning look. Soup glances over to the now open adjoining door between their rooms and smiles. "My dad was a locksmith, remember?" She drops the skinny metal lamp, the base now bent from its collision with Allan's head.

"Cheap piece of junk, but it did the trick." Marki surprises herself with her confidence and assumes command. "We need to get the fuck out of here."

"How? There are no windows, two clowns down the hall are guarding the only way out, and I need to pee so bad my teeth hurt."

"I have a way out, but you'll have to hold on to your problem. Let's drag him over to the far corner."

They each grab a leg and not so gently pull the limp Allan to the far side of the room, away from the door. "Do you think he's dead?" Carolyn asks.

"I doubt it, but he'll wish he was when he wakes up." Marki gently closes the connecting door, located kitty corner right to the hallway entrance. "Grab his keys and follow me."

Carolyn delicately reaches into his right pants pocket, withdrawing the keyring she knew she'd find.

"There are three, which one is the door?"

Marki examines the keys carefully, selecting one between thumb and index finger. "This one, the big one's probably the front door, the other one, I don't know, but it's odd, not a door key. You're in charge of them."

"What are you in charge of?"

"This." She picks up the broken lamp.

"You think you can take them both out with that?"

"If I have to, but I probably won't need to if you're fast enough with the key."

"Oh, I get it. Wait, my Wombat." Carolyn scurries back to Allan, adrenalin flowing like Niagara. She reaches into his suit coat pocket, retrieving her treasure. "Cripes! His eyes are open."

Marki calmly walks over, lamp poised. "Maybe I did kill him," she says nonchalantly. "He's definitely out. No, he's breathing . . . barely. Let's snuggle up against the wall opposite the door."

They walk tentatively to their strategic position, tingling as they put Marki's plan into effect.

"I sure hope this works," Marki whispers. "We get one shot at this."

She hammers the wooden door three times with the lamp base, and then pauses to listen. Nothing. She hammers again. *Footsteps, they're coming. Both of them. Good.*

The door springs open, almost pinning them to the wall. The men race to Allan, now moaning from his position at the foot of the bed. They react to the sound of the closing door too late, and Carolyn succeeds in locking them in.

"Run!" Marki barks. "That door won't hold them long!" Already they hear the wood giving way as they approach the front door. No one there, and it's unlocked! They breeze to Carolyn's rented Runabout.

"What's the pass key, what's the pass key?" Carolyn panics.

"Like I know! Slow down and think, Carolyn. You get one more chance."

"66543. That's it, we're in!" The canopy gently rises in silence, allowing them access. They pile in, Soup taking command of the controls. "Right now I wish this was a Corvette." She floors the Runabout and the electric engines respond, quickly accelerating in all their quiet efficiency to the car's top cruising speed of 73 miles per hour. Plenty under most circumstances, but totally insufficient now.

"I hope we have a good head start," Marki says with false bravado.

"I'll drive it like I don't own it," Carolyn answers, echoing the words her father spoke to Michelle under similar circumstances years ago in the countryside around Ada.

They move forward at what feels like a snail's pace, racing up the dirt road towards Philadelphia freedom. Two headlights flicker in the rearview, somewhat distant, but slowly gaining. "I remember an approach road a couple of miles on the other side of the bridge," Marki says. "That might be our best bet. There was a sign that said New Hope. It must be a back way into the town."

◆ ◆ ◆

"Okay, this is interesting," Livermore says. "Allan Bruce is not answering his phone—not directly, not through the senate page, not at all. What could he be up to? Sam Meade doesn't know his exact whereabouts either, a situation I find a bit odd. I have not alerted Senator Meade at this point, but that will soon change. A high-level warrant has been issued to search the senator's office for clues. The cat will be out at that point."

"They were heading north by northwest. We traced Carolyn's Wombat near the outskirts before it was turned off. Marki's remains in Carolyn's room where she left it, presumably after talking to you, Hedley. There are a lot of rural areas to navigate through, but there's not much else we can do at this point. Something will turn up if we keep slogging, something positive. It always does." *I only hope not too late*, he thinks to himself.

"What about dead spots?" Hedley asks. "I mean, they're covert, it stands to reason they would have a location in a dead zone."

"We're on it. The only one around is up near New Hope along the river valley. Not dead exactly, but fuzzy. Good thinking, though. We have people in the area."

"I feel out of my mind and helpless," Michelle says. "There must be something, anything I can do."

"We're doing it," Livermore replies. "Think, reflect, any little detail may help. Wrack your brains, people."

"What? It's Carolyn!" Brian exclaims. "She's trying to reach me, but the signal is weak."

Technicians lock on to the feed, attempting a trace. Livermore reacts, clasping his own device to his ear. "Get to the New Hope area now! We have contact."

"Carolyn! Where are you? What's that sound?" Brian panics at what he thinks he hears, not wanting to believe.

◆ ◆ ◆

"They're gaining, Carolyn. Punch it!"

"I'm punched out! This is all we've got."

"Oh god, they're closing!" Marki screams, losing control when they are rammed from behind. She is tossed around by the impact, her shoulder harness rendered useless on the trip out. Carolyn fights for control, barely managing to keep the Runabout level to the road. "Brace yourself!" she screams at the sound of the powerful engine revving for a new assault. It comes with a loud crunch, sending the Runabout into a sliding skid, but again, Carolyn somehow keeps them stable.

"I don't like this," Marki says as they head into a curve. Just beyond lies the quaint wooden bridge that seemed so hospitable on the way out. The same thought hits them both, paralyzing them with fear as the pursuing engine screams almost in agony as it accelerates forward. The terrible crunch sends the Runabout into a tailspin Carolyn cannot control. They scream in unison as the Runabout breaks through the wooden railing, plunging ten feet down the embankment into the river below.

Carolyn is dazed but conscious. Fear grips her as the wetness intrudes, and she hears it: the water. She screams, now fully aware. The Runabout is upside down and sinking, the wraparound canopy a fragile shield between her and the water. "Marki? MARKI?"

Marki is gone. The bubble canopy, mostly intact, was forced shut again by the impact of the Runabout hitting the water, the same water that is finding its way in through a massive crack running across the canopy's girth. She coughs as the trickling water fills her nostrils. *Think, girl, think.* She undoes her restraint and rights herself above the rising danger, feet now planted precariously against the curved bubble which itself rests on the river bed. The force widens the breech, increasing the trickle to a small gush. She knows time is precious. Eerily calm now, she reaches for her Wombat, still safe and dry in her pocket case. Brian's face fills the screen, blurry but perceptible.

"Carolyn, Carolyn! Where are you? What's that sound?!" She hears the panic in Brian's voice and smiles.

"I can barely see you, the picture's dark. I hear water. Are you okay?"

"Carolyn, tell us where you are," Michelle says

"I'm in trouble, Mom, I haven't got much time. You need to listen to me." She coughs as water starts to make its way in into her mouth. She shifts as best she can, elevating herself out of the rising water as high as the upside-down floor of the Runabout will allow.

"I love you, Soup, please don't leave us," Hedley says as he realizes.

"I love you too, Hedley, you know that, but you all need to listen to me. Brian . . ."

Hedley surrenders his place to Brian, standing behind for a glimpse of his sister. Michelle is also focused on the small screen, quietly composed, her arm comforting Hedley as Jeff's arm comforts her.

"Listen to me." She coughs again but remains focused. "We've got him. I'm sending the proof. Stop him, don't let it happen. God I'm cold, the water is so cold, Brian. Help me!"

The screen goes dead as water floods the inside of her Wombat. *Did it go?* she wonders. *Daddy? I'm scared.*

I've got you Soup. Take my hand. Warmth and light is everywhere, and she's gone.

◆ ◆ ◆

Now

We all get lost along the way
We all hurt and we all pay
Depending on your point of view
It's the same for me and you

And as I lie awake at night
Blinded by my lack of sight
I close my eyes I feel no pain
Yet it hurts me
Yet it maims

My face is pressed against a window am I
Looking out or looking in
Neither side holds my redemption
I can't lose I can't win

What I really want to say
As tomorrow becomes today
I don't believe you have the right
To win the battle and lose the fight

I brace myself against the fall
Use my strength to build a wall
Against the things that cannot be
Stop them from falling down on me

My face is pressed against a window am I
Looking in or looking out
The world outside holds no beginning
The view inside is wrapped in doubt
Oh oh

Hedley returns his guitar from whence it came.

Come on, Soup, wake up.

The last massive crunch caught the Runabout squarely on the left rear, cata-pulting it to the right and through the bridge railing. The canopy flew up as the car hit the embankment before bouncing into the river, throwing Marki clear. She was out, she didn't know for how long, but long enough.

The pursuers were still there, looking down from the bridge. She was hidden from their sight; she dared not move. She heard it first, the gurgling as the river swallowed the Runabout whole, the rippling surface bubbling like a cauldron of witch's brew. Carolyn was nowhere, but Marki dared not call or move. Panic set in as precious time ticks away; still, the watchers remain.

After an eternity they leave, satisfied the deed is done. The red taillights shimmer as they drive away, but Marki does not see. She is already in the water, down seven feet to the overturned Runabout. It is dark, she cannot see Carolyn, but she knows she's there. Every ounce of discipline her years of competitive swimming have taught her is with her now as she struggles to smash the canopy with a rock. She returns to the surface, oxygen starved, exhales, takes a gulp, and plunges again. She is calm, but she knows the risks. Her CPR training provided her with more knowledge than she wishes for at the moment. How long Carolyn has been without air is anyone's guess, she dares not speculate. She feels along the canopy, finding what she hopes to find. She leans into it with both hands, smashing the jagged rock against the weak point of the crack. The canopy gives. She tears a small section free, not wanting to weaken the canopy completely, and she is in. Carolyn is floating against the upturned floor, uncon-scious. *Do not pass out,* Marki tells herself as dizziness assails her.

She pulls Carolyn from the car, one hand clasping her waist while the other helps her legs backpedal away from the opening. Free now, she pushes against the canopy with her feet, catapulting herself and Carolyn upwards. She breaks the surface and gasps as the dizziness almost takes her. *Get her to the shore NOW*, her mind screams. As they reach the riverside she positions Carolyn flat on her back and applies two-handed pumps to her chest. She alternates with mouth to mouth and curses leaving her own Wombat behind. She continues, scared out of her mind for Soup, but rational and calm in her task. Minutes go by; nothing. Still she works.

After an eternity, Carolyn gurgles like an engine sputtering to life. A small amount of water is discharged. *Not enough*, Marki thinks, *not enough*. Still she works, fighting back the tears, listening for signs. She hears breathing, shallow, but breathing, signs of life. But Carolyn does not move. She does not shake, she does not twitch, she is as still as the night around them. Marki dares not quit, and as the early morning light breaks the horizon, she hears a car, or more correctly, a truck. The vehicle slows to a crawl as it takes the bridge, stopping completely at the gaping hole.

"Down here," Marki yells. "Help me please, she's hurt!" The young farmhand scurries down the embankment to her. "She drowned, she's alive, but I don't know ..." She loses it then, sobbing uncontrollably while continuing to pump.

"I'll get help," the young man says. He scurries back to the truck for his communicator. Twenty-five minutes later, they are in a Pulse air hover rescue vehicle en route to Philadelphia, Marki swamped by grief as Carolyn lies still.

They are all there at emergency, waiting for news. Hedley spots them first, joining one hand to Maki, the other to Soup, walking briskly with the stretcher bearers as they propel Carolyn to the entrance.

"Sir, step aside," a uniformed female attendant says with authority. He obeys, letting go of Carolyn's hand. He looks at Soup, then Marki, his anguish written in every fiber of his being. Michelle remembers a similar scene from long ago in LA and prays for the same outcome. It was Scott's turn then, airlifted to emergency after his near-fatal encounter with Scheck in the Sierra Mountains. The Scheck incident dominated the news then, as Carolyn's plight would now. *The future is past and present.* Tracy's words echo in her mind. Brian pleads in vain to go with her as Carolyn disappears through double swinging doors leading to the intensive care unit. He breaks in the arms of his sister, a new pain foreign to his being sapping his strength. The prospect of losing her is too much to endure. Michelle walks to them, gently stroking Brian's hair. "Faith, Brian, and strength. She needs us strong."

They take their places in the waiting room and the vigil begins. All is quiet save the hustle and bustle of the emergency ward around them. They soon realize Carolyn is only one of many in dire need of help, one of many fighting their way back from the land of the dead. Marki leans into Michelle while Hedley chats with Jeff opposite them. Karin and Tracy make a sandwich of Brian, better now but worse for wear. They can only wait.

Danny Livermore returns, hoping to question Marki, but thinks better of it, at least until word comes on Carolyn's condition. They do not wait long. A middle-aged doctor approaches the group, scrubs ruffled, facemask dangling to one side around his throat.

"Mrs. Yonge?" A flash of recognition shines as his eyes fall on Michelle. "Carolyn is in a coma. Her vitals are strong, but she was deprived of oxygen for a long time. I believe she will come out of the coma. It would be a different story if her friend hadn't been so diligent. There is no way of knowing when she will wake or what the final effects of the oxygen deprivation will be, but her eyes are alive. There is reason for hope."

"Thank you," Michelle says. "Can we take her home? I can make arrangements."

"She needs to stay with us for at least a week. We'll make a decision then."

"Yes, of course. Can we see her?"

"For now, no. Let her rest. You could all use some rest."

They disperse, returning to Tracy's. Michelle and Jeff have rooms, but they choose to stay together at Tracy's request, at least for the time being.

Livermore takes the time to talk to Marki one on one while the story is fresh in her mind. It is hard, he knows, but any detail may be the tipping point in a case. After several hours, they are exhausted, but he has the information he needs. He drops her at Tracy's and continues to the Bureau's downtown office.

The file made it to Brian's Wombat and is now in the hands of the FBI investigative division. The names are known. The roundup will soon begin. As expected, Allan Bruce has gone the way of Hugh Peterson. He is gone to the world, but this time, his disappearance will be harder to sustain.

June was hit hard. She feels the weight her son has put on the Yonge family is on her, but she is strong. Michelle insisted she come to Ada. "Family should be together in a crisis," she told her. Michelle would not accept anything else. Margret, too, made the journey, once Soup was released to their care. Brian also made the trip, taking a leave of absence to be at Carolyn's side. He is determined to be there when she wakes up.

◆ ◆ ◆

Hedley wanted to cancel the rest of the tour, but Michelle thought it best that he fulfill his obligations. She sensed that being out there would do him nothing but good. "Waiting around is not your thing," Michelle said. "Those are my shoes to fill." The close dates of Albuquerque on the fourteenth, Seattle on the sixteenth, and Portland on the eighteenth were rescheduled, tacked on to the end of the tour in the first week of September.

The shows took on a whole new perspective and dynamic. Hedley was overwhelmed to find that the whole country, those at the shows anyway, were also on vigil, with Carolyn's plight at the front of their minds. He draws strength from their common concern. Marki was torn, but in the end, she wanted to be with Hedley. She travelled with him, as does Sheila with Kenny, and a new friendship is formed.

Jeff remained forever at Michelle's side, his natural place now in Ada. Business could finally wait. For the first time in his life, he was needed, and he would respond. Del and Gloria made the trip, as did Tom Brascoe, so the house was full, even with Hedley and Marki's absence. But as time passed, only Brian and Michelle remained. Their bond grew with each passing day.

Brian was indeed with Soup when she woke in early September. Her eyes opened suddenly. She looked at him and squeezed his hand. She was cognizant but could not speak. He looked back and smiled. She returned his smile, weak but full of life. He reached over, pressing the buzzer. He soon heard the footsteps of Michelle and the on-duty caregiver. Michelle saw her daughter and wept, gently caressing Soup's face. And soon the world knew. Soup was awake.

LATE SEPTEMBER 2021

The thunderous ovation drones on. It began as they crossed the stage and has continued for two minutes, and still it grows. Michelle is there in all her finery, beautiful beyond her years and glowing. Hedley is with her, as is Marki, glued to his side. Tracy and Karin flank them on either side, but Brian could not find a way to attend, not yet.

They are in Washington, DC, as guests of the Peace Initiative. The gathering, three thousand and counting, is there to honor the sacrifice.

Addressing an audience that in her mind amounts to nothing more than a convention was not on the top of Michelle's list of priorities, but she felt it right to attend this function. She is at peace with herself and her life. She hopes to help Hedley reach the same plateau.

Full of confidence, she advances to the podium as the applause finally wanes.

"We are here today on a wave of optimism," she begins with dignity. "In an increasingly complex world, solutions to our challenges seem less tangible, harder to hold in our hands. But today we embrace solid results, real hope for our future. Our troops are coming home!"

The applause breaks out again. She patiently waits for an opening.

"The Peace Initiative can trace its roots to a small gathering on the steps of the Liberty Hall. The date was June 19, 2009. They were there to protest the reinstatement of the draft. Each of those thirty people had lost family members to the Middle East Crisis and wanted the killing to stop. They wanted their own silent pain to stop, so they stood on those steps and sang the words to 'MaryAnn Said,' a song my husband wrote."

It started then, the chant growing quickly with each word. Soon it was three thousand strong.

MaryAnn said Bobby's dead
MaryAnn said Bobby got angry
Bobby took a gun to the shed
The very one he brought home from the army
MaryAnn said Bobby's dead

They repeat the mantra for several minutes until Michelle raises her hands in a silent plea. They quiet themselves, the room suddenly drowning in silence.

"They were hurting," Michelle continues. "They wanted people to feel their anguish. They wanted to be noticed, to be heard. Who could have known what that day would lead to? And yet, here we are, twelve years later. Because of the efforts of one woman to organize one small group on one small day, we have a real, tangible shot at living in a world at peace with itself. Because of Tracy

Albright, we live in a better world." They respond, on their feet en mass, to acknowledge Tracy as Michelle walks to her, hugging her close. Tracy releases and waves a shy wave, embarrassed by the attention.

"I am not a member of the Peace Initiative," Michelle says. "My husband was not a member of the Peace Initiative. My son is not a member of the Peace Initiative. But like our daughter Carolyn, we carry your message, your hopes for a better future in our hearts. Carolyn, my Soup, *our* Soup, was drawn like a moth to the flame. It was in her nature to be so consumed. Her wish was to stay in Philadelphia and align herself to the movement. Her beliefs compelled her to risk everything to do what she felt should be done. Her contribution to the demise of the latest AFF plot cannot be underestimated. Her contribution to all the lives that have known her cannot be weighed and measured, yet all of us here, everyone everywhere is better off for her efforts. The connections between my family and the initiative are well known, but not well understood.

"The now famous rally of June 27, 2009, is looked upon as the origins of the initiative, and Scott Yonge regarded as the catalyst. Some would go as far to say he was the father of the movement, but such is not the case. He was there as a musician, nothing more, a musician encouraging us all to find our own way through the wilderness, just as he had found his. Yet he believed in his heart, as you do, that we need to find answers for the common good of us all, for the common good of the planet, and most of all, for our children. He once said to me that a society is worth nothing if it can't protect its children. Now his child has risked everything to protect all of us. I believe that to be a beautiful thing. As a mother, I would not have chosen her for the task, but I could not be more proud. Carolyn would love to be here if she could be, but of course she cannot."

Michelle stammers, losing her composure momentarily, then recoups. "She's a strong girl, she's improving daily. If not for the efforts of Marki," she turns to Marki and smiles. "If not for the efforts of Marki Devron, Soup would not be with us at all. She spoke for the first time since waking up last week. Brian Hamm is with her, she leans on him for love and strength. We can ask no more of life than life itself, but we can give back what we can to enrich each other, and in so doing, enrich ourselves. So my friends, remember those who did that. Salute their efforts, and when you leave today, do everything in your power to follow in their footsteps. But always, always wear your own shoes, the shoes you were given, for they were given with a greater purpose. We are all a part of everything. Thank you."

She steps down from the podium to the loudest ovation of her life. Choked with emotion, Hedley runs to her, followed by Karin Hamm and Tracy Albright, each taking their turn in the receiving line. Marki waits her turn, her large oval eyes brimming. They embrace, clinching as the clapping and whistling goes on and on. Time moves gently as the others circle them, applauding as though they were rock stars. The audience still stands, everyone trying somehow to be a part of the inner circle. Marki finally sees. She is a part of it, a part of the whole story. She was meant to be there for Carolyn, it was her destiny. And she is, as Michelle said in Philadelphia, as much a part of Hedley as he is himself. What the future holds she cannot say, but the future looks bright from her place in life. Soup is awake, the universe is aligned again.

Marki Smiles.

♦ ♦ ♦

Michelle - 2001

MARCH 13, 2051

He stands behind them, looking over the couch as they sit, their eyes focused on the screen. The room is dim, an eerie light cast by the old reel-to-reel projector the only source of illumination as the antique machine ticks.

"Who are we watching, Great Gram?" Franklyn asks with six-year-old curiosity.

"That man is your great grandfather," Michelle answers in a shaky voice. She sits, covered in a shawl, stooped and cold despite the warmth of the room.

"He looks funny," the boy says.

"Yes, I suppose he does." Her eyes dance at the memory, as fresh as yesterday in her mind.

"What's he doing? I can't hear anything."

He's singing, child, and playing guitar, just like your grandfather. I'll play you the music later if you like. Right now, I just want to see."

The image flickers and dances at the damaged spots, sometimes revealing flashing bright white holes where little of the film remains. Michelle does not mind, she is able to fill in the blanks.

"Mom, care for some tea?" Carolyn asks.

"That would be nice, Soup, thank you."

"Juice please," Franklyn requests with a smile.

Carolyn affectionately rubs his head. "Coming up, little man."

"Is that you, Gram? You were pretty!' Franklyn laughs, delighted with his observation.

"I was, wasn't I?" She has a jump in her voice. "Not so much anymore."

"I think you are," Frankie says.

"And aren't you a Yonge." They laugh and continue to watch.

"Did he love the geese too, Gram?"

"Very much so. He was the first of us to see them. He told us about them."

"Really? Thank you, Mr. Great Grandfather."

"Scott, his name was Scott."

"Are we going again this year?"

"We most certainly are, and for always."

"Wouldn't it be nice if Great Granddad could be there?"

She nods and turns suddenly as a memory jostles her. She feels him as she often does, this time strong.

Soon my love, soon.

Acknowledgements

No one gets here alone.

I'd like to thank my friends who helped me along the way. The Lesage family in Winnipeg, who practically adopted me in a time of great need. The Craw family in Calgary: Haley for her beautiful pencil sketches; Bruce for his friendship, inspiration and digital art; and Heather for keeping them all alive. Len Milne at Bedside, and Scott Pinder at Polyphonic Mastering Labs, both there every step of the way. Randy (and Biff), for reading the book as a stranger and pulling no punches on his way to becoming a friend. CP, my lifelong musical brother, and Lor, his lifelong bride, partners in everything.

There are others, too many to name, but you are there in my heart, and my thoughts. To all the players over the years, and to the musicians who played on my project, I thank you. You have shaped me. Special thanks to Eric the editor for trying to teach me how to write. I'm not there yet, but I hope to be, one day.

This story is dedicated to Mom and Ralph and all members of the Haugen/Wright clan, and descendants thereof. It is their story as well as mine. I would especially like to thank NC for inspiring the color blue, though she never makes me feel that way. She changed the story. She changed me.

Thank you Gordie, for starting the journey so many years ago. You will be remembered.

Chronology

1924 – Gordon Richter is born

1925 – Duke Peterson is born

1926 – Helen Richter is born

1934 – June Ashcroft is born

1935 – Martin Zoe is born

1944 – Margret Ashcroft is born

1944 – Margret Ashcroft is adopted by the Zoe Family

1957 – Scott Yonge is born

1960 – Martin Zoe and Arlene Jenkins are married

1962 – Michael Zoe is born

1963 – Darren Zoe is born

1964 – Jim Yonge leaves Helen

1964 – June Ashcroft marries Harold Peterson

1966 – Michelle Zoe is born

1967 – Friday August 25–the accident

1968 – Hugh Peterson is born

1968 – March 2 Helen Yonge dies at 42.

1981 – Scott Yonge and Delbert Gould Meet

1999 – Summer – Kevin Manning and Scott Yonge meet at the St. Germane

2001 – March 13 the Garrett Awards

2001 – December – Duke Peterson dies in Calgary

2002 – March – Scott and Michelle marry

2003 – Carolyn Yonge is adopted

2003 – Hedley Yonge is born

2009 – Scott Yonge dies
2022 – Simon Yonge is born
2046 – Franklyn Yonge is born

Louisiana Hayride

Addendum Links

SOUP
Link To
Addendums

www.soupsyz.com
From there, you can access the addendum link

ADDENDUM

Song Links

SOUP
Link to Music

www.soupsyz.com

SONGS

Contact Page

Enjoyed *Soup*? Sign up to be notified of
The next book in the One Song Series.
Visit www.travishaugen.com

Invite the author to YOUR book club? Library? Or School?
Invite Travis Haugen to answer your questions, play some music and discuss
Soup at your book club, library or school. For contact information, email
travis@onesongsyz.com, or candy@onesongsyz.com or call 1 780 757 6580.

Interested in hearing more music, or learning more about
Travis Haugen? Visit www.travishaugen.com

Want to give *Soup* as a gift? Or purchase multiples for your book club?
To find a list of available *Soup* e-book formats,
visit www.travishaugen.com and click the book link.

To find a list of stores from which to purchase a soft or hard cover copy,
please visit www.travishaugen.com and click the book link.

Contact travis@onesongsyz.com or candy@onesongsyz.com
and ask about discounts off the cover price for bulk purchases.